"I need a favor. A big one. I need you to marry me. _Tonight._"

The look Jericho gave her let Laurel know that he thought she'd lost her mind. Maybe she had. But she didn't exactly have a lot of options, and Jericho was still her best bet.

"Marry you?" he repeated.

He was no doubt remembering the bad history between them. "What's going on?" He turned as if he was about to show her to the door but then stopped. And studied her with those cop's eyes. The warm amber-brown-colored eyes weren't so warm right now, but Laurel had firsthand knowledge that they could be.

Every part of Jericho could be _warm_.

Again, it was firsthand knowledge fed by years of experience of kissing him. Touching him, wanting him.

TAKING AIM AT THE SHERIFF

BY
DELORES FOSSEN

Published in Great Britain 2015
by Mills & Boon, an imprint of Harlequin (UK) Limited,
Eton House, 18-24 Paradise Road, Richmond, Surrey, TW9 1SR

© 2015 Delores Fossen

ISBN: 978-0-263-25325-2

46-1215

Harlequin (UK) Limited's policy is to use papers that are natural, renewable and recyclable products and made from wood grown in sustainable forests. The logging and manufacturing processes conform to the legal environmental regulations of the country of origin.

Printed and bound in Spain
by CPI, Barcelona

Delores Fossen, a *USA TODAY* bestselling author, has sold over fifty novels with millions of copies of her books in print worldwide. She's received the Booksellers' Best Award and the RT Reviewers' Choice Best Book Award. She was also a finalist for a prestigious RITA® Award. You can contact the author through her webpage at www.dfossen.net.

Chapter One

Sheriff Jericho Crockett didn't have time to react. The SUV flew out from the side road and slammed right into the side of his truck.

The jolt was instant, tossing him around, and the seat belt snapped like a vise across Jericho's body. It knocked the breath out of him and dazed him for a couple of seconds.

He couldn't say the same for the driver of the SUV.

No dazed moments for the person behind that heavily tinted windshield. The driver backed up a few yards and came at Jericho again. This time, the front end of the SUV collided with his pickup's engine and then pulled back before coming onto the main road behind Jericho.

Much to Jericho's surprise, the guy didn't bolt. The SUV stayed put, the driver revving up the engine as if it were some kind of wild animal on the verge of pouncing for an attack.

What the hell was going on here?

Was someone trying to kill him? Or at least put him in the hospital? Jericho wasn't about to let either of those things happen. He drew his Smith & Wesson from his waist holster and threw open his door.

The blast of December air came right at him, spiking a

chill in him that went bone deep. But the cold didn't stop him. Jericho leaned out just enough so that he'd still have some cover but so this clown would see his gun.

What Jericho still couldn't do was get a glimpse of the person inside. Of course, the darkness didn't help. Nor did the fact that the driver didn't even have on his headlights.

"I'm Sheriff Crockett!" Jericho shouted. "Get out of your vehicle now!"

Since this crazy attack had come out of the blue, Jericho wasn't sure what to expect, but he braced himself in case someone in that SUV tried to take shots at him.

But that didn't happen.

The SUV came at him again, slamming into the back of his truck and causing Jericho's arm and shoulder to bash against the steering wheel. He held on to his gun, thank God, and he used it. Jericho sent two bullets into the SUV's engine, but they ricocheted off. Obviously, it'd been reinforced in some kind of way, because the front fender wasn't even crushed.

"The next shot goes through the windshield," Jericho warned him. Easier than putting bullets through metal, anyway. "And right into you."

The warning must have worked because this time the guy didn't crash into him. The driver threw the SUV into Reverse and hit the accelerator, the tires kicking up smoke and stench as they squealed away.

Since this was a farm road, less than a quarter of a mile from Jericho's family ranch, there wasn't much traffic, but he didn't want an innocent bystander hit by someone who was either drunk or just plain dangerous. He was more than ready to go after the idiot, but the spewing steam from his engine stopped him. The radiator had probably been busted in the collision, and he wasn't going to get far. Best to try to get to the ranch and regroup.

Cursing, Jericho took out his phone and pressed his brother's number. Jax, who was a deputy and still at work, answered on the first ring.

"I think somebody just tried to kill me," Jericho said instead of a greeting. He eased his foot down on the accelerator, hoping the truck would make it home.

"Again?" Jax asked. It wasn't exactly a smart-mouthed question. Earlier in the day, Jericho had been shot at during a domestic dispute. Now, this.

"A black SUV rammed into me three times, tore up my truck and then drove off. Run the plates for me." Jericho rattled off the license numbers, and he heard the clicks his brother was making on the computer keyboard back at the sheriff's office in the nearby town of Appaloosa Pass.

"You okay?" Jax sounded considerably more concerned with this question than his last one.

"I'm fine." Well, except for what would no doubt be a god-awful bruise on his shoulder. It was already throbbing like a toothache.

"The plates aren't registered," Jax provided a moment later. "They're bogus."

Of course they were. "Find this moron and arrest his sorry butt. Once I'm at my house, I'll get another vehicle and help you look for him."

"I can handle this. No need for you—"

"I'll be there," Jericho insisted, and he ended the call.

Well, there went his plans for a quiet night. Dinner and sleep. Maybe not even in that order since he was fully spent after pulling a twelve-hour shift. But apparently his shift wasn't over. Yes, his brother could handle this. Jax could handle pretty much anything when it came to a lawman's work. But this was personal, and that meant Jericho would have his hands in it.

The truck engine continued to chug and spew steam, but he was finally able to reach his place. Thankfully, it was at the front of the ranch property, the house that'd once belonged to his great-aunt and -uncle.

Jericho kept watch around him, just in case the bad-driving nut job returned, and he hurried up the back steps and into his kitchen so he could get the keys for his spare truck. He instantly spotted the note taped to his door.

"'I put up a tree for you. Love, Mom,'" he read aloud.

He automatically scowled. He wasn't much of a Christmas person. Definitely didn't put up trees—even though Christmas was only two days away. But he made a mental note to thank his mother, anyway.

Jericho stepped inside and cursed again once he turned on the lights and noticed the blood on his shirt.

Then, on his shoulder.

He peeled off his jacket and cowboy hat, dropping them on the table, and after he removed his badge, he sent the shirt flying straight toward the washer in the adjoining laundry room. It wasn't a deep cut, barely a nick, but it was bleeding enough that he'd need a bandage.

Jericho made it one step into the living room when he heard someone moving around.

And he put down his badge and drew his gun.

Great day in the morning, had the idiot in the SUV gotten here ahead of him?

"Jericho," a woman said. Her voice was a whisper.

He picked through the dark room and located her. Right next to a Christmas tree with all the trimmings. Even though he could barely see the brunette sitting on his sofa, he knew exactly who she was.

Laurel Tate.

She wasn't the very last person on earth that he would have expected to see in his house, but it was close. Jericho hadn't laid eyes on Laurel in over two years, since she'd moved from her father's nearby ranch to Dallas where she was supposed to run one of her family's businesses.

A shady one, no doubt.

Which pretty much described all her family's businesses.

Heck, Jericho's nights with her had been shady of a different sort since she was hands off. But those nights had been memorable, as well. He wasn't very happy about that. Wasn't happy about giving in to this scalding heat that'd always been between them.

Still was.

Much to his disgust.

"Nice tree," she remarked. "Your mother's doing?"

"Really? I doubt this visit is about Christmas trees. Or my mother. Why are you here?" he growled. "And how'd you get in?"

She fluttered her fingers toward the back door. "It wasn't locked, and I had to see you, *alone*, so I didn't want to go to your office," Laurel said, as if that explained everything.

It didn't explain squat. "Well, you can use that same unlocked door to let yourself out. I don't have time for a visit."

Laurel got to her feet. Slowly. Her cool blue eyes fastened to him. Not just on his face, either. Her gaze slid over his upper body, reminding him that he was bleeding and shirtless. Jericho hoped it was the blood that caused her breath to go all shivery like that, because he wasn't the least bit interested in having her react to his body.

They were enemies now. But lovers once.

Okay, not just once.

They'd been sixteen when they'd first discovered sex together, in this very house the summer he'd been staying at the place when his great-aunt and -uncle had been away. Jericho had actually discovered sex a year earlier with the cute cheerleader whose name he couldn't remember, but he'd been Laurel's first. A first had turned to a second, third and so on until his father's murder two years later.

Things had changed big-time between them then.

Everything had changed.

But he damn sure remembered Laurel's name.

Every inch of her body, too. A reminder that Jericho told to take a hike.

"You're bleeding," she said.

"And you're leaving so I can take care of it." But then he got a bad thought. *Really bad.* "Did you have something to do with the guy in the SUV who ran into me? Let me rephrase that. Did your scummy father have anything to do with it?"

Because Laurel wasn't the sort to get her hands dirty. She just associated with the lowlifes who did.

Her eyes widened and she shook her head. "Someone tried to hurt you?" And yeah, it sounded like a genuine question from a concerned, surprised woman.

"Is your father responsible for my bloody shoulder and bashed-up truck?" he pressed.

It wouldn't have been Herschel Tate's MO to be so obvious. He was more a knife-to-the-back sort of guy. Too bad Jericho had never been able to pin any crimes on him. Especially one big crime.

The murder of Jericho's own father.

Twenty years later, the pain of that still cut him to the bone. And that pain spilled over onto Laurel because she'd refused to see the truth or help him put her murdering father behind bars.

"I don't think my father was involved with anything that happened to you tonight." Laurel shook her head again. "But I can't be positive."

Well, that was a first—having her admit that her precious daddy could do anything wrong. But Laurel didn't elaborate. She hurried past him, and for a moment Jericho thought she was leaving. Instead, she came back from the kitchen with some paper towels that she pressed to his shoulder.

Jericho eyed her. Her nursing attempt put her fingers in contact with his bare skin. "How'd you get here?" he snapped. "Did your father or somebody else drop you off?"

Though he couldn't imagine why Herschel would do that. The hatred Jericho felt for the man was mutual.

"No. My father doesn't know I'm here. No one does. I parked behind your barn."

Since he had a big driveway and side yard, there was only one reason to park behind the barn. To conceal the vehicle. Jericho couldn't think of a single good reason for her to do that, but since he was a cop, he could think of some bad ones.

"Start talking," he insisted.

Laurel didn't do that, though. She kept dabbing at the cut. And more. Now that she was this close to him, Jericho could see her bottom lip tremble a little. He could also see that the whites of her eyes had some red in them.

Had she been crying?

"Your hair's longer," she said, her breath hitting against his neck right next to the hair she was apparently noticing. "It suits you."

That earned her a flat stare, and to end the little touching session, Jericho snatched the paper towels from her. "Are you really here to chat about my infrequent trips to the barbershop?"

"No." She moved away from him, repeated her answer and tucked a strand of her own loose hair behind her ear. "But we need to talk."

"So you've said. Well, start talking. Jax is waiting on me to come back to the station so we can go after the guy who hit my truck."

Jericho made sure he sounded impatient enough. Because he was. But Laurel didn't seem to be in a hurry to start this conversation that he didn't exactly want to have. So, Jericho started it for her.

"If you're here on your father's behalf—to try to make some kind of truce or deliver a threat—I'm not in a truce-making or threat-listening kind of mood."

"It's not anything like that." Laurel paused, pulled in her breath. "It's about…marriage."

Jericho went still. The woman sure knew how to keep him surprised. After all, Laurel was already married. Or at least she was supposed to be. But now that he had a better look at her left hand, she wasn't sporting a flashy diamond or a wedding band.

She followed his gaze to her ring finger and shook her head. "I didn't go through with the wedding. I called it off." Laurel looked up at him, clearly waiting, as if she expected him to ask why.

He'd rather eat a magazine of bullets first. But if the gossip was right, Laurel was supposed to be married to one of her father's rich lackey lawyers. Considering that she, too, was an equally rich lackey lawyer, it was no doubt a match made in some place other than heaven.

"Look, Laurel, like I keep saying, this isn't a good time—"

The rest of what he was about to remind her just stopped there in his throat when she opened her hand, and Jericho saw the small blue stone. She'd obviously been holding it for a while, because there was a mark on her palm.

"You remember what this is?" she asked.

Yeah, he did. And while it would seem petty to deny that, Jericho nearly went with petty.

Nearly.

"It's the rock we found on the banks of Mercy Creek twenty years ago," he supplied.

"We went walking there after we, well, afterward." Laurel tipped her head toward the bedroom, to the very place where she'd lost her virginity to him. "We found the two rocks. They were almost identical in size, shape and color. We'd never seen rocks that color before, so we decided it was some kind of sign, maybe even good-luck charms."

Jericho couldn't remember if he'd paid his electric bill this month, but he remembered that twenty-year-old conversation with Laurel. Every blasted word of it. And he knew that silly teenage notions of signs and charms like that came with a price tag attached.

"You said we'd each keep one, and that this rock could be a marker of sorts. Payment for any favor down the road. *Anything*," Laurel added. "In all these years, I've never used it because we said it should be for something very important. And we'd know just how important it was because we'd used this marker."

Jericho nodded. "I figured that'd come more in the form of a favor, like buying you a horse or something.

Or if you needed me to whip somebody's butt for messing with you."

And then it hit him. What this visit might really be about. "You don't think we're going to make the same mistake again of having sex?" he asked.

"A mistake," she said under her breath. Not exactly an agreement, but Jericho couldn't quite put his finger on the tone in her voice. And he certainly didn't see a let's-have-sex look in her eyes.

Not exactly, anyway. Of course, when it came to Laurel and him, there was always heat. Unwanted heat. But heat nonetheless.

"No. I'm not here for *that*," she verified.

"Good."

His body didn't exactly agree with that. Never did when it came to Laurel, but after that last fiasco together, Jericho had learned his lesson. Play with fire. Get burned. Or in their case, get burned *bad*, because for a couple of hours, it had made him forget her scummy family.

And Jericho had paid for it.

Hell, he was still paying.

It was a good reminder because it made Jericho realize it was time for Laurel to leave. However, before he could even point to the door again, Laurel took his hand and put the rock in it.

"I do need a favor. A big one." She swallowed hard. "Jericho, I need you to marry me. *Tonight*."

Chapter Two

Laurel wished she'd been able to come up with a better way to do this. Hard to come up with anything, though, with the tornado of emotions going on in her head. Of course, Jericho now had some emotions, too.

Bad ones, obviously.

Because the look he gave her let Laurel know that he thought she'd lost her mind. Maybe she had. But she didn't exactly have a lot of options here, and Jericho was still her best bet.

Even if he didn't believe that right now.

"Marry you?" Jericho repeated.

He was no doubt remembering the bad history between them. And he probably included their last one-nighter in that heap of bad history.

"It'll take more than a rock to make that happen." He cursed, dropped it on the table. "What's going on here?"

Laurel had figured that would be his first response— anger and demands. It was certainly hers when this idea had first come to her. Still, she was hoping the blue rock and the promise that had gone along with it would buy her enough time so she could explain things before Jericho kicked her out.

No such luck.

He turned as if he was about to show her to the door, but then stopped. And studied her with those cop's eyes. The warm amber-brown color wasn't so warm right now, but Laurel had firsthand knowledge that they could be.

Every part of Jericho could be *warm*.

Again, it was firsthand knowledge fed by years of experience of kissing him. Touching him, wanting him. And then having that warmth vanish and cool to iceberg temperatures like those outside right now.

Well, except for that night over two years ago.

Those two years seemed like a lifetime. For her, anyway. Jericho looked the same except for the slightly longer brown hair. In other words, he still looked like the hot cowboy he'd always been. Maybe it was his DNA, those eyes or the fit of his jeans, but when a woman saw Jericho Crockett, she noticed.

Laurel had been no different.

"I need an explanation," he pressed. "Like right now."

Where to start?

She doubted Jericho would want her to get into the little details. Not just yet, anyway. Judging from the impatient stare, he was looking for the condensed version of why she'd called in a very old marker that to him was probably worthless.

Laurel picked up the rock, slipped it into the front pocket of his jeans, careful not to touch too much of him.

"I had a baby," she finally said. "A son named Maddox. And my father is challenging me for custody."

It crushed her to say that.

Crushed her even more to think that her father might succeed.

The tears came again, and Laurel tried to blink them back. She'd already cried an ocean of tears, and they didn't help. Now she had to focus on a fix for this. She had to do whatever it took to save her son.

"A baby?" His gaze skimmed over her body. "You don't look like you've had a kid. And the gossips around town sure haven't gotten hold of that tidbit."

"I guess being several hundred miles away has kept the gossips from putting their noses in my business." Added to that, she'd worked very hard to make sure the news stayed within her family and a very small circle of friends.

For all the good that'd done her.

Jericho huffed, and his hands went on his hips. "So, your father's challenging you for custody, huh? Guess that means you two had some kind of falling-out. Or maybe you finally learned what a sack of dirt he really is."

"I've always known." She let that hang in the air for a few moments. "But I stayed for my mother's sake. As sort of a buffer between him and her."

He studied her. With some obvious skepticism in his gaze. There was a reason for that. Laurel had indeed defended her father over the years. Had believed his lies when he'd told her that his businesses would all be legitimate. Most of his lies, anyway.

And even that little shred of belief had cost her, bigtime.

It'd cost Laurel her freedom. Her safety. It'd also cost her Jericho. What she needed to tell him wouldn't help, either.

"My mother had cancer and passed away," Laurel said. "She died two weeks ago."

"I'm sorry. Losing a parent is hard." The look of sympathy that he gave her was genuine, but it didn't last. "I'm guessing after her death was when things fell apart with your father?"

"More or less." Mainly *less*, but she'd save that for another time. "I don't think it'll come as a surprise to you
that my father has influence over several judges. Doctors
and psychiatrists, too. He's trying to declare me mentally
and morally incompetent to raise my son. There's no truth
to it," she added, just in case Jericho doubted it.

Which he probably did.

But he also no doubt believed that her father wasn't
competent to raise Maddox, either.

Jericho stayed quiet a moment. "And you think if you're
married, *to me*, that your father will…what? Step back
from this fight he has with you? Herschel's never backed
off from anything, period."

Her father wouldn't do that this time, either. Unless
he had no choice. She had to make sure he didn't get that
choice.

Because she needed it, Laurel took a moment, too. "If
we're married, I'd sign over custody to you. Immediately.
My father might have enough dirt on me to declare me
incompetent, but he can't do the same to you."

She hoped.

After all, Jericho had been the sheriff of Appaloosa
Pass for well over a decade. He was respected by some.
Feared by others. It would be next to impossible to fab-
ricate enough to smear his reputation, and Laurel was
hoping a corrupt judge would back down from trying to
go after Jericho.

"What kind of dirt does Herschel have on you?" he
asked. Of course, Jericho wasn't going to let that slide.

"My father manufactured some of it. Some of it was my
own stupidity in handling one of his business accounts."

And again, that was an explanation best saved for another day. She hadn't done anything knowingly, but she

had known her father. Had known what he was capable of doing. Now that her father knew the whole truth, he would use anything to hurt her where it hurt the most.

By going after Maddox.

Jericho's stare got worse. So did his profanity. "Surely there's somebody other than me who can do this for you. Like your ex-fiancé?"

"He can't help," she settled for saying. And, in fact, he was a big part of the problem.

"Really? You'd think the kid's father would have something to say about you asking another man to marry you." A muscle flickered in his jaw. "What's your ex's name, anyway? Leo-something-or-other."

"Theo James," she supplied.

Jericho lifted his right eyebrow. "Oh, I get it now. Theo doesn't have a clean record, either, and your father will use that to get custody of his only grandson." His eyebrow went higher. "You probably should have picked a different guy to hook up with, Laurel."

She had. And Laurel would have told Jericho that, too, if the sound hadn't shot through the room. Since her nerves were already right there at the surface, she gasped, her body readying itself to fight yet another battle.

But it was just Jericho's phone.

"It's Jax," he said, and quickly answered it.

Even though Jericho didn't put the call on speaker, Laurel was close enough to hear what Jax told him. "We caught the guy in the SUV. He was on the side of the road trying to switch out the bogus plates. I'm bringing him in now."

The news caused Jericho's shoulders to relax a little, but that quickly ended when his gaze snapped back to her. "Good," he said to his brother. "Has he said anything about why he did it?"

"Not a word. He's already lawyered up, but I'll see if I can get anything from him."

"I want to talk to him," Jericho insisted. "I won't be long. Laurel Tate's here, and I need to finish up some things with her."

Jax paused. For a long time. "Laurel," he repeated, the venom clearly in his voice. "Why the heck is she at your place?"

"You wouldn't believe me if I told you."

No, he wouldn't. Nor would Jax approve. Because like the rest of the Crocketts, Jax blamed her in part for his father's death. They'd never forgive her for that.

Laurel wouldn't forgive herself, either.

She wouldn't forgive herself for a lot of things.

Jax cursed, and she had no trouble hearing it. "Please tell me you're not getting mixed up with Laurel again," he said to Jericho.

"No." Jericho didn't hesitate. Of course, Laurel had known he wouldn't simply agree to marry her. But hopefully he would when he understood the big picture.

She could practically see Jax's puzzled expression, but he didn't press things. "I'll see you when you get here."

And at that time, Jax would no doubt want a full explanation as to why their enemy's daughter was in his brother's house.

Jericho pushed the end call button and walked right past her. First to the kitchen so he could retrieve his badge from the counter. Then, toward his bathroom, she quickly realized, when she followed him.

"Look, I sympathize with this problem you're having with your father," he said, taking a bandage from the medicine cabinet. "Herschel shouldn't be raising any kid. But I can't help you." Jericho slapped the bandage on his shoulder and then went into his bedroom.

She followed him there, too.

Even though there were dozens of things on her mind, important things, Laurel still felt the punch from the old memories here. The room hadn't changed much in the twenty-two years since she'd been here for the first time.

Since she'd landed in that bed with Jericho.

Laurel made the mistake of looking at him before she could rein in the heat that trickled through her. A big mistake. Because Jericho saw that heat, and he scowled at her.

"My answer's not going to change," he insisted, taking a gray shirt from the closet. Once he had it on, he clipped on his badge. "It doesn't matter what happened between us on that bed. Or what happened over two years ago."

Laurel was about to tell him that it did indeed matter, but this time it was her phone that rang. She took it from her pocket, and when she saw her father's name on the screen, she let it go to voice mail—along with the other dozen messages he'd left her in the past couple of hours. She didn't have to listen to the message to know what he was demanding again.

That she hand Maddox over to him.

Or else agree to every detail of his sick plan.

She didn't intend to do either one of those.

"I can't let him get his hands on my son," she whispered.

"Good luck with that." It sounded like a dismissal, but she thought she saw some concern in Jericho's eyes. "I take it you've hidden the baby so that Herschel can't find him?"

She nodded. "He's with a friend I trust."

"A friend," he repeated, that cop's stare coming at her again. "But I'm guessing this is a friend who can't help you with your marriage problem."

"No."

He huffed, scrubbed his hand over his face. "I can't do this. What I can do is make some calls and arrange a safe house where you can stay until you work things out with Herschel. For now, I need to get to the station to question this dirt-for-brains suspect."

Yes, Jericho had made it crystal clear that he had more important things to do and no intention of helping her. So, Laurel pulled out the big guns. Or rather, the picture. It was the screen saver on her phone, and she held it up for him to see.

"That's my son, Maddox," she said.

Laurel didn't need to see the picture to be able to describe it in complete detail. The precious little boy with the blondish-brown hair, amber eyes and a melt-your-heart kind of smile.

Not a newborn baby.

As Jericho had likely been expecting.

Since Laurel was watching him so closely, she saw the change in his expression when he began to connect the dots. It wasn't a huge change. Just the muscles in his face going tight for a moment. Followed by a head shake, and then that lethal stare came back to her.

"How old is he?" Jericho asked. Except it wasn't just a question. It was a demand spoken through clenched teeth, and he practically ripped the phone from her hand for a closer look at the picture.

Laurel tried to steel herself for what was no doubt about to be a fierce storm. "He's eighteen months."

There. That was the last bit of information that Jer-

icho needed so he could finally understand why she'd
had come to him. Why their marriage had to happen and
happen fast.

Why she couldn't turn to anyone else.

"Yes," Laurel verified. Her voice cracked, and she had
to clear her throat before she could continue. "Maddox
is your son."

Chapter Three

The blood rushed to Jericho's head.

It happened too fast for him to get hold of himself before it felt as if someone had slugged him with a hammer.

So many emotions went through him. The shock. The anger. The feeling that his life had just turned on a dime.

Because it had.

Everything had just turned.

Laurel and he had been together two years and three months ago, the perfect timing for them to have an eighteen month old son.

"Why?" he managed to say, though it would be the first of many questions. Questions that Laurel had darn sure better be able to answer.

Laurel didn't exactly jump to answer, but then she didn't back away from him, either. Even though he had to be giving her his worst glare, she held her ground.

"You should probably sit down," she suggested.

No way would sitting help. Nothing could at this point. His entire body was a tangle of nerves and fresh adrenaline—all caused by that picture of the little smiling face on Laurel's phone.

Everything about that face was familiar.

Because it was practically identical to pictures he'd seen of himself when he was a baby.

"Why?" he repeated, his jaw so tight now that he was hurting.

"I didn't tell you because I didn't want my father to find out. I was afraid he would kill you."

"He would have tried," Jericho conceded. Now the profanity came, and he couldn't stop himself from cursing Laurel. "You still should have told me."

Her chin dropped a little, and while she still held her ground, the tears shimmered in her eyes again. He wasn't immune to those tears, but right now he had no intention of giving Laurel one ounce of comfort.

How dare she do this.

"I already had your father's death on my conscience," she said. "I didn't want your death there, too."

"That's no excuse." He jabbed his index finger at her and considered punching the wall just to release some of this dangerous energy revving up inside him. Hardly a mature reaction, but this had shaken him to the core.

A baby!

Except he wasn't exactly a baby now. He was eighteen months old. Born nine months after Laurel and he had ended up in bed. And she'd kept it from him this entire time.

"You had no right," he warned her.

"Maybe not, but what's done is done. I'm sorry I can't give you more time to come to terms with this. I'm sorry about a lot of things. But right now, we have to stop my father from taking him."

Jericho got a new surge of anger, too. Except this was more rage, and it was aimed at Herschel. "That won't happen. No way will I let that snake take custody of…" But the words wouldn't come so he could finish that.

My son.

However, it was exactly what Jericho meant. It wasn't happening. It already sickened him to realize that Herschel had been part of the little boy's life this entire time.

And that Jericho hadn't been.

Later, he'd *address* that with Laurel.

"Why is Herschel trying to take custody?" Jericho asked. "*How* is he trying to do it?" he amended.

"My father has two fake psychiatric reports on me," Laurel explained. Not easily. The words seemed to stick in her throat. "Both claiming that I'm mentally unstable."

"You could counteract those with your own real psychiatric reports." Because Laurel had been careless and irresponsible when it came to her father, but she wasn't crazy.

"I could, but I don't own the judge that'll be presiding over the hearing. Plus, my father has a document I signed that's connected to some illegal funds that were transferred from an offshore account. I did sign it, but I had no idea it was a part of a money laundering scheme."

So, Herschel was coming at her from two angles, but it did surprise Jericho there was only one document with her signature on it that could have criminal ties. After all, Laurel had worked for her father for nearly a dozen years, and she'd no doubt come in contact with plenty of his dirty businesses and schemes.

"I want the names of every person involved in that deal," Jericho insisted.

Laurel nodded, but there was plenty of hesitation in her expression. "My father said if I came to you for help, that he'd only make things worse for both of us."

Yeah, that sounded like Herschel. A man of threats.

Though he didn't know how much harder her father could make things, considering he was trying to take Laurel's child.

Jericho's child, too.

The reminder didn't settle easily in his mind. Of course, nothing about this would.

"You don't doubt he's yours?" she asked.

"No." How could he? The proof was right there in front of him. "How much does Herschel know about Maddox's paternity?"

"Everything. *Now*," she added in a whisper. "At first, I'd told him Theo was Maddox's father, and Theo went along with it. But when I broke off the engagement, Theo told him the truth. That's why Herschel wants custody right away. You know how much he hates you, and he hates me even more now that he knows I kept the truth about Maddox from him."

Jericho was betting there was a whole other story to go along with that one. Theo had probably squealed to get back at Laurel. He didn't know this Theo idiot, but he'd settle things with him later.

With Herschel, too.

Not just for this stunt he was trying to pull with getting custody, but because it was possible that Herschel had indeed been behind the hit-and-run idiot that Jax now had in the holding cell. Jericho didn't know exactly what Laurel's father would hope to gain by that, but anything was possible when it came to Herschel.

Especially anything illegal.

"Your father must have seen the resemblance between Maddox and me," Jericho said, handing her back the phone.

"He did," Laurel readily admitted. "He didn't know

about that night we were together. I'd managed to keep that from him, but he asked me point-blank if I'd been with you. I denied it, and I falsified the results of Maddox's paternity test so I could try to get him off your trail."

Jericho hadn't wanted Herschel off his trail. Especially not for something like this, something that would keep Maddox from him. The best way to deal with a snake was to confront it.

"Where's Maddox now?" Jericho asked.

"With a friend, Sandy Singer. She's a former cop, and she took him to her parents' house in Sweetwater Springs. Her parents are out of town so the place was empty."

So, Maddox was about thirty miles away. Close. But any distance wouldn't have mattered.

"I want to see him." And the glare Jericho gave Laurel dared her not to refuse him.

She didn't refuse him, though. She gave a shaky nod. "We'll just have to make sure we aren't followed."

He would make certain of that because he wouldn't put it past Herschel to take the boy, all in the name of keeping him safe from Laurel. Later, Jericho would have to do something about those false reports, but for now he had a more immediate problem on his hands.

"I have to call Jax and tell him I won't be able to question the man in custody until, well, until later," he settled for saying. Because Jericho had no idea how much time he'd need to start fixing this mess Herschel had created.

That Laurel had created, too.

"I'm sorry," she repeated, no doubt after she saw the latest round of anger go through his eyes.

Not in the mood for an apology that wouldn't help one bit, Jericho waved her off and took out his phone to call his brother. However, he stopped when he heard the sound.

A vehicle was approaching the house.

"Oh, God," Laurel whispered, her fingertips going to her mouth.

"It might be nothing," he assured her.

After all, his family's ranch was huge, and people came and went all the time. It could be one of the ranch hands, his mother or maybe even his sister, Addie, and her fiancé, Weston. Since Addie was pregnant, they were often making night runs to get whatever she was craving.

Heck, it could even be one of his other brothers, Levi or Chase. Both had houses on the grounds of the ranch.

"Wait here," Jericho told her, and he headed to the living room window to look out. He braced himself for the worst.

And the worst was exactly what he got.

The moment he pulled back the curtain, he spotted the man who'd stepped from the black car now stopped in front of Jericho's house. It was dark enough that Jericho couldn't make out the guy's face, but he had no trouble seeing his gun.

Or hearing it.

The bullet slammed into the windowsill just a couple of inches from where Jericho was standing.

"Get down!" he shouted to Laurel.

But he did something to make sure that happened. Jericho hurried to her, hooked his arm around her waist and pulled her to the floor behind the couch. It wouldn't be much protection against bullets, but it was safer than her standing in a room with windows on the front and side.

"Call Jax for me," he said, tossing Laurel his phone. "I need backup and everyone in the main house warned that we're under attack."

Despite Laurel yelling for him to stay down, Jericho

headed back to one of the windows so he could figure out who this idiot was and how to stop him.

From what Jericho could tell, the guy was alone. At least he was the only one out of the car. Of course, someone could be inside, waiting, so that's why he went to the window on the other side of the room. He wanted as much of an element of surprise as he could manage when he fired at this nut job. Maybe the guy wouldn't see him before Jericho got off the finishing shot.

"Jax is on the way," Laurel relayed to him. "He's bringing one of the deputies with him. Dexter Conway. He'll also call your mother and the rest of your family on the drive over."

Good. It'd take at least twenty minutes for Jax and Dexter to arrive, but maybe the attack was confined to just here. He didn't want Herschel's brand of violence spreading to the rest of his family.

"Now, please get down," Laurel added. "I'm calling Sandy to make sure everything is okay with Maddox."

Even though what Laurel was saying was important, Jericho shut her out, knocked out the pane of glass with his gun and took aim. He pulled the trigger, and though he couldn't be sure, he thought he might have hit the shooter in the shoulder. The guy ducked down and jumped into the car. Just in case he intended to get back out, Jericho sent another shot his way.

"Do you know for sure who's doing this?" Jericho asked Laurel.

"No. My father hates me now, but I can't believe he'd try to kill me."

"Believe it," Jericho said just as he got another surprise of the night.

Another bullet came right at him. Not from the idiot

in the car this time. This shot had come from somewhere across the road. The land was level pasture there, and it would have been easy for a gunman to stand out, which meant the guy was likely hiding in the ditch.

Had he come with his partner in the car?

Probably.

Herschel no doubt wanted some kind of backup to make sure this attack was a success. After all, if Herschel got rid of both of Maddox's parents, then there'd be no fight for custody. However, that only led Jericho to yet another set of questions.

Did Herschel really want Maddox enough to kill for him?

And why?

Because Jericho wasn't sure a man like Herschel was capable of loving a child this much.

Jericho didn't have time to dwell on that because another shot came crashing through the window, and it spewed broken glass all over the room. Some of it even flew behind the couch.

Worse, it didn't stay a single shot.

The bullets began to rip through what was left of the window. Tear through the walls, too. It was an old house with a wood frame, and if the shooters were using the right kind of bullets, they could do some serious damage before Jax and backup could even arrive.

"Crawl to my bathroom," Jericho told Laurel. "Get in the tub."

"You can't stay out here, either," she insisted.

"I'll be right behind you."

Maybe. But he immediately had to rethink that *maybe* when he finally spotted the shooter in the ditch. Jax would be there soon, and this guy was right next to the road.

Jericho didn't want his brother getting hurt. Losing one family member to Herschel's schemes was more than enough.

Jericho moved to the side of a bookcase. Like the couch, it wasn't ideal coverage, but it would do. Hopefully. Since there wasn't any glass remaining in the window, he leaned out and fired right at the shooter in the ditch.

The guy dropped back down. But Jericho didn't think he'd managed to hit him.

Still, if he could keep both of these idiots pinned down, that would keep Laurel and the rest of the ranch safe. That thought had barely crossed his mind, however, when he heard a sound he definitely didn't want to hear.

More shots.

Coming from the car.

Shooter number one was back at it again, and this time the bullets weren't coming at Jericho. They seemed to be going on the other side of the house. Right in the direction of the bathroom where he'd just sent Laurel. And right in the direction of where there were sounds of yet more broken glass.

It didn't help when he heard her scream.

"You can't do this!" Laurel shouted. "Please. No!"

Hell.

Jericho raced from the living room, praying that one of those bullets hadn't hit her or that a third gunman hadn't managed to get into the house. Either was possible. He didn't have a security system and rarely even locked the windows or doors. Anyone could have gotten in.

Jericho kept as low as he could when he approached the bathroom. The light wasn't on, but there was a small window near the ceiling, and it gave him just enough illumination to see Laurel in the tub.

She had her left hand covering her head, and there were shards of glass on her from the broken window.

"Are you hit?" Jericho asked.

Her breath was gusting, and when she turned to look at him, that's when he saw that she had her phone against her ear. Despite the fact the bullets were coming at them nonstop, she still got out of the bathtub and would have bolted out the door if Jericho hadn't caught her.

"What's wrong?" he demanded, and he pulled her to the floor to get her out of the path of those shots.

Laurel frantically shook her head, fighting to get away from him. "They went after Maddox."

That handful of words sent his stomach straight to his knees. "Who did?"

"Kidnappers." Her answer rushed out with her breath, and Laurel scrambled to her feet again. "We have to get to him. Sandy said the kidnappers broke into her house, and they're trying to take Maddox right now."

Chapter Four

Laurel tried to push Jericho aside so she could run to
her car. It didn't work. He held on, cursing at her to stop.

"Is your friend alone in the house with Maddox?"
Jericho asked. "Has she called the Sweetwater Springs'
cops?"

Laurel nodded to both his questions and tried to break
free again. Everything inside her was spiraling out of
control, and she was within a breath of a panic attack—
something that wouldn't do her or Maddox any good—
but she couldn't seem to stop herself.

"Getting yourself killed won't help Maddox," he
snarled.

That helped with the panic. Well, it helped enough so
that she could level her breathing and try to fight through
the need to run.

Jericho took her by the arm and maneuvered her toward
the kitchen. He slapped off lights along the way, pausing
only long enough to put on his jacket and grab a set of
keys before they went to the back door.

"Keep low and move fast," he ordered.

The relief flooded through her. They weren't going to
hunker down and wait. They were going after Maddox.
But that relief was short-lived when they stepped outside,

and the bullets came. Not directly at them. The shooter was still firing into the front and side of the house, but without the walls to buffer the sounds, the shots were deafening.

And worse.

The shots started coming toward them.

"They're using infrared," Jericho said under his breath.

Someone obviously wanted them dead, but Laurel couldn't give in to the fear and panic that was snapping at her like the bitter wind. She had to get to Maddox.

Obviously, Jericho felt the same way because despite the shots, he practically dragged her onto the porch with him. With his hand on her back, he kept her low. Kept her running, too, toward his truck that was parked between them and the barn. That's when Laurel spotted the other damaged truck by the side of the house.

Soon, very soon, she'd need to find out if her father was responsible for that attack and this one. But for now, she had more pressing matters.

Jericho threw open the driver's side of his truck, shoving her inside and onto the floor. He shut the door, and in the same motion, he started the engine.

"Call Jax again." He tossed her his phone and hit the accelerator. "Tell him what's going on. And stay down."

Despite her shaking hands, Laurel found Jax's number in the recent calls and pressed it. "I'm almost there," Jax greeted her.

Laurel was about to tell him they were on the run, but the bullet blasted through the side window. The safety glass held, but it wouldn't for long.

"We're on our way to Sweetwater Springs," she said to Jax. "You need to get all the help you can out to 225 Anderson Lane to stop a kidnapping."

"A kidnapping? What's going on there?" Jax asked. At least he didn't hesitate, or curse her, after hearing her voice.

"Someone's trying to take…my son." Not exactly a lie, but Jericho would have to explain the full truth later: that Maddox was his son, too.

Now Jax cursed. Maybe because he'd already filled in the blanks or maybe because he had a child of his own and knew that this was a parent's worst nightmare.

"I'll make the call and get every available lawman in the area out there." And Jax cursed some more when another bullet slammed into the truck. A bullet that he no doubt heard. "Tell Jericho to be careful," he added before he ended the call.

She relayed all of that to Jericho, emphasizing the last part. Did he listen? Of course not. And she was partially thankful for that. She didn't want Jericho hurt, but she also didn't want to waste any time getting to Maddox.

"Hurry," she said purely out of frustration.

Jericho was already hurrying, because she heard the tires squeal against the asphalt as he took a turn. Likely the one to the main road that would lead them to Sweetwater Springs. It was cold, just below freezing, and it was possible there was some ice on the roads. That didn't help the panic, either, but she was thankful that Jericho didn't slow down.

"Are they following us?" Laurel asked.

A muscle flickered in his jaw. "Yeah."

They couldn't lead the gunmen straight to Sandy's house. Of course, it was highly likely that both the gunmen and the kidnappers were working for the same person.

Her father.

"This is all my fault," she whispered. "I should have never left Maddox with Sandy."

"Herschel knows who Sandy is?" Jericho asked without taking his attention off the road.

"No, my father doesn't know her, but he must have found out about her." Laurel hadn't expected that. Especially not so soon. She'd only left Maddox with Sandy a little over two hours ago, and she hadn't thought anyone was following her.

She'd clearly thought wrong.

And her precious son could suffer because of her mistake.

"If Herschel's the one behind this," Jericho said, "then he won't hurt Maddox. Will he?" His jaw muscles tightened again, and there was a low, dangerous tone to that question.

"No. Not intentionally." But her baby was in the middle of an attack, and plenty of things could go wrong. Especially since both Sandy and the kidnappers would be armed, and Sandy wouldn't just let the kidnappers take Maddox without putting up a fight.

Oh, God.

Those hired guns could hurt Sandy. Or kill her. Her father would have given them orders to keep Maddox safe, but he wouldn't have extended such an order to the woman hiding his grandson.

Even though Jericho didn't say anything to her, Laurel could almost feel him trying to work out some kind of plan. Good. Because they needed something—anything—to save their son. No, her father wouldn't hurt Maddox, but if he got his hands on Maddox, he would hide him away so she could never find him.

"Hold on," Jericho warned her. "I have to do something about these SOBs behind us."

He slammed on the brakes, turning the steering wheel and bringing the truck to a stop sideways on the road. Laurel couldn't see the men following them, but she heard the squeal of their brakes as they approached. Felt the cold blast of air when Jericho lowered his window. He took aim.

Then, nothing.

Jericho just waited. The seconds crawling by. Precious time that they should be using to get to Maddox. Laurel knew they didn't have a choice. They couldn't arrive at Sandy's house with gunmen on their tail, but the waiting only caused the panic to smother her again.

Her heartbeat was already crashing in her ears. Her chest so tight that she couldn't breathe. But she could think, and her mind was coming up with all sorts of worst-case scenarios.

Even though she knew Jericho wouldn't approve, she lifted her head just enough so she could see out the side mirror. Laurel immediately spotted the black car. The passenger's door opened, and a man leaned out. He had a gun, and he pointed it right at them.

The shot blasted through the air.

It took her several heart-stopping moments to realize the gunman hadn't fired the shot. Jericho had. And their attacker dropped, falling out of the car and onto the ground.

Jericho fired another shot, this one slamming into the windshield right in front of the driver. The glass was tinted and there wasn't much of a moon, so she couldn't tell if the bullet hit the guy or not. Jericho maybe couldn't tell, either, because he sent two more shots in the same spot.

Nothing.

"Which word of *stay down* didn't you hear me say?" Jericho snarled. He didn't even spare her a glance, but he threw his truck into gear and got them moving again—fast.

She'd heard every word just fine, but Laurel had to see for herself if the gunmen were going to follow them. They didn't. Much to her relief, the black car didn't move when Jericho sped away.

Laurel got back down but gasped when another sound shot through the truck, and for one terrifying moment she thought the gunmen had returned fire, after all. But it was just Jericho's phone that she still had gripped in her hand.

"It's Jax," she said, glancing at the screen. Laurel answered the call and put it on speaker.

"I'm not far behind you—" Jax started.

"Look out for the black four-door car that's maybe still in the middle of the road near the creek," Jericho interrupted. "The guys inside are the ones who attacked Laurel and me."

"Did you kill them?" Jax asked.

"Maybe. But even if I didn't, I doubt they're in any shape to drive."

Good. It seemed wrong to celebrate anyone being shot or killed, but the men were another obstacle they didn't need.

"If they're alive," Jericho continued, "arrest them. Get answers from them and get them fast. But be careful. I don't know what kind of orders they have."

Neither did Laurel, but she did know that wounded men could still kill, and she didn't want that happening to Jax and Dexter.

"I'll keep an eye out for the men and the car," Jax

assured him. "I just got off the phone with Sheriff Cooper McKinnon over in Sweetwater Springs. He and two deputies are at the residence. Two men fled on foot, and the deputies are in pursuit."

"Did they take Maddox?" Laurel couldn't ask fast enough.

"They didn't have a baby with them, but Cooper said he'd call me back once he was sure the residence was secure. I'll let you know as soon as I hear anything." And Jax hung up.

Her stomach tightened. It wasn't over. Just because those would-be kidnappers were running, it didn't mean there weren't other hired guns inside the house. Maybe holding Sandy and Maddox hostage.

Or worse.

"Don't go there," Jericho warned her. The glance he gave her this time let her know that he didn't want to deal with a hysterical woman. "You said your friend was a former cop, and I'm guessing she can handle herself or you wouldn't have left Maddox with her."

Laurel managed to nod. Sandy could indeed handle herself. But that didn't mean something couldn't have gone wrong. She should have hired a team of bodyguards to help, but there hadn't been time.

Maybe still wasn't.

"Any chance we'll be able to link any of these hired guns to your father?" Jericho asked.

"No chance whatsoever. My father is thorough." Among other things. She'd always known he was capable of breaking the law, but Laurel hadn't realized until recently just how far he would go to make sure he got what he wanted.

And what he wanted was Maddox.

"Now that I've defied him," she said, "my father will stop at nothing. *Nothing*," Laurel repeated.

Jericho stayed quiet a moment. Kept driving, the tires squealing when he took the curves too fast. "And you really think marriage will stop him?"

"No," Laurel readily admitted. "He'll put me in jail or a mental hospital. But what the marriage can do is prevent him from taking Maddox."

She hoped.

Still, it was a long shot. And judging from the way Jericho's forehead bunched up, she hadn't convinced him this was the way to go.

"Hang on," he said just as he took another sharp curve. The truck went into a skid, but Jericho quickly regained control.

Laurel was far enough down on the seat that she couldn't see out the windshield, but she did see the lights filtering in. No doubt from the town of Sweetwater Springs. That meant they were only minutes from Sandy's parents' house. However, it seemed to take an eternity for those minutes to pass.

She finally saw the swirl of blue lights from a police cruiser. Red lights, too. Probably from an ambulance.

That put her heart right back in her throat.

Laurel sat up, her gaze firing all around while she tried to spot Maddox and Sandy. No sign of them, but she'd been right about the cruiser and the ambulance. Both were in front of Sandy's parents' house, and there were several lawmen milling around in the yard.

Before Jericho even pulled the truck to a full stop, Laurel tried to bolt out, but as he'd done at the house, he caught onto her arm and stopped her.

"I have to get to Maddox," she insisted.

"No. You have to wait here," he ordered. "And I mean it."

With his gun already drawn, Jericho threw open the door and made a beeline toward the tall, lanky man on the porch. Laurel recognized him—Sheriff Cooper McKinnon. Like Jericho, Cooper had had some run-ins with her father, but she hoped that wouldn't prevent him from doing his job and saving Maddox.

Laurel did wait in the truck. Several painful seconds. As long as she could manage. And then she got out, running toward the two sheriffs. Another lawman in the yard, a deputy, tried to stop her from getting closer, but she batted his hands away.

"My son is in there!"

"It's okay," Cooper assured the deputy. "Let her through."

Laurel didn't take the time to thank him or to respond to the glare Jericho was giving her for disobeying his order. She rushed past the men and hurried into the house. The room was dark, only a corner lamp for illumination, so she needed a moment for her eyes to adjust and take everything in.

Some of the furniture and a Christmas tree had been toppled over. Things were strewn around. Evidence of the struggle that'd taken place here.

Then her heart bashed against her ribs.

Because she saw the blood. On the floor. And on the front of Sandy's white T-shirt.

"Oh, God." Laurel's gaze flew past her friend and to the medic.

Who was holding Maddox.

"He's all right," Sandy quickly told her. The medic repeated a variation of the same thing.

Laurel didn't believe either of them. She hurried to her son, praying there'd be no blood on him. There wasn't. She took him from the medic's arms, trying to check every inch of him. Maddox didn't cry, didn't seem upset, but he did look a little confused about what was going on.

"He wasn't hurt," Sandy insisted.

Laurel shook her head. "But the blood."

"It's mine." Sandy lifted the sleeve of her T-shirt, and Laurel saw the angry gash on her friend's arm.

That gave Laurel a new burst of emotions. Concern and the sickening dread that she'd put her friend in danger. "I'm so sorry."

Sandy shrugged. "I just got grazed by a bullet, that's all. Nothing serious. The medic will stitch me up, but I wanted him to check out Maddox first."

"The kid's fine," the medic assured her. He goosed Maddox in the belly and went toward Sandy to start examining her.

"I can't ever thank you enough," Laurel told the woman.

"No thanks needed." Sandy's attention went to Jericho. "But I'd appreciate it if you caught the scum who did this."

Jericho nodded. "I will." And it sounded like a promise. One that Laurel hoped he could keep.

"Boo-boo," Maddox said, pointing to Sandy's arm.

Since Laurel didn't want him to see that, she sheltered his face against her shoulder and moved to the other part of the room.

And practically ran right into Jericho.

The moment seemed to freeze. Or maybe she felt that way because Laurel's feet suddenly seemed anchored in place. But then, Jericho didn't move, either. He just stood there, his attention fixed on Maddox.

Maddox gave him a wary look, his gaze sliding from Jericho's cowboy hat, face and finally to the shiny badge on his shirt. Maddox smiled.

Jericho sure didn't.

Laurel saw all the emotions go through his eyes. The love, instant and strong. The fear that he'd come so close to losing him. And finally the hatred. Not aimed at Maddox but at her.

For keeping Maddox from him.

"We need to leave," Jericho said to her. Not easily. His jaw muscles were as hard as granite.

Well, they were until Maddox smiled again.

Jericho's expression softened a bit. Then it softened a lot when he reached out and touched his son's cheek. That seemed to be the only invitation Maddox needed, because he reached for Jericho and that badge.

But Jericho didn't get a chance to take him.

Because Cooper stuck his head through the partially opened door. The lawman's attention went straight to Jericho. Then her. "My deputy caught one of them," Cooper said. "It's not good."

No. Laurel wasn't sure she could handle any more bad news tonight.

"What's wrong?" Jericho asked, walking closer to his fellow sheriff.

"I have to get all of you out of here now," Cooper insisted, glancing at both Jericho and Laurel. "The kidnapper we caught told my deputy that more men were on the way here, and they have orders to shoot to kill."

Chapter Five

Shoot to kill.

Not exactly orders that Jericho had wanted to hear, but it'd gotten Laurel, Maddox and him hurrying away from the scene and to the sheriff's office in Appaloosa Pass. That wasn't exactly ideal for a toddler, but it would have to do until Jericho could make other arrangements.

And put an end to the danger.

The first would be a whole lot easier than the last.

Sandy didn't have any info about the kidnappers, and the one captured kidnapper was no longer talking, other than to tell them that those shoot-to-kill orders were meant only for Laurel and him. Jericho felt no relief about the fact that Maddox had been excluded in that hit plan because the baby could have easily been hurt in the attack.

Someone would pay for that.

Herschel, no doubt. But it was going to be a bear to prove his involvement.

Too bad Jax hadn't found the two gunmen in the black car who'd followed Jericho after the attack at his house. Jericho had indeed wounded at least one of them, because his brother had found blood on the road. But neither the car nor the men had been there by the time Jax arrived.

Not good.

He needed all these thugs in jail to up their chances of finding information to stop Herschel. Or anyone else who might be involved in this.

Jericho finished up his latest round of calls and made his way to the break room at the back of the building. Hardly living quarters, but there was a small bed that he and the deputies sometimes used when pulling double shifts. Tonight, however, Laurel and his son were sleeping in it.

It might take a while before those words—*his son*—didn't sound foreign to him. Not because of his feelings for the baby. No, he already loved the little boy. But his son was still a raw reminder that Laurel had kept Maddox from him.

Jericho didn't knock on the door because he didn't want to wake Laurel and the baby, but when he stepped inside the room, he saw that only Maddox was on the cot. The little boy was on his stomach, snuggled in some blankets. No snuggling for Laurel. She was pacing.

And crying.

Jericho saw that right off, though she did quickly wipe away the tears and turn from him. He shut the door so the noise from the squad room wouldn't disturb Maddox.

"Sandy just called," Laurel relayed before Jericho could say anything. "The doctor at the hospital checked her out and released her. She's on her way to Houston to stay with friends, and she told her parents not to come home until she's sure it's safe."

That was a smart move. The hired guns probably wouldn't go back to her place, but there was no sense taking that kind of risk, especially since they might see Sandy as a possible witness who needed to be eliminated. Jericho made a mental note to call Houston PD and arrange for some extra security for her.

"Please tell me the kidnapper you arrested is talking," she added. "And that he's got evidence to lead to my father's arrest."

"Afraid not." But she already knew that would be the answer. If he'd gotten big news like that, he would have come straight to her with it, and he darn sure wouldn't have been sporting a scowl.

A scowl that faded considerably when he went closer to his son.

Hard to scowl when looking at Maddox's face. Jericho could see so much of himself in the boy. Some of Laurel, too.

"What about the other man?" she asked, walking to Jericho's side. "The one who tried to run you off the road. Is he talking?"

Jericho had to shake his head. "We know from his prints that his name is Travis DeWitt. He's got a record, a long one, but so far we haven't been able to connect him to your father."

"There's probably a connection." Laurel gave a heavy sigh and turned away from him again when she swiped at more tears.

She had plenty of reasons to cry. Someone had tried to kill her tonight, and that *someone* apparently wasn't giving up.

Part of him wanted to put his arm around her and try to comfort her. Thankfully, that part of him didn't win out, because the last thing he should do was have Laurel in his arms. Despite the bad blood, the attraction was still between them, too. No sense flaming that kind of heat when it would only make things more complicated than they already were.

She went to the table, picked up a notepad and handed it to him. "Those are the names of the people involved in the money laundering deal."

The deal that Herschel was using to try to have her arrested. There were only two names: Quinn Rossman and Diego Cawley.

"I've tried to dig up anything on them, of course," Laurel continued. "But so far, nothing. I thought it was just a simple real estate deal."

Because her father had no doubt wanted it to look that way.

"That's also the time line, as best as I can remember." She pointed to some dates, times and a brief description of phone conversations she'd had with Rossman and Cawley. "I didn't have any face-to-face meetings with either of them."

Jericho checked through the time line and saw that something was missing. "I'll need the exact dates of your mother's death and when you broke off your engagement." Because one or both of those could have triggered what was happening now.

While Laurel jotted down those dates, Jericho fired off a text to his brother Levi, who was a cop at the San Antonio Police Department, and asked him to run background checks on both men. Maybe Levi could dig up more than Laurel had. He also told his brother that he'd be faxing him a copy of the time line Laurel had just provided.

"So, what happens now?" she asked, handing him back the notepad.

Good question. But Jericho didn't have anything remotely resembling a good answer. "We keep looking for the idiots who attacked us. Keep looking for anything we can use to stop Herschel." He paused. "Please tell me you've got some dirt on him. Any kind of dirt that I can use to start legal proceedings for an arrest."

"No." Another heavy sigh. "Within minutes of Theo telling him that he wasn't Maddox's father and that I'd broken off the engagement, all my computer files and backups disappeared. They were corrupted by a virus that someone triggered."

That someone was no doubt one of Herschel's lackeys. "What about paper files?"

She shook her head. "All missing. By the time I got to my office, everything was gone."

Herschel had worked fast. But then, he'd probably had this backup plan ready to go for years just in case Laurel turned against him. Still, there was something about this that didn't make sense.

"You must have known your father would retaliate when you stopped being the perfect daughter."

"I did. But I didn't think he'd go this far." Her voice broke, and again Jericho had to stop himself from lending her a shoulder to cry on.

Hell.

He only managed to hold himself for a couple of seconds, and then, as if it had a mind of its own, his arm eased around her and pulled her closer. Until they were touching far more than they should. Of course, any kind of touching was out between Laurel and him. That didn't stop him.

Nope.

Jericho just waited until she wrestled with more of those tears. Thankfully, it didn't last long. But it was long enough for his body to get really stupid ideas about the touching.

"Sorry," Laurel said, and moved away from him.

Jericho got the feeling that the apology extended to a lot of things. Things he didn't want to get into right now since he was still seething over the fact that Laurel had kept his son from him. And all because she was afraid Herschel would have tried to kill him.

Which Herschel would have tried to do.

All the more reason to figure out how to put that idiot behind bars.

"I guess you didn't know Theo was going to tell your father the truth about Maddox when you broke off the engagement?" Jericho asked.

"I figured he would. Just not so soon." She pushed her hair from her face. "I wasn't thinking straight. My mother," Laurel added.

Yeah, he figured her grief for her mother had played into this. From all accounts, they'd been close.

"So, after your mother's death, you decided…what?" Because Jericho was having a little trouble filling in the blanks. "That you didn't want to live by your father's dirty rules?"

Her gaze slowly came to his. "I think my father murdered my mother." No tears this time. There was a totally different emotion in her eyes and voice.

Anger.

And lots of it.

"You said she died from cancer," Jericho pointed out.

"I think he helped her death along with an overdose of pain meds." Laurel folded her arms over her chest. Started pacing again. "My mother wanted me to break off my engagement to Theo. She wanted me to leave and tell you the truth about Maddox."

Jericho didn't cheer out loud, but he was on her mother's side on this. "She was right."

"She was. And I think my father eavesdropped on our conversations and arranged for her to get an overdose of painkillers. Yes, she was sick. Very sick. But the chemo was working, and she wasn't so much out of it that she would have taken too big of a dose by accident. I think my father might have put them in her food or something."

That gave him a new surge of anger, too. Herschel preying on a sick woman because she wasn't toeing the line. "Was there an autopsy?"

"No. And my father had her cremated the same day she died."

Jericho wanted to curse. Hell. Now they were looking at murder. Two counts of it, since he was certain Herschel had also been responsible for his father's death.

"I was grieving," Laurel added, "and by the time I figured out what might have happened, it was already too late. Any evidence proving his guilt was cremated with my mother."

Which Jericho was betting wasn't an accident.

There was a soft knock on the door, and a moment later Jax opened it. "DeWitt's lawyer is here."

Good. Maybe the lawyer would convince his scummy client to talk.

Jax walked closer to them, and his gaze slid from Jericho to Laurel. Then to Maddox.

"He's your son." There wasn't a shred of doubt in Jax's voice. "How long have you known?"

"A couple of hours." That alone said plenty, but his brother deserved a whole lot more, especially since Jax knew the emotional wringer he'd been through over the years with Laurel and her father. "Herschel's trying to get custody."

Jax didn't look surprised, just as disgusted as Jericho was. "By trying to eliminate Laurel and you?"

"It looks that way. Herschel has dirt on Laurel to have her arrested." Jericho handed Jax the notepad with the time line and names. "I need that faxed to Levi so he can try to help with the threat of Laurel's arrest. But Herschel also has fake dirt to have her committed to the loony bin. Laurel wants me to marry her so she can transfer custody of Maddox to me."

His brother didn't say anything for several moments. "So, you'll marry her?"

That question just hung in the air, and before Jericho could even attempt an answer, he heard voices in the squad room. Loud ones.

"Wait here with Laurel," he told Jax, and Jericho drew his gun.

Bracing himself for another attack, Jericho hurried out of the break room and down the short hall to the squad room. But there was no attack. Their loud-talking visitors—a tall, bulky-shouldered man and a gray-haired woman—didn't appear to be armed. However, one of the deputies, Dexter, was frisking them, and neither seemed especially happy about that. The unhappiness went up a significant notch when the man's gaze landed on Jericho.

"Sheriff Crockett," he said like venom.

Jericho didn't recognize the guy, but venom like that was almost certainly personal.

"Theo James." Jericho put some venom in his voice, too.

"We want to see Laurel now," the woman demanded. And there was no doubt that it was a demand.

"And you are?" Jericho made sure he sounded like the sheriff when he asked that question.

"Dorothy James. Theo's mother."

Of course.

He didn't see much of a resemblance. Maybe because of the woman's slight build. She looked on the frail side, and her skin was as thin and white as paper. Unlike her son, who towered over her and had a tan despite it being the dead of winter.

Jericho knew that Theo James was a lawyer, like Laurel, but he could have passed for a bouncer. A well-dressed one, though. Jericho figured that suit had come with a big price tag. Ditto for the haircut. And it looked as if he'd had a manicure. As a general rule, he didn't trust men who had manicures.

Of course, he hadn't needed a manicure to feel that way about Theo James.

And Jericho was certain that jealousy wasn't playing into this.

Almost certain, anyway.

"Why do you want to see Laurel?" Jericho pressed.

Dorothy wasn't the sort of woman to hide her emotions. She huffed, glared and generally looked ready to run right over him to get to Laurel. "We heard about the attack, and I want to make sure she's okay. She's my son's fiancée."

"Ex-fiancée," Jericho corrected.

Oh, that did not please either Theo or his mom.

"The breakup is all just a misunderstanding," Theo answered. "And a temporary one. Once I speak with Laurel, we can sort it all out—"

"I doubt that. What do you know about the attack?"

"I don't like your tone," Dorothy snapped. "Are you implying we had something to do with it?"

Jericho stared at her. "Did you?"

"No!"

Man, the woman could yell, and all in the same breath, she belted out a denial and a threat to slap him with a defamation-of-character lawsuit. However, Theo wasn't denying much. That's because he had his attention nailed to the hall. More specifically, to the doorway of the break room where Laurel was standing.

"Laurel," Theo said on a rise of breath, and he started toward her.

He didn't get far because Jericho latched onto his arm. Yeah, the guy was big. Strong, too. But Jericho shoved him back.

"Stay put," Jericho warned him.

"Theo just wants to go to his fiancée." Dorothy again. The woman turned her attention to Laurel. "Are you going to come out here and stop this asinine interrogation of the man you love?"

"No. She's not." And Jericho gave Laurel a warning glance. She didn't say anything, but she also didn't stay put. Not exactly a compromise since he didn't want Laurel in the same general area as the pair.

"Laurel, we need to talk," Theo said. He threw off Jericho's grip but didn't go closer. *"Alone."*

"Then talk. But it won't be alone," Laurel added. "Whatever you have to say, you say here."

Laurel took the words right out of Jericho's mouth. Except he'd intended to glare more than she had. Theo sure added some glare and snarl though—he aimed it at Jericho—before turning back to Laurel.

"Certainly you must know by now that calling off the engagement was a mistake," Theo said to her. "You've upset your father. Us. And yourself."

"Upset?" Laurel threw her hands in the air. "Gunmen attacked Jericho and me. That's why I'm upset." She walked toward them. "If you know anything about those gunmen, tell us."

"Of course we don't know anything," Dorothy insisted. "Now, get Maddox and come home with us. We'll make sure you're both safe." The woman paused. "Where is Maddox, anyway?"

"He's already safe," Jericho assured her.

Partly true. Jax was back there with Maddox, and a gunman would have to break into the back exit or come through the front to get to them. Still, Jericho wasn't about to share that with these two.

A staring match started between Theo and him. Dorothy joined in on it, but Jericho pretty much ignored her and focused on Laurel's ex.

"You think Theo here could be in on the attacks?" Jericho asked Laurel. He knew the question would rile mother and son. And it did.

Dorothy made a sound of pure outrage. "Theo had nothing to do with this. He loves Laurel. He only wants to marry her and be a father to Maddox."

"Maddox already has a father." Laurel's voice was hardly more than a whisper, but it was obvious Dorothy heard it loud and clear. She jerked back as if Laurel had slapped her.

"It's true," Theo said, his voice quiet, as well. "We'll discuss it later, Mom."

Okay, so Dorothy didn't know about Maddox's paternity, but like Jax, she had no trouble putting two and two together. Except in Dorothy's case, there was more disapproval than Jax had shown.

A lot more.

"Later," Theo warned his mother when it appeared she was ready to launch herself at Jericho. He gently took hold of his mother's arm. "Laurel's tired and upset," he repeated, as if making a point. "I can talk to her in the morning when her head is clearer."

Jericho tapped his badge, pulling the lawman card, and he put his gun back in his holster. "You'll talk to me. And not in the morning. You'll do it right now. Is Herschel behind the attacks?"

"Of course," Dorothy answered without hesitation. "Who else?"

Jericho was thinking the *who else* could apply to the woman asking the question. And her hulk of a son. "If you disapprove of her father so much, then why insist Laurel marry Theo?" he asked.

Dorothy gave him an isn't-it-obvious? huff. "Because they're right for each other, that's why. And besides, even if Theo isn't Maddox's biological father, he's been a father to him. He deserves to raise that little boy."

"Theo's hardly seen Maddox." Laurel went to Jericho's side, stared at Dorothy. "For that matter, Theo's hardly seen me over the past six months."

Six months? The more Jericho learned about this unholy union, the less he liked it. Soon, very soon, he'd want to know why Laurel had gotten involved with the guy in the first place.

"Theo hasn't seen Maddox or you much because he's been working out of state, that's why. And I'm betting Theo's seen more of Maddox than his so-called birth father has." With that zinger, Dorothy added a smug nod. No doubt to rile Jericho.

It worked.

However, Jericho reined in his temper so he could try

to get some usable info from these two clowns. Except he realized it would have to wait a second or two when he heard footsteps. They weren't coming from the break room but rather from the side hall where the holding cell was located. The man who appeared was wearing a pricey suit like Theo's.

DeWitt's attorney, no doubt.

"Did you get your client to talk?" Jericho asked him.

The lawyer didn't introduce himself, didn't even spare Jericho a glance. "I've advised him to remain silent. If he's smart, he'll listen." He went past Dexter and let himself out. He shut the door so hard that it shook the nearby Christmas tree and sent the sparse ornaments jangling.

A moment later, Mack, the other deputy, came out from the holding-cell area. "DeWitt's all locked up." He volleyed his attention between Theo and his mother. "Want me to arrest somebody?"

"Not yet. Maybe soon." Jericho turned back to Theo. "Okay, I'll bite. If you know Maddox isn't yours, then why would you want to marry Laurel?"

Theo looked at Jericho as if he'd sprouted horns. "Because I love Maddox and her, that's why."

Maybe. But something about this felt as wrong as wrong could feel. "I don't know all of what's going on, but I suspect there's either money or power involved. Money and power you'll lose somehow if you don't have your ring on Laurel's finger."

Bingo.

Dorothy got some fire in her dust-gray eyes. Theo's teeth came together for a moment. Neither of them, however, jumped to volunteer anything.

However, Laurel did. "Theo and my father were involved in several business deals. Major ones. And some of the investors pulled out when I broke off the engagement."

All right. Now, *that* was motive.

"How big were these business deals?" Jericho asked.

"Millions," Laurel provided.

Yeah, definitely motive.

"A misunderstanding, that's all," Theo insisted. "A few of the investors were worried that I didn't have Herschel's backing. I do. And once that's made clear, then they'll pony up the money again."

"So, you've got Herschel's backing even if he's trying to murder the woman you want to marry?" Jericho concluded.

"My mother accused Herschel of wrongdoing. You didn't hear that from me. And you won't," Theo added. "Because I don't believe Herschel would do anything like this."

Interesting. Dorothy's reaction was interesting, as well. She turned those frosty eyes on her son.

"If Herschel's not behind this, then who is?" Jericho asked Theo.

"You and your family maybe," Theo answered. "From everything I've heard, none of your siblings or your mother wants you involved with Laurel."

They didn't. But Jericho had no intention of admitting that to this beefed-up jerk. He tapped his badge again. "I'm a lawman. My brothers are all lawmen, too. That means we're not into attempted murder or other assorted felonies. Now, talk. If not Herschel, then who? And this time, I want your answer to make sense."

Theo's mouth tightened. "You'd have to ask Laurel. I suspect she was involved with someone else, or she wouldn't have ended our engagement. Someone who's angry enough to want her dead."

Laurel cursed, something he'd rarely heard her do over the years. "There was no one else."

"Right." Theo shot Jericho a glare.

"It appears you've got something to say to me?" Jericho challenged.

Oh, Theo wanted to say plenty, all right, but Jericho saw the moment the man reined in his manicured claws.

Dorothy, however, appeared to be sharpening hers. "When you look at other suspects, look at a businessman named Quinn Rossman."

The very man involved in the money laundering scheme that Herschel was trying to use to have Laurel arrested. Theo clearly knew the name, too. Clearly didn't like his mother mentioning it, because he glared at her.

A glare that the woman ignored. "Rossman's the one who'll take the biggest financial loss because of these failed deals," Dorothy added.

So, the claws weren't for Jericho but for this Quinn Rossman.

Laurel nodded. "Quinn Rossman will lose several of those millions, but like everyone else involved in this, I haven't found anything to link him to what's going on with the attacks."

"Then, keep looking," Dorothy insisted. "You don't have to worry about his moron of a partner, Diego Cawley. He doesn't have the stones or the brains to do something like this."

"Mom," Theo whispered. And it was indeed a warning. "You've said enough."

Jericho didn't agree. He wanted to hear a whole lot more. "You seem to know plenty about these two,

Rossman and Cawley. How much do you know about their money laundering deal?" He stared at Dorothy, waiting for an answer.

"She knows nothing about that," Theo snapped, and he took his mother's arm. "If you want to question us further, then contact our attorney." He rattled off his lawyer's name and left, practically dragging his mother with him.

"Want me to stop them?" Mack asked.

Jericho gave it some thought, and while it would give him some instant gratification to grill Theo like a common criminal, he wasn't likely to get any other answers from the pair. Not tonight, anyway.

"No, let them go," he told Mack before turning to Laurel. "You need to be back in the break room. Away from these windows." They were bullet resistant and the blinds were pulled all the way down, but there was no sense taking any chances.

Laurel motioned toward the break room. "What about the door that's in there?"

"It leads to the parking lot, and it's reinforced and locked. Wired to the security system, too. If anyone tries to come in that way or through the windows, the alarm will sound."

Apparently satisfied with that, she nodded. However, Jericho and Laurel had only made it a few steps when he heard a thudding sound coming from the other side of the building.

From the holding cell.

Both deputies went running in that direction. Jericho nearly followed them but instead decided it was wise to move Laurel into his office just off the hall. There was a single window in there, but it stayed locked. It was also bullet resistant and wired to the security system.

"What's going on?" Jericho called out to the deputies.

No answer. But he could hear them moving around and cursing. What had gone wrong now?

"Wait here," he ordered Laurel.

With his gun drawn, Jericho hurried to the other hall, and he didn't have to go far before he saw the deputies in the holding cell. His first thought was that DeWitt was trying to escape.

But he wasn't. DeWitt was sprawled on the floor.

Dead.

Chapter Six

Laurel opened her eyes and nearly bolted from the bed. It took her a moment to realize where she was.

In the guest room at the Appaloosa Pass Ranch that the Crocketts owned.

Not Jericho's place, either, but the main house. Where most of his family still lived. The same family who despised her. And they had reasons for hating her. Her father's possible involvement with Sherman Crockett's murder, and now she'd kept Jericho in the dark about Maddox.

Her being here would only rub salt in a still-open wound.

Along with possibly bringing the danger to their doorstep. The danger was still there because they didn't have the answers to stop it. Answers they definitely wouldn't get from DeWitt, the man who'd rammed into Jericho's truck.

That's because DeWitt had committed suicide.

The cause of death was a dose of poison that his lawyer had likely slipped him. Of course, last she'd heard, the lawyer was nowhere to be found. The man could have been another hired killer like the ones who were already after her.

Yet, Jericho had insisted on bringing Maddox and her here to the ranch. Despite her objections. He'd said they could discuss it after a good night's sleep and by then she would see that this was the right move.

Well, it was morning, the sunlight seeping through the edges of the blinds, and Laurel still wasn't convinced coming here had been the right thing to do.

Easing out of the bed, she glanced down at the borrowed T-shirt she'd used as a gown. Maybe Jericho's. But thankfully, it didn't carry his scent. She already had too many reminders of the man without having that.

She checked on Maddox, who was still asleep in the crib in the corner of the room. Thankfully, Jericho hadn't had to go to any trouble to find the crib. It was already set up because Jax's fifteen-month-old son sometimes stayed over. Also thankfully, Maddox had slept through the night. Probably because he'd been as exhausted by their ordeal as she'd been.

Laurel looked at the clock on the nightstand, almost seven, and she hurried to the adjoining bathroom so she could grab a shower. Even though the steamy water felt heavenly on her tight muscles, she stayed in the shower only a couple of minutes because Maddox would be up soon. Someone—Jericho's mother, Iris, or maybe the housekeeper—had left her clean underwear and toiletries.

Since she hadn't gotten any clothes from her house, Laurel was forced to put back on the jeans and red sweater she'd worn the night before when she had gone to Jericho's house to ask him to marry her. Clearly, that plan hadn't worked.

Nothing had.

She'd need a change of clothes soon. And a change of location. That meant hiring bodyguards and moving

Maddox to some kind of safe house. No way could she stay at the Crocketts' ranch another night.

Laurel hurried back into the bedroom and practically skidded to a halt when she spotted Jericho. She hadn't heard anything to indicate he was in the guest room. But there he was.

Holding Maddox.

"I didn't hear him wake up," she said. "I didn't hear *you*."

Jericho looked up at her, a half smile on his face, but the smile vanished as quickly as it'd come, and he made a manly sounding grunt. It took Laurel a moment to realize that had something to do with the fact that she was still pulling down her sweater. She hadn't exactly flashed him, but since her bra was nothing but flimsy white lace, he'd gotten an eyeful. She quickly fixed that.

"I heard Maddox and came in to check on him." Jericho turned his attention back to the baby.

"He was fussing?" She wanted to kick herself for not hearing it. And for taking a shower. And for the bra peep show.

"Not exactly. He was just moving around in the crib. I tapped on the door, and when you didn't answer, I came in to make sure he was okay."

Well, Maddox certainly wasn't fussing now. Jericho had taken off his badge, and Maddox was playing with it. Smiling, too. And yes, it was the same half smile that she'd just seen on Jericho's face.

She went to them, expecting Maddox to reach for her, but her son clearly was more interested in the badge and the man holding him.

"Tar," Maddox babbled. His attempt at saying star—the

shape of the badge. Something that Jericho had obviously already taught him. But that wasn't all Jericho had done.

"You changed his diaper?" she asked when she saw the fresh one Maddox was wearing.

Jericho nodded. "He'd stripped off the other one. When I came in, he was bare-butt naked."

Not unusual. Maddox often did that. In fact, she was surprised he still had on the cotton T-shirt, since he'd recently learned to pull that off, as well.

"Anyway, I found the diaper bag and put a fresh one on him," Jericho finished.

It was as if she'd stepped into an alternate universe. "You know how to change a diaper?"

Maybe her tone was a little insulting, because she got a flash of a scowl. "Jax is a dad. We've all had some practice."

"Of course." In fact, since Jax was a widower and worked both at the sheriff's office and the ranch, he and his son probably spent a lot of time here.

But not now.

She'd heard Jericho say the nanny had taken Jax's little boy to relatives who lived out of the county. Wise move, considering it wasn't safe to be around her. Still, it meant Jax wasn't with his son right now, and with Christmas so close, she figured Jax wasn't happy about that.

She certainly wasn't.

"How is Jax?" she asked. "I mean, since his wife died." And not just died. His wife, Paige, had been murdered by a vicious serial killer called the Moonlight Strangler, who'd been murdering women for over three decades.

"Jax's dealing as best he can." As if it was the most natural thing in the world, Jericho took a pair of overalls from the diaper bag and put them on Maddox. "It'd help if we could catch the bastard who killed her. Well, it'd help Jax to better deal with her murder, anyway."

What Jericho wasn't saying was that the Moonlight Strangler had more than one emotional hold on his family. The killer was also the biological father of Jericho's adopted sister, Addie. So, yes, catching the Moonlight Strangler would give Jax and plenty of other families some much-needed justice, but if and when that happened, it wouldn't be easy for Addie to have to deal with the man who'd fathered her.

Of course, other than Jax's wife, the Moonlight Strangler had left Addie and her adopted family alone. And even more, it was rumored that the serial killer had developed an eerie attachment to the Crocketts and had even helped them solve a recent case where Addie had been in danger.

"Jax's son is much too young to remember his mom," Jericho added a moment later. "I guess that's both good and bad. He doesn't remember she was killed. And it helps that Jax has family to step in and try to fill the void."

"You've stepped in," she pointed out. "I just hadn't expected you to be a hands-on kind of uncle."

All right, that earned her another scowl. She was batting a thousand in the piss-off-Jericho-this-morning department.

But then Jericho shrugged and smiled when Maddox looked up at him. "Guess that means you didn't expect me to be a hands-on kind of father, either. Well, expect it because that's exactly what I'll be."

That sounded like a threat. And it probably was. Laurel hadn't thought for one second that she could tell Jericho about Maddox and that he'd then quietly step away.

Jericho wasn't the *quietly* type.

But she also hadn't expected to feel, well, *this*. Maybe a little jealousy. Was that it? Apparently so. For eighteen months, it'd just been mainly Maddox, her mother and her. Theo and her father had rarely been in the picture. Laurel hadn't braced herself nearly enough to share Maddox with his own father.

Nor had she braced herself for being so close to Jericho again.

She'd thought that over two years would be enough to make herself immune to him. No such luck.

"There should be a vaccination that women can take for when they're around men like you." She hadn't intended to say that aloud. It just slipped out. And she thought maybe Jericho would be puzzled by it.

But no.

She got that brief half smile again. The one that turned her brain to mush and made her feel like a hormone-raged, sixteen-year-old girl again.

The heat came. Of course it did. Sliding through her. Jericho dropped his gaze to her mouth, and even though there were still several inches of space between them, she could have sworn she felt him kiss her.

"Yeah," Jericho said. He didn't look any happier about this heat than she was. But he looked just as affected.

Good grief.

Laurel shook her head to clear it. "I'll need to make other arrangements for a place to stay."

"Already in the works. But I figure we'll be okay here for a while."

She didn't like the sound of that. "How long is awhile?"

Jericho's forehead bunched up. "As long as it takes. Maddox's safety has to come first, agreed?"

Laurel nodded, but her agreement was just for the

Maddox-coming-first part of that. "As long as it takes?" she repeated. "Because you know I can't stay here. Your family—"

"Won't be a problem. They know I'm Maddox's father. I told all of them."

All of them, meaning his mother, three brothers, his sister and her fiancé. Laurel had expected it, of course. News like that wouldn't stay secret for long, especially since Jericho was close to his family.

"They'll hate me now even more for keeping Maddox from you all these months," she said on a heavy sigh.

"Well, it didn't earn you any gold stars." He tipped his head to her face. At least, she thought it was her face. She realized he was actually looking at her mouth. "That won't, either."

"That?" Again, it was something she shouldn't have asked out loud. No need to clarify anything when it came to her mouth and his.

"That," he verified, and touched her lips with his index finger. Like the previous look, it felt very much like a kiss. "We're good together like *that*, but it's the only way we're good together. My family knows it, and they won't want me tangled up with you again."

It was true. They were good together when kissing. And in bed. But they couldn't live in bed forever, and the real world always came crashing in. After all, she'd always be Herschel's daughter, and in the eyes of his family, she would always be the one who helped her father get away with murder.

Too bad it was partly true.

If she'd just figured out a way to stop him. Or at least have found some evidence that would lead to his arrest. But nothing.

"Don't worry," Jericho added. "No one will object to you being here."

Only because of Maddox. And it made her wonder— would the Crocketts soon want her out of the picture?

Probably.

That wouldn't happen. Despite the mess she'd made of her life, Maddox was her son, and even though he had Crockett blood, she wouldn't just let Jericho push her out of their son's life.

"I'm bringing in your father for questioning this morning," Jericho tossed out there.

That got her attention. "You talked to him?"

He shook his head. "Only spoke to one of his lawyers and told him if Herschel didn't come in, that I'd put out a warrant for his arrest."

Her gut twisted. Not because her father shouldn't be questioned. He should be. But an ultimatum like that was like poking a stick at a bed of rattlers.

"Maddox and you will stay here while I talk to him," Jericho went on. Not really a request. More of an order. "Chase and Levi will be coming to the ranch, to make sure you're safe."

"But what about you? Someone tried to kill you, too."

He tapped his badge. "That goes with the territory."

As arguments went, that one sucked. Because she was the reason he was in this *territory*.

"Talking to my father won't help," she reminded him. "In fact, prepare yourself because he'll probably have some out-of-county lawman with him who'll insist on you turning me over to him so I can be arrested or locked up in a mental hospital."

"Yeah, I figure he'll try to pull something like that. But I've got three hours before the meeting, and I'm hoping

between now and then we can find something to connect him to the hired guns who've been coming after us."

"Good luck with that." Sarcasm aside, she meant it.
And then she had a thought. "Maybe while you're with my
father, I can somehow get into his office and find something. Not just connected to this, but also to your father's
murder. My mother's death, too."

Jericho didn't shake his head. He just gave her a flat
look to let her know that wasn't going to happen. "Just
in case he's the one who wants you dead, let's not make
it easy for him."

"Just in case?" she repeated. "You're thinking maybe
it's not him, after all?"

"I'm thinking there are other suspects. Theo and his
Mommy Dearest. Diego Cawley and Quinn Rossman.
And no, adding Theo to the suspect list doesn't have any-
thing to do with the fact that he's your ex-lover."

"My ex-fiancé, not my lover," she corrected without
thinking.

She should have thought first.

Because Jericho honed right in on that. "Something
you want to tell me, Laurel?"

"No." And she was certain of that. Best not to get into
why she'd allowed herself to accept a proposal from Theo.
Jericho already thought too little of her, and that wouldn't
help.

Besides, it wasn't any of his business.

Though Jericho's look said differently. Still, he didn't
press it, thank goodness. "Levi called earlier about those
two men, Rossman and Cawley, who were involved in the
money laundering deal."

"And?" she couldn't ask fast enough.

"Lots of shady deals but no arrests. Also, just as you

said, there's no obvious link to your father. *Obvious*," Jericho repeated. "But one of Rossman and Cawley's companies did business with Theo's mother. And I'm not talking about the deal your father's trying to use to put you in jail. This was something that happened well over a year ago."

"How'd Levi find that?"

"Apparently, the FBI had Rossman and Cawley under surveillance for a while. Nothing turned up, but the agent kept track of all the men's contacts. Dorothy was one of them. So were you." Jericho paused. "Who did the initial paperwork for the money laundering deal?"

She huffed. "My father, of course."

"So, there had to have been some kind of communication between him and Rossman and Cawley. I'll have Levi keep digging."

It was a long shot, but maybe, just maybe, something would finally turn up.

"Maddox will be hungry soon," she said, forcing the conversation in a different direction. "He doesn't take a bottle, but he'll need cereal or something."

"I'm pretty sure Ellie and Mom will be fixing some oatmeal," Jericho finally said, a muscle flickering in his jaw.

Ellie, their longtime housekeeper. She probably wouldn't care for Laurel being there, either.

"I can't make this perfect for you," Jericho said as if reading her mind. With Maddox still in his arms, he headed toward the door and the stairs.

Laurel followed after them. "At least tell me someone found the kidnapper and he's been arrested."

"Afraid not." Jericho glanced back at her. No heat this time. Just the same worry she figured was in her own eyes. "Not yet, anyway. But Jax and the other deputies are working on it."

Jericho likely had been, too. There was more than worry and brief flashes of forbidden heat for her in those amber eyes. There was also plenty of exhaustion, which probably meant he'd been up most of the night—something she should have done, as well. But the adrenaline crash had gotten the best of her and, despite the nightmares, Laurel had gotten some sleep.

He led her through the family room, and the Christmas tree with the twinkling lights instantly caught Maddox's attention.

"Pretty," he said. Or rather he said a baby version of the word. And he repeated it with each new decoration. The wreaths on the walls and the gold angels and a trio of stuffed Santas on the mantel.

"My mom really gets into Christmas," Jericho said as they passed another decorated tree in the hall. There was yet another small one in the eating area just off the kitchen.

Normally, Laurel made a big deal out of the holidays, too, but with grieving over her mother's death and trying to escape her father, the holidays hadn't exactly been in the forefront of her thoughts. Too bad, because Maddox deserved Christmas. Instead, they'd dodged bullets.

And she would have to dodge more. Not literal ones this time. But rather, Jericho's mother. Iris was at the stove, stirring a pot of oatmeal. She looked up, sparing Laurel a frosty glance, but her expression warmed considerably when she spotted Maddox.

"There he is." Smiling, Iris put aside the wooden spoon, and wiping her hands on her apron, she walked toward them. She held out her arms, and Laurel got yet another surprise when Maddox went to her.

Maddox had *met* his grandmother hours earlier when they had first arrived at the ranch house, but Maddox hadn't been fully awake then. And Iris hadn't exactly been in a chatty mood, especially since she'd just learned that Jericho was Maddox's father. Laurel was certain Jericho had gotten an earful about that after Laurel had gone to bed.

"He's usually a little shy around strangers," Laurel remarked. Obviously, though, he didn't consider Iris a stranger. Or the enemy.

Unlike the way Iris felt about her.

After a few snuggles with Maddox, Iris finally made eye contact with her. "I can't forget that my husband is dead. Murdered. And it's all because of your family. You might not have pulled the trigger, but you also didn't help us put Herschel behind bars. Now it's led to this."

Laurel nodded, was about to assure her that she couldn't forget it, either, but Iris continued before she could say anything.

"But we need a truce," Iris said. "Certainly not for your sake but for Maddox's. Agreed?"

"Agreed." It definitely wasn't a warm fuzzy welcome, but then Laurel hadn't expected one.

Iris's smile returned. Aimed at Maddox, of course. "Are you hungry, sweetie?" Iris asked him. "Because Grandma and Ellie made some oatmeal. Scrambled eggs, too."

Laurel noticed the easy way *Grandma* had rolled off her tongue. It had to be hard because of the bad blood between their families. Still, Iris was either putting on a good show or else she wasn't letting any of that bad blood extend to Maddox.

"The oatmeal will be fine." Laurel went to the stove to dish him up a bowl so it could cool.

"Tar," Maddox said, showing Iris Jericho's badge.

"Yes, it is. A pretty one. And there's another star. A gold one." Iris pointed to the one on top of the Christmas tree by the breakfast table, and she went in that direction with Maddox. Maddox discarded the badge when Iris plucked off a horse ornament for him to play with.

That's when Laurel noticed the blinds were down. Not just in the breakfast area, either, but in the kitchen, as well. That probably wasn't their usual position, but she was thankful for it. The ranch was likely well protected, but that didn't mean someone with a rifle couldn't fire a shot into the house, as they'd done to Jericho's the night before.

Not exactly a good thought to settle her already churning stomach.

And speaking of unsettling things, Laurel glanced around at the empty kitchen. She'd known Chase and Levi wouldn't be there yet, but she'd expected to see the others. "Where is everyone?"

Iris and Jericho exchanged an uneasy glance before Jericho answered. "Addie and Weston are in Austin visiting his sister. Jax's son is staying with his other grandmother for a few days."

Laurel understood the uneasy glance then. "They're not here because of me. Because of the danger." She huffed. "Maddox and I should have been the ones to stay elsewhere."

"Nonsense." Iris got another ornament off the tree for Maddox. "Addie and Weston understand."

Laurel didn't get a chance to argue about that because

Jericho's phone rang, and she saw Jax's name on the screen. Since this probably had something to do with the investigation, he stepped out of the breakfast area and into the hall.

"I'll feed Maddox," Iris volunteered, taking the bowl of oatmeal from Laurel.

"Thank you." And Laurel meant it. She was thankful because it gave her the opportunity to go into the hall with Jericho and listen in on his conversation.

Jericho didn't put the call on speaker. Probably because he didn't want his mother to hear if it turned out to be more bad news. That meant Laurel had to go close to him.

Very close.

And despite the fact her mind should be on anything but Jericho, her body gave her a little nudge to let her know Jericho would always be on her mind.

"We haven't found anything on DeWitt's lawyer," she heard Jax say. "He used a fake ID when he checked into the sheriff's office, and we can't get any usable fingerprints off the sign-in sheet."

All planned, no doubt. Heck, the man probably wasn't even a lawyer.

"I reviewed the surveillance footage from the camera outside the holding cell," Jax continued, "and he did hand DeWitt some papers. It's possible that's when he passed DeWitt the poison he used to kill himself."

"So, he didn't actually murder him," Jericho concluded. "Any reason why DeWitt would commit suicide?"

"Nothing I can find so far." Jax added something under his breath she didn't catch. Profanity, maybe. "In fact, I'm not finding anything on anybody that'll put an end to this danger."

Jericho whispered some of that profanity himself. "Get some rest. I'll be there in about an hour."

He pushed the button to end the call but didn't budge. Maybe because Jericho needed a moment to take some of the gloom and doom off his face. Laurel was sure there was plenty of it on her face, as well.

"What now?" she asked.

Jericho stared at her and touched her arm, rubbed gently. "I'll make arrangements for a safe house for the three of us."

She was partly relieved that Jericho would be going with her. No one would protect Maddox the way he would. But Laurel reminded herself that being under the same roof with Jericho just wasn't a good idea.

Jericho must have gotten that same jolting reminder because he glanced down at where he was rubbing her arm and eased back his hand. He looked ready to apologize.

Or kiss her.

That stupid part of Laurel was hoping for the kiss. But he didn't get a chance to do either because the phone in the kitchen rang. Jericho hurried to answer it, but his mother beat him to it.

"Teddy," Iris greeted. She was still holding Maddox in her arms. Still smiling, but the smile quickly faded. "I'll let Jericho know."

"Teddy's a ranch hand," Jericho explained to Laurel. "What'd he want?" he asked his mother the moment she hung up.

"We have a visitor," Iris said, her voice practically trembling. "Herschel Tate just arrived, and he's demanding to see his daughter."

Chapter Seven

Hell. This was not the way Jericho had wanted to start the morning. Yes, he'd braced himself to interrogate Herschel. But not now and not here at the ranch.

And definitely not with Laurel and Maddox around.

"Oh, God," Laurel said under her breath.

He hated that her father could put that kind of fear on her face. Hated even more that the fear was warranted.

Jericho took the phone from his mother, but for Maddox's sake, he tried to appear calm. He figured he was failing, but maybe Maddox wouldn't be as frightened as Laurel was.

"Teddy," Jericho greeted the ranch hand, and he put the call on speaker so Laurel could hear. His mother moved into the hall with Maddox. "Where's our visitor now?"

"Herschel's still in his car in the driveway. I've got a gun pointed at him. That was the right thing to do, wasn't it?"

"Absolutely." Jericho had instructed all the hands to keep an eye out for a possible attack, and this could be the start of one. Of course, it'd be pretty stupid of Herschel to come to the ranch and personally try to attack them. "Keep the gun on him. Is he alone?"

"No. There's a woman and another fella with him. And

a driver. The woman says her name is Nan Winston, Herschel's lawyer, and the fella introduced himself as Laurel's fiancé."

Laurel groaned. "Ex-fiancé. And what the heck is Theo doing here? Why are any of them here?"

Both good questions, but Jericho doubted their visitors would provide the answers to Teddy.

"I want to see my daughter," he heard Herschel insist. Not exactly a shout but close enough.

With Herschel's temper and mean streak, the man might provoke Teddy into a fight just so he could shoot the ranch hand. Of course, Teddy knew how to handle a gun. That's why Jericho had posted him out front. Still, it was best if Jericho went outside and faced down this idiot and his entourage. Besides, he might even get Herschel to say something incriminating so he could arrest him.

Or so Jericho could shoot him.

It was probably wrong to wish that, but after the things Herschel had done, he deserved a bullet or two.

"Wait inside," Jericho told Laurel. "And I mean it. I don't want your father to even know you and Maddox are here."

Laurel suddenly no longer looked afraid, and she darn sure wasn't trembling. "He already knows or he wouldn't have shown up. I need to stand up to him."

"Admirable. But it's not the right time."

She shook her head, no doubt ready to launch into an argument. One that Jericho intended to nip in the bud. He took hold of her arm and moved her deeper into the kitchen so Maddox wouldn't hear. Maddox probably wouldn't be able to understand what was being said, but Jericho didn't want to risk it.

"Both the so-called lawyer and driver could be armed,"

Jericho reminded her. "Plus, you don't need to go another round with delusion-boy Theo. At best, he has a serious issue with reality by still referring to himself as your fiancé. At worst, he wants you dead and is trying to goad you into coming out."

Her chin stayed firm. "I need to stand up to him, too."

"Again, admirable. But it's not going to happen. Not until one or both of them are behind bars."

Jericho took his badge from the table and clipped it on. He was already wearing his holster and weapon, something he normally didn't do around the house, but then just about everything that'd happened in the past twenty-four hours had been far from normal.

"They could gun you down, too," Laurel said, following him to the front.

Jericho took hold of her. There were sidelight windows on both sides of the door, and while there was holly and such rimming the glass, he didn't want to risk Herschel's seeing her. Jericho glanced out, though, and saw not only Teddy but three other ranch hands.

All armed.

Their visitors were still inside the car. Or rather the limo. But the left-side passenger's door was open.

"I'll be okay." Jericho put on his jacket and Stetson. "And remember that part about staying inside." He shot her a warning glance he hoped would do the trick and make her stay put.

He didn't open the front door until he made sure Laurel wouldn't be in anyone's line of sight, and he went onto the porch, closing the door behind him. It was cold, and he got a full blast of that cold when the wind battered into him. The temperature was yet another reason to end this conversation fast so he could get Herschel and the others off the ranch.

The moment Jericho went down the stairs, someone stepped out of the limo. Herschel. He'd always been a big man, and he still was, even in his late sixties. Not overweight, just bulky. He'd always looked formidable to Jericho.

That hadn't changed, either.

He, too, was wearing a cowboy hat and a heavy jacket. Jericho didn't care much for that jacket because it could conceal a weapon.

"What the hell do you want, Herschel?" Jericho didn't want to sound even marginally pleasant.

His question must have spurred the others into action, because Theo stepped out, and he was soon followed by a leggy blonde wearing a red dress. Hardly the right garb for butt-freezing weather. This was no doubt Nan Winston, Herschel's lawyer.

"You know what I want—to see my daughter. Tell her to come out."

Jericho would take a hit with a hot branding iron first. "Who says she's here?"

Herschel jammed his thumb against his chest. "I do. My daughter's predicable."

He made a sound to let Herschel know he didn't agree with that. Laurel was far from predicable.

"Tell your driver, aka thug, to get out of the car, too," Jericho ordered. "I expect this little chat to be short and sweet. Emphasis on the short part. But I want everyone to keep their hands where I can see them."

Herschel chuckled, obviously trying to dismiss any danger that Jericho might pose to them. "You're going to shoot us, *Sheriff*?"

"Maybe. Haven't had my coffee yet, and I'm a bit testy. My advice—don't test me anymore. Do as I've said, speak your piece and then get the hell out of here."

No more chuckling, but his words did spur some glares from the trio. The driver also stepped out. He didn't lift his hands in the air, but he did put them on the car door in plain sight.

"I know my daughter's here," Herschel argued. "I had someone watching the sheriff's office, and they called and said you brought her and Maddox to your family's ranch. I gotta say, that wasn't very predictable."

Jericho shrugged, not fessing up to anything.

But Jericho had to admit to himself that it was possible for someone to have followed him from the sheriff's office. Not all the way to the ranch however. Even though he'd been bone tired, he would have noticed another vehicle on the rural road, but Herschel's hired morons could have seen the route he was taking and figured out he was going to the ranch.

"I'm here to take my daughter and grandson home," Herschel insisted.

"Really?" Jericho challenged "You honestly think I'd let that happen?"

"The law's on my side, Jericho. I have proof Laurel's not mentally fit to be a mother."

"Says you."

"And a team of respected psychiatrists," Herschel countered.

"Which you bought and paid for," Jericho countered right back.

Herschel didn't deny it. "She got involved with you and got pregnant. That proves she's not stable."

"No." Jericho stretched that out a few syllables. "It proves she was once attracted to me, that's all."

Oh, Herschel didn't like that one bit. Herschel really wouldn't like it if Jericho pointed out that the attraction was still there. Jericho certainly wasn't pleased about it, either.

"Laurel committed a crime," Herschel tried again.

"That's the pot calling the kettle black. Or did you think I'd forget all about you ordering my father's murder?"

Now Herschel got a smug look. So did the skinny lawyer. "But there's proof of Laurel's crime," the lawyer said. "No proof whatsoever of Herschel's wrongdoing. Unlike his daughter, he has a spotless record."

No smug look for Jericho. He huffed, and because he really was testy, he put his hand over his gun. "You know, I'm getting a little tired of you bantering around this so-called proof you have against Laurel. Where is it?"

"You'll see it soon." Herschel checked his watch. "The warrant for her arrest will be finalized within the hour."

"Finalized unless I hand over my son to you," Jericho finished for him.

It wasn't Herschel who answered but rather Theo. "You don't have the right to raise that little boy."

Jericho was about to assure Theo and these other three that he did indeed have that right, but then he heard a sound he definitely didn't want to hear. The front door of the house opening.

And Laurel stepped onto the porch. She didn't stay on the porch, however. She marched down the steps toward them.

"Which part of *stay inside* didn't you hear me say?" Jericho whispered to her through clenched teeth.

"I can't let you fight my battles for me."

He would have liked to remind her this battle wasn't just hers. It was for custody of Maddox. But there was no sense letting her father know they were still at odds.

"You'll be arrested soon," her father said. "I plan to wait here until the cops from Dallas show up and take you away in handcuffs."

So, the Dallas PD had drawn the short straw. They probably didn't know this was part of Herschel's sick plan—especially since there was almost certainly some evidence against Laurel. *Some.* Her father would have seen to that.

Too bad Herschel hadn't sought out help from the SAPD. Jericho's brother Levi could have possibly helped put an end to this already. Of course, Herschel was probably insisting the crime had taken place in the Dallas PD's jurisdiction.

"I guess this means I won't be going to a mental hospital," Laurel remarked. She folded her arms over her chest, faced their enemies head-on. Well, at least she wasn't looking afraid now. Just riled to the core.

"That was only if the warrant fell through," her father answered. "It didn't. But I can always use it as a backup."

"Or you can come to your senses and do the right thing," Theo said to Laurel.

When Theo took a step toward Laurel, Jericho drew his gun. Aimed it at the man. "First warning. Don't come closer. You don't get a second warning."

Theo's expression turned to iron, and his eyes were still narrowed when he looked at Laurel. "You can marry me and put an end to all of this."

"Marry you?" she repeated. "And that'll make the

criminal charges and the insanity allegations go away? That's not going to happen."

"Then prepare yourself to go to jail," the lawyer said, her tone sassy enough to put Jericho's teeth on edge.

"I'm already tired of you and I barely know you. Get back in the limo," Jericho ordered her. "Teddy, shoot her if she manages to get her hands on a gun while she's in there."

Clearly, Nan wasn't accustomed to being put in her place. She cursed at him. A vanilla kind of profanity that a third grader would have used. But she got her butt back in the limo.

One down, three to go.

Jericho pointed to several heavily treed areas around the ranch and then got the attention of the other two ranch hands. "Keep watch, because our visitor here likes to hire killers. Which is why you should be inside," he added to Laurel.

"I'm staying put until they leave," Laurel insisted.

Of course she was. And besides tossing her over his shoulder and hauling her back into the house—something that Jericho briefly considered—there was no way to get her to budge. That meant he really needed to hurry this conversation along.

"All right, let's just get this out on the table," Jericho said to Theo. "Laurel's not marrying you." After clearing that up, he turned to Herschel. "And she's darn sure not going anywhere with you."

"Then be prepared for me to take custody of my grandson, because the warrant will include a court order for me to do just that."

Doubtful. Still, Herschel could have manipulated that some way, too. It didn't matter. Jericho usually didn't have a shades-of-gray approach to the law, but in his son's case, he'd make some exceptions.

"I'm Maddox's father," Jericho said, just in case these two nut jobs had forgotten that significant detail.

Hell. Herschel's smug look returned. "You have no legal right to him. Your name's not even on the birth certificate. Plus, I have DNA results that my own daughter gave me. Results that prove that Theo is the baby's father."

"Those results are a lie!" Laurel snapped.

"Are they?" Herschel's smug look got worse.

"You know they are. I couldn't put your name on the birth certificate," Laurel whispered to Jericho. "I couldn't let my father know. And I would have had to let you know, too."

Yes, because she couldn't have added Jericho's name without his knowledge. Considering she thought it would be a death sentence for him, there was no way Laurel would have done that. But that blank space and the fake DNA results were going to give Theo some leverage.

If Jericho allowed it to happen.

He wouldn't.

Herschel shrugged. "It'll take a while for you to redo the DNA test. Until then, Theo has a right to take his son. Go inside, Theo, and get Maddox. You know he's in that house."

"And I have a right to shoot Theo if he tries to go inside," Jericho insisted right back.

Maybe Theo wasn't so stupid, after all, because he didn't make a move. "We'll be back when that court order arrives, and Herschel and I will take custody."

Jericho wanted to use the cliché *over my dead body*, but since that's exactly what someone wanted, he kept it to himself. Besides, he didn't need to say anything. Herschel knew what kind of man Jericho was, and even with all this bluster and talk, he also knew Jericho wouldn't just hand the child over to Theo or him.

"Think of the danger," Theo said, looking at Laurel now. "Someone's obviously trying to kill Jericho and you. Maddox shouldn't be near you, or he could get caught in the crossfire."

"He's already been caught in it." And that's all Laurel said for several moments. The anger was there in her voice, but there was also plenty of hatred. "If you're so concerned about his safety, then come clean and tell us who's behind the attacks."

She stared at her father, maybe waiting for Theo to acknowledge in some way that Herschel was responsible.

Theo didn't utter a word.

But Herschel did. "I'm not trying to kill you."

"Then who is?" Laurel pressed.

Herschel blew out a long breath, rubbed the space between his eyebrows as if fending off a headache. "Maybe someone involved in that money laundering deal you orchestrated."

"I didn't orchestrate it. I was set up, probably by you. So, who other than you would want me dead?"

"Dorothy," Herschel finally admitted.

Theo opened his mouth as if to deny that, but he only shook his head. "Maybe," he conceded.

What Theo didn't concede, however, was that he had just as much, if not more, motive than his mother. Something he'd never admit.

This was another of those not-over-my-dead-body situations. One they'd never resolve. But in the meantime, the minutes were just ticking away, and if Herschel was telling the truth, it wouldn't be long before the Dallas police arrived. That meant Jericho had to get Laurel and Maddox out of there fast.

"Come on." Jericho slipped his arm around Laurel's waist and got her moving toward the house.

"You can't run!" Herschel called out to them. "I have someone watching the ranch and the roads. Of course, if you try to run, I can have you charged with obstruction of justice. Then, Theo won't have any trouble claiming that boy."

Jericho didn't trade barbs with the man. Didn't even acknowledge him. He just hurried Laurel inside.

"Get Maddox's things," Jericho told her once he'd shut the door.

Her eyes widened for a moment. "We're leaving?"

"Yeah. Herschel might be watching the roads, but we can get out to the highway using the old ranch trails." Jericho didn't see another way around leaving.

Another way around something else that had to be done, too.

"We're going to a safe house," Jericho told her. "And then we're getting married—*today.*"

Chapter Eight

As a young girl, Laurel had fantasized about her wedding.

To Jericho, of course.

However, she hadn't imagined her wedding would happen while she was wearing jeans, a purple top and while hiding out in a safe house. In her fantasy, Jericho hadn't been scowling, either.

Too bad that was what he'd been doing a lot since they'd arrived at the safe house. Of course, there was plenty to scowl about.

Moving her from the ranch and hiding her wouldn't put him in the good graces of the Dallas PD. Something that clearly didn't please him since he'd been the sheriff of Appaloosa Pass for well over a decade. This had also put his brothers in a bind since they, too, were lawmen, and the Dallas PD would be pressing each one of them to tell them where Jericho had taken her.

They wouldn't tell.

His brothers were loyal to him.

But that didn't mean this kind of pressure couldn't hurt their careers. Plus, as long as there was danger of an attack, Jericho's family would have to continue watching their backs. Because the person after them could use Jericho's family to get to him.

She definitely wasn't getting on their good sides like this.

The only upside to this was that for the moment Maddox was safe. And this marriage would ensure his safety even if she was arrested.

Laurel checked her hair in the dresser mirror. Yes, it was silly to be concerned with such things, but it was her wedding day, after all. Her hair was fine, but there was no way she could conceal the worry in her eyes.

Thank goodness Maddox was too young to notice it, and so far he'd acted as if coming to the safe house was an adventure. Laurel could partly thank Iris for that. Jericho's mother had come with them. Along with Levi. Iris and Levi had spent the past couple of hours entertaining him in the large family room of the rural ranch house.

Jericho, too.

She wasn't sure why she was surprised by it, but Jericho seemed to slide right into daddy mode. And it wasn't as if he didn't have other things to do. He had plenty, what with all the arrangements for the so-called wedding, and for transferring custody of Maddox to him. Jericho had taken care of those things. Had continued to get updates about the investigation and some other cases he was in the middle of.

But it certainly felt as if he'd put Maddox first.

Since her bedroom door wasn't shut, Laurel had no trouble hearing the footsteps in the hall, and a moment later Jericho appeared in the doorway.

Still scowling.

Like her, he was dressed casually, wearing jeans and a gray button-up shirt.

"How's Maddox?" she asked.

"Napping on a quilt in the family room."

Not unusual since Maddox still took two naps a day. At least they'd managed to maintain parts of his routine.

"I think we tired him out," Jericho added. "Does he always have that much energy?"

"Always. Between him and me, you won't be getting much sleep for a while." She winced because that sounded a little more intimate than she'd intended.

Thankfully, Jericho ignored it and glanced in the direction of the family room. No doubt where his mother and Levi still were, before he stepped inside and shut the door.

"The justice of the peace will be here in about an hour," he explained. "Keep your fingers crossed that the weather cooperates."

Yes, that. As if they needed more obstacles. The sky was iron-gray, and it was cold. Anything that fell now was more likely to be ice than snow. A white Christmas was rare in this part of the state. However, ice could definitely slow down or even stop the justice of the peace from getting out to the safe house.

"You trust this person?" she asked.

Jericho nodded. "Jax will be driving him out and will make sure they aren't followed."

Good. Jericho had already told her that only a handful of people, mostly his family and his deputies, knew about the location of the safe house. It wasn't one that any other law enforcement agencies used but rather belonged to a friend of one of the deputies.

"I've also started the paperwork for you to sign over custody of Maddox to me," Jericho added.

That was what Laurel wanted. Or rather what she

needed to happen. Still, it felt like a punch, and the doubts came. So did the tears that she tried to blink back.

"Your family hates me," she said.

"Yeah, they do. But that has nothing to do with giving me custody. I'm doing this to stop Herschel, not to claim Maddox."

Laurel heard the accusation in his voice, and it was there for a good reason. She'd kept Maddox from him. "What I did was wrong. But please believe me, I thought I was doing the right thing."

Jericho didn't give her any indication he agreed with that. The pain was still too raw over having been shut out of his son's life for eighteen months. Maybe it always would be. The current situation certainly wasn't helping matters.

He glanced at her. Specifically at her tear-filled eyes. He mumbled something she didn't catch, and as if it was the last thing on earth he wanted to do, Jericho slipped his arm around her. Pulled her to him.

Laurel hated that it was a dose of instant comfort.

Instant attraction, too.

He made a sound deep within his chest, and backed away. Physically, he did, anyway. The attraction was still there. His scowl, too, though he had toned it down at bit. It made her wonder, though, if it'd ever go away.

"You don't really want to do this with me," she said.

"What?" No scowl, just some confusion in his eyes. "The marriage? Or…"

"Of course. Oh." They were talking about the forbidden attraction now. The kind of attraction that would cause a rift the size of Texas in his family. "Nothing will happen. We've got this under control."

Laurel hadn't realized Jericho would take that as a

challenge, and maybe he hadn't wanted it to be one. He cursed again. Not general cursing, either. It had her name in it. And judging from the profanity, she thought he was about to call off the wedding and storm out of there.

He didn't.

Still cursing her, and adding some raw words for himself, Jericho took hold of both her arms and snapped her to him. Laurel didn't even manage a sound of protest before his mouth was on hers.

The feelings came in a flash. The memories and the attraction. Always the attraction. But the pleasure was there, too, simmering right along with other things—including the reminder that this wasn't a good thing for them to be doing.

Her body didn't listen.

It never listened when it came to Jericho.

For just a couple of moments, she wanted to get lost in the pleasure. In the kiss. Not hard to do. The heat warmed her from head to toe. His mouth took the heat to a slow burn, and it didn't take long for Laurel to do something about that. She slipped her arms around his neck and pulled him closer.

He had the beginnings of an erection. She found that out when she brushed against him. That should have been a big red flag to put a stop to this, but her body seemed to think it was a good thing. Jericho still wanted her. Of course, the deep kiss was already proof of that. She got more proof when he dropped some of those kisses on her neck.

And lower.

Mercy, she wanted him to go lower.

More profanity from him. Not exactly traditional foreplay, but then this wasn't foreplay.

Was it?

She tested that by brushing her sex against his.

All right, it felt like foreplay, which meant it had to end. There was no way she could have sex—

Jericho groaned and jammed his hand between them to block the *foreplay*. Not a good idea because it meant his hand was practically between her legs. Exactly where that part of her wanted it to be.

Without warning, Jericho turned her, pressing the front of her against the door. And pressing his body against her back. Definitely not the way to continue the foreplay.

Or so she thought.

It slowed things down. No more frantic kisses. No more testing the limits of his jeans by brushing against his erection.

But the kissing didn't stop.

With his breath gusting and hot on her skin, Jericho cupped her chin with his left hand and kissed the back of her neck. He kept his other hand on her lower stomach, and he lowered it even more. Touching her until Laurel's vision blurred and she lost what little breath she had.

She didn't get a chance to regain her breath because Jericho pressed himself, hard and hot, against her. And just when Laurel was within a heartbeat of an orgasm, he stepped back.

All the way back.

So that no part of him was touching any part of her.

Laurel stayed there a moment. Not wanting to face him. But knowing she couldn't put that off forever. She eased around, fixing her clothes to avoid eye contact with him. However, Jericho forced that, too, by catching onto her chin again.

"Yeah, we've got it all under control," he snapped. "I don't think it's a good sign when we start lying to ourselves."

No. But then making out with him wasn't a good sign, either.

She glanced at his zipper area. "Are you going to do something about that?" Good grief. "I mean, you can't go out there like that."

"And you can't go out there like that." He dropped his gaze to her breasts. Her nipples were still hard and pressed against her top.

Since there wasn't much else she could do, Laurel laughed. Not actually from humor. More from the absurdity of this. "Guess we're both wearing our lust on our sleeves."

"We always have." He scrubbed his hand over his face. "Look, we can go ahead and finish what we started, but it'd be a mistake. Agreed?"

"Yes."

She couldn't say it fast enough. Especially not with his brother and mother just a few walls away. Mothers and siblings tended to have a sixth sense about that sort of thing, and she already had enough on her plate without incurring another dose of Crockett anger.

Since some of that anger would also be aimed at Jericho.

They would forgive him, eventually, for fathering a child with her, but that forgiveness wouldn't extend to starting up their relationship again.

"I should check on Maddox," she said, though she knew he was fine. Laurel just didn't want Iris and Levi to notice that Jericho and she had been behind a closed door for much too long.

"Do we look guilty of…something?" Laurel asked him as she opened the door.

He didn't answer, other than emit a soft grunt, which let her know they did indeed look guilty.

They went into the family room, and yes, both Levi and Iris were still there. Levi was at the window, keeping watch, but he glanced in her direction, giving her one of those Crockett snarls. He was like Jericho in so many ways. Just slightly less intense. But he made sure she got some of that intensity.

Iris, too.

Except her expression was one of apprehension. She stood, facing Jericho. "Are you sure this marriage is the only way?" Iris asked.

"It's the fastest way," Jericho assured her. "If all goes well, I'll have custody of Maddox in a day or two, and then we can focus fully on dealing with Laurel's legal issues. We're already working on that, but Herschel has a lot of judges and important people in his pocket."

"Maybe a lot of hired guns, too," Laurel added.

"Maybe?" Iris questioned. Despite the truce Iris had offered, it was clear it was going to take a while for the woman to fully trust Laurel. "Even now you doubt him."

Laurel looked her straight in the eye. "No. I don't. I know what he is, but there are other suspects. Theo and his mother. Plus, it might be someone who's upset about the business deals that fell through when I broke off my engagement with Theo."

Obviously, Iris wasn't buying any of that. And she might be right. Her father was certainly the top suspect for the attacks, and that's the main reason Laurel didn't want to exclude the others. Someone, like Theo, could be using this to get revenge on her while her father would get the blame.

"I don't like this." Iris shook her head, looked at Jericho. "If you're her husband and if it comes up that she knows something about Herschel murdering your father, then you can't testify against her."

Oh, so that was the reason Iris was worrying. Well, one reason, anyway. The bad blood was playing into this, too.

"As my husband, Jericho can't be forced to testify. But if Jericho found anything, I'm sure he would testify even if it meant putting me behind bars." That kiss had made her weak in the knees, but she wasn't delusional. "I promise you, though, I had nothing to do with your husband's murder."

Iris's chin came up. "But you never tried to have your father convicted of it, either."

"True. I looked, but I didn't look hard enough." Because she'd known that her father would get back at her through her mother.

And he had.

"Mom," Levi said, "it's okay. Jericho knows what he's doing." However, despite the lack of bite in his voice, Levi didn't sound any more convinced than Iris looked.

Jericho's phone buzzed, and she saw Dexter's name on the screen. Laurel hoped the deputy wasn't calling with another round of bad news. Jericho went into the kitchen to take the call, and Laurel followed him. This time, he put the call on speaker. Probably because he didn't want any more close contact with her. After what had just happened in the bedroom, that wasn't a bad idea.

"Jericho, we've got a problem," Dexter greeted. "There were just two cops here from the Dallas PD, and they were looking for Laurel and you. I told them I didn't know where you were."

"Thanks." Jericho paused. "What else did they say?" he asked, because he no doubt heard the hesitation in his deputy's voice.

"I tried to buy you some time. Said I'd need a day or two to find you. But they didn't believe that. They left, but they said they'd be back. They're giving you six hours to turn over Laurel, or they'll swear out a warrant for your arrest. And for me and all the other deputies. They said they'd get the Texas Rangers in here to take over the whole sheriff's office."

Jericho said a single word of profanity under his breath. Laurel silently said a whole lot more. She didn't want anyone to go to jail to protect her, but she also didn't want to hand over her son to her father.

"I'll handle this," Jericho assured Dexter at the same time that Levi called out from the living room. "Jax and the justice of the peace are here."

"Good." Though there was nothing in Jericho's body language that indicated anything about this latest news was *good*. "I'll phone you back," he added to Dexter, and he ended the call.

"I'll have to turn myself in," Laurel insisted. And her mind began to whirl with the possibilities of how to do that while keeping Maddox safe.

Jericho gave her a look that could have withered an entire forest, and he took hold of her hand to lead her back into the living room. "Come on. Once the vows are finished, we'll work out what the hell we're going to do."

Chapter Nine

Jericho checked the time. Laurel and he had been married exactly one hour, and he was already on his sixth phone call. He'd never really given much thought to his wedding day, but he sure as heck hadn't figured that he'd be spending his time trying to keep himself and his entire department out of jail.

But that's exactly what he was doing.

Along with putting some things into motion that he hoped would buy Laurel and him some time. Time he needed, because the only way to put a stop to this situation was to find the link between those hired thugs and Herschel.

"I might have something," Levi said the moment Jericho finished his latest call.

Since Levi, too, was working on his own string of phone conversations, Jericho hoped his brother had a whole lot better news than he did.

"It's about Rossman and Cawley," Levi explained. "The FBI wiretapped their office months ago and recorded all their calls. There are several from Laurel to discuss a real estate transaction. But there's one from a man who doesn't identify himself. It could be Herschel. There's nothing that out and out incriminates him. Only one sentence—'Let's get this done.' If it's Herschel's voice, then we'll at least have proof that he was in on the deal."

"You can access my phone messages if you need a sample of my father's voice to compare to the recording," Laurel said, walking into the kitchen. She'd obviously been listening. "I don't have my phone with me. Jericho said maybe it could be traced, so I took out the memory card and left it at the ranch."

"I can access your phone messages from here," Levi assured her.

She blew out a breath of relief and turned her attention to Jericho. Laurel was obviously waiting for good news. Too bad Jericho didn't have a string of good news to give Levi or her. But he did have something.

"The custody papers have been filed," Jericho explained to them. "They're being walked through, so they'll be done before the judge and his staff leave for Christmas break."

Jericho hoped. That was the plan, anyway, but it was possible that key players needed for the process had already left work for the holidays.

"Good," Laurel said under her breath and then repeated it. "And what about the arrest warrants for you and the deputies?"

Jericho looked at Levi, hoping he'd made some progress in that area. But Levi shook his head. "The warrants haven't been sworn out yet, but the Dallas PD has probable cause if they believe you're harboring a fugitive."

Yep, there it was in a nutshell. He was indeed doing just that. And in this case, he was now married to the fugitive.

His *wife*.

The word didn't exactly stick in Jericho's throat, but it was close. He'd had no plans for marriage, but he'd always thought when and if he got around to saying I do, that it wouldn't have been to save his son. Or to save Laurel.

"I'm really sorry," she said as if she knew exactly what he was thinking.

"Don't," Jericho warned her. He would have liked to have added that this wasn't of her own making. But that was only partly true. She had brought some of this mess on herself by not seeing the truth about her father sooner.

She didn't listen to his warning. "I'm sorry," she repeated. First to Jericho. Then to Levi. "How much time do we have before I turn myself in and stop those arrest warrants from being issued?"

"I've already told you, that's not going to happen," Jericho snapped.

"No, you glared at me when I said I was going to do it. Now that you've got the custody papers started, I can turn myself in."

Jericho got to his feet so he could make eye contact with her and so she could see that he wasn't leaving room for argument. "Your father's past the brow-beating stage with you. He wants you behind bars, and he wants Maddox. Turning yourself in won't stop that."

Laurel lifted her hands in the air. "Then how do we stop him?"

He had a plan, all right. Jericho just wished it was a whole lot better than it was. "I've asked the county sheriff to file charges against Herschel for trespassing on the ranch."

Levi looked at him as if he'd sprouted an extra nose. "That won't put Herschel behind bars."

"No, but it'll keep him occupied for a few hours while he's trying to sort it out." Maybe. "In the meantime, Jax and Weston are digging into the backgrounds on the shrinks who gave fake reports regarding your mental health. They're looking to find a way to connect Herschel to the illegal activity."

Laurel didn't exactly jump for joy. Probably because she knew her father would have covered his tracks well.

"Chase will help them when he can, but he's on a lead right now to find the Moonlight Strangler," Jericho added.

He hated he couldn't pull Chase away from that case, but it was critical that the Moonlight Strangler be stopped. Especially since the snake would no doubt strike again. And soon.

She stayed quiet for a few seconds before her gaze drifted toward the living room. "Maddox deserves better than this," she whispered.

Yeah. He did. A whole lot better.

Jericho didn't know a lot about babies, but he knew this should be a time of celebration. Presents, Christmas trees, lots of excitement. Well, there was excitement, all right, but it was the wrong kind.

"I'll make sure he has some gifts," Jericho assured her. He wasn't certain how he would manage that, yet, but he'd get him something even if he had to download some games and books from the internet.

Levi must have decided this wasn't a conversation he needed to be in on, because he took out his phone again and headed out of the kitchen. "I'll see what I can do about speeding up the process for that voice comparison."

Jericho thanked his brother, was ready to launch into some calls himself, but he stood so he could glance into the living room and check on Maddox. Still asleep. So was his mother. She was napping in the recliner next to Maddox.

He went closer, his attention on his son's face, and he

wondered if it would always be like this when he looked at him. That strong wash of love. So strong that it seemed to crush his chest. Twenty-four hours ago, Jericho hadn't even known Maddox existed, and now he couldn't imagine a life without him.

That meant a life with Laurel, too.

Even after they put an end to the danger and sorted out all her legal troubles, she would still be in his life. Jericho was guessing she'd want some kind of split-custody arrangement. And maybe that'd work. But he didn't want to lose another minute with his son, much less the time he wouldn't have with Maddox if he had to share custody with Laurel.

He glanced at Laurel and realized she was staring at him. "What?" Jericho asked.

"Magical, huh? I mean, people tell you what it's like to love a child, but you can't imagine it until it happens to you."

Jericho didn't trust his voice and settled for a nod. But Laurel kept staring. "Something else on your mind?"

She waved it off, literally, but then shook her head. "You didn't cough or choke when you said I do."

"Neither did you."

"It was different for me." Laurel sank down in the chair across from him. "You're the one doing me the favor. I wanted the marriage."

"This isn't a favor." Or a real marriage, for that matter. "I did this for my son." Which seemed a stupid thing to say since Laurel was doing it for the same reason.

She nodded. Paused, then nodded again. "Did you keep your blue rock?"

Now, here was the part where he could be ornery and say no, that he didn't have a clue what'd happened to it.

But considering that he and Laurel had been through hell and back, it didn't seem fair.

"Yeah. It's in the junk drawer in the kitchen."

"A good place for it." And yes, there was a touch of sarcasm in her tone.

"I was going to toss it, changed my mind, and the drawer was nearby."

Best not to tell her that he also kept his father's badge in that drawer. And some family photos. A drawer he walked by and saw every time he came in and out of his house.

"It was a silly memento, anyway," Laurel added.

She looked up at him, their gazes connecting, and it seemed as if a dozen things passed between them without them saying a word. Of course, most of those dozen things included the puppy-love kisses when they'd found those rocks.

And the lust-induced kissing session they'd had just before the wedding.

Nothing puppy love about that.

Hell, he still was having trouble walking. He didn't want to know how long it'd be for the memory of her taste to fade.

Maybe never.

Since this wasn't something he wanted on his mind, Jericho was thankful when his phone buzzed. That thankfulness didn't last long, though, when he saw Theo's name on the screen.

"I'll take this in the bedroom so I don't wake up Maddox and Mom," Jericho said, showing Laurel the screen.

She followed him, of course, and once Jericho was in his bedroom with the door shut, he put the call on speaker.

"Where are you?" Theo demanded the moment Jericho answered.

"Really? You think that's any of your business?"

"It's my business because I'm worried about Laurel. Is she with you?"

"Again, none of your business. And if this is the only reason you called, then you're wasting my time and yours—"

"It's not the only reason." But Theo didn't exactly hurry to continue that explanation. "I found something. About Herschel."

Laurel opened her mouth, no doubt to ask what, but Jericho shook his head. Even though Theo no doubt thought they were together, Jericho didn't want to confirm that for him.

"What'd you find?" Jericho snapped. "And this better not be a waste of my time."

"It's not a waste." Still, Theo took several moments to add something to that. "Herschel had fake psychiatric evaluations done on Laurel."

This time, Jericho huffed. "Tell me something I don't know. Laurel's sane. Herschel's not. Of course he faked them."

"Yes, but I can prove it."

Laurel's gaze flew to his, and he saw the hope in her eyes. Hope that Jericho wasn't ready to feel just yet. After all, this was Theo. And it wasn't jealousy playing into his dislike of the man. Well, maybe it was still a small part of it, but Jericho didn't trust anyone who was in cahoots with Herschel.

"How can you prove it?" Jericho pressed.

"I talked to the psychiatrist, and then sent a follow-up email. He admitted in a roundabout way that he never even saw Laurel for evaluation."

That hope in Laurel's eyes got even stronger, but thankfully she stayed quiet.

"The shrink put that in writing?" Jericho asked.

"Yes, in an email. But it's not an outright admission of wrongdoing. He just says he made his recommendation based on the medical records Herschel provided to him."

Fake records, no doubt. "I want that email," Jericho ordered.

"I figured you would. It might not keep Laurel out of jail, but you could perhaps use it to discredit Herschel in some way."

Oh, yeah. And he could do that by giving it to the press.

"But the email's not all I have," Theo added. "Herschel's using two reports by two different psychiatrists, and I believe I can discredit the other one, as well."

Jericho didn't care for the way Theo let that hang in the air for a while. "I'm guessing you want something in exchange for this?" Jericho asked.

"I want to talk to Laurel. Face-to-face."

Hell. Jericho figured there'd be a catch. "You're withholding evidence in an active criminal investigation. I can have you charged with obstruction of justice if you don't turn over the information."

"You could, but I could also destroy the evidence, and Laurel could end up in a mental hospital or jail for years. I doubt either you or Laurel want that."

He didn't, but Jericho didn't want to deal with this snake, either. "Why is it so important for you to speak to Laurel?"

"There are things I need to tell her, and I can't do it over the phone."

Probably a ploy to try to win her back so he could

salvage those business deals. Or maybe Theo did love her in his own sick way.

"As you can imagine, it's not a good idea for Laurel to be meeting anyone right now," Jericho reminded him. "Including you."

"I know about the arrest warrant for you and your deputies. I know you have a matter of only a few hours to turn her in or you'll be taken into custody, too. It's my guess neither Laurel nor you want that to happen." Theo didn't wait for confirmation. "So, meet me at the sheriff's office in Appaloosa Pass this afternoon. I can talk to Laurel before the deadline for you to turn her over to the Dallas PD."

Jericho stared at her. That hope was still there in her eyes, but this was hope with a big string attached. He didn't want her to have to deal with Theo. Hell, he didn't want her arrested.

"Why should I believe that you're willing to throw Herschel to the wolves?" Jericho asked.

Another long pause from Theo. "Because I don't think this is the way to change Laurel's mind."

"It's not. But you've gone along with it so far."

"Let's just say I've had a change of heart. The plan was never for Laurel to be put in danger."

"Really? Then, what was the plan?"

"I'll tell Laurel when I see her. And I'm emphasizing that *her* because if she's not there, then I won't be, either. The only way you're going to get what I have is for us to meet face-to-face."

"All right," Laurel said, moving closer to the phone. "I'll do it. I'll meet you at the sheriff's office in a couple of hours, you and I can talk, and then you can give us the evidence."

Jericho didn't bother to curse because he'd known this was what she'd do. He didn't like it, but then there wasn't much he liked about this, especially since he was still trying to prevent that arrest by completely clearing Laurel's name.

"Good. I'll see you both then." And Theo ended the call before Jericho could say anything else.

"I have to do this," Laurel immediately argued. "I've known all along I'd have to turn myself in before the deadline the Dallas PD gave us. I can't risk having you arrested, not when we're so close to you getting custody of Maddox."

Part of that made some sense, though it was a bitter pill to swallow. He didn't want to think of Laurel in jail even for a short period of time.

"I don't want Maddox near Theo," Jericho insisted.

"Neither do I. Maybe he can stay here with your mother, Levi and one of the deputies."

Jericho would make sure there was at least one deputy at this safe house, and he would do whatever else it took to protect Maddox.

"When I'm arrested, I'll need you to bail me out," she added.

He would, of course, but she'd still have those mental-instability accusations hanging over her head. The mental instability could cancel out the other charges, since a lawyer could argue that if she was indeed crazy, then she wasn't fit to stand trial for money laundering. Either way, though, Laurel would be locked up somewhere until Jericho could prove she should be set free.

"What does Theo want to talk to you about?" he came out and asked.

She blew out a long breath, pushed her hair from her

face. "He probably just wants to try to win me back. He can't."

"Obviously. You're married to me now, so that shoots to hell his notion of winning you back." He paused. "Doesn't it?"

That got him a huff and an eye roll. "Now that I know we can keep Maddox from my father, nothing would make me go back to Theo. *Nothing.*"

There weren't any doubts in her voice. And that got Jericho thinking about something else she'd let slip the day before.

"You said Theo wasn't your lover. Explain that."

"Your memory is a little too good." She sighed, looked away, dodging his gaze. "Theo knew I didn't love him, but I agreed to the engagement to get my father off my back. And my mother's. My father was always pressuring her to pressure me, and I finally just gave in and said yes. I know, that makes me weak."

He didn't verbally argue with that, but he made to let her know he didn't totally agree. "And the part about him not being your lover?"

Laurel shrugged. "I told Theo we'd have to wait until we were married before we had sex."

"And he agreed to that?"

"I didn't give him a choice."

Well, great day. "He didn't press you to change your mind?"

"He did. I stopped him." She glanced away again, but when her attention came back to him, there was a little fire in her eyes. "Satisfied?"

Jericho played around with some answers to that and decided there wasn't a good one. Was he satisfied she hadn't slept with Theo?

Yeah.

And yeah, that made him somewhat of a jerk.

"Theo might have had the hots for you, but I still believe it's mostly about business when it comes to you," Jericho settled for saying. "So yes, I guess I am satisfied that you didn't end up in bed with a man who wanted to use you."

No more gaze dodging. She stared at him. "And that's the only reason you're *satisfied*?"

No. Laurel knew that, too, because of those scalding kisses they'd just shared. Kisses he could still feel in every inch of him.

He was betting she could feel them, too, because her breathing became uneven, and her face flushed.

"Don't answer that," she insisted. "It's technically our wedding night, and please don't say or do anything that would make me want to get in your bed."

Jericho was about to make a big mistake and point out that'd there be a lot of wanting going on tonight, whether she was in his bed or not. Of course, admitting that want would be the very thing that would make them forget all of the damage they could do by sleeping together again. Thankfully, he was saved from saying something like that because of the knock at the door.

"Jericho," Levi said, "we have a problem."

Heck. What now? Jericho hurried to the door and threw it open. Even if his brother hadn't mentioned something was wrong, he would have been able to tell just by looking at Levi's face.

"Jax and the other deputies are on their way back out here and will be here any minute. We'll need to leave as soon as they get here." There was just as much concern in Levi's voice as there was in his expression. "Jax believes our location has been compromised."

Chapter Ten

Laurel's heart went to her knees. No. This couldn't be happening. Her baby was in danger again.

"Grab your things and Maddox's diaper bag," Jericho told her. He didn't seem nearly as shaky as she was, but Laurel figured he was just as concerned.

"How did this happen?" she asked, hurrying across the hall to her room. Thankfully, the house wasn't so large that she couldn't hear Levi's answer.

"When Jax picked up the justice of the peace, he told him to leave his phone behind, that it could be traced. Well, he left his business one but forgot he had his personal one in his briefcase."

All right, that wasn't as bad as the wild ideas running through her head. Ideas of kidnappers and gunmen on the way. Still, Jax was right and most cell phones could be tracked.

"Jax is pretty sure that someone, maybe Herschel, hired people to watch all the justices of the peace in the area. Ministers, too. Jax knows they weren't followed, but if the spy saw the JP leave with Jax, then they could have tapped into the GPS tracker on his phone."

So, moving was just a precaution. That didn't cause

Laurel to slow down, though. It was best to get Maddox away from here.

"Jax and the deputies are here," Iris called out to them.

That sent Levi hurrying to the living room. With her own bag and the diaper bag in hand, Laurel was about to head there, too, but Jericho stopped her in the hall. Now she saw more emotion on his face, and she knew he was about to tell her something she didn't want to hear.

"I need to go to the office and meet with Theo," Jericho said. "You're still sure you want to come with me?"

"Of course. Theo won't give us the recording or anything else if I'm not there." And Laurel was positive that wasn't a bluff. If she wasn't there, they wouldn't get the proof that could clear her of the false psychiatric reports.

If Theo actually had a recording, that is.

Theo likely had something. Something that he was sure he could use to get her to talk to him. Laurel only hoped it was worth the risk and the emotional toll it would take for her to be away from Maddox. Even though she hoped she wouldn't have to be away from him for too long.

"How will this work?" she asked Jericho.

He scrubbed his hand over his face. Clearly frustrated. "I'll have Jax and the deputies take Mom and Maddox to a new location. Another safe house. Levi, you and I can go to the office."

"Levi could go with them, too," she suggested.

"No way. I want backup with us when we're on the road."

Laurel nodded, finally, and with that green light given, Jericho rushed her back into the living room. Iris already had Maddox bundled in her arms, ready to go. Her son was still half asleep, but he smiled when he looked at her. His smile got even bigger when he looked at Jericho.

"Tar," Maddox muttered, pointing to Jericho's badge.

Jericho returned the smile and stepped away to tell the others the plan. Laurel used the time to say goodbye to her son.

"Be a good boy for Mommy." She pressed some kisses on his cheek. "I'll see you soon." Laurel hoped. It was possible that it would be days, since, with the holidays, it might not be easy for Jericho to post bond for her.

"I'll take good care of him," Iris assured her.

"Thank you." And she meant it. It was easy to see that Iris loved Maddox. Jericho, too. That would make it easier for him if things turned from bad to worse and Laurel ended up with a long jail sentence.

"You ready?" Jericho asked her when he'd finished talking to his brothers and the deputies.

Laurel nodded. Kissed Maddox again. Jericho did the same, brushing a kiss on his forehead. That was it, the only goodbye before he got them outside.

Jax had parked an SUV directly in front of the door, and Laurel was relieved when she saw the infant seat. It probably belonged to his own son since this was Jax's personal vehicle.

Iris got Maddox strapped in, with Dexter getting into the backseat with them. Jax and Mack took the front seat, and Jax didn't waste any time speeding away.

"Best to get moving," Levi reminded them, and they hurried to his truck on the side of the house.

It was still bitterly cold, but thankfully there was no ice or snow falling. Not yet. Maybe it wouldn't start until Maddox and the others had arrived at the new place. She definitely didn't want her baby on icy roads.

Laurel kept her gaze nailed to Jax's SUV, watching it while she ran to the truck and got on the seat between

Levi and Jericho, with Levi behind the wheel. She could have sworn a hand squeezed around her heart when the SUV was out of sight.

"It'll be okay," Jericho said to her.

She hated that the tears came, but this had been an emotional overload of a day, and it wasn't over yet. "Please tell me the new place will be safe."

"It will be." Almost idly, Jericho brushed a kiss on her forehead, much as he'd done to Maddox just minutes earlier.

Levi made a soft grunt. Probably of disapproval, and he took something from his pocket. A plain gold wedding band.

"Jax brought it with him," Levi said, passing it to Laurel. "He thought it would be a good idea for you to wear it."

Because her head was in such a muddle, Laurel looked at Jericho for an explanation.

"It might get Theo to back off. From pressuring you about getting back together with him, anyway. It might also help if you have to appear before a judge. It makes the marriage seem, well, real, and not something we slapped together so Herschel can't get Maddox."

Of course, the marriage had indeed been slapped together, and while it might not sway a judge, it was a nice finishing touch. Laurel slipped the ring on and then had a horrible thought.

"The ring doesn't belong to Jax's late wife, Paige, does it?" Laurel knew Jax and Paige had divorced shortly before she'd been murdered, but the ring would still have sentimental value for Jax and Paige's son.

Levi shook his head. "It belonged to our grandmother. Jax meant to bring it with him when he drove out with the JP, but he forgot."

"I can't wear this. It's…real. It's a family heirloom." She started to take it off, but Jericho stopped her by sliding his hand over hers.

"Keep it on." He didn't add more than that. Didn't move his hand from hers, either.

Laurel hated that something as simple as Jericho's touch would help her calm down, but it did. However, it didn't do the same for Levi. Jericho's brother didn't say a thing, but she saw a flash of disapproval in his eyes. First the kiss, now this. Levi was probably ready to give her an earful.

But he didn't.

In fact, he didn't say anything, and that's when she noticed he was volleying his attention between the rearview mirror and the road ahead. Jericho was doing the same thing, but he took it one step further.

Jericho drew his gun.

That caused the skin to crawl on the back of her neck.

"What's wrong?" Laurel tried to turn and look behind them, but she didn't get the chance. Jericho pushed her down on the seat.

"Maybe nothing."

However, it didn't feel like *nothing*.

"That person in the black SUV behind us could be following us," Levi supplied. "Let's find out."

That was the only warning she got before Levi made a left turn. And she waited. Breath held. Her mind and heart racing.

She wasn't familiar with this part of the county. It was all rural, just ranch land and woods, and from her position on the seat, Laurel could tell the road was bumpy, coiling its way through the trees that were practically a canopy over them.

"Hell," Jericho said. And she knew then that whoever had been behind them had made that same turn.

"Can you see how many are in the vehicle?" Levi asked.

Jericho shook his head. "The windows are too dark. Take that next turn. That'll get us headed toward Miller Road."

Which would lead them back into town. Eventually. By her estimation, they were at least twenty minutes out. Maybe more, since they were on the back roads.

Laurel forced herself to remember that this could still turn out to be nothing. After all, it could be someone who lived in the area.

Levi took the next turn as Jericho had told him. And the wait began again. Laurel wasn't sure how time managed to crawl and fly by at the same time, but it felt as if that's what was happening.

Jericho cursed again and pushed her farther down on the seat. That meant they had their answer.

They were being followed.

And worse.

"Watch out!" Jericho shouted to his brother.

Just as the bullet slammed into the roof of the truck.

JERICHO DIDN'T HAVE time to curse. Though that's something he'd be doing plenty of later. For now, he had to do something to make sure all three of them got out of there alive.

"Just focus on the road," Jericho told his brother. "I'll see what I can do about the idiot who just fired that shot."

A shot that Jericho had barely seen coming. He hadn't noticed the passenger's-side window of the SUV was down, but he'd darn sure seen the person's hand snake out with that blasted gun. A gun he'd quickly used to fire a shot at them before pulling his hand back inside.

Jericho doubted it'd stay that way.

No, this was an attack, and it was clear from the shot that the thugs inside didn't care if they killed them or not.

Now, the question was—who had ordered the thugs to attack?

Jericho would find out, but first things first. He lowered his own window. Leaned out just enough to take aim. And he sent a shot right into the windshield of the SUV. The bullet slammed into the glass, creating a small circle, but it didn't go through, which meant their attackers had come prepared. The glass was bulletproof.

Unlike their truck.

And the thug must have known that because the passenger's hand came out again and he fired another shot.

This one slammed into the side of Jericho's door but, thankfully, ricocheted off. Of course, a ricocheted bullet could still hit one of them.

"I'm turning," Levi warned them a split second before he took a left on another farm road. Jericho wasn't familiar with this particular one, but most of the roads led back toward Appaloosa Pass. He hoped this one did because he didn't want to have to dodge bullets any longer than necessary.

"Maddox," Laurel said on a rise of breath. There was plenty of panic in her voice.

Plenty of panic inside Jericho, too. He prayed attackers hadn't gone after Maddox, as well.

"Call Jax," Jericho said, and tossed her his phone.

He glanced at her to make sure she stayed down when she did that. She did. And Jericho tried to tamp down his fears for his son while he kept an eye on the shooter behind them.

The guy didn't reach out again, probably because the road was a series of curves, and it would be nearly impossible to take aim. That was something, at least, but the curves probably wouldn't go on for long.

"Someone's shooting at us," Laurel said the moment Jax answered her call. "Is Maddox all right?"

How could just a few seconds seem like an eternity? Jericho wasn't close enough to hear Jax's answer, so he could only wait. And pray.

"They're okay," Laurel relayed. "No one's following them."

He released the breath he'd been holding, but Jericho didn't have time to celebrate his son's safety. The hand came out of the window again, and the shooter pulled the trigger. This time, though, the shot slammed into the rear windshield and sent the safety glass spewing right at them.

Jericho tried to cover Laurel as best he could. Which wasn't much coverage at all. Still, the protective coating around the glass had saved them from getting cut to shreds. However, with the giant gaping hole, the bitter cold came in, and it didn't take long for the temp inside the truck to plummet.

"Another turn," Levi announced.

He took the turn on what had to be two tires, at best, and Jericho's heart thudded against his chest when the truck went into a skid. Levi quickly got control, thank God, but Jericho knew there wouldn't be much time before another bullet came their way.

"Jax wants to know how far we are from town," Laurel asked. She looked up at him, meeting his gaze for just a moment, and Jericho saw the terror in her eyes.

"About ten miles," Levi answered.

Even at the speed they were going, which was too fast for these curvy country roads, that was still way too much time for these idiots to take this situation from bad to worse.

Laurel passed along that information to Jax. "Jax will have someone tap into the GPS to get our location," she relayed when she ended the call. "He'll get backup out to us as fast as he can."

Jericho had no doubt his brother would do just that, but it was a long shot for backup to arrive in time.

Which meant he had to do something now.

Jericho got a confirmation of that when another bullet came through the vehicle and bashed into the front windshield. Like the glass in the back, it didn't shatter, but it broke like a giant spiderweb, making it next to impossible for Levi to see.

"Stop when you can," Jericho instructed. "We need to try to put an end to this."

Levi nodded, knowing they didn't have another option. He couldn't drive blind on these roads, and he certainly couldn't stick his head out the side window to see.

"They'll try to kill us if you stop," she said, her voice trembling.

"They're already trying to kill us." And were doing too good of a job at it since two more shots came their way, both of them hitting the side of the truck. These shots were definitely lower, which meant the guy was probably trying to shoot out a tire or two.

"Levi, the second you stop, get your gun ready. Aim for their tires," Jericho instructed. Because two could play at this game. "Laurel, so help me God, you'd better stay down."

"But I could help you return fire. I know how to handle a gun."

The glare Jericho tossed her let her know that wasn't going to happen. Still, he didn't want her unarmed just in case things got even worse than they already were, so he threw open the glove compartment, took out a backup weapon that he knew Levi kept there and tossed it to her.

"Stay down," Jericho warned her again.

She did, and he hoped she didn't get up, no matter what. Of course, he couldn't swear she'd be completely safe, but he did know that he and Levi were darn good shots, and it'd be much easier to shoot these clowns if they both weren't in moving vehicles.

"I'd like to keep one of them alive," Jericho said to Levi, and his brother nodded.

Not that they'd had good luck when it came to getting the other thugs to talk, but one of these might. And if not, then maybe Jericho could force him to talk.

This had to end.

He couldn't continue to allow Laurel and Maddox to be in danger, and that meant he might end up bending the law by forcing the guy to cough up some answers.

"How about stopping there?" Levi tipped his head to a small clearing in front of a cattle gate. There was a cluster of trees just to the left and an irrigation ditch on the right.

"Do it," Jericho answered.

The words had hardly left his mouth when Levi hit the brakes, hard, and he skidded into the narrow clearing. But he didn't just park. He maneuvered the truck around so that it was facing the SUV head-on.

Using the truck doors for cover, they both got out. Both took aim at the SUV's front tires. The SUV driver slammed on his brakes just as Levi and Jericho fired into them. Jericho was positive his bullet went into the tire, but it didn't go flat.

Hell.

Probably puncture resistant. Yeah, these guys had come prepared. But they probably hadn't expected the Crockett brothers to take a stand.

The SUV tires squealed, digging into the asphalt until it came to a stop about ten yards from them. No one got out, but the driver did lower his window. He stayed inside so that Jericho couldn't see him. He probably wouldn't have recognized him, anyway, since these were almost certainly hired killers.

"Well?" Jericho called out.

He didn't wait for a response. Not that he would have gotten one, anyway. Hired guns usually weren't big on talking.

Jericho fired a shot into the SUV's engine. Finally. He hit something that wasn't reinforced, because the bullet went through. However, it didn't immediately disable it because the engine continued to run.

So, Jericho continued to shoot at it.

Levi did the same. And soon they had a barrage of bullets slamming into the SUV hood.

Jericho had to stop to slap another magazine into his gun, and he was in the process of taking aim again when the driver threw the SUV into Reverse and hit the accelerator. He peeled out of there, fast.

Doing the one thing Jericho didn't want them to do.

They were getting away.

Chapter Eleven

Laurel couldn't stop shivering. Something she'd been doing on the entire drive to the sheriff's office. And despite the ample heat in the building, she was still shivering, the cold going all the way to the bone.

Thanks to those latest gunmen, she had a new set of memories to give her nightmares and make her tremble. A new set of worries, too.

Because the gunmen had gotten away.

That meant they could return for another attempt to kill Jericho and her. Of course, Jericho and his brothers were trying to stop that, but Laurel had to wonder what the heck she could do to put an end to this.

Maybe turning herself in to the police would work.

Maybe.

Or maybe that would just make her an easier target to kill.

Either way, it wasn't a theory Jericho wanted to test, and he'd spent the last half hour since their arrival at his office making calls to the Dallas PD. Trying to stop the warrant for her arrest. Judging from the amount of his profanity and his scowl, it wasn't going well.

"Here, try this." Levi handed Laurel a cup of coffee.

Laurel took a sip of the coffee, nearly choked on it. It

would need a lot of improvement just to classify as horrible, but it was hot, and with the hopes it would take away her chill, she drank some more.

"We should have heard from Jax by now," she said.

Levi made a sound of disagreement. "He's just being cautious. Jax is driving around to make sure they aren't being followed before he goes to the safe house with Maddox."

Yes, Jax had already told her exactly that in the three calls she'd made to him. Laurel didn't dare make another so soon since he'd warned her with the last one that he needed to concentrate on his driving. The temps were dropping, and he wanted to be careful.

Laurel wanted that, as well, but more than anything, she just wanted her son to be safe.

"Jax will take good care of him," Levi added. "And Jericho will find whatever he needs to find to put an end to this."

She desperately wanted to believe that. But it was easy to lose hope when they'd come so close to dying again.

"What about the kidnapper already in custody?" Laurel asked. "Is he still not talking?"

Levi shook his head. "We do know his name is Otto Palmer. We got that from his prints, so he obviously has a record. I think he would have talked, but he got spooked after DeWitt's death. He probably thinks the same thing will happen to him."

Yes, that would spook anyone, especially since they still weren't sure if DeWitt had taken his own life or if his so-called lawyer had murdered him.

Jericho stood when he finished his latest call, and that seemed to be Levi's cue to start moving away from her.

"I'll see if I can find out what's happening with Rossman and Cawley."

Good idea, since the pair was yet something else they had to deal with, especially if they could help clear her name of the money laundering charges. "How about the wiretap recording you're trying to match to my father's voice?"

"Still working on it. I'll let you know the minute the FBI lab calls me back." Levi went to a desk in the corner and started another call.

"Did they find those men who shot at us?" she asked Jericho.

"Afraid not. But the county sheriff and his deputies are still out looking."

That was probably the last thing they wanted to do right before the holidays, but that area had come under the jurisdiction of the county sheriff. That meant Levi, Jericho and she would soon have to write statements of the incident so there could be an official investigation.

As if that would help.

She was betting those men were well out of the reach of the law. For the time being, anyway.

"I ran the plates on the black SUV," he continued. "They're not registered, of course, which means they're fake, but I also alerted car repair shops that someone might be bringing in a vehicle that matched the description."

He was covering all the bases as best he could. She hated to take a glass-half-empty outlook on this, but a person who had enough money to hire multiple hit men probably wouldn't care about having a vehicle repaired. Especially one that could be traced back to him or her.

"You're shaking," Jericho said.

He went closer to her, and barely touching her, he put his hand on the small of her back to get her moving toward his office. Maybe because he thought it'd be warmer there. Or maybe because he realized she was on the verge of tears. Of course, there could be another reason for the privacy.

"Do you have more bad news?" Laurel came out and asked.

He took a moment, put his hands on his hips. "Not as bad as it could be. Dallas PD won't kill the warrant against you, but they're giving me some more time. I told them you'd been shaken up pretty bad in the latest attack."

That certainly wasn't a lie. "How much time?"

"Tomorrow morning."

Laurel groaned. Tomorrow was Christmas, and she hadn't wanted to spend it being arrested. "And what about the warrant for your arrest?"

Jericho flexed his shoulders. "They're not killing that, either. The captain at Dallas PD insists if I don't turn you in, they'll arrest me, the deputies and then bring in the Rangers to take over the sheriff's office. But they're giving me until tomorrow, too."

What a mess. Jericho loved his badge. Loved being sheriff. And now he had to choose between it and her. Laurel figured she would always be on the losing end when it came to his badge.

"I'll bet you wish you'd never met me," she whispered.

"Some days." He paused. Looked at her. Cursed. "Not today, though."

He turned, and as if part of a dance, he slipped his arm around her, drawing her to him.

And he kissed her.

There it was. The heat. Jericho could take her from

shivering to hot in a matter of seconds. But this was more than just the fire from the attraction. The pull seemed to go even deeper, and it slid through her, head to toe.

As always, his mouth was clever, tasting and taking at once. And Laurel let him. She just tried to hang on, bracing herself for the onslaught of need. It came, all right. It always did and made her long for a real marriage.

He deepened the kiss. Tightened his grip. It robbed her of her breath and any clear thoughts she should be having. Well, she did have one clear thought—about his bed— but that vanished when she heard the bell jangling. The sound let them know that they had a visitor.

"Stay here." Jericho pulled her behind him and drew his gun.

"Laurel?" Theo called out. "Are you here?"

She certainly hadn't forgotten about Theo's planned visit, but with everything else going on, Laurel hadn't realized it was time for him to arrive.

Jericho stepped into the hall, and Laurel could tell from the way he stiffened that something wasn't right. One glimpse in the reception area, and she understood why he'd had that reaction. Theo wasn't alone.

Dorothy was with him.

Since Dorothy was a suspect, and Theo hadn't mentioned bringing her along, Jericho had reason for concern. That was probably why he didn't holster his gun.

"Why is she here?" Jericho tipped his head to Dorothy.

"Because I need to talk to Laurel, too," the woman insisted.

Theo huffed. "She followed me. Or rather, her driver did. He's parked just outside, waiting for her."

Laurel had no idea why Theo would be keeping things from his mother. Nor did she care. She only wanted this to be a short, productive visit. "Did you bring the evidence?" she asked.

Theo held up a manila envelope. "I did. But you'll get it only after we talk. That was the deal."

"So, talk," Jericho snapped, and he stayed between Theo and her.

Well, partially. Laurel's hand wasn't hidden, and Dorothy's attention snapped right to the wedding ring she was wearing.

"Did you marry him?" Dorothy howled. "Did you actually marry this cowboy cop?"

"I did." And Laurel braced herself for their reactions.

She didn't have to wait long. Dorothy started shaking her head, mumbling how stupid Laurel was, and as if she'd gone weak in the knees, the woman sank down into one of the chairs.

Theo, however, just stared at Laurel, and by degrees, she saw the changes in his expression. Surprise, at first. Quickly followed by some disappointment and then the anger. His jaw went tight. His eyes narrowed. Levi didn't miss the reaction, either, because he also drew his gun.

"Why the hell did you marry him?" Theo asked. He stormed toward her, but Jericho stepped in front of him, blocking his path.

"Why the hell do you care why she did it?" Jericho retorted. "Laurel broke off your engagement. That means she's free to marry me or anybody else, for that matter."

"No!" Theo shouted. "She definitely wasn't free to marry you." He went from anger to enraged, and Laurel thought about grabbing that envelope from him before he did something stupid.

Like try to destroy it.

But Jericho did the grabbing for her. He snatched it

from Theo, and motioned for Levi to take it. Levi came across the room to do just that.

"Get started on that right away," Jericho told his brother without taking his narrowed gaze off Theo.

Theo, however, looked past Jericho, his glare fixed on her. "Do you think I'm saving you from going to jail so you can be with the likes of him?"

Oh, that was not the right thing to say, and Laurel took hold of Jericho's arm in case he was about to punch Theo. Not that she would have minded that. Theo deserved a good punch or two for the remark, but she didn't want a fight in the sheriff's office. Especially since they had other more important battles.

"The likes of him?" Laurel repeated. Because she wanted to calm things down, she tried not to glare at Theo. "He's my son's father, along with being the sheriff here. Seems like a good match to me."

"Well, it's not! He didn't even know about Maddox until you went running to him. You should have let it stay that way."

"And lose custody of Maddox to my father?" she snapped. "I don't think so."

It appeared to take Theo a moment to rein in his temper enough just so he could speak. "I would have taken custody of him while I helped you work through the charges."

Jericho took a step toward him, narrowing the already narrow space between them. "That was never going to happen. Maddox is my son, not yours. And Laurel is my wife."

She could tell Theo wanted to start that fight with Jericho. One that he wouldn't win. Jericho didn't just look dangerous.

He *was* dangerous.

"Did you sleep with him, too?" Theo snarled.

Nearly. And part of Laurel wanted to throw that at Theo, but it would be like gasoline on a fire, and she was too exhausted to drag out this argument.

"What I do with Jericho is my business," she settled for saying. Still a bit of gasoline, but anything she could have said probably would have been. Theo was spoiling for a fight.

The trick would be to make sure Jericho didn't give him one.

"I loved you," Theo said to her. "I loved you more than anyone or anything ever. And I would have done whatever it took to protect you. You should have trusted me to deal with your father."

"How? By marrying me? Because that's what triggered all of this," Laurel reminded him. "I ended things between us and all hell broke loose. I have to believe you're at least partially responsible for that."

Theo didn't deny it. Not with words, anyway. But the look he gave her was filled with disbelief.

Maybe some hatred, too.

Even though Laurel had had some doubts that Theo was actually in love with her, she knew he had some feelings for her. In his own obsessed kind of way. However, she had also known that a one-sided relationship would never work.

Of course, now she was repeating that with Jericho.

Definitely one-sided. Yes, he'd kissed her several times, but that was just lust. There'd always be lust. But when he was thinking straight, and that would happen, he would remember that he would lose his family by being with her. Jericho wouldn't allow that to happen.

And neither would Laurel.

"There's a USB with an email conversation between Theo and a shrink named Dr. Marvin LaMastus," Levi relayed to them. He was still examining the envelope while volleying glances between it and them. "And there's also a statement from the nurse of the second psychiatrist. She says she never saw Laurel in the doctor's office, and there's no record of any appointment. Both the emails and the statement look legit."

"Of course they are," Theo snapped. "Both psychiatrists were pressured or bribed into giving their diagnoses."

"I don't suppose the shrink said anything in that email about Herschel hiring him?" Jericho asked.

Theo's jaw tightened even more. Maybe because they weren't jumping for joy over what he'd brought them. "You don't know what I had to do to contact Dr. LaMastus. I had to risk your father finding out."

"You poor thing." Jericho's voice was loaded with sarcasm. "Laurel was shot at. If you cared one ounce about her, you should be doing any and everything to help her get out of this mess."

Theo looked down at the wedding ring. "No. Not now. I'm done with her. As far as I'm concerned, you two deserve each other."

Normally, that would have been an insult, but considering Laurel had spent most of her adult life playing with the idea of marrying Jericho, she decided it wasn't much of an insult, after all.

Theo glanced at his mother before he stormed out the door.

But Dorothy didn't budge. She lifted her suddenly weary gaze to Laurel. "You have no idea what you've done."

Jericho glanced at Laurel to see if she knew what the

woman was talking about. She didn't. Because this seemed to be a whole lot more than just a broken engagement, especially since Dorothy had never seemed that fond of her.

"Why don't you explain to me what I've done," Laurel insisted.

Dragging in a long breath, Dorothy got to her feet. "You need to annul this marriage and try to smooth things over with Theo. I'm not saying you have to go through with marrying my son, but you need to make it look as if you two have kissed and made up."

Was the woman insane? "Kiss and make up? Dorothy, someone's trying to kill Jericho and me. I'm on the verge of losing my son. My freedom. And you think all I have to do is kiss and make up with Theo?"

Dorothy nodded, and she must have worked her way through the shock of all of this because she suddenly looked a lot stronger. "I know you haven't forgotten about Rossman and Cawley. They'll kill you because of those failed business deals."

Laurel hated how those two, Rossman and Cawley, kept popping up, especially since no one had been able to find them. Was it really that simple—did the pair want her dead because of the money they'd lost from the broken business deals?

Because it felt like more than that.

"Do you have any proof whatsoever that Rossman and Cawley hired someone to attack us?" Jericho asked. And yes, he was all lawman now.

"None." Dorothy didn't hesitate, either. "And you won't find anything, either. They're thorough, and they won't resurface until they've tied up every loose end in this mess."

Laurel was a loose end. Well, she was if she believed what Dorothy had said.

"You stand to lose a lot of money from those business deals, too," Laurel reminded the woman.

Dorothy stayed silent a moment. "Go ahead. If it makes you feel better, accuse me of this. But it won't help you. Nothing will, except your crawling back to Theo and begging for his forgiveness."

Laurel was just punchy enough to laugh. "That's not going to happen."

"Then I guess I'll be attending your funeral soon. Yours, too," Dorothy added to Jericho, and she walked out. Not in a hurry, either. More like a woman out for a Sunday stroll.

Jericho and she stood there, waiting until they saw Dorothy's limo drive away. Jericho holstered his gun, put his arm around her again, and it took Laurel a moment to realize why. She'd gone past the trembling stage, and her legs had nearly given way.

"I'm sorry," she said as tears watered her eyes.

Jericho cupped her chin, forced eye contact. "Not your doing."

"But it is. God, Jericho. I could cost you everything."

The anger flashed through his eyes. For just a moment, anyway. When their gazes connected again, there was a lot more than anger in them. There was a swirl of all the things that Laurel herself was feeling.

Including the heat.

Oh, yes. It was there, all right, thanks to that latest kissing session in his office. She had to do something to avoid kissing him again, and even as the thought flew through her head, Laurel knew there was zilch she could do about that. Jericho's lifted eyebrow let her know that he was right there on the same page with her.

Jericho's phone buzzed, and her heart skipped a beat or

two when she saw Jax's name on the screen. Laurel held her breath, waiting and praying for good news.

"We made it to the safe house," Jax said when Jericho answered the call and put it on speaker. "We're all okay."

Once again, Laurel's legs turned wobbly—this time from sheer relief—and she leaned against Jericho to keep her balance. "Can I talk to Maddox?"

Even though you really couldn't have a phone conversation with an eighteen-month-old, Jax didn't hesitate. "Tell Mommy hello," Jax instructed Maddox.

"Mama," Maddox said.

The warmth and the love went through her, head to toe. "Maddox, I love you."

And Jericho said the same thing to their son.

Maddox attempted to say it, as well, with love coming out as *wuv*. It was exactly what she needed to hear. Apparently, it worked for Jericho, too, because he smiled right along with her.

"Sorry, but he just spotted a toy chest," Jax said, coming back on the line. "Looks like he'll be busy for a while."

Laurel heard Maddox babble bye-bye.

She had no idea where this safe house was, but Laurel was glad it contained something to keep Maddox entertained. Glad, too, that he would have family with him. And that she'd gotten to hear his precious voice.

"We'll stay here until we hear from you," Jax added.

Heaven knew how long that would be, and it broke Laurel's heart to think she might not be able to spend Christmas with her son. Of course, that was the lesser of two evils. She didn't want Maddox to be in any danger.

"Is everything all right there?" Jax asked.

Definitely no smile from Jericho this time. "Still working out some things. Thanks for everything, Jax." His gaze slashed to the front of the building. "Gotta go. I'll call you when I can."

Laurel tried to see what had caused Jericho's reaction, but as he had done with Dorothy and Theo, he pushed her behind him and drew his gun. Sweet heaven. Was there about to be another attack? Had those men in the SUV followed them here?

"What the hell is he doing here?" Jericho said under his breath.

However, she didn't have to see their visitor to know who it was. Because she soon heard his voice.

"Laurel," her father said, his voice syrupy sweet. "I thought I might find you here."

Chapter Twelve

Jericho's happy meter was at zero, and he was so not in the mood to deal with Laurel's father. Yet, here he was.

"You can wait in my office," Jericho said to Laurel. She didn't, of course. Not that he'd thought for one second that she would.

She was exhausted. Still unsteady on her feet. But Herschel's mere presence seemed to give him a jolt of energy and put some fire in her eyes.

"What do you want?" she snapped at her father. Definitely not a trace of affection.

Not that Jericho could blame her. Herschel was a snake of the worst kind. A man who'd destroy, or maybe even kill, his own child, to get what he wanted.

"You managed to delay the arrest warrants," Herschel said. "Clever. But not clever enough. Tomorrow morning, those warrants will be served."

"Predicting the future now? *Clever*," Jericho repeated. "And please don't tell me you came all the way here to toss that puny threat at us."

"No." That's all he said for several moments. "A little bird told me Theo and Dorothy were just here." Herschel's gaze slid from Jericho and her to the papers that Levi was holding. "What did they give you?"

"Evidence to prove you're lying so you can frame Laurel," Jericho quickly answered.

There was a moment, just a moment, when there was some uncertainty in Herschel's body language, but it vanished, and he became the dirtbag father again.

"Whatever Theo gave you is a lie," Herschel insisted.

Jericho took a step toward the man. Hopefully, the look on his face was as mean-spirited as Jericho felt. "Oh, yeah? Why would Theo do that?"

"To cover his tracks, that's why. He's behind all of this."

"Really?" Laurel took a step closer to her father, too. "Theo has nothing to gain from having me committed to a mental hospital. Or nothing to gain from being tossed in jail. And he certainly has no solid reason to want me dead."

Herschel huffed. "Ever hear of revenge? Payback? Laurel, the man's obsessed with you. He'd rather see you dead than with someone else. Especially Jericho Crockett."

Theo was indeed obsessed. Furious, too, about the broken engagement. Add to that the money he had lost in the broken business deal with Rossman and Cawley, and yeah, that all added up to motive. But Herschel had the same motives. And more than that.

He wanted custody of his grandson.

"And you're obsessed with getting Maddox," Jericho spelled out for him. "Why, exactly? Is it to get back at Laurel? To put the screws to me? Or did you just wake up one morning and decide you wanted to be a bigger jackass than usual?"

Herschel had to do another quick wrestling match with his temper, but as he'd dealt with the surprise of Theo's evidence, he quickly corralled it. "I love Maddox. You know that."

"Do I?" Jericho asked. "Because you've said the words, but I'm just not feeling it. Maybe because you're not capable of love."

"I'm capable!" No corralling that time. Oh, boy. That was a little temper tantrum that Jericho was pleased to see. Pissed-off people usually said a lot more than calm ones. "And I don't want you or any Crockett raising my grandson."

There it was. In a nutshell. Despite the fact Herschel had almost certainly ordered Sherman Crockett's murder, it still wasn't enough. He wanted the rest of them to suffer, too.

And why?

All because Jericho's father had made it his business to put a stop to Herschel and his scummy dealings.

"I'm tired of talking to the two of you," Herschel grumbled. "And now I see you're married."

Jericho hadn't seen the man even glance at Laurel's wedding ring. Or maybe he'd heard the news from his *little bird* source. Probably some idiots he had spying on the sheriff's office.

"If you think a marriage will stop me from getting custody," Herschel added, "think again."

"The marriage alone might not," Jericho countered, "but I have a legal right to take custody of my son."

"Not if you're in jail. And I'll do anything to make sure you join my daughter behind bars. *Anything!*" Herschel took a huge risk by smiling, and Jericho had to do some temper corralling of his own so he didn't beat the man to a pulp.

"I'll add that threat to the evidence I have here," Levi said. He clicked off the tape recorder he was holding.

There was no temper in his brother's voice. Just a calmness with the edge of the dark storm brewing beneath it.

Oh, Herschel didn't like that, either. "You can't just record me."

"Sure he can," Jericho argued. "This is an interview of a potential suspect. It's procedure to record it."

Levi nodded. Smiled, too. "I can turn it over to the Dallas PD so they know the real Herschel Tate." And as if it was a done deal, Levi picked up his phone.

Herschel volleyed some nasty glares among all three of them. "Trust me. You don't want to cross me."

Jericho went closer. Not quickly. He made sure Herschel heard each step. "Too late. The crossing's already been done. On my part. And yours." He leaned in, violating a lot of personal space. "Big mistake, Herschel. I *will* bring you down."

And it wasn't a bluff. Somehow, someway, Jericho would make it happen. Apparently, Jericho got his point across, because Herschel whirled around and left.

Jericho immediately turned to make sure Laurel was okay. She wasn't trembling, but he had no trouble seeing the worry in her eyes.

"This has to end," she said, her voice barely a whisper.

It wasn't a smart thing to do, but Jericho pulled her into his arms again. He was doing that a lot lately.

Wanting to do it, as well.

He didn't bother to curse the attraction. Or their situation. Hell, Laurel and he just seemed to end up together, no matter what.

"Let me make some calls, finish up a few things here, get you something to eat," Jericho told her, turning her toward his office, "and I'll get you to another safe house. Not with Maddox," he added. "It's clear Herschel has someone watching the place, and it'd be too risky for you to go there."

She nodded. Blinked back tears. And just like that, she was back in his arms. Good grief. He hated seeing her put through the wringer like this. She was still in his arms, too, when Levi cleared his throat.

"I just got a call about Rossman and Cawley," his brother announced.

That got Laurel and Jericho moving apart, and they made their way to the desk Levi had been using. Levi put the call on speaker.

"This is Detective Mark Waters from the San Antonio PD on the line," Levi explained to them. "Mark, why don't you tell my brother what you just told me."

"Cawley's dead," Waters immediately explained. "He was killed in a car accident yesterday."

"Accident?" Jericho questioned. Because the timing of it sure was suspicious.

"That's what it's being called for now. Dallas PD is investigating since it happened in their jurisdiction. If they come up with anything, they said they'd call."

Jericho figured if Cawley had been murdered, there wouldn't be any evidence to find.

"What about Quinn Rossman?" Jericho pressed.

"Plenty of shady deals as Levi suspected, and the FBI's getting ready to arrest him for money laundering. I did find something interesting, though. Levi mentioned that Cawley and Rossman had lost a boatload of money from some failed business deals. One involving Laurel and Herschel Tate."

Beside him, Laurel pulled in her breath. Maybe because she thought this detective had found something else to incriminate her.

"Well, it turns out that Cawley and Rossman didn't lose a cent in those deals," Waters went on. "They moved what they'd planned to invest into something else and made a bundle. Turned out to be a very good thing for them. The only ones who lost money in that deal were Herschel, Theo James and his mother, Dorothy."

Bingo. That wasn't proof of which one was behind these attacks, but it did help Jericho narrow down his suspect pool from five to three.

"I need to talk to Rossman," Jericho insisted. "Even if it's a phone interview."

Because if he could get Rossman to admit that Laurel hadn't known anything about the money laundering, it could negate the charges against her. It would keep Laurel out of jail and go a long way to putting Herschel behind bars for orchestrating this.

"I'll see what I can do," Waters assured him.

Jericho thanked him and then stepped away when his phone buzzed. Laurel moved quickly to look at the screen. Probably because she thought it was from Jax. But it wasn't. The call was from his other brother, Chase. Since Chase was a marshal, Jericho hoped that something else hadn't gone wrong.

"I don't want any bad news," Jericho greeted him.

"Sorry."

Even without the sorry, Jericho knew something wasn't right. "Are you hurt?"

"Some. I'll be fine." But Chase's voice said otherwise.

"What the hell happened?" And a lot of bad possibilities started going through his head. Laurel's, too, since she gasped and pressed her fingers to her mouth.

"Jericho," Chase finally said, his voice sounding even weaker. "There's been a murder."

* * *

OH, MERCY.

The fear roared through her head like a piercing scream. "Maddox?" Laurel managed to say.

"Not Maddox," Chase answered. "This wasn't family."

That helped, but the fear already had her by the throat, and Laurel couldn't just turn it off. Jericho put her in the chair next to the desk, turned down the volume on the speaker function of his phone and continued the conversation with Chase.

Levi stayed right there next to him, listening, no doubt to see if there was something they were going to have to buffer for her.

But Laurel didn't want a buffer.

If this murder had something to do with her or this situation she was in, she wanted to know. Too bad she could only hear snatches of the conversation, thanks to her own heartbeat throbbing in her ears. However, she did hear something that sent her pulse racing even more.

The Moonlight Strangler.

She prayed he didn't have anything to do with this. The man was a vicious serial killer. More than a dozen victims. And he was very good at murder, because he hadn't been caught in over thirty years. No one knew his name, but Laurel did know he was the biological father of Jericho's adopted sister, Addie.

He'd also murdered Jax's wife.

Had the Moonlight Strangler gone after Chase now?

His victims were usually young women, but maybe he'd made an exception.

"Read it to me," Jericho said to Chase.

Again, Laurel couldn't hear, but whatever Chase said to them had Levi and Jericho exchanging puzzled glances.

"Go ahead and get in the ambulance," Levi added, still talking to Chase. "I'll see if I can get there to check on you soon. When you can, tell one of the officers on the scene to fax us a copy of that note." He paused. "Hell, don't do that—

"He hung up," Levi said, adding some profanity. "Talk about being hardheaded. He's bleeding like a stuck pig, and he insisted on taking a picture of the note. Said he'll text it to you."

That had Jericho repeating Levi's *hell*.

Laurel wanted to curse, as well. What the devil was going on?

The moment Jericho finished the call, Laurel stood, faced him. "Is Chase all right?"

"I'm not sure," Jericho admitted. "The Moonlight Strangler clubbed him on the head and then knifed him in the chest. He's on his way to a San Antonio hospital right now."

This was bad. An injury like that could be fatal. "Levi, you'll need to go to him."

Levi nodded. "I will. After things are settled here."

She was about to remind him that might not happen, that he should be with his brother, but Jericho's phone dinged, indicating he had a message. Most likely from Chase.

"I'll get someone over to the bank," Levi told Jericho, and he stepped away to make a call, leaving Jericho to explain what the heck was going on.

"The Moonlight Strangler left a typed message on his latest victim's body," Jericho said. "It's about your father."

Of all the things she'd been expecting Jericho to say, that wasn't one of them. "My father? Why would the killer do that? And what did it say?"

Jericho shook his head. "I'm not exactly sure of the why part. Maybe because I'm Addie's brother, and he feels this warped family connection. Maybe he just hates your father as much as I do."

Laurel still didn't understand, but she got a better idea when Jericho handed her his phone so she could read the note for herself.

Doing you a little favor here, Sheriff Crockett. Not the dead body. Guess you wouldn't see that as a favor since you're one of the good guys. But you might want to hear a secret or two about the man who's after your honey and you. Herschel Tate. Funny, I got the label of a killer and he doesn't. Sometimes, the law doesn't have a long arm, after all, does it?

Laurel frantically scrolled down to read the rest. What would the Moonlight Strangler possibly know about her father?

She soon found out.

A little over thirty years, Herschel-boy was involved in a little gunrunning operation with me. You know all about it because you investigated it a couple of weeks ago.

Jericho had. Laurel knew all about it because it had been on the news. A man named Canales had tried to kill Addie because he'd been afraid she would remember he'd been involved in that gunrunning operation. An operation she might have witnessed as a child before being abandoned by her murdering birth father. But now, Canales was dead.

There are photos and such to prove Herschel was involved, Laurel read on. You can find that in a safe-deposit box rented to Wilbur Smith at the First National Bank over in Sweetwater Springs. Now, that's not my real name, so don't go off half-cocked. Just use what's in there to create a little justice for Herschel-boy. You're welcome, Sheriff Crockett.

Laurel read it again to make sure she hadn't misunderstood. "You really think there's proof?"

"We'll know soon," Levi answered. "I've got the bank manager and the Sweetwater Springs sheriff headed over there right now. The bank manager agreed to open the box because it could be connected to the Moonlight Strangler."

That was good since there could be other evidence in the safe-deposit box. But then she went through the details again. "A gunrunning operation over thirty years ago? The statute of limitations plays into this. My father can't be arrested for the crime even if there's proof."

"Unless he murdered someone," Jericho corrected. "No statute of limitations for that."

True. And the killer hadn't mentioned any proof of murder. Still... "Maybe if the evidence is strong enough, we can present it to a judge. It would go a long way toward preventing my father from getting custody of Maddox."

On its own, it wouldn't be enough, and they'd have to find a judge who wasn't in her father's pocket, but coupled with the info Theo had given them, then maybe they could use it to stop him.

Jericho glanced around as if trying to figure out what to do next. His gaze finally settled on Laurel. "I need to take you someplace safe so I can free up Levi to go check on Chase, and I'll get someone to cover the office. Don't tell Mom about any of this," he added to Levi. "Not until we know just how badly Chase is hurt."

Iris would no doubt be frantic once she heard about the attack, and she, too, would likely want to go to her son.

"With your mother gone, I'll need to be at the safe house with Maddox," Laurel insisted.

She expected Jericho to argue, to tell her that Jax and the two deputies could manage it. And they probably could. But Laurel wanted the three lawmen guarding her son to focus on protecting her son, not taking care of him.

"We have some time," Jericho finally said. "And if Chase's injury isn't that bad, we can keep the arrangement as is. If not, well, we'll just have to be careful when I take you there."

Part of Laurel was happy that she might soon be with Maddox again, but she didn't want Chase's injury to be so serious to make that happen. Plus, there was the risk of going to the safe house.

"Is it possible to find the people my father has watching us?" she asked.

Jericho went to the window, lifted one of the slats on the closed blinds and looked out, though he already knew what was out there.

Buildings. Lots of them.

Not just across the street but on each side of the sheriff's office. Her father's spy could be on the roof of one of those or maybe even inside. With long-range equipment, the spy could be anywhere on the street.

"Herschel probably has someone watching the roads, too." Jericho shook his head. "We could probably flush out someone nearby, but there's no telling how many people he hired."

True, and it wasn't as if her father was lacking for money.

Levi's phone rang, and he glanced at the screen. "Sheriff McKinnon from Sweetwater Springs." Thankfully, he put the call on speaker.

"It's here," the sheriff greeted. "Some old photos of what appears to be the sale and transfer of arms. There are also some notes with dates, names and such. And yes, Herschel Tate's name is included on them."

"But is he in the photos?" Levi asked.

"Hard to tell for sure, but it could be him. I'll have to send them to the lab, of course, but I'll fax you some copies."

"Thanks. I'm at the sheriff's office in Appaloosa Pass." Levi thanked him, ended the call and looked at his brother. "I'll wait here until you get someone to cover the office. It isn't a good idea to keep Laurel here much longer, though."

No. Because if her father's little bird told him about the contents of the safe-deposit box, then he might get desperate. There could be another attack.

Jericho nodded, took out his phone, but it buzzed before he could even make a call. Laurel figured it was an update on Chase.

It wasn't.

Quinn Rossman's name appeared on the phone screen.

"Sheriff Crockett," Rossman said the moment Jericho answered. "I understand you want to talk to me about Laurel and the money laundering charges against her. Well, let's talk. I'll be at the sheriff's office in just a few minutes."

Chapter Thirteen

Jericho felt as if he was being buried by an avalanche.

So much was coming at Laurel and him. Their impending arrests. The danger. Chase's injury. The new info from both Theo and the Moonlight Strangler.

Now, this.

Rossman would be arriving soon, and while Jericho did indeed want to have a chat with the man, he didn't want that to happen at Laurel's expense.

"What can I do to help?" Levi asked.

Jericho went with the most pressing problem—making sure Laurel was safe. "Call in the reserve deputies. I want at least two of them, and tell them to get here ASAP."

He used the computer to pull up the personnel roster for Levi. The deputies wouldn't be pleased about being called in since they were probably spending time with their families, but it couldn't be helped.

While Levi started to make the calls, Jericho turned to Laurel. Like him, she looked overwhelmed. Scared, as well. Too bad there was a reason to be scared. After all, Rossman hadn't been ruled out as a suspect, and with his partner, Cawley, now dead, Rossman could be looking to blame Laurel in some way for this mess they were all in.

"I know," she said before he could speak. "You want

me to hide in your office. But until Rossman gets here, I can help."

Jericho was about to assure her that he had everything under control, but then he heard the whirring sound of the fax machine. No doubt, copies of the photos and notes from Sheriff McKinnon.

He tipped his head to the papers that the machine was spitting out. "Why don't you take those and go in my office."

She nodded, probably because she was interested in seeing if it was her father in the old photos, but she would also be safer in there than in the squad room. However, Laurel didn't jump to get the faxes. She stood there, staring at him.

"You'll be careful, right?" she asked.

"Yeah." But they both knew that being careful hadn't stopped the other attacks. It might not stop this one, either, if Rossman came in with guns blazing.

Since Jericho thought they both could use it, he brushed a kiss on her forehead. Then, her mouth. He could definitely be doing other things right now, but this seemed just as important as everything else.

"Go," he insisted before he kissed her again. "While I'm waiting for Rossman, I'll start to work on a place for us to stay."

Laurel finally got moving. She gathered up the papers and went to his office. "Don't open the window in there," he reminded her. Not that she would. "And just in case something happens, there's a gun in the center desk drawer."

Another nod, and he hated that Laurel barely had a reaction to being told about the gun. She was probably still partially in shock from the last attack because there was no way she could become immune to the possibility of someone trying to kill her again.

At least he hoped not.

No one should get used to that.

Jericho waited until she was inside his office before he took out his phone and went to one of the front windows to look out. He didn't raise the blinds. He looked out the side.

Since it was still butt-freezing cold, there weren't many people out and about, though there were several folks eating at the diner across the street. Jericho could also see cars pulling in and out of the parking lot of the grocery store just up the block. No one seemed to be focused on the sheriff's building. And there was definitely no sign of Rossman. Thankfully, Jericho had seen a photo of the man in the background report, so he should be able to recognize him.

Jericho made his call to a friend, Marshal Dallas Walker, and asked him to arrange a safe house. He had to add another ASAP to the request, and the marshal assured him he'd get right on it.

"The deputies are on their way," Levi relayed to him when he finished his calls. "What next?"

"Call and get an update on Chase. If it's good news, I'll phone Jax." He'd need to call Jax, anyway, to let him know what was going on, but Jericho preferred to have some good news before he did that.

Jericho returned to keeping watch. Still no sign of Rossman, but he heard Laurel step out of his office, and he pivoted in that direction. Considering all the bad stuff that'd been going on, he almost expected her to say they were under attack. Instead, she held up the handful of faxed photos.

"It's my father," she said. "Of course, he's a lot younger in the photos, but it's him, all right."

Good. The lab would still have to verify it, but this was a start. "What does it say about your father in the notes?" Jericho asked.

"He's mentioned in one of the deals to buy illegal weapons." Laurel blew out a frustrated breath. "But they're just notes. I can't imagine them being admissible in court."

They wouldn't be. But maybe the photos and notes together would be enough to get Herschel to back off. Jericho hated to bargain with the snake, but if Herschel thought he was fighting a losing battle to get Maddox, then maybe he'd call off his dogs.

Jericho motioned for her to go back in the office, and he made another sweeping glance of the street.

"Chase will be okay," Levi relayed while he was still on the phone. "He's got a concussion, and he'll need about a dozen stitches to the chest, but the cut isn't that deep. Once that's done, he should be able to leave the hospital."

That was even better news. Too bad getting the photos and notes had come at such a high price. A woman's murder and Chase's injury. Of course, the Moonlight Strangler had likely planned on murdering the woman, no matter what, but Jericho hated that the killer had done it this way.

"Chase said one of the Sweetwater Springs deputies can bring Chase here to the sheriff's office," Levi added.

"Not here." Jericho didn't even have to think about that. "Tell Chase to go to the ranch." At least there were plenty of ranch hands who could help guard him, and their long-time cook had some decent nursing skills.

Jericho listened to Levi relay the message. Braced himself in case Chase argued about it.

But then something caught his attention.

A man in a dark, heavy coat was coming up the sidewalk across the street near the diner. No hat so Jericho got a good look at him. Dark hair, thin face.

It was Rossman.

Every nerve in Jericho's body went on alert.

"Rossman's here," he called out to Levi. "Laurel, don't come out."

"Is he armed?" Levi asked, joining Jericho at the window.

"Hard to tell." Jericho could see his hands, and Rossman wasn't carrying a gun, but that coat was big enough to conceal plenty of weapons.

Rossman turned his gaze toward the sheriff's office, and in the same motion, he caught onto the side of the diner. But he didn't just catch onto it. The man sank to his knees.

"What the hell?" Jericho went to the door, opened it, and with his gun ready, tried to get a better look.

And he got one, all right.

A gust of wind flipped back the side of Rossman's coat, and Jericho saw the front of the man's shirt was bright red.

Blood.

"Call for an ambulance and cover me," Jericho said to Levi, and he stepped out, praying this wasn't some kind of ruse so that hired thugs could go after Laurel again.

Rossman lifted his head, made eye contact with Jericho. No ruse. Well, not on Rossman's part, anyway. The man was indeed hurt.

Maybe dying.

It was a risk. Anything he did at this point was. But Jericho kept watch around him and hurried across the street. Once he was closer, he saw there wasn't much color left in Rossman's face, and the man's breathing was thin and ragged.

"What happened to you?" Jericho asked, stooping down beside him. He tore open the shirt.

More blood.

Too much of it.

Rossman was bleeding out, and since the ambulance might not get there in time, Jericho held his hand against the gaping wound to try to staunch the blood.

"What happened?" Jericho repeated.

"I got shot." Rossman motioned up the street.

That's when Jericho saw a dark green car at the traffic light. The car's headlights and engine were still on, and the driver's-side door was wide-open. Someone had shot through the window, and the bullet had no doubt gone into Rossman.

Considering what'd happened to Rossman's business partner, Jericho figured the man had been followed and targeted.

Since the shooter could come back for another round, Jericho pulled the man into the narrow alleyway. A couple of the diners came outside, no doubt to see what was going on, but Jericho motioned for them to get back in.

"The ambulance will be here soon," Jericho told Rossman. "Just hold on a few more minutes."

"I don't have minutes. I'm dying." The hoarse breath he dragged in sure sounded like a man on his deathbed.

"Did you see the person who did this to you?" Jericho asked.

Rossman nodded, and his eyelids fluttered down. "He said I was to give her a message. Tell her that he's coming to kill her. To kill Laurel."

Well, hell. That was not a message Jericho wanted to hear. "Who's coming?" Jericho pressed.

"Herschel." That was all Rossman said for several long moments. "I didn't see him, but I heard his voice. He's the one who shot me."

Jericho got right in his face. "You're sure it was Herschel?"

But there was no way for Rossman to hear the question. No way for him to answer.

Because the man was already dead.

Chapter Fourteen

There was blood on her hands.

Not her own. And thankfully, not Jericho's. She wasn't exactly sure how it got there, but it belonged to Rossman.

After the ambulance had taken the man's body away and Jericho had come back into the sheriff's office, she'd ended up in Jericho's arms. Laurel was fuzzy about how that'd happened, too, but she'd pretty much lost it when he had told her what Rossman had said.

Of course, she'd known all along that her father was capable of murder. Had known he would do anything to get Maddox and get back at her. But now a man was dead, and he'd used his dying breath to deliver a message.

Tell her that he's coming to kill her.

There it was in a nutshell. So what if they had proof now to discredit her father and get the charges against her dismissed? That wouldn't matter if he was hell-bent on making sure she was dead.

And that riled her to the core.

Rossman's blood angered her, too, because it was yet another reminder of a life lost in this ordeal. Too many lives, including Jericho's father and her own mother. Added to that were the injuries and the fear that seemed to be crushing her lungs.

One way or another, Herschel was going to pay.

She heard the footsteps, and several moments later, Jericho appeared in the doorway of his office where she was waiting. He, too, still had blood on him and was sporting a very concerned expression. Something he'd had for the past hour, since Rossman had been murdered.

"Did you find my father?" she asked.

Some of the concern vanished, replaced by frustration when he shook his head. "Not yet. The deputies looked for him, but I brought them back in so the office—and you—would be protected. The Rangers just arrived so they'll take over the search."

If her father was indeed still out there, he was probably staying well hidden. Until it was time for the final attack against her.

"I'm making arrangements for a safe house," Jericho continued. "The Sweetwater Springs's sheriff has offered to lend me two of his deputies to do backup for us while we're at the safe house. But I'm also making this place as safe as possible in the meantime. We've got the security system turned on. And as I said, the reserve deputies are here. Levi, too. He's staying now that Chase doesn't need him."

She certainly hadn't forgotten about Chase, but with everything else going on, she'd pushed him to the back of her mind. "How's Chase?"

"He'll be okay. He's a Crockett, and along with a hard head, he's got thick skin like the rest of us."

Laurel appreciated Jericho's attempt to lighten things up, but nothing was going to work right now.

"Did you get a chance to call Jax?" Jericho asked her.

She nodded. "Everything's okay, but Maddox was

asleep, so I didn't get a chance to talk to him. He doesn't usually go to sleep this early."

"Between the deputies, my mom and Jax, he's got four playmates. I'm betting they tired him out."

Maybe. She hoped that was true and that her little boy wasn't picking up on all the stress from the danger.

She certainly was.

Laurel felt wired and exhausted at the same time. There was so much nervous energy bubbling up inside her and nowhere to aim it. Too bad her father wasn't around so she could give him a piece of her mind.

"Come on," Jericho said, helping her to her feet. "There's a bathroom just off the break room. Well, sort of a bathroom. No shower, but there's a sink. The water pressure's practically nonexistent, and the hot-water heater taps out after about a minute, but we can both wash off some of the blood."

Yes, they could wash it off, but Laurel would still see it. Still feel it, too.

"Laurel's going to get some rest," Jericho told Levi when he leaned around the hall corner to look into the squad room.

His brother was obviously busy, but Levi muttered something about that being a good idea. And it was, in theory. But that didn't mean it was going to happen. Not with her mind in tornado mode.

"I wish my father was dead," she said.

Jericho made a quick sound of agreement and led her toward the break room. A place she already knew too well since she'd stayed there for hours the night after the first attack. Maddox had slept on the small bed tucked against the wall while she paced and worried about, well, everything. She wasn't pacing now, but the worry was still there in spades.

He opened one of the metal lockers positioned against the wall and took out a gray T-shirt. He held it up, glancing at it, then at her.

Jericho tossed her the T-shirt. "It won't be a good fit, but it'll be better than nothing."

It would be. She didn't want any more reminders of the violence that'd just taken place.

The blinds were still closed, and he slapped off the overhead lights. However, it didn't plunge them into total darkness because of the light coming from the hall. There were also lights threading in around the edges of the blinds. Plenty of light for her to see the worried look on his face.

"Is there something you aren't telling me?"

He looked down at the blood on her hands. On the front of her top, too. "I just don't like seeing that on you."

"I could say the same thing." She touched the front of his shirt. Of course, that meant she touched his chest, too. Not a good idea, considering her raw nerves and spiked adrenaline.

Also not a good idea because of the attraction.

Jericho didn't exactly step back, but it was close. He glanced away, dodging her gaze and dodging her touch in the process. Wise decision. His mind was likely in tornado mode, too.

"Go ahead. Wash up," he said, opening the bathroom door for her.

Laurel didn't turn on the light, and since there was no window, there was even less light in here than in the break room itself. Still, she found her way to the sink and began to wash off the blood.

"My father took a huge risk by shooting Rossman," Laurel said, thinking out loud. Thinking quietly about it, too. There was something about this that just didn't add up.

Jericho made a sound of agreement, but she could still see his face, and that wasn't agreement in his expression. "Think this through. Pulling the trigger himself just isn't something Herschel would do. So, why do it now? Especially when he has his spies planted all around. Why not just get one of them to do his dirty work?"

Good question. Too bad Laurel didn't have a good answer. "You think Rossman would use his dying breath to lie?"

"He might if he was dying, anyway, and wanted to get back at Herschel. Heck, Rossman could have even shot himself. A suicide so he could incriminate your father. After all, Rossman was about to be arrested for money laundering. His partner's already dead, so he might have figured this was the easy way out."

She splashed some water on her face while she thought about that. Yes, a suicide was possible. But it was also possible that either Theo, Dorothy or both had ordered the hit on Rossman.

Laurel groped around until she located a towel. Dried her face. And then debated how to change out shirts. She didn't especially want to close the door between Jericho and herself, but it probably wasn't a good idea to strip down in front of him, either, so she stepped back into the corner of the bathroom to change. When she came back out, she realized he was staring at her.

Judging from the heat in his eyes, maybe she hadn't been in the shadows as much as she thought. Best not to bring it up, though. And it wasn't as if they didn't have anything else to think about. Or talk about.

"My father has a strong motive for wanting Rossman dead," she reminded him. Reminded herself, too.

Jericho nodded. "But it still doesn't feel right. Herschel would have found another way. Maybe a car accident like the one that Rossman's partner had. Now, that's something Herschel would do."

"But Rossman said he saw my father."

"He could have lied about that. Or maybe he did see him. Herschel's probably still in town somewhere, and Rossman could have been at the wrong place at the wrong time."

Or else someone could have made sure he was there by luring him to the area. Theo or Dorothy could have certainly managed that. And that meant they were back to square one again.

Well, almost.

"You can still use Rossman's accusation to arrest my father." Her father might be able to wiggle out of the charges, but that would take time, and it would give him something else to focus on rather than Jericho and her.

"Oh, yeah," Jericho quickly agreed. "And trust me, that's exactly what'll happen when he's found. I've asked the Rangers to assist in the search."

Good. So, not square one.

"But we need more," he added. "I'm playing around with the notion of trying to set some kind of trap to lure your father or anyone else involved in this."

"What kind of trap?"

He shook his head. "Not sure yet. I'm still trying to work it all out. But once I have the details set in my mind, you'll be the first to know."

Jericho peeled off his blood-stained shirt and headed into the bathroom. As she'd done, he scrubbed his hands, hard. His face, too. But since she was holding the only towel, he came back into the doorway to take it from her.

"You're worrying," he pointed out, frowning. Maybe because she was frowning at herself. "You shouldn't. There's good news in all of this. With Herschel arrested and charged with murder, that'll make it easier to ax the arrest warrants against both of us. Ax his custody petition, too."

Laurel heard every word he said. Felt the relief that the danger might finally be ending. But she also had a shirtless Jericho standing in front of her, and he hadn't even attempted to find a shadowy corner to hide while he dried off.

She saw it then. The faint scar on his chest where her name had once been.

"What?" he asked. But then he scowled when he followed her gaze. "Yeah, I had it removed."

That was to be expected. But Laurel couldn't help remembering the time he'd first gotten it when they were still teenagers. A tattoo to prove to her that she'd always be part of him.

As if she needed ink to prove that.

If there was a test for it, she was sure Jericho was in her veins, in her blood. He was certainly in her heart.

"What can I say? I was young, and in those days words alone didn't seem to be a strong enough man-statement." He walked past her, heading toward the locker again. No doubt for another shirt. But he didn't take out anything. He just stared inside the locker as if expecting to find some kind of answer there.

"It was a statement. I remember you trying to pretend

it didn't hurt like crazy. The tattoo," she clarified when he turned around to face her again.

Still no shirt. Just that intense stare that only Jericho could manage. "It hurt," he verified.

And they were no longer talking about the tattoo.

She shouldn't touch him. Laurel knew that. Touching Jericho was never as simple as just touching, and it could be dangerous.

It didn't stop her.

As if her hand had a mind of its own, it went to his chest, and the moment she felt him beneath her fingers, the relief came. Washing over her. Through her. For this brief time, she hadn't lost him. He was still hers to touch.

Hers to take.

Of course, it was pure fantasy. He was no one's for the taking, especially hers, but when it came to Jericho, she'd spent most of her life weaving fantasies, and tonight was apparently no different.

He glanced at her hand. "You plan on doing something about that?" Those sizzling amber eyes came back to hers and held. Waiting.

Without lifting her hand, Laurel inched it lower. To his stomach. She hadn't thought she could ache more for him, but she'd been wrong. Every part of her was aching now. Every part wanting him. Wanting more. She was so close to his zipper. Close enough that she could *do something about that.*

Something she was sure they'd regret when they came to their senses.

But not now.

No regrets now.

She leaned in to kiss him, but Jericho beat her to it. His rough hand went around the back of her neck and dragged her closer. Not for a kiss, though. He just stared at her, studying her. So much emotion in his face. A tangled mix that Laurel was feeling, too.

"Damn you," he growled. He shut the door. Locked it. And he kissed her.

Laurel had wanted that kiss more than her next breath, but she still wasn't ready for it. Jericho mouth's came to hers, and she remembered that he kissed with the same intensity that he did everything else in his life. No gentle lead-in. Just the sweet assault of his taste and his body against hers.

He took her hand, put it over the front of his jeans. "Are you going to do something about that?" he demanded.

She did. Laurel unzipped him, slowly, eased her hand into his jeans and beneath his boxers. And she got the reaction she wanted. Not only was he hard as stone, he made a sound, deep in his chest.

Before he dragged her to the bed.

It was exactly what Laurel wanted. This fire. This need that only Jericho could fix. And he fixed, it all right.

Everything was urgent. Fast. As if this had become a life-and-death matter. He stripped off her borrowed T-shirt. Her bra, too. And Laurel got the full impact of having his bare skin against hers. It didn't rob her of her breath exactly, but Jericho did something else to make sure that happened.

As she'd done with him, he slipped his hands into her jeans, into her panties, touching her while slipping off her jeans at the same time. Laurel wanted to help him. She freed him from his boxers but wanted to get rid of any and all barriers between them. His touch stopped her from doing that.

No ordinary touch.

No.

His fingers went inside her, and just like that she went from being on fire to being very close to climaxing. Something she didn't want to happen. Not until he was inside her, anyway.

Laurel tried to distract him with a kiss. Tried to get off his jeans, too. But Jericho kept on touching her, his fingers sliding in and out of her. Until she couldn't hold on any longer.

In the milky light, their gazes met. Held. And he sent her flying right over the edge.

Even as the pleasure wracked her body, she cursed him. "I wanted us to do this together."

"We will." It almost sounded like a threat.

Laurel wasn't sure if she should laugh or be worried. But she didn't have time for either. He rid her of her panties. Didn't bother with his jeans, though. Maybe because the need was too urgent. He kneed her legs apart and robbed her of her breath again when he pushed inside her.

The pleasure was blinding.

Not that she'd expected anything less.

The earlier climax now felt like foreplay. Jericho's version of foreplay, anyway. This was the real deal. The avalanche of emotions and pleasure that only he could give her. No pleasure on his face, though. Just the intensity to finish this.

To finish her. Again.

And he would. He always did.

Her body knew this rhythm they created together. Knew just how to move with him.

Or so she thought.

But Jericho made a move inside her that robbed her of what little breath she had left. It fueled the urgency for both of them. Turned his need-laced battle into an out-and-out war.

With their gazes still locked, Jericho pushed into her. Faster. Harder. Deeper. And even when her vision started to blur again, Jericho caught onto her chin, forcing her to hold the eye contact.

As if he'd rehearsed every moment, every move, he pushed into her one last time. The climax came. Even stronger than the last one. It came for him, too. Laurel felt his body surrender. And heard the single word he said loud and clear even though it barely had any sound.

"Hell."

Chapter Fifteen

Jericho gave himself a minute to let the feeling of release slide through him. It was a darn good minute, too, what with the intense pleasure and the feel of a naked Laurel beneath him. But he'd known right from the start that the minute and the pleasure couldn't last.

Time to deal with some reality.

Especially since reality was staring him right in the face.

Laurel's eyes were still a little glazed. His probably were, too. Great sex could do that, and there was no doubt about it. It'd been great. Always was when he was with Laurel. But great didn't mean there wouldn't be some serious consequences.

"Hell?" she said, repeating what he'd just gutted out.

"I didn't mean it like that."

Jericho rolled off her, damn near fell on his butt because the bed was so narrow. The jolt of having to keep his balance caused the last aftershocks of pleasure to vanish.

It wouldn't be long though before the need for her returned.

Always did.

"Then how did you mean it?" she asked. Laurel got

up when he did, and she started to dress. It was a shame. Because the view of her naked was amazing.

Hard to give her a flat look when her breasts were still bare. She quickly did something about that and put her bra back on.

"You know what I mean," he insisted. "This complicates things."

She nodded. Sighed. And then she put on her jeans and the peep show was over. "Because your family will never accept me. Because *you'll* never accept me."

Jericho's flat look turned to a scowl. And because that last part riled him, he hooked his hand around the back of her neck and kissed the living daylights out of her.

"Trust me, I've *accepted* you," he snarled. And gotten himself worked up again in the process.

Laurel's mouth twitched. Maybe from the hard kiss. Maybe because she was fighting back a smile. Since she was a smart woman, she won. The smile didn't.

"Just so you know. I haven't been with anyone else since that last time with you," she added.

The night he'd gotten her pregnant. The reminder hit him like a punch. "I didn't use a condom." A first. Oh, man. He was clearly losing it. "I don't guess you're on the pill?"

She shook her head and didn't look nearly as alarmed as he did. "No need for it. Well, not until tonight, anyway. It's okay. It's the wrong time of the month."

Maybe. But considering he'd used a condom the last time and Laurel had still gotten pregnant, then maybe there was no *wrong time of the month* when it came to the two of them.

"At least we're married," he said, because he had no idea what else to say.

Now her smile won out. Jericho didn't join in on it.

"You're a serious distraction, you know that?" He dropped another kiss on her smiling mouth and unlocked the break room door so he could go and do all the things he should have been doing instead of having sex with Laurel.

Too bad he couldn't say it wouldn't happen again. And soon.

Yeah, he was losing it, all right.

"Good news," Levi said the moment Jericho glanced into his office, where Levi was working at the desk. A place Jericho should be. "We got a warrant for Herschel's arrest for Rossman's murder."

That was indeed good news. Jericho needed a whole lot more, though. Because as long as Herschel and those hired guns were at large, the danger would still be there for Laurel and Maddox.

"And the FBI got a match to Herschel's voice on the recording from those surveillance tapes involving the money laundering," his brother added. "There'll be a warrant coming for that, too."

Levi glanced at him. Did a double take. Then stared at Jericho—specifically at Jericho's rumpled clothes and not-quite-right expression.

"Want to talk?" Levi asked him.

"Not about *that*." Jericho huffed. "Why, do you want to tell me how wrong it is to get involved with Laurel again?"

"No."

All right. That was a surprise. "Then what do you want to tell me?"

"That you're human."

Jericho huffed. "What the hell is that supposed to mean?"

"It means you and Laurel have skirted this attraction

for years. Fighting it. Giving in to it. Cursing yourself. Did you curse her, too?"

Yeah, in an indirect way he had. He'd said that *hell*. No plans to admit it, either. "Is there a point to all of this?"

"There is. If you two decide to quit skirting, then the family will eventually accept it. Hear me out," Levi added when Jericho was about to argue with that. "Laurel and you have a child. That'll bring Mom around. She's already said she wants a truce with Laurel, and I believe she means it."

But that was only one piece of this messy puzzle. "What about Herschel killing Dad?"

"What about it? True, Herschel almost certainly did kill him. But there's never been an ounce of proof that Laurel had any part in it either before or after the fact."

"But I knew," Jericho heard Laurel say, and he cursed himself for not hearing her walk up behind them. In addition to his mind, his ears were going, too. "I didn't have any proof, but I knew he'd done it."

"And without proof, there wasn't a damn thing you could do about it," Levi reminded her. Something that Jericho should have been telling her.

Laurel shook her head. "Still, I stayed under his roof. I continued to work for him."

Levi jumped right on that, too. "Because of your sick mother. I get that. I'd do the same if it were my mother."

Jericho scowled at Levi. It was the right thing to say. Right time to say it, too. But those right words should have been coming from Jericho's mouth.

"All right." Levi held up his hands. Obviously, Levi hadn't missed Jericho's sharp look. "Then you tell her. And this time try it without scowling. Without cursing."

It got so quiet in the room that he could have heard

an eyelash fall, and it took Jericho a lot longer to gather his thoughts.

Too long.

Because Laurel leaned in and kissed him. Hard. "It's okay. We'll work it all out later. For now, we'll work on keeping Maddox safe. Christmas is only a matter of hours away, and I'd like for us to spend that day with him. With all of us safe."

Well, hell's bells. Now she was saying the right thing, too. And she was right.

"You said something earlier about possibly setting a trap," she added.

"What kind of trap?" Levi immediately asked.

One that could out and out fail. Still, Jericho hadn't been able to come up with anything else to bring the danger to a quick end. Laurel was right. Time was ticking away.

Jericho made sure they didn't have any visitors in the squad room just in case Herschel had sent in one of his spies pretending to need some kind of help. But the only people out there were the two reserve deputies who were both busy working.

"Earlier, while the deputies were looking for Herschel, I spoke to Sheriff McKinnon over in Sweetwater Springs about possibly leaking some false information." Jericho hoped this made sense when he said it aloud. "Information about what was in the message that the Moonlight Strangler left at the crime scene."

Laurel shook her head. "What kind of false information?"

"The press has made a big deal out of the fact that the Moonlight Strangler hasn't gone after Addie. Or anyone else in the family since they found out that she's his daughter. I've seen some reporter speculate that the serial killer is actually helping us on cases."

Jericho wanted to put that speculation to good use.

"I want it leaked that the Moonlight Strangler has evidence that could prove who's been trying to kill Laurel. Evidence he intends to send to the cops tonight." Jericho continued, "It'd have to be something specific."

"Like proof of payment to the hired guns," Levi supplied. "Or photos of the person meeting with one of the men."

"Exactly like that. Something that could be used to trace the thugs back to the person who hired them. And it'll help that it's probably already leaked that the killer left something on his latest victim's body. We could say that a courier will bring the evidence to the Sweetwater Springs's sheriff office tonight, where it'll be prepped to be sent to the crime lab."

Another headshake from Laurel. "But what if the person who wants me dead goes after the sheriff and deputies in Sweetwater Springs? Or what if he goes after the courier?"

"The courier will be guarded, and Sheriff McKinnon will be ready for an attack." At least that's what McKinnon had assured Jericho. He hoped that was true because he didn't want this to turn out badly for the fellow sheriff who was trying to do them a huge favor.

"It might not work," Jericho added. "The person responsible could see right through the ruse and attack us here or while we're on the way to the safe house. We have to be ready for that."

More silence. But this time it didn't last very long, and Laurel nodded. "Let's do it. Anything to put an end to this."

Levi stayed quiet a moment longer. Then nodded. "I'm in."

Jericho added his own nod and took out his phone to call Sheriff McKinnon. He just hoped like the devil that this was the right thing to do.

And that he wasn't about to set another attack in motion.

THERE WAS NOTHING to do but wait. Something Laurel had been doing for the past two hours. She just wasn't good at it, especially when lives were on the line to save Maddox and her.

She was tired of the danger. Tired of hiding. Tired of being away from her son. And especially tired of people dying because of some stupid plan that'd been set in motion by her father. Maybe by Theo or Dorothy. They might soon know if the trap that Jericho set worked.

The sheriff's office was quiet. For a change. The two deputies were keeping watch at the back of the building. Jericho and Levi were at the front. Laurel was in Jericho's office, away from the wall of front windows. It would be a gutsy move for someone to attack a building with four cops inside, but the other attacks had been gutsy, as well. Added to that, the person might be as desperate as Laurel was to put an end to all of this.

She leaned back in the chair, tried to settle her nerves. No chance of that happening, so she used one of the secure phones to call Jax. But it wasn't Jax who answered. It was Iris.

Laurel's heart went straight to her throat. "Is something wrong? Why didn't Jax answer?"

"Everything's fine. Jax is eating, that's all, and when I saw the number on the screen, I thought it might be you calling. Maddox is still sleeping," Iris went on. "I think he got tired out from all the ride-the-horsey games he played with Jax. Maddox is such a sweet little boy, Laurel."

"Yes, he is. Thank you."

"You're welcome. And I should have said it sooner. I should have said a lot of things sooner." Iris paused. "Like welcoming you to the family since Jericho and you are married now."

"I'm not sure how long that'll last." The moment Laurel heard her own words, she winced. "I mean, you know he only married me so he could keep my father from getting custody of Maddox. But it looks as if my father won't stand a chance at doing that now."

"Yes, Jax told me about that. It'll be an answer to a lot of prayers if Herschel is stopped." Another pause. "But that doesn't have anything to do with Jericho and you and your marriage. You two have always been together, even when you weren't. And you're good together."

Laurel got a flash of a naked Jericho with her in the break room, and despite everything else, she felt a trace of pleasure ripple through her again.

"I guess what I'm saying is I won't stand in the way of making this marriage permanent," Iris continued. "In fact, I think you should make it permanent."

Laurel certainly hadn't seen that coming. "You mean for Maddox's sake."

"No. For you and Jericho. Just think about it."

She was about to assure Iris that she would. She was about to thank her, as well, but Laurel heard Jericho and Levi talking in the squad room. Their voices weren't raised or frantic, but there was something in Jericho's tone that put Laurel on full alert.

"I need to go," she said to Iris. "I'll call you back."

Laurel clicked the end call button and went to the doorway so she could see Jericho and Levi. Levi was on the phone, but Jericho immediately turned to her. Yes, she could tell from the look on his face that something had indeed happened.

"Your father was spotted in town," Jericho said. "Just a couple of blocks from here."

All right. That required her to take a deep breath. Of course, she'd known he was nearby. Well, he was if Rossman had been telling the truth, that is.

"I'd faxed your father's picture to all the businesses that were still open, and the security guard at a storage facility spotted him a couple of minutes ago. Not alone. There were two other men in the car with him."

Hired guns no doubt. "Is he coming here?" she asked.

"Maybe." But his expression said *definitely*. She was the reason her father had come here, and his spies had likely already told him exactly where she was.

Laurel wasn't afraid. She was well past that point when it came to her father. It was pure anger now. In fact, if she knew that Jericho and the others wouldn't be hurt, she would demand a showdown with him.

But maybe there was something she could do.

"I'm calling my father," she said, and Laurel didn't wait for permission from Jericho. Something he'd never give her, anyway.

"Laurel," Jericho snapped, his voice a stern warning.

However, she had already pressed in the number, and when her father answered on the first ring, she put the call on speaker.

"Jericho?" Her father's greeting was as frosty as Jericho's glare. The one he was volleying between the phone and her.

"No, it's me," Laurel said. "I understand you're in town. Are you coming to see me?"

"Right. As if I'd let you know where I am or where I'm going. You'd just tell Jericho, and he'd arrest me. Or kill me."

"Jericho's not a killer. But you are."

Her father cursed, and like Jericho's glare, some of it was aimed at her. "I didn't kill Rossman."

"That's not what he said," Laurel argued.

"Well, he was mistaken. I was there, yes, because I got a call from one of my men. He said there was something I needed to see. Turned out to be a trap. Somebody shot Rossman, and now I'm getting the blame."

That was possible, for her father to have been set up, but it was just as possible that he was lying.

"Rossman isn't the only death connected to you," she said.

"Ah, now we're talking about Sherman Crockett. Since I suspect your *husband* is listening to our every word, then that's one topic that's not up for discussion."

Jericho opened his mouth, no doubt to return verbal fire, but Laurel lifted her hand, motioned for him to stay quiet. Yes, her father probably did know that Jericho would be there with her, but she figured she would get more information out of him than Jericho would.

Well, maybe.

At the moment her father probably hated her more than he hated Jericho, and she might be able to strike a nerve. One that would get him to blurt out a confession.

"First Sherman, then my mother," Laurel said.

Silence. For a long time. "Your mother was dying."

"Possibly. Did you help that process along by giving her an overdose of painkillers?"

More silence. "She was in a lot of pain. No matter what you think of me, I loved her in my own way. I couldn't stand to see her suffering."

It took her a moment to rein in her own temper just so she could speak. "You didn't love her. And she didn't love you. She was terrified of you, and so help me, you'll pay for killing her."

"I didn't kill her!" he shouted. "What, are you recording this? You think you can use it against me?"

"There's already enough evidence against you. And there's already a warrant out for your arrest."

"A warrant, yes," her father agreed, "but they'll have to find me to serve it. In the meantime, I've got my entire legal team working to clear my name. And it will be cleared… What the hell…"

Laurel was about to ask him why he'd said that, but Jericho's phone buzzed. He glanced at the screen and immediately stepped away and answered it.

Laurel hurried after Jericho. "What's wrong?"

Jericho was already talking to the person on the other end of the line, but he paused to answer her. "Someone just fired shots into the Sweetwater Springs sheriff's office."

Chapter Sixteen

So, someone had taken the bait.

Jericho was partially happy about that, but he darn sure wasn't pleased that Sheriff McKinnon and his deputies were under fire.

"Are they okay?" Laurel asked. The color had drained from her face.

He considered going with a lie so that maybe he could ease some of the fear in her eyes, but Laurel was right in the thick of this with him. "I don't know," Jericho answered honestly. "Sheriff McKinnon only had a few seconds to tell me what was happening. I heard shots in the background," he added.

She nodded. And, yep, the fear stayed. "What if they don't capture one of their attackers alive?"

"They will." Okay, that was possibly a lie, one that Jericho had to believe. If they didn't or if they couldn't get the hired gun to talk, then all of this danger had been for nothing.

Well, except for the fact that if the hired guns were there in Sweetwater Springs, they weren't anywhere near the safe house that contained Maddox. Jericho hated to put fellow lawmen's lives on the line, but if their situations were reversed, Jericho would have done the same for them.

Jericho went back to the window to keep watch, but he also tipped his head to the phone she was holding. "Is your father still on the line?"

She shook her head. "He hung up."

That was just as well. Herschel had come darn close to incriminating himself, but he was too clever to spill anything important. Especially anything that would get him the death penalty. Of course, he might not have to spill anything if they could get the murder charges to stick. Or if Sheriff McKinnon managed to get a confession from the thugs who were now shooting at him.

"Is anyone out there?" Laurel asked. Still too pale, and he was pretty sure she was trembling now. Jericho wanted to go to her, but the shooting at Sweetwater Springs could be a ruse to get them to lower their guard.

Wasn't going to happen.

"You should go back in my office," he insisted. Fewer windows there. "Make sure you leave the light on."

That was a departure from what he usually told her, but Jericho had turned on every light in the place. Including the bathroom. He hoped that way, if hit men did show up, they wouldn't know what room Laurel was in. Plus, the interior lights helped illuminate the front sidewalk and the sides of the building.

"Be careful," Laurel said.

Jericho glanced back at her, their gazes connecting. Usually when that happened, he felt a punch of heat from the attraction, but now he saw something else.

Something he didn't like.

"I'm not going to get shot," he let her know. Possibly

another lie, but there was no need for her to be worried about him.

"See anything?" Jericho asked Levi once Laurel was back in his office.

"No. You?"

"Nothing." Jericho reminded himself that was a good thing, but he still had a knot in his gut. A knot that tightened when his phone buzzed, and he saw the caller's name.

Theo.

Jericho didn't want to tie up his hands for the call, so he hit the answer button, sandwiched the phone between his shoulder and ear. "Make it quick," Jericho snarled. "I'm busy."

Plus, Theo could be calling to try to distract him, which meant Jericho didn't care to have a long chat.

"Is Laurel okay?" Theo asked.

That didn't help his uneasiness, and Jericho made another sweeping glance of the area around the building. "Why do you ask?"

"Because she's in danger, that's why. Hell, we're all in danger."

"Some of us more than others," Jericho remarked. "Unless you've got something new and interesting to tell me— like a confession—then this call is over."

"Don't hang up!" It wasn't a shout. More like a plea. But it took Theo a few seconds to continue. "I think someone wants me dead."

"That's not a confession. Heck, it's not even a surprise. You piss people off, Theo. Me included."

"But you didn't just try to kidnap me. Did you?"

"No. That wasn't on my to-do list tonight." Now it was Jericho's turn to pause. "First, did this so-called kidnapping attempt really happen? And if so, did it happen in my jurisdiction?" Because if it didn't, then that was yet another reason to end the call and have him whine to somebody else.

"It happened just a few minutes ago. I'm a couple of streets away from the sheriff's office near the hotel. Two big guys jumped out of a black car when I was at the traffic light, and they tried to Taser me. I got away."

"Convenient." And possibly the truth. Because it could be true, Jericho had to use his lawman's voice. "Were you hurt?"

"Just some scrapes and bruises. I carry a concealed .38. Yes, I have a permit," he added before Jericho could ask. "Anyway, I managed to draw it, and I think I hit one of them when I fired."

Hell. Discharge of a weapon. Possible injury along with a possible kidnapping attempt. It would have to be investigated, but this was one duty Jericho would have to delegate.

"Call the Rangers," Jericho told Levi. "Tell them there's a situation I need them to handle at the Saltgrass Inn."

"You're not coming to help me?" Theo asked. Clearly, the man had heard what Jericho had said to his brother.

No way. Jericho had no intention of leaving Laurel to walk into what could be a trap or a ploy to get him away from Laurel. "Why are you here in town?"

"I got a call from one of your deputies who told me Laurel was in trouble, that I needed to go to the sheriff's office and check on her because she wanted to see me."

Theo hadn't hesitated, which meant it could be the truth or he could have just practiced the lie until it rolled right off his tongue. "Laurel doesn't want to see you, and no deputy of mine called you."

"But he did. He said his name was Mack Parkman—"

"Was his name on the caller-ID screen?" Jericho snapped.

"No. It said unknown number. But I figured your deputies were just using secure cells."

Mack was, since he was at the safe house with Jax and Maddox, but there would have been no reason for Mack to call Theo. Still, the lawman in him had to rule it out. Jericho jotted down a note for Levi to call Mack and verify that he'd had no phone contact with Theo.

"I want to come to the sheriff's office and see Laurel," Theo started up again. "And don't say she's not there, because she'll be wherever you are."

"Don't be so sure of that."

"I need to talk to her," Theo said, not even addressing Jericho's comment.

"Mack didn't call him," Levi whispered to Jericho.

Just as Jericho had figured. And yes, he trusted Mack, had known him his entire life. Theo, however, had reason to lie—so he could try to worm his way in and see Laurel. And if he wasn't lying, then someone like Herschel or Dorothy could have hired anyone to make the call to lure Theo out so he could be kidnapped.

And there's where Jericho's theory came to a sudden stop.

Would Dorothy really try to hurt her own son?

Probably, if she blamed Theo for blowing the engagement with Laurel. That broken engagement had cost Dorothy a bundle. Then there was also the possibility that she hadn't wanted to hurt Theo but rather had wanted to set up someone to make it look as if they had murder or kidnapping on their mind.

Someone like Herschel.

Because if Dorothy was riled at Theo for losing those big bucks, she might aim the same venom at Herschel.

Or vice versa.

Herschel definitely wasn't a saint.

"Well, can I see Laurel?" Theo pressed.

Jericho was about to tell him a loud no, with some curse words added to it. But he didn't get the chance to say anything.

Because a blast shook the entire building.

THE SOUND WAS DEAFENING, and Laurel caught on to the wall to steady herself. Not a gunshot. This was something much bigger and louder.

What the heck had Theo done now?

She'd known that Jericho was talking to him, but from what she could hear, it didn't seem as if he'd been threatening Jericho. However, something had definitely happened.

Laurel didn't bolt from the office, but she peered out the door. Jericho was still at the window where she'd last seen him. One of the blinds had fallen to the floor, and she could see the fireball in the street directly in front of the sheriff's office.

"Stay back," Jericho warned her. "It was a bomb."

Her heart was already pounding, but that news made it worse. "How did Theo get close enough to use a bomb?"

"I'm not sure it was Theo. I think someone on the roof of the diner tossed it down."

Oh, mercy. That meant they could have been aiming for the building itself. It also might mean this bomb wasn't the only one they had.

"Get under my desk," Jericho added.

"You should, too." Though she knew it wouldn't do any good.

Jericho just shook his head. "Go!"

Laurel did as he said. She scrambled under his desk just as she heard another sound. Not the blast from a second bomb.

But rather a gunshot.

Then, another.

She couldn't be sure, but Laurel thought maybe they'd been fired into one of the front windows. The glass was bullet resistant, she remembered Jericho saying that, but it didn't mean the shots couldn't eventually get through. She prayed that Jericho and Levi were staying down.

"The shots stopped at the Sweetwater Springs office," Levi relayed to Jericho. "No one was hurt, and the shooters ran off."

That was good. The lawmen there were no longer under attack, but it was clear the shots hadn't stopped here. Because she heard several more of them crack into the windows.

Laurel gasped when another sound shot through the room. Since she was already bracing herself for the worst, it took her a moment to realize it was a landline phone on Jericho's desk. She wasn't sure if she should answer it or not, but when it kept ringing, Laurel thought it might be someone calling to report a sighting of their attacker. She grabbed the phone and got back under the desk.

"Who is this?" the caller immediately asked.

Laurel groaned. Because it was Dorothy on the line. "It's me. And I don't have time to talk."

"Then, make time," the woman insisted. "Because what I have to tell you could save your life."

All right. That grabbed her attention. "What do you mean?"

"I mean, Theo has gone stark raving mad, that's what.

He's trying to get to you so he can kill you. And he's trying to do the same thing to me. Don't trust him, Laurel."

"I won't. I won't trust you, either." Laurel could also add her father to the list of people who might want her dead. She had no plans to trust any of them.

"Somehow, he'll get to you," Dorothy added. "Jericho, too. Theo wants him dead because of what you two did to him. He blames both of you for ruining his life. Just be careful."

"Is Theo the one shooting at the sheriff's office right now?" Laurel asked.

But Dorothy didn't answer her. "No!" the woman shouted, and it was followed by an ear-piercing scream.

And a gunshot.

This one hadn't come from immediately outside the building, either. It had come from the other end of the phone.

"Dorothy?" Laurel said. "What happened?"

Nothing. The line was dead.

Maybe Dorothy was, too. Did that mean Theo had had his own mother shot? Or was this some kind of trick?

Laurel debated whether she should tell Jericho about the call, but it would have to wait. The bullets were still slamming into the front of the building, and she didn't want to say or do anything to distract him. Hopefully soon, the Rangers or backup would arrive and help put a stop to this.

Whatever *this* was.

Two attacks of sheriff offices in the same night. Yes, the one in Sweetwater Springs was no doubt to get the fake evidence that Jericho had leaked. But then why had it stopped? And why were the gunmen now attacking them here? They must know there were lawmen inside.

Four of them. Hardly a fortress, but the gunmen, and their boss, had to be desperate to try to shoot their way inside.

"Hell," she heard Jericho say, and again she nearly bolted out from beneath the desk to make sure he hadn't been hurt. By now, some of those bullets had to be getting through.

But Laurel didn't get the chance to bolt.

Everything happened fast. There was a crashing sound behind her, followed by the howl of the security alarm. Before she could even turn around, the glass from the window came flying out over the room. If it was bullet resistant, then something big had shattered it.

Then a hulking-size man wearing dark-colored camouflage scrambled through the gaping hole and grabbed her. She fought him. Tried to scream out for help. But she didn't manage even that before another man on the other side of the window took hold of her and pulled her through.

"Laurel!" Jericho shouted. And even over the sounds of the continuing shots and the alarm, she heard him running toward the office.

But it was too late.

She landed on the ground outside the window. So did both of her attackers. One turned and fired shots into the office window.

Right where Jericho would be.

Oh, God.

Had the man managed to shoot him?

Laurel couldn't see. Couldn't hear much of anything now with the roar of her heartbeat in her ears and the shots that were no longer buffered by the wall. They were loud, thick blasts.

Too many of them.

One of the men stuffed a gag in her mouth, and they

continued to drag her away from the window. Away from Jericho.

There was white smoke snaking through the air. From the explosion, no doubt, but part of it also seemed to be freezing fog. The men ran right into it, using it to conceal them.

Using it to kidnap her.

She stumbled, on purpose, and when the thug on the right reached for her, she brought up her foot and kicked him. He growled in pain, latched on to her hair and kept moving.

When the smoke cleared, Laurel saw where they were taking her. To a black car parked beside a Dumpster. If they got her inside, they'd be able to speed away, so she knew she had to keep fighting. Because this wasn't just a kidnapping. Laurel had no doubts that she'd soon be dead if she didn't do something right away.

She twisted her body. Tried to fall again. But the man still had hold of her hair, and he used that to control her. The pain watered her eyes. The fear had her by the throat. But she kept fighting. Kept trying to get away.

"Laurel?" Jericho shouted again.

He was alive. For now. But the gunman turned again and fired a shot in the direction of Jericho's voice.

She prayed he hadn't been hit. Prayed that Jericho would get to her in time.

But he didn't.

The moment the men reached the car, the door flew open. And the men began to drag Laurel inside.

Chapter Seventeen

Jericho couldn't believe what was happening. One second Laurel had been in his office. Now she wasn't.

He had to get to her. Had to stop whatever was happening to her because he knew whatever it was—it would only get worse.

"What happened?" Reese Jenkins, the reserve deputy, came rushing to the doorway.

"They got Laurel."

Jericho scrambled through what was left of the window. And immediately had to duck right back down to dodge the bullet that blasted through the air. However, he did get a glimpse of Laurel.

And the two armed thugs that were on either side of her. He also got a glimpse of the car that'd been hidden by the Dumpster. Since it was out of line of sight of any part of the sheriff's building, Jericho had no idea how long it'd been there, but there was a road just behind it. The men were heading in that direction, and heading fast, so it was clear that's how they planned to escape with Laurel.

Jericho called out to her. Only to have another bullet come his way.

Still, he could see that she was fighting to get free. Could also see that one of the men had her in a fierce grip—literally dragging her by her hair and trying to put her in the car.

"Cover me," Jericho shouted to Reese. "And don't you dare hit Laurel with friendly fire."

He doubted that it was possible for Reese to actually cover him since the gunmen at the front of the building were still shooting. But Jericho couldn't just stay put. He had to try to get to Laurel and stop those hired guns.

Reese gave a shaky nod and hurried to the side of the window. He leaned out, took aim while Jericho climbed through and dropped to the ground. The bitter cold hit him right off. So did the smoke lingering from the explosion. Jericho ignored both and started running.

He didn't get far.

The thug on Laurel's left turned, fired. Jericho had to drop down behind a cruiser. It wasn't just one shot, either. At least six bullets came his way, pinning him down.

Reese didn't fire. Probably because he didn't have a clean shot. But Jericho heard a sound he damn sure didn't want to hear.

The roar of the car's engine.

He peered around the cruiser and his heart missed a couple of beats. Because the driver hit the accelerator. They were getting away.

Cursing, Jericho fished through his pocket, found the master key for the cruiser and managed to get the door open. Not easily. Because the gunmen out front started shooting at him. He practically jumped inside once he had it open, and the moment he had the engine started, he hit the accelerator, heading after the black car.

The road behind the sheriff's office was narrow, coiling through a neighborhood with walls of houses on each side. Plenty of trees, too. Lots of places for hired guns to wait so they could attack. He only hoped that bullets didn't start flying here or plenty of innocent people could be hurt.

Finally, they reached the edge of the neighborhood, and the black car took a turn into the town's park. Onto an even more narrow road. Sometime during the past hour or so, a light mist had started to fall, and it had created some ice scabs on the road. Jericho hit one, went into a skid but fought to regain control of the cruiser.

Ahead of him, the driver of the black car wasn't so lucky.

Jericho could only watch as the car veered hard to the right. The wheels clipped the sidewalk, ricocheting the vehicle to the left.

And it slammed into a streetlight.

Oh, man. It was as if a Roman candle went off in his head. Laurel could have been hurt or worse. The front end of the car was a tangled mess, and there was steam spewing out of what was left of the engine.

Jericho brought the cruiser to a quick stop just a few feet behind the wrecked car, and he hurried out, leaving the door open in case he had to grab Laurel and jump right back in. That's when he spotted the swirling blue lights from a cruiser coming up the road behind him. Reese, no doubt. Maybe even Levi.

Good. Because Jericho would probably need plenty of backup.

Maybe an ambulance, too.

With his gun ready, Jericho approached the car. However, before he got there, the back door opened and someone got out. Not easily. The person was groaning as if in pain.

Laurel.

She looked up, and when she spotted him, she started to run toward him. Jericho ran, too, and quickly ate up the distance between them. She was alive, but there was blood on her head. Maybe other injuries that he couldn't see.

Nor could Jericho take the time to find out.

Because a second person came out of the car. It was the same thug that'd dragged Laurel by the hair. The guy was still armed, and even though he staggered a little, he still managed to point the gun at Laurel.

He fired.

Jericho hooked his arm around Laurel's waist and yanked her behind the door of his cruiser. Not a moment too soon, because another shot came right at them. Apparently, the gunman hadn't been injured in the wreck. And neither had his shooting buddy, Jericho quickly learned, when the second gunman got out, too. He didn't waste any time joining in on the shooting fest.

This was exactly what Jericho had hoped to avoid. Here, Laurel was under attack again, and all those stray bullets could be going into the nearby neighborhood.

"Get in," Jericho told her.

She was still wobbly, so Jericho gave her a shove. He also sent a couple of rounds in the direction of the gunmen, but was careful to keep the shots low, so if they missed the men completely, they'd go into the ground.

Behind him, the other cruiser braked to a stop. Levi stepped out, using his own door for cover. A good thing, too, because the idiots started sending some of their shots his way.

"We need to get out of here," Jericho called out to his brother. Levi darn sure didn't argue with that.

Laurel crawled to the passenger's seat so that Jericho could get behind the wheel. He threw the car into gear, ready to hit the gas, but an SUV came flying out from a side road to their right. Jericho couldn't see who was inside. But it didn't take him long to figure out what they wanted.

Whoever was inside the SUV opened fire.

THEY WERE CAUGHT in a crossfire.

The blood rushed to Laurel's head, and the punch of fear robbed her of what little breath she had left. She was thankful to be out of the car with the men who'd taken her, but now Jericho was right back in the middle of a deadly situation.

His brother and the deputy, too.

And there was nothing she could do but stay down and pray that they would all get out of this alive.

The gunmen in the SUV didn't waste any time shooting at the tires of the cruiser, and Laurel felt the exact moment they managed to do just that. Jericho still threw the cruiser into gear, no doubt ready to try to get them out of there.

But then Laurel heard the plinging sound.

Someone in the SUV had tossed something onto the road just in front of them.

"Get down!" Jericho shouted. "It's a grenade." He threw himself over her, pushing her down on the seat.

Just as the blast tore through the air.

The impact was so hard that it lifted the front of the cruiser and sent it flying back several feet before they crashed to the ground. Because of the way Jericho and she were hunkered down, their heads hit the dashboard, hard. Hard enough for her to see stars.

Laurel immediately looked back to check on Jericho and gasped when she saw the blood trickling down his forehead.

"It's just a cut," he explained. "Same with you."

She touched her fingers to her own forehead, felt the warm blood, but she was too shaken to feel the pain. Too shaken to move.

But Jericho didn't seem to have that problem.

He'd managed to keep hold of his gun, and he took another one from the glove compartment. "Stay down," he insisted.

However, he didn't do that. He sat up, his gaze darting around and pausing for a moment on the rearview mirror.

"Levi and the deputy," she said, trying to get up. "Are they okay?"

"They appear to be." Jericho pushed her back on the seat and tried to start the cruiser engine.

Nothing.

It'd obviously been damaged too much in the explosion. No doubt what their attackers had planned. Now they were sitting ducks in the crossfire. But maybe they could somehow get to Levi's vehicle. Or better yet, maybe they could take out these gunmen.

"The men in the SUV aren't shooting at us," Jericho mumbled.

Because her ears were still ringing, it took Laurel a moment to understand what he'd said. And to realize it was true. The men in the SUV were shooting at the thugs in the black car. And vice versa. The bullets were no longer coming at Jericho and her.

What the heck was going on?

From the moment she'd seen that SUV come out from the side road, Laurel had assumed they were working with the men in the black car. But clearly they weren't if they were trying to kill each other. However, Laurel doubted that meant whoever survived would just let them walk away.

"Will backup come?" she asked.

"Eventually. I figure Levi probably called the second reserve deputy, Shane. He might respond alone, but Shane's a rookie. No experience with chasing down bad guys. He'll probably wait for the Rangers to arrive so he can bring them here."

"Where are the Rangers?" was her next question.

"Too far away. It'll be a good half hour."

She groaned. So they were on their own, because she doubted this attack would last that long.

Laurel tried to steady her nerves. Hard to do with the danger right on top of them. Added to that, she was past the stage of just shivering. When the men had dragged her through the office window, she hadn't been wearing a coat, and now that the engine was disabled, it was getting cold fast in the interior of the cruiser.

Jericho's phone buzzed, and he passed it to her to answer. That's when she saw Levi's name on the screen.

"Were you hurt?" Levi asked before she could say anything.

"Just minor stuff." Laurel wiped the blood from her head, reached up and did the same to Jericho. "How about the two of you?"

"We're both fine. But we got an even bigger problem than the SUV and the black car. Another vehicle just pulled up behind us. A limo. The headlights are off, but when one of the people inside opened the door, I got a glimpse of a two guys in the front seat with guns. I'm betting we've got more gunmen joining this sick shooting party. I'll call you back if I can figure out what the heck is going on."

God, no. Not more of them. Whoever was behind this had hired an army to kill them.

Laurel was about to relay the info to Jericho, but his attention was on the rearview mirror again. "I see the limo." And he added some more profanity.

"Are they shooting, too?" Laurel asked. There were so many bullets being fired that it was hard to tell.

"Not yet." But Jericho no longer had his attention on the newcomers. He was watching the exchange of gunfire between the others. "Two down," he said. "Lots more to go."

And then the gunfire stopped.

Laurel lifted her head just enough to see that the two men in the black car were down. Literally. They were both sprawled out on the ground and likely dead.

But why?

The men in the SUV certainly weren't shooting at whoever was in the limo. Did that mean they were working together?

Before she could even try to come up with what'd just happened, Jericho's phone buzzed again. She answered it without looking at the screen because Laurel figured the call was from Levi.

It wasn't.

"Sheriff Crockett," the man said. Laurel didn't recognize his voice. She put the call on speaker so that Jericho could hear it. "Are you listening, Sheriff?"

She connected gazes with Jericho, silently asking if she knew the caller, but he shook his head.

"Who are you and what do you want?" Jericho snarled.

"I'm in the limo behind your brother. Let's just say

I'm a friend trying to do you a favor. We don't want you. Only Laurel. Hand her over, and you, your kin and the deputy can leave."

Laurel hadn't thought her heart could beat any faster, but she was wrong. This attack was all for her. And it didn't matter exactly that she didn't know who was doing it or why it was happening, she'd put Jericho and heaven knew who else in danger.

"That's not going to happen," Jericho answered, still keeping watch around them. "Now, who the hell are you?"

"My name's not important."

"Yeah, it is. Because I want to know who to arrest or kill. Your choice. Either way is fine with me, but you're not getting Laurel."

"Then you'll have to pay a big price for that decision. There are roadblocks in every direction. Explosives. Anyone who tries to get to you now will pay. Is that what you want?"

"Text Levi," Jericho mouthed to her. "Let him know."

Even though her hands were shaking, Laurel managed to do what Jericho asked without hanging up on the snake who was making these threats.

"Why do you want me?" she asked the man once she was finished sending the text.

Jericho shot her a nasty look, probably because he hadn't wanted her to have any verbal contact with the goon, but Laurel wasn't going to stay quiet.

"It's nothing personal," the man answered. "Just doing my job."

Well, it was very personal to her. People she cared about were in danger. "And who paid you to do that job?" she pressed.

The man didn't answer, and even though she couldn't

be sure, it seemed as if he was having a whispered conversation with someone. Probably someone in the limo with him.

Laurel pushed the phone against her chest so the caller wouldn't be able to hear what she was about to say, and she looked up at Jericho. "I don't want you to die, but this might—"

"No way," he interrupted. "I'm not handing you over to them."

It was exactly what Laurel had expected him to say. But she had to make him at least consider it. "I don't want to die, but if those men manage to kill both of us, then Maddox will be an orphan. I don't want that, either."

"You really think our *friend* will let us all live? Not a chance. Because if he lets me walk, I'll hunt him down. And I'll kill him."

Yes, Jericho would. And the man on the other end of the line almost certainly knew that, too.

"Enough of this." Jericho snatched the phone from her hand. "Who the hell hired you to come after Laurel?"

More silence. It went on so long that Laurel thought the line might have gone dead. But it hadn't.

"I hired him," someone finally answered.

And this time, it was a voice that Laurel had no trouble recognizing.

Chapter Eighteen

Dorothy.

Jericho wasn't sure which of their suspects would turn out to be behind this, but none of them would have been a surprise. All had motive.

Or at least they thought they had motive.

"You're doing this because of the money you lost on those business deals?" Jericho snapped.

"In part," Dorothy admitted. "But I really don't want to discuss that now. Is everything in place?" she asked, and it took Jericho a moment to realize that she wasn't talking to him.

"It's in place," a man verified. The same man who'd been talking to them earlier. One of Dorothy's hired thugs.

Jericho was about to demand to know what exactly was *in place*, but then he heard Reese's shout. "I'm sorry, Jericho. I didn't see them in time."

Heck. That couldn't be good. Jericho turned around, trying to pick through the darkness, and he finally saw what he didn't want to see.

Levi and Reese.

Their hands were in the air, and there was a gunman on each side of the cruiser his brother had been driving.

"Don't blame the deputy or your brother." Dorothy's

voice had gone from sarcastic to taunting. "I brought plenty of backup with me, and there were men waiting in the ditch."

And it'd worked. It also meant Dorothy had at least six gunmen with her. Two in the SUV, the two guarding Levi and Reese, and the two that Levi had spotted in the limo when it first arrived.

Of course, there could be more.

Not to mention Dorothy was probably armed. He hoped she was because he couldn't shoot an unarmed woman, but he darn sure could shoot an armed one. Especially this one.

"Is Theo helping you?" Jericho came right out and asked.

"Please. I have a coward of a son. He hired those men in the black car to save you, to kidnap you."

Laurel shook her head. "Why?"

"Because Theo was going to keep you all for himself so he could try to convince you that he's the man for you. Laughable, isn't it?"

"Not really," Jericho growled. "Nothing laughable about this. So, you lost money. Boo-hoo—"

"I lost more than that!" Dorothy paused, and Jericho figured she was trying to get hold of the temper tantrum she'd just started. "I lost my reputation. My so-called friends whisper behind my back now. And that's all because of Laurel."

"How do you figure that?" Jericho asked.

"She was supposed to marry Theo. I told everyone it was finally going to happen. I made plans for business deals that hinged on Theo and Laurel being man and wife."

All right. Jericho didn't want to have this conversation,

but it might give him time to figure out what to do next. "You mean plans with Rossman and Cawley? Who, by the way, are both dead. Your doing?"

She didn't confirm the part about having them murdered. "Bigger plans than that. Ones that would have made me richer than my wildest dreams."

"Ah, I get it now. You made those plans because of Laurel and her father's connections. When the engagement ended, so did the connections, and you were left holding a very empty bag that you hoped would be filled with money."

Again, Dorothy didn't verbally confirm it, but judging from her ripe profanity, he'd hit pay dirt.

"Laurel ruined us," Dorothy said a moment later. "Both Theo and me."

"I didn't ruin you," Laurel argued. "You did it to yourself."

"You did this!" she shouted. "And after all that, Theo still wants you back. Even after I told him that you had crawled into bed with that cowboy."

Even though Laurel was scared spitless, that put some fire in her eyes. "Jericho's my husband."

"Right," Dorothy said with a serious dose of sarcasm. "A marriage of necessity to stop your father from getting custody of your son. Well, I don't think you have to worry about that anymore."

Jericho wondered if that meant that Dorothy had killed Herschel. No such luck. Because a moment later, Herschel got out of the limo. Not voluntarily. A heavily muscled armed goon shoved him out.

Herschel staggered, and it took him several wobbly steps to regain his balance. The man's hands were cuffed in front of him, and he looked disheveled. Definitely not a happy camper right now.

"Give me Laurel or Herschel dies," Dorothy threatened.

Jericho so wished the woman could see the flat look he was giving her. "Do you think I really care a flying fig what you do to Herschel?"

Laurel made a sound of agreement. After everything Herschel had tried to do to her, Jericho thought she might be willing to pull the trigger herself. She certainly wasn't going to sacrifice herself for him.

And that sent an uneasy feeling snaking up his spine.

If Dorothy thought she could use Herschel to lure out Laurel, then the woman had something up her sleeve.

Something dirty, no doubt.

"Oh, you should care about what happens to Herschel," Dorothy said. She was back to being as cold as ice. No sign of that hot temper right now. "If you want to know the truth, that is."

"What truth?" Laurel and Jericho asked at the same time.

Herschel certainly didn't jump to answer. Thanks to the interior lights from the limo, Jericho had no trouble seeing the man's expression. Not defeat. He was riled to the core.

"The truth about your father's death," Dorothy finally said. She stepped from the limo wearing a thick fur coat. And she was smiling. "Or should I say, his murder? Because Sherman Crockett was indeed murdered."

That uneasy feeling inside him turned to a full roar. "What do you know about that?" Jericho demanded.

"Plenty. I know Herschel murdered him, and I have proof. Not with me, of course. I'm not stupid. But I have it tucked safely away."

Jericho figured this was about the time for Herschel to

blurt out his innocence. He didn't. Nor did he deny that Dorothy had such proof.

"Let's just say Herschel had too much to drink one night and got very chatty," Dorothy explained. "He didn't know I was recording every word he said."

Now Herschel responded. His narrowed gaze cut to Dorothy, and he cursed her. "You'll burn in hell for this."

"Maybe, but you'll be right there with me." Dorothy patted his cheek before looking toward Jericho again. "Hand over Laurel, and I'll give you Herschel and the proof."

So, that's what was up her sleeve. Laurel for the thing that Dorothy thought Jericho wanted the most.

"You can be the one to arrest Herschel. And you can be there when he gets the needle shoved into his arm," Dorothy continued. "Think about it, Jericho."

He didn't have to think about it. Yes, he wanted justice. He wanted it so much that he could taste it.

But there was no way he'd trade Laurel for it.

"No deal," Jericho let the woman know.

"Too bad." Dorothy answered quickly enough that she'd no doubt considered that's how this would play out.

"Why do you want Laurel alive, anyway?" Jericho asked.

"Because she'll force me to go through with those business deals," Laurel provided. "She needs my contacts, and my signature. And once she has that, she'll kill me."

Jericho had no doubts, none, that it was exactly what Dorothy had in mind. Either way, she'd kill Laurel first chance she got.

"I suggest you change your mind," Dorothy warned him. "Because if you don't hand Laurel over to me, I'll give my men the order to start shooting. You're outnumbered, Jericho. Outgunned, too. They'll kill all of you, including Laurel."

Jericho knew this wasn't a bluff. If Dorothy couldn't have Laurel, then she'd have them all killed. Or try.

That was a risk. One that cut him to the core. But at least Laurel was inside the cruiser, and even though the engine was damaged, the windows and the sides were bullet resistant. His brother and Reese were also still close enough to their cruiser that they could use it for cover when all hell broke loose.

He hoped.

"Stay down," Jericho whispered to Laurel. He took another gun from the glove compartment and also handed her extra magazines of ammo. "No matter what happens, don't get out."

Laurel's eyes widened, and she shook her head. "What are you going to do?"

"Stay down," he repeated, and brushed a kiss on her mouth.

"Levi, you ready to do something about this?" Jericho shouted.

"Oh, yeah," his brother confirmed without hesitation.

Just as Jericho had thought. That was the only green light he needed.

Jericho came out of the cruiser with guns blazing.

"No!" LAUREL SHOUTED to Jericho. But it was already too late. He was out of the cruiser, and the shots started flying.

Sweet heaven, he was going to get killed.

Maybe Levi and the deputy would be, too. Of course, it wasn't as if Dorothy had given them too many options. And now Laurel could only pray that they got out of this alive.

Dorothy screamed out her own "No!" and Laurel wondered if she'd been shot. Maybe. But she quickly had to amend that when the woman belted out another order. "Kill them all. Do it now."

Laurel lifted her head just enough to see out the back window. No sign of Dorothy. The woman had probably gotten back in the limo. Laurel's father was on the ground, his hands covering his head. Trying to protect himself.

Dorothy's gunmen were doing the same thing—they'd gotten behind the back of the limo. Out of the line of fire but still in a position to shoot and carry out Dorothy's orders. It was the same for Levi and Reese. They were on the side of their cruiser, both of them shooting.

Jericho ducked down behind the door of the cruiser, once again using it for cover, but he continued to lift his head enough to return fire. So many shots came at him. Too many, and Laurel sat there, feeling helpless. And furious that Dorothy wanted her dead all because of money and revenge.

She thought of her son, and it broke her heart to think that she might not see him again. But at least he wasn't here in the middle of the attack.

From the corner of her eye, Laurel saw the movement. The two gunmen from the SUV were getting into position to help out their fellow hired thugs. One of them scrambled toward the hole in the pavement created by the grenade.

Coming toward Jericho and her.

And not just coming toward them. The guy was trying to sneak up on Jericho so he could gun him down from behind.

Laurel didn't think. She just reacted. She opened the cruiser door just enough so that she could take aim and stop him. But he must have seen what she was doing because he pivoted in her direction, bringing up his gun to shoot her.

But Laurel shot first.

The recoil of the gun stunned her a moment, but she quickly fired another shot. Both of the bullets slammed into the man's chest. However, he didn't drop to the ground. He stood there, frozen, his gun still pointed at her for what seemed an eternity.

Before he finally collapsed.

Jericho snapped toward her, and Laurel braced herself for his usual protest—*what word of* stay down *didn't you hear?*—but he muttered, "Thanks," followed by "Now, get down and stay there."

The words had barely left his mouth when he levered himself up, turned and fired in the direction of the SUV. But not at the SUV itself. At the second gunman. Laurel had been so focused on Jericho and the man she'd killed that she hadn't noticed the second one.

But he'd seen her.

He had his gun aimed right at her and was no doubt within a split second of pulling the trigger.

Jericho beat him to it.

He finished off the gunman with a shot to the head, and in the same motion, Jericho turned his gun toward the limo. He fired. And he took out the gunman on the left-rear side.

Laurel hated to feel relief that she'd just killed a man and had watched another die, but the relief came, anyway. They were winning. Except she knew that could change on a dime.

"Don't shoot!" someone yelled. It was the final remaining gunman. "I'm surrendering."

Laurel wasn't sure if it was some kind of trick, but then she saw the man slowly get up from the limo's right side. He still had hold of his gun, but he raised his hands in the air.

"Drop your weapon," Jericho ordered. He stayed behind the cover of the door. Good. Because this still wasn't over. "Are there any other gunmen in the limo?"

He tossed down his gun, shook his head. "Just the boss lady. Don't shoot me. Arrange for me to get a plea deal, and I'll tell you whatever you want to know."

"Where's the proof that Herschel killed my father," Jericho demanded.

The gunman shook his head. "I don't know that, but I know plenty about the men she hired to kill you. That's something you'll want, right? It'll be enough to put her in jail for the rest of her life."

Before Jericho could answer, Laurel heard the sound. It didn't even sound human at first, more like something that would come from a feral animal. But it was Dorothy. And it was the sound of pure outrage.

"Coward!" she screamed.

"Dorothy, get out of the car," Jericho ordered her.

"If you kill me, you'll never get the evidence I have against Herschel. Never," Dorothy threatened.

Laurel figured the woman would use that to bargain while she stayed in the limo. She didn't. Making another of those feral sounds, Dorothy came out from the backseat. A gun in each hand.

And she fired shots at Jericho.

Jericho ducked down in the nick of time, the bullets slamming into the cruiser door.

The woman didn't give up. She kept firing. Kept screaming. Until Levi took aim at her and brought her down with a shot to the chest.

Dorothy fell, the guns clattering to the frozen ground with her.

"I'm sorry," Levi immediately said to Jericho. "I wanted to take her alive."

Laurel understood that. She also understood it'd been impossible to do that. It was clear Dorothy would have murdered them all if she'd gotten the chance.

"Don't get out," Jericho insisted when Laurel pushed open the door. He glanced around, no doubt looking for more of Dorothy's hired thugs. Laurel didn't close the door, but she did duck back inside.

"There aren't any more of us, I swear," the lone surviving gunman insisted, and he repeated his earlier offer. "I'll tell you what you want to know."

But Jericho didn't turn his attention toward the gunman. He went to Dorothy. Leaned down and checked her pulse. He didn't have to confirm that the woman was indeed dead because Laurel could tell from his expression that she was.

Levi hurried to the gunman, kicking his gun aside and cuffing him. Reese headed out to check on the other gunmen. No doubt to make sure they were dead, as well.

However, Jericho went to her father. Jericho caught onto the collar of Herschel's coat and dragged him to his feet. "Where's the proof that you murdered my father?"

It wasn't exactly a request. Jericho moved until he was right in Herschel's face.

But Herschel just laughed.

She saw Jericho struggling to hold on to his temper. Laurel didn't blame him. He'd loved his father, and now Sherman's killer was right there in front of him.

Despite Jericho's order for her to stay put, Laurel got out. She was already chilled to the bone, and the gust of bitter wind didn't help. Nor did the fact that it'd started to snow.

Laurel hurried toward the others and hoped there was a shred of fatherly love left in Herschel. Enough of a thread for him to come clean.

"Where's the evidence Dorothy had?" Laurel asked him, moving next to Jericho.

Her father's gaze went from Jericho to her. Then to the wedding ring she was wearing. He smiled. Not an ordinary one. Definitely not one filled with any fatherly love whatsoever. Laurel had always figured he hated her, but that smile and the look in his eyes was all the proof she needed.

Jericho looked ready to unleash his temper and his fists on Herschel, but then his gaze met hers. She could almost see the battle going on inside him. Could feel it. That's why she was surprised when Jericho took a step back.

"Levi, I need some cuffs." Jericho's voice wasn't exactly calm, his muscles weren't anywhere near relaxed, but he sounded exactly like the lawman that he was. "Herschel, you're under arrest for Quinn Rossman's murder." And Jericho continued to read him his rights.

"I didn't kill him," her father insisted. "And I can prove I was lured to the crime scene so his death could be pinned on me. Hell, I'm betting Dorothy's hired idiot will tell you the same thing."

Judging from the gunman's stark expression, he would do just that.

Levi handed Jericho the cuffs, and he slapped them on her father.

But Herschel only laughed when Levi took him toward

the cruiser. "With the lawyers on my payroll, I'll be out of jail in no time," her father insisted. "This isn't over."

And, yes, it sounded exactly like the threat that it was.

Chapter Nineteen

Jericho cursed the whole white-Christmas thing. It was snowing, and yeah, it was pretty all right. It'd make for a picture-perfect holiday, but with the ice already on the road, it was slowing down the drive to the safe house.

Laurel was next to him in the front of the cruiser; Levi, in the back. His brother was on the phone, but Laurel leaned forward and stared up at the night sky as if cursing it, too. It was a toss-up as to who was the most antsy about getting to the safe house so they could see Maddox. They knew the baby was fine, thanks to several conversations with Jax, but Jericho wouldn't rest easy until he saw his son. Of course, resting easy was a pipe dream, anyway.

No doubt for Laurel, as well.

They both had nicks on their faces. Both looked as if they'd been through the wringer and back. That's why it surprised him when she looked at him and smiled.

"It's still a couple of hours until Christmas," she said. "We didn't miss spending it with him. Well, we won't if the weather doesn't slow us down too much."

"We'll be there soon."

They were only a few miles away, but Jericho needed to drive around a little longer. The only thing good about going at a snail's pace was that he could make sure Laurel and he weren't being followed.

Not that the chances were high they would be.

Jericho hadn't started the drive to the safe house until the Rangers were fairly sure they'd rounded up all of Herschel's hired thugs. While the Rangers had been doing that, Jericho had arrested Herschel, and Theo and Dorothy's gunman who'd surrendered at the scene. All three were behind bars.

"I killed a man," Laurel said. It wasn't exactly out of the blue. Jericho figured it'd been weighing on her mind along with everything else.

"You killed a *bad* man," he clarified. "One who would have murdered all of us if he'd gotten the chance. You stopped him."

She made a sound of agreement followed by a sigh. Of course, she knew that already, but it would give her nightmares for a while. Him, too. Jericho had gotten a few years shaved off his life when he'd seen her open the cruiser door, putting herself in the line of fire. For him.

"You saved my life," he added. "Thanks for that."

Laurel brushed a kiss on his cheek. "And you saved mine. But I need to thank you more than once since I lost count of how many times you saved me."

He looked at her, barely a glance because he had to keep his eyes on the road. However, he wished he could just hold her.

All right, kiss her, too.

Just being with Laurel would make him feel a whole lot better.

"Keep pressing him," Levi insisted to the person on the other end of his phone. He finished his latest call with one of the Rangers, but judging from the way he shoved his phone back in his pocket, he wasn't happy with the outcome of the conversation.

"A problem?" But Jericho hated to even ask. Hated more to hear the answer because it was probably one he didn't want to hear. "Are Herschel and Theo still behind bars?"

"They're still there. For now. Theo's been officially charged with kidnapping Laurel from the sheriff's office."

"Good," she said, but there wasn't much joy in her tone, and when she settled her head against his shoulder again—something she'd been doing on and off since the drive started—Jericho noticed she was still trembling.

"Dorothy's gunman is cooperating," Levi went on. "That's the good news. The bad news is that he confessed to assisting in both Cawley's and Rossman's murders."

Hell in a handbasket.

That didn't help Laurel's trembling. Because she knew what it meant. With that confession, Herschel wouldn't be charged with those murders.

"Is my father getting out of jail?" she asked.

"Not tonight. The Rangers can hold him for questioning while they go through the evidence we got from Theo. There should be enough in that to make some charges stick for his attempt to have Laurel declared mentally incompetent."

Yeah, but those weren't charges for murder. Not for Rossman's, anyway. And not for Jericho's father. Levi's and Laurel's silence let him know that they were thinking the same thing.

"I'm sorry," Laurel finally said. She paused. "Can you get the DA to offer Theo a deal? If he knows where his mother put the recording of my father's drunk confession, then could he exchange that for a lesser sentence?"

"No. I want Theo behind bars for a long time for what he did to you."

"So do I. But more than that, I want justice for your father. Think it through," she added when Jericho opened his mouth to argue. "If my father's out of jail, we'll never be free to live our lives with Maddox."

Well, he certainly couldn't argue with that. "We can get Herschel some other way."

"Not as fast as you can by having the DA strike a deal with Theo. Theo's facing several felony charges, and he'll get years of jail time. My father could get life in prison. Maybe even the death penalty."

"Laurel's right," Levi piped in.

She was. But it felt as if he was minimizing what'd happened to her. Still, Herschel would do far worse than kidnapping if he got the chance. Now that Laurel had rejected him, Herschel would be even more intent on seeing them all dead.

"Make the call," Jericho told his brother. "See if Theo's willing to deal, and if he is, contact the DA and work it out."

That caused Laurel to settle even closer to him. He probably should have told her to tighten her seat belt, but Jericho wanted this contact as much as she seemed to want it.

"You said 'free to live our lives with Maddox.' Did you mean it?" Jericho asked.

Laurel lifted her head. Blinked. "Of course." Then her eyes widened. "Oh, I guess that sounded bold. I need to give you a free pass."

"Excuse me? What the heck does that mean?"

She glanced back at Levi, maybe to make sure his

brother was on the phone and not listening to them. He was. Well, he was on the phone, anyway.

"A free pass for the sex," she said. "Just so you know, I don't expect anything because we slept together. And I don't expect anything because of this." She lifted her hand, tapped the wedding ring.

"Well, you should." He said that a whole lot louder than he'd intended. And yes, it got Levi's attention, but Jericho didn't care. This conversation couldn't wait. "You should expect everything from me."

"Everything?" Laurel asked, sounding very uncertain of what that meant.

Jericho wasn't exactly certain, either. Not of the details, anyway, but he had a bead on the big picture. "I'm your husband, and I'd like to keep it that way."

He shot his brother a glare in the rearview mirror when Levi smiled. Maybe the smile meant that Levi approved of this marriage, or maybe it was just that whole thing of him watching his big brother squirm.

"You'd like to keep it that way?" Laurel repeated, still sounding uncertain.

Jericho would have attempted to clarify that, but that's when Levi's smile vanished, and he slid his hand over his phone.

"Theo didn't ask for us to work out a plea deal with the DA for him to get a lighter sentence. He told the Rangers where they could find the evidence against Herschel," Levi interrupted. "It's at Dorothy's house in San Antonio. The local cops are headed over there now."

That was great news, but that wasn't a great-news kind of look on Levi's face. "What's wrong?" Jericho asked.

"Theo's on the line, and he wants to talk to Laurel."

Jericho wanted to growl out a "no way in hell," but it

wasn't his call, and Laurel reached for the phone before he could say anything.

She jabbed the speaker button. "Thank you for doing the right thing about the evidence," Laurel greeted Theo. "I appreciate it. So do the Crocketts. But I'm not getting back together with you."

"I know," Theo readily admitted.

"But yet you'll give us the evidence. Why?" she demanded.

A good question. Jericho hoped Theo had a good answer.

"Let's call it a wedding gift. With no strings attached," Theo said. "I know you don't believe me, but I sent those men to save you tonight. I knew my mother was going to try to kill you, and I thought if I could hide you away, she wouldn't be able to get to you."

"Laurel was already safe," Jericho snarled. "You could have gotten her killed."

"I know that now. And I'm sorry."

Theo sounded sincere enough, but Jericho would make sure he got the maximum sentence.

"I don't want you in my life," Laurel said to Theo.

"I won't be. Good luck, Laurel. I sincerely hope you're happy, even if that happiness happens to be with Jericho."

Laurel didn't respond. She just handed the phone back to Levi. "You believe him?" she asked.

Jericho was surprised that he did. "With all the charges against him, Theo's looking at a decade or two in jail. He could have withheld the evidence as part of a plea deal with the DA. He didn't."

That didn't mean Jericho wouldn't be checking to make sure Theo did all the jail time and then stayed far away from Laurel.

She nodded. "Good. Then, we can get Maddox and move on with our lives."

There it was again. Not yours or mine. *Our lives.*

Jericho liked the sound of that. Figured he would like the sound of it even more when they saw their son. He took the final turn toward the safe house.

The snow was coming down harder here, and the house was already dusted with it. His son would wake up to a white Christmas. No gifts, though. But Jericho would remedy that. Unless the snow piled up, they'd be able to leave in the morning, and he could call the owner of the department store and beg him to open so that Jericho could do a quick shopping trip.

The moment he pulled the cruiser to a stop, the door opened, and his brother Jax came out. As expected, Jax had his bag ready and looked more than ready to leave. And no doubt was. He wanted to get home so he could spend Christmas with his own son.

"Glad you're in one piece," Jax greeted them, and then he glanced at the cuts on Laurel's and his head. "Well, for the most part."

"Thanks for everything," Jericho told him. He used his sleeve to wipe the blood from Laurel's and his face. Best for his mom and Maddox not to see that. "You should get going before the roads get bad."

Jax nodded, started toward his car but then stopped. "Are you two back together?" But he waved off the question. Smiled. "Of course you are. Heck, you were never really apart. Merry Christmas."

It was Jericho's go-to reaction to scowl at a remark like that, but he had to admit to himself that it was true. Laurel and he were back together.

He hoped.

Now he needed to see how Laurel felt about that.

However, Jericho didn't get the chance to say anything because the door opened again, and his mother gathered the three of them inside. There was a fire snapping and flickering in the stone fireplace, and the deputies were at the small kitchen table drinking what smelled like hot chocolate.

"Where's Maddox?" Laurel and Jericho asked in unison.

His mother put her finger to her lips and motioned for them to follow her to one of the bedrooms. Levi didn't follow them. His phone buzzed, and he stayed in the living room to answer it.

There wasn't a crib in the safe house, but they found Maddox sleeping on the center of the bed with pillows around the edges so that he wouldn't fall off.

Laurel got to him first, and she pressed a flurry of kisses on Maddox's face. Jericho soon got his turn, and even though he wanted his son to get plenty of sleep, he wasn't disappointed when Maddox opened his eyes. The little boy gave a sleepy yawn, but then he smiled the moment his gaze landed on them.

"Da-Da," Maddox babbled, his smile aimed at Jericho.

Jericho nearly lost it.

"I've been showing him your picture and telling him you're his daddy," Iris explained. "I hope you don't mind," she said to Laurel.

"No, I don't mind at all."

Hearing that one word was one of the best Christmas presents he'd ever gotten.

And then he got another one.

"Wuv you," Maddox said, and he repeated it to Laurel as his eyelids drifted back down.

Jericho couldn't help himself. He had to kiss his boy again. Laurel did, too. And then they eased out of the room and into the hall. They didn't close the door, though. They just stood there and watched Maddox sleep.

"Fatherhood looks good on you, son." Iris gave him a pat on the arm and then did the same to Laurel before she strolled away.

Jericho had so many things to say to Laurel, but the moment he opened his mouth, Levi started toward them. Jericho groaned at the interruption until he remembered they had important business still up in the air.

"SAPD found the evidence at Dorothy's house," Levi explained. "It was exactly where Theo said it would be. And yes, in the recording, Herschel does confess to having Dad murdered."

Jericho's breath rushed out. Pure relief. Laurel's reaction was pretty much the same. It'd been a long wait for justice, but it'd finally come.

"My father will be charged with murder," she verified. "He'll stay in jail."

"For a very long time," Jericho assured her. There was no bail for murder, so he would stay behind bars while awaiting trial. Considering everything Herschel had done, it was another good Christmas present.

And now Jericho had just one more.

Levi had the sense to go back in the living room and give them some privacy. Well, as much privacy as they could have in a small house filled with people.

"You know what I want for Christmas?" he asked.

Laurel obviously hadn't been expecting that question because she gave him a funny look.

"I want you." Jericho snapped her to him. Kissed her. Not exactly a chaste kiss, either.

She smiled when he finally broke the kiss so they could catch their breath. "I want you, too."

That was a good start, but it wasn't quite enough. So, Jericho kissed her again. He wanted to remind her of what had brought them here.

And it wasn't just the attraction.

It was something much, much more.

He took out the blue rock. The one she'd used when she asked him to marry her. Or rather, when she'd told him that was the way things had to be. Now, he dropped it into the palm of her hand.

"I'm calling in the marker," he said. "I'm in love with you."

Tears watered her eyes, but he was pretty sure they were happy ones. She kissed him. And she was very good at it. Jericho felt himself go warm and then hot in all the right places.

Including his heart.

"Jericho, I've been in love with you most of my life. All of my life," she added.

Now it was his turn to smile. Probably a goofy one, but it was genuine. Laurel loved him.

He brought her closer to him and spelled out the rest of his wish list. "I want you and Maddox. I want this marriage and our family to be real."

"It already is," she said. Smiling again, Laurel pulled him to her for a long, slow kiss.

* * * * *

She had too many responsibilities to have time to be interested in any man.

She saw the screen saver picture had come up— a picture of Trent Dixon, a longtime friend and coworker. Trent was carrying her son on his big shoulders. Both guys were smiling as if they'd had the time of their lives—and she suspected they had.

Katie quickly pushed a key and sent the image away before melancholy could take hold. She'd made her choices—and a relationship with Trent wasn't one of them. She needed the brawny KCPD detective as a friend—Tyler needed him as a friend—more than she needed Trent to be a boyfriend or lover or even something more.

Even if every cell in her body screamed to allow this man into her heart.

KANSAS CITY CONFESSIONS

BY
JULIE MILLER

All rights reserved including the right of reproduction in whole or in part in any form. This edition is published by arrangement with Harlequin Books S.A.

This is a work of fiction. Names, characters, places and incidents are purely fictional and bear no relationship to any real life individuals, living or dead, or to any actual places, business establishments, locations, events or incidents. Any resemblance is entirely coincidental.

This book is sold subject to the condition that it shall not, by way of trade or otherwise, be lent, resold, hired out or otherwise circulated without the prior consent of the publisher in any form of binding or cover other than that in which it is published and without a similar condition including this condition being imposed on the subsequent purchaser.

® and ™ are trademarks owned and used by the trademark owner and/or its licensee. Trademarks marked with ® are registered with the United Kingdom Patent Office and/or the Office for Harmonization in the Internal Market and in other countries.

Published in Great Britain 2015
by Mills & Boon, an imprint of Harlequin (UK) Limited,
Eton House, 18-24 Paradise Road, Richmond, Surrey TW9 1SR

© 2014 Julie Miller

Published in Great Britain 2015
by Mills & Boon, an imprint of Harlequin (UK) Limited,
Eton House, 18-24 Paradise Road, Richmond, Surrey, TW9 1SR

© 2015 Julie Miller

ISBN: 978-0-263-25325-2

46-1215

Harlequin (UK) Limited's policy is to use papers that are natural, renewable and recyclable products and made from wood grown in sustainable forests. The logging and manufacturing processes conform to the legal environmental regulations of the country of origin.

Printed and bound in Spain
by CPI, Barcelona

Julie Miller is an award-winning *USA TODAY* best-selling author of breathtaking romantic suspense—with a National Readers' Choice Award and a Daphne du Maurier Award among other prizes. She has also earned an *RT Book Reviews* Career Achievement Award. For a complete list of her books, monthly newsletter and more, go to www.juliemiller.org.

For my dear friend and fellow author Laura Landon.

She's a sweetie to travel to conferences with,
and a tough ol' bird when it comes to motivating me.
Love her!

Oh, and she writes wonderful historical romances, too.

Chapter One

"'God bless us, every one.'"

Katie Rinaldi joined the smattering of applause from the mostly empty seats of the Williams College auditorium, where the community theater group she belonged to was rehearsing a production of Charles Dickens's *A Christmas Carol*. The man with the white hair playing Ebenezer Scrooge stood at center stage, accepting handshakes and congratulations from the other actors as they completed their first technical rehearsal with sound and lights. The costumes she'd constructed for the three spirits seemed to be fitting just fine. And once she finished painting the mask for the Spirit of Christmas Future, she could sit back and enjoy the run of the show as an audience member. Okay, as a proud mama. She only had eyes for Tiny Tim.

She gave a thumbs-up sign to her third-grade son and laughed when he had to fight with the long sleeves of his costume jacket to free his hands and return the gesture. His rolling-eyed expression of frustration softened her laugh into an understanding smile.

She mouthed, *Okay. I'll fix it.* Once he was certain she'd gotten the message, Tyler Rinaldi turned to chatter with the boy next to him, who played one of his older

Cratchit brothers. One of the girls joined the group, bringing over a prop toy, and instantly, they were involved in a challenge to see who could get the wooden ball on an attached string into the cup first.

Although extra demands with her job at KCPD and the normal bustle of the holidays meant Katie was already busy without having to work a play into her schedule, she was glad she'd brought Tyler to auditions. The only child of a single mother, Tyler often spent his evenings alone with her, reading books or playing video or computer games after he finished his homework. She was glad to see him having fun and making friends.

"Note to self." Katie pulled her laptop from her lime-green-and-blue-flowered bag and opened up her calendar to type in a reminder that she needed to adjust the costume that had initially been made for a larger child. What was one less hour of sleep, anyway? "Shorten sleeves."

"I think we might just have a show." Katie startled at the hand on her shoulder. "Sorry. I didn't realize you were working."

Katie saved her calendar and turned in her seat to acknowledge the slender man with thick blond hair streaked with threads of gray sinking into the cushioned seat behind her. "Hey, Doug. I was just making some costume notes."

The play's director leaned forward, resting his arms on the back of the seat beside her. "You've done a nice job," he complimented, even though she'd been only one of several volunteers. His professionally trained voice articulated every word to dramatic perfection. "We're down to the details now—if the gremlins in this old theater will give us a break."

"Gremlins?"

Doug looked up into the steel rafters of the catwalk two stories above their heads before bringing his dark eyes back to hers. "I don't know a theater that isn't haunted. Or a production that feels like it's going to be ready in time. Those were brand-new battery packs we put in the microphones tonight, but they still weren't working."

"And you think the gremlins are responsible?" she teased.

Laughing, he patted her shoulder again. "More likely a short in a wire somewhere. But we need to figure out that glitch, put the finishing touches on makeup and costumes, and get the rest of the set painted before we open next weekend."

"You don't ask for much, do you?" she answered, subtly pulling away from his touch. Doug Price was one of those ageless-looking souls who could be forty or fifty or maybe even sixty but who had the energy—and apparently the libido—of a much younger man. "It's a fun holiday tradition that your group puts on this show every year. Tyler's having a blast being a part of it."

"And you?"

Katie smiled. Despite dodging a few touches and missing those extra hours of sleep, she'd enjoyed the creative energy she'd been a part of these past few weeks. "Me, too."

"Douglas?" A man's voice from the stage interrupted the conversation. Francis Sergel, the tall, gaunt gentleman who played the Spirit of Christmas Future, had a sharp, nasal voice. Fortunately, he'd gotten the role because he looked the part and didn't have to speak onstage. "Curtain calls? You said you'd block them this evening."

"In a minute." Doug's hand was on her shoulder again. "You want to go grab a coffee after rehearsal? My treat."

Although she knew him to be divorced, Doug was probably old enough to be her father, and she simply wasn't interested in his flirtations. She had too many responsibilities to have time to be interested in any man besides her son.

"Sorry. I've got work to finish." She gestured to her laptop and saw the screen-saver picture had come up—a picture of Trent Dixon, a longtime friend and coworker. Trent, a former college football player, was carrying her son on his big shoulders after a fun day spent in Columbia, Missouri, at a Mizzou football game. Dressed in black-and-gold jerseys and jeans, both guys were smiling as if they'd had the time of their lives—and she suspected they had. Trent was as good to Tyler now as he'd been to her back in high school when she'd been a brand-new teenage mom and she'd needed a real friend. As always, the image of man and boy made her smile…and triggered a little pang of regret.

Katie quickly pushed a key and sent the image away before that useless melancholy could take hold. She'd made her choices—and a relationship with Trent wasn't one of them. She needed the brawny KCPD detective as a friend—Tyler needed him as a friend—more than she needed Trent to be a boyfriend or lover or even something more. She'd nearly ruined that friendship back in high school. She'd nearly ruined her entire life with the foolish impulses she'd succumbed to back then. She wasn't going to make those mistakes again.

Katie pointed to the small brown-haired boy onstage. All her choices as an adult were based on whatever was best for her son. "It's a school night for Tyler, too. So we need to head home."

But Doug had seen the momentary trip down memory

Iane in her lengthy pause. He reached over the seat to tap the edge of the laptop. "Was that Tyler's dad?"

The scent of gel or spray on his perfectly coiffed hair was a little overpowering as he brushed up beside her. Katie leaned to the far side of her seat to get some fresh air. "No. His father signed away his rights before Tyler was born. He's not in the picture."

She realized the tactical error as soon as the words left her mouth. Doug's grin widened as if she'd just given him a green light to hit on her. She mentally scrambled to backtrack and flashed a red light instead.

Easy. She clicked the mouse pad and pulled up the screen saver again, letting Trent's defensive-lineman shoulders and six feet five inches of height do their intimidation thing, even from a picture on a small screen. "This is Trent Dixon. He's a friend. A good friend," she emphasized, hoping Doug would interpret her longtime acquaintance with the boy who'd grown up across the street from her as a message that she wasn't interested in returning his nightly flirtations. "He's a cop. A KCPD detective."

If Trent's imposing size wasn't intimidating enough, the gun and badge usually ensured just about anybody's cooperation.

"I see. Maybe another time." Doug was king of his own little company of community theater volunteers and apparently didn't accept the word *no* from one of his lowly subjects. "I'll at least see you at the cast party after opening night, right?"

For Tyler's sake, she'd go and help her son celebrate his success—not because Doug kept asking her out. Katie lowered her head, brushing her thumb across the bottom of her keyboard, studying Trent's image as plan B popped into her head. Trent was Tyler's big buddy—the main male role model in her son's life besides her uncle Dwight, who'd taken her in when he'd married Katie's aunt Maddie nine years ago. Trent would be at the show's opening night. She'd make sure to introduce the big guy to Doug and let the handsy director rethink his efforts to date her. Katie was smiling at her evil little plan when she looked up again. "Sure. All three of us will be there."

"Doug?" Francis Sergel's voice had risen to a whiny pitch. "Curtain call?"

"I'm coming." The director waved off the middle-aged man with the beady dark eyes. "By the way, Tyler's done a great job memorizing his lines—faster than the other kids, and he's the youngest one."

Katie recognized the flattery for what it was, another attempt to make a connection with her. But she couldn't deny how proud she was of how her nine-year-old had taken to acting the way she once had. "Thanks. He's worked really hard."

"I can tell you've worked hard with him. He stays in character well, too."

"Douglas. Tonight?" Francis pulled the black hood off his head, although his dark, bushy beard and mustache still concealed half his face. "I'd like to get out of this costume."

"Coming." Doug squeezed her shoulder again as he stood. "See you tomorrow night." He clapped his hands to get everyone's attention onstage and sidled out into the aisle. "All right, cast—I need everybody's eyes right here."

But Francis's dark gaze held hers long enough to make her twitch uncomfortably in her seat. The man didn't need the Grim Reaper mask she was making for him. With his skin pinched over his bony cheeks and his eyes refusing to blink, he already gave her the willies. When he finally looked away and joined the clump of actors gathering center stage, Katie released the breath she hadn't known she'd been holding. What was that about?

Dismissing the man's interest as some kind of censure for keeping the director from doing his job, Katie turned to Tyler and winked. She tilted her head to encourage him to pay attention to Doug before she dropped her focus back to the computer in her lap. Francis was a bit of a diva on the best of nights. If he had a problem with Doug trying to make time with her, she'd send the actor straight to the source of the problem—aka, not her.

Feeling the need to tune out Doug and Francis and the prospect of another late night, Katie turned back to her computer. Blocking the final bows and running them a few times would take several minutes, leaving her the opportunity to get a little work done and hopefully free up some time once she got home and put Tyler to bed.

With quick precision, she keyed in the password to access encrypted work files she'd been organizing for the police department—sometimes on the clock, sometimes in her own spare time. Katie had spent months scanning in unsolved case files and loading the data into the cross-referencing computer program she'd designed. Okay, so maybe her work as an information specialist with KCPD's cold case squad wasn't as exciting as the acting career she'd dreamed of before a teenage pregnancy and harrowing kidnapping plot to sell her unborn son in a black-market baby ring had altered her life plan. But it was a good, steady paycheck that allowed her to support herself and Tyler single-handedly.

Besides, the technical aspects of her work had never stopped Katie from thinking, imagining, creating. She loved the challenge of fitting together the pieces of a puzzle on an old unsolved case—not to mention the satisfaction of knowing she was doing something meaningful with her life. She hadn't had the best start in the world—her abusive father had murdered her mother and been sent to prison. Helping the police catch bad guys went a long way toward redeeming herself for some of the foolish mistakes she'd made as an impulsive, grieving young woman trying to atone for her father's terror. Working with computers and data was a job her beloved aunt Maddie and uncle Dwight, Kansas City's district attorney, understood and respected. She would always be grateful to the two of them for rescuing her and Tyler and giving her a real home. Although she knew they would support her even if she had chosen to become an actress, this career choice was one way she could honor and thank them for taking her in and loving her like a daughter. Plus, even though he didn't quite grasp the research and technical details of her job, Tyler thought her work was pretty cool. Hanging out with all those cops and helping them solve crimes put her on a tiny corner of the shelf beside his comic book and cartoon action heroes. Making her son proud was a gift she wouldn't trade for any spotlight.

Katie sorted through the first file that came up, highlighting words such as the victim's name, witnesses who'd been interviewed, suspect lists and evidence documentation and dropping them into the program that would match up any similarities between this unsolved murder and other crimes in the KCPD database. The tragic death of a homeless man back in the '70s had few clues and fewer suspects, sadly, making it a quick case to read through and document. Others often took hours, or even days, to sort and categorize. But she figured LeRoy Byrd had been important to someone, and therefore, it was important to her to get his information out of a musty storage box and transferred into the database.

"There you go, LeRoy." She patted his name on the screen. "It's not much. Just know we're still thinking about you and working on your case."

She closed out his information and pulled up the next file, marked *Gemma Gordon*. Katie's breath shuddered in her chest as she looked into the eyes of a teenage girl who'd been missing for ten years. "Not you, too."

The temperature in the auditorium seemed to drop a good twenty degrees as memories of her own kidnapping nightmare surfaced. This girl was seventeen, the same age Katie had been when she'd gone off to find her missing friend, Whitney. Katie had found her friend, all right, but had become a prisoner herself, kept alive until she could give birth to Tyler and her kidnappers tried to sell him in a black-market adoption scheme. Thanks to her aunt and uncle, Tyler was saved and Katie had escaped with her life. But Whitney hadn't been so lucky.

She touched her fingers to the young girl's image on the screen and skimmed through her file. The similarities between the old Katie and this girl were frightening. Pregnant. Listed as a runaway. Katie had fought to save her child. Had Gemma Gordon? Had she even had a chance to fight? Katie had found a family with her aunt Maddie and uncle Dwight and survived. Was anyone missing this poor girl? According to the file, neither Gemma Gordon nor her baby had ever been found.

"You must have been terrified," Katie whispered, feeling the grit of tears clogging her throat. She read on through the persons of interest interviewed in the initial investigation. "What…?" She swiped away the moisture that had spilled onto her cheek and read the list again. There was one similarity too many to her own nightmare—a name she'd hoped never to see again. "No. No, no."

Katie's fingers hovered above the keyboard. One click. A few seconds of unscrambling passwords and a lie about her clearance level and she could find out everything she wanted to about the name on the screen. She could find out what cell he was in at the state penitentiary, who his visitors were, if his name had turned up in conjunction with any other kidnappings or missing-person cases. With a few keystrokes she could know if the man with that name was enjoying a healthy existence or rotting away in prison the way she'd so often wished over the years.

When a hot tear plopped onto the back of her knuckles, Katie startled. She willed herself out of the past and dabbed at her damp cheeks with the sleeve of her sweater. Beyond the fact that hacking into computer systems she didn't officially have access to without a warrant could get her fired, she knew better than to give in to the fears and anger and grief. Katie straightened in her seat and quickly highlighted the list of names, entering them all into the database. "You're a survivor, Katie Lee Rinaldi. Those people can't hurt you anymore. You beat them."

But Gemma Gordon hadn't.

After swiping away another tear, Katie sent the list into the database before logging out. She turned off the portable Wi-Fi security device on the seat beside her and shut down her laptop. She squeezed the edge of her computer as if she was squeezing that missing girl's hand. "I'll do whatever I can to help you, too, Gemma. I promise."

When she looked up, she realized she was the only

parent left in the auditorium seats. The stage was empty, too. "Oh, man."

How long had she been sitting there, caught up in the past? Too long. Her few minutes of work had stretched on longer than she'd thought, and the present was calling. She stuffed her equipment back into her flowered bag and stood, grabbing her wool coat off the back of her seat and pulling it on. "Tyler?"

Katie looped her bag over her shoulder and scooted toward the end of the row of faded green folding seats. As pretentious and egotistical as Doug Price could be, he also ran a tight ship. Since they were borrowing this facility from the college, there were certain rules he insisted they all follow. Props returned to backstage tables. Costumes on hangers in the dressing rooms. Rehearsal started when he said it would and ended with the same punctuality. Campus security checked the locks at ten thirty, so every night they were done by ten.

Katie pulled her cell phone from her bag and checked the time when she reached the sloping aisle—ten fifteen. She groaned. The cast was probably backstage, changing into their street clothes if they hadn't already left, and Doug was most likely up in the tech booth, giving the sound and light guys their notes.

Exchanging her phone for the mittens in her pocket, Katie hurried down the aisle toward the stage. "Tyler? Sorry I got distracted. You ready to go, bud?"

And that was when the lights went out.

Chapter Two

"Ow." Disoriented by the sudden darkness, Katie bumped into the corner of a seat. Leaning into the most solid thing she could find, she grabbed the back of the chair and held on while she got her bearings. "Hey! I'm still in the house."

Her voice sounded small and muffled in the cavernous space as she waited several seconds for a response. But the only answer was the scuffle of hurried footsteps moving over the carpet at the very back of the auditorium.

She spun toward the sound. "Hello?" She squeezed her eyes shut against the dizziness that pinballed through her brain. Only her grip on the chair kept her on her feet while her equilibrium righted itself. She heard a loud clank and the protesting squeak of the old hinges as whoever was in here with her scooted out the door to the lobby. Opening her eyes, Katie lifted her blind focus up the sloping aisle. "Tyler? This isn't a good time to play hide-and-seek."

Why weren't the security lights coming on? They ran on a separate power source from the rest of the theater. "Did we have a power outage?"

Why wouldn't anybody answer her? Panic tried to lock up the air in her chest. The dark wasn't a safe place to be. She'd been reading those old case files, had lingered over knew she hadn't imagined those footsteps earlier. She wasn't alone.

"Tyler, honey, if you're playing some kind of game, this isn't funny." She shouted for the security guard who worked in the building most nights. "Mr. Thompson?"

Was Doug Price playing a trick on her for turning him down again? Did he think she'd be freaked out enough that she'd run to him and expect him to be her hero? If that was what this was about... Her blood heated, chasing away the worried chill. Oh, she was so never going out with that guy. "Tyler? Where are you?"

Why didn't he answer? Had he fallen asleep? Had something happened to him?

Uh-uh. She wasn't going there.

Katie shined her light into the men's dressing room. Lights off. Room empty. She sorted through the costumes hanging on the rack there, peeked beneath the counter. Nothing. She opened the door to the ladies' dressing room, too, and repeated the search.

"Tyler Rinaldi, you answer—"

A boot dropped to the floor behind the rack of long dresses and ghostly costumes. Katie cried out as the layers of polyester, petticoats, wool and lace toppled over on top of her. Hands pushed through the cascade of clothes, knocking her down with them. "Hey! What are you...? Help! Stop!"

She hit the tile floor on her elbows and bottom, and the impact tingled through her fingers, jarring loose her grip on the phone. Her assailant was little more than a wisp of shadow in the dark room. But there was no mistaking the slamming door or the drumbeat of footsteps running across the concrete floor of the work space and storage area behind the stage.

Katie's thoughts raced as she clawed her way free through the pile of fallen clothes and felt around in the darkness to retrieve her phone. Had she interrupted a robbery? There were power tools for set construction and sound equipment and some antiques they were using as props. All those things should be locked up, but an outsider might not know that. Was this some kind of college prank by a theater student? Could it be something personal? She wouldn't have expected Doug to get physical like that. Had she offended someone else?

Her fingers brushed across the protective plastic case of her phone and she snatched it up. She pushed to her feet and smacked into the closed door. "Let me out!" She slapped at the door with her palm until she found the door handle and pulled it open. "Stay away from my son! Tyler!"

But by the time she ran out into the backstage area in pursuit of the shadow, the footsteps had gone silent. The exit door on the far side of the backstage area stood wide open and a slice of light from the sidewalk lamp outside cut clear across the room. After so long in the darkness with just the illumination from her phone, Katie had to avert her eyes from even that dim glow. She saw nothing more than a wraithlike glimpse of a man slipping through the doorway into the winter night outside.

Following the narrowing strip of light, she stumbled forward, dodging prop tables and flats until the door closed with a quiet click and she was plunged into another blackout.

She stopped in her tracks. The one thing she hated more than the darkness was not knowing if her son was safe. And since she couldn't find him…

She pushed a command on her phone and raised it to her lips. "Call Trent."

Inching forward without any kind of light now, she counted off each ring of the telephone as she waited for her strong, armed, utterly reliable friend to pick up. She thought she could make out the red letters of the exit sign above the door by the time Trent cut off the fourth ring and picked up.

"Hey, sunshine," he greeted on a breathless gasp of air. "It's a little late. What's up?"

Oblivious to the current irony of his nickname for her, Katie squeezed her words past the panic choking her throat. "I'm at the theater… The lights…" She bumped into the edge of a flat and shifted course. "Ow. Damn it. I can't see…"

A warm chuckle colored the detective's audible breathing. "Did you leave your car lights on again? Need me to come jump-start it?"

"No." Well, technically, she didn't know that, but she didn't think she had.

"Flat tire? Williams College is a good twenty minutes from here, but I could—"

"Trent. Listen to me. There is some kind of weird…" As his deep inhales and exhales calmed, she heard a tuneless kind of percussive music and a woman's voice laughing in the background. *The man is breathless from exertion, Katie. Get a clue.* "Oh, God," she mumbled as realization dawned and embarrassment warmed her skin. "I'm so sorry. Is someone with you?"

Instead of answering her question, Trent's tone changed from winded amusement to that steely deep tone that resonated through his chest and reminded her he was a cop. "Weird? How? Are you all right? Is Tyler okay?"

Trent Dixon was on a date. He might be in the middle of *more* than a date. She'd forgotten about setting him up with that friend from the coffee shop a few weeks back. Trent wasn't her knight in shining armor to call whenever she had a problem she couldn't fix. He wasn't Tyler's father and he wasn't her boyfriend. Trent was just the good guy who'd grown up across the street and had a hard time saying no to her. Knowing that about him, because she was his friend, too, she'd worked really hard not to take advantage of his good-guy tendencies and protective instincts. "Is that Erin Ballard? I'm sorry. I wasn't thinking. You have company."

"I dropped Erin off an hour ago after dinner. I stopped by the twenty-four-hour gym because I needed to work off some excess energy. And it's too cold to go for a run outside." He paused for a moment, wiping down with a towel or catching his breath. "Apparently, I'm not the only night-owl fitness freak in KC."

He felt energized after his date with Erin? Was that *excess energy* a code for sexual frustration? Had he wanted something more from Erin besides dinner and conversation? Or had he gotten exactly what he wanted and was now on some kind of endorphin high that wouldn't let him sleep? The momentary stab of jealousy at the thought of Trent bedding the willowy blonde she'd introduced him to ended as she tripped over the leg of a chair in the darkness. "Damn it."

"Katie?"

"I'm sorry." She should be thinking of her son, not Trent. Not any misplaced feelings of envy for the woman who landed him. Tyler was the only person who mattered right now. And a panicked late-night call to a man she had no claim on wasn't going to help. "Never mind. I'm sorry to interrupt your evening. It's late and I need to get Tyler home to bed. Tell Erin hi for me."

"Katie Lee Rinaldi," Trent chided. "Why did you call me?"

"I'll handle it myself."

"Handle what? Damn it, woman, talk to me."

"Sorry. I don't need you to rescue me every time I make a mistake. Enjoy your date."

"I'm not on a... Katie?"

"Good night." She disconnected the call, ending the interrogation.

Seconds later, the phone vibrated in her hand. The big galoot. He'd called her right back. Not only did she feel guilty for interrupting his evening, but now she realized just how crazy she'd sounded. Practically perfect Erin Ballard would never panic like this and make a knee-jerk call to a friend for help.

Pull it together and think rationally. She should simply call 9-1-1 and report a break-in or say that an intruder had vandalized the lights in the theater. She could call Uncle Dwight. But as Kansas City's DA, it would only be a matter of minutes before half the police department knew that she'd lost her son and wasn't fit to be his mother.

Katie inhaled a deep breath, pushing aside that option as a last resort. She didn't ever want to be labeled that impulsive, needs-to-be-rescued woman she'd been as a teenager again. Katie Rinaldi stood on her own two feet. She took care of her own son. The two of them would never end up like the girl in that file again.

"Tyler!" With her phone on flashlight mode once more, she hurried as quickly as she dared toward the exit sign. "If you are playing some kind of game with me, mister, I'm grounding you until you're eighteen."

Silence was her only answer.

Had Tyler gotten tired of waiting for his flaky, work-obsessed mother and headed on out to the car? Or was he still inside someplace, trapped in the darkness like she was? Why didn't he answer? *Could* he answer?

First that damn case file and now this? She couldn't stop the nightmarish memory this time. Her feet turned to lead. Katie didn't have to close her eyes to remember the hand over her mouth. The prick of a needle in her arm. Her limbs going numb. Cradling her swollen belly and crying out for her baby as she collapsed into a senseless heap. The night she'd been abducted she'd gone to help Whitney and wound up in the same mess herself. A few weeks later, she'd given birth to Tyler in a sterile room with no one to hold her hand or urge her to breathe, and she'd nearly given up all hope of surviving.

But the tiny little boy the kidnappers laid in her arms for a few seconds had changed everything, giving her a reason to survive, a reason to escape, a reason to keep fighting.

If anything happened to her son…

If he'd been taken from her again…

Finally. Her palm flattened against ice-cold steel. Burying her fears and summoning her maternal strength, Katie shoved open the back door. A blast of bitter cold and snowy crystals melting against her nose and cheeks cleared her thoughts. "Tyler!"

It was brighter outside the theater, even though it was night. The campus lights were on, and each lamppost was adorned with shiny silver wreaths that shimmered with the cold, damp wind. The rows of lights illuminated the path down into the woods behind the auditorium and marked the sidewalk that led around the back of the theater to the parking lot on the north side. New snow was falling, capturing the light from the lamps and reflecting their orange glow into the air around her.

There were dozens of footprints in the first layer of snow from where the cast and crew had exited out to their cars. But there was one set of man-size prints leading down the walkway into the trees, disappearing at the footbridge that arched over the creek at the bottom of the hill. Good. Run. Whoever had been in the darkened building with her was gone.

But the freezing air seeped right into her bones when she read the hastily carved message in the snow beside the tracks.

Stop before someone gets hurt.

She shivered inside her coat. "Gets hurt?" She looked out into the woods, wondering if the man who'd trapped her in the dressing room was still here, watching. "Stop what? What do you want? Tyler?"

Confusion gave way to stark, cold fear when she zeroed in on the impression of a small, size-five tennis shoe, left by a brown-haired boy who hated to wear his winter boots. She hoped. The prints followed the same path as the senseless message. "Tyler!"

Thinking more than panicking now, Katie searched the shadows near the door until she found a broom beside the trash cans there. She wedged the broom handle between the door and frame in case the footprints were a false hope and she needed to get back inside the theater and search some more. She followed the smaller track down the hill. Had the man taken her son? Convinced him to come along with him to find his missing mother? Had she been stuck inside the building for that long?

But suddenly, the boy-size footprints veered off into

the trees. Katie stepped knee-deep into the drift next to the sidewalk, ignored the snow melting into her jeans and headed into the woods. "Tyler!"

She heard a dog barking from somewhere in the distance. Oh, no. There was one thing she knew could make her son forget every bit of common sense she'd taught him. The boy-size prints were soon joined by a set of paw prints half the size of her fist. Both tracks ran back up the hill toward the parking lot, and Katie followed. "Please be chasing that stupid dog. Please don't let anyone have taken my son. Tyler!"

The trail led her back to the sidewalk and disappeared around the corner of the building. Katie broke into a run once she cleared the snow among the trees and followed the tracks into the open expanse of asphalt and snow. She was almost light-headed with relief when she spotted the boy in the dark blue parka, playing with a skinny, short-haired collie mix in the parking lot. "Tyler!"

A blur of tan and white dashed off into the woods, followed by clouds of hot, steamy dog breath and a boy's dejected sigh.

Thank God. Tyler was safe.

Sparing one moment of concern for the familiar collarless stray disappearing into the snowy night, Katie ran straight to her son and pulled him into her chest for a tight hug. She kissed the top of his wool stocking cap, hugged him tighter and kissed him again. "Oh, thank goodness. Thank goodness, sweetie."

"Mo-om," Tyler whined on two different pitches before pushing enough space between them for him to tilt his face up to hers. "You scared him away."

Katie eased her grip around her son's slim shoulders and brought her mittened hands up to cup his freckled cheeks and look down into those bright blue eyes that matched her own. "I was so scared. There was a black-out inside the theater and I couldn't find you." Since running across the parking lot in panic mode and hugging the stuffing out of him had probably already worried him enough, Katie opted to leave out any mention of the cryptic message in the snow or the man who'd pushed her down in the dressing room. "I kept calling for you, but you didn't answer. What are you doing out here?"

"Feeding Padre. Doug told me he was out here again tonight, so I came to see him."

"Doug did?" Why would the director send her child out of the theater on such a bitter night?

"He said he'd tell you where I was." But Doug hadn't. "I think Padre's hungry, so I saved my peanut butter sandwich from lunch for him."

Still feeling uneasy, her breath came in ragged puffs while Tyler knelt down to stuff an empty plastic bag into the book bag at his feet. Katie looked all around the well-lit but empty lot to verify that her red Kia was the only vehicle there and that no one else was loitering about. If Doug had meant to tell her Tyler's whereabouts, he'd forgotten amid the busyness of shutting down a tech rehearsal and had apparently gone home without giving her mother's concern a second thought. Maybe the mix-up was all perfectly innocent. But if he'd done it on purpose...

"Come on, sweetie. We need to go." Katie draped her arm around Tyler's shoulders when he stood back up and hurried him along beside her to the car. "Didn't you eat your lunch?"

"Most of it. But I can always have a bowl of cereal

when we get home, and Padre doesn't have anybody to feed him."

"Padre?" She swapped her phone for the keys in her coat pocket and unlocked the car.

Tyler opened the passenger door and climbed inside on his knees, tossing his book bag into the backseat. "Did you see the ring of white fur around his neck? It looks like the collar Pastor Bill wears, and everybody calls him Padre."

Katie closed the door and hurried around the front of the car to get in behind the wheel. Naming a dog she knew he couldn't have was probably a bad thing, but she was more worried about blackouts and intruders and not being able to find her son. She placed her bag in the backseat beside Tyler's, locked the doors and quickly started the engine so she could crank up the heat. "Why didn't you wait for me? Or come get me as soon as you'd changed? I'm sorry I got distracted, but I was sitting out in the auditorium. I would have come to feed the dog with you. You shouldn't be out here by yourself, especially at night."

Tyler turned around and plopped down into his seat. "I know. But I wanted to see Padre before one of the other kids got to him first. He likes me, Mom. He lets me pet him and doesn't bite me or anything. Wyatt already has a dog, and Kayla's family has two cats. So he should be mine."

She grimaced at the sad envy for two of the other children in the play. "Tyler—"

"When everybody else started to leave, I tried to get back in, but the door was locked. So I stayed outside to play with Padre."

"Is that the real story? I don't mean the dog. Doug sending you outside? Getting locked out?" She pulled off her mitten and reached across the car to cup his cheek.

Chilled, but healthy. She was the only one having heart palpitations tonight. "There wasn't anyone left in the cast or crew to let you back in?"

"Maybe if I had my own cell phone, I could have called you."

"Really?" She pushed his stocking cap up to the crown of his head and ruffled his wavy dark hair between her fingers. "I was scared to death that something had happened to you, and you're playing that card?"

He fastened his seat belt. "I put a phone on my Christmas list."

"We talked about this. Not until middle school."

"Johnny Griffith has one."

"I'm not Johnny Griffith's mom." Katie straightened in her seat to fasten her own seat belt. "You're up past your bedtime. Let's go home before your toes freeze."

"Did Doug ask you out again?" Tyler asked. "Is that why he wanted to get rid of me?"

She glanced over at the far too wise expression on her son's freckled face. "He did. I told him no again, too."

Tyler tugged off his mittens and held his pink fingers up in front of the heating vent. "I thought maybe you were still in there talking to him. He's a good director and all, but I don't want him to be my dad."

Katie reached for Tyler's hands and pulled them between hers to rub some love and warmth into them. "He won't be." Not that he'd had a chance, anyway. But endangering her son certainly checked him off the list. "I can guarantee that."

"Good." When he'd had enough of a warming reassurance, Tyler pulled away and kicked his feet together, knocking snow off his shoes onto the floor mat. "Do you think Padre's toes will freeze out there tonight? Dogs have toes, right?"

"They do. But he must have dug himself a snow cave or found someplace warm to sleep if he's survived a whole week outdoors in the wintertime. I think he'll be okay. I hope he will be." Katie smiled wryly before turning on the windshield wipers and clearing away the wet snow. She shifted the car into gear, but paused with her foot on the brake to inspect the empty parking lot one more time. Maybe Tyler hadn't been in any danger. Maybe she hadn't really been, either. But why leave that message? And if the intruder had run along the pathway, had Tyler seen him either sneak into the building or run out of it? The man could easily have parked in another area of the campus so she wouldn't be able to spot him. But could Tyler have gotten a description that might put him in some kind of future harm? Her grip tightened around the steering wheel. "Did anybody talk to you while you were out here by yourself?"

"Wyatt and Kayla said goodbye. Kayla's dad asked me if you were still here. I told him as long as the car was, you were, too."

She'd make a point to thank Mr. Hudnall for checking on her son tomorrow night. "I meant a stranger. Anybody you didn't know? Was anyone watching you or following you?"

Tyler dropped his head back in dramatic groan. "I know about stranger danger. I would have shouted really loud or run really fast or gotten into the car with Kayla's dad because I know him."

"Okay, sweetie. Just checking."

He sat up straight and turned in his seat. "But if I had a phone—"

"Maybe later." She laughed and lifted her foot off the brake. "I need to talk it over with Aunt Maddie and Uncle Dwight first. We're on their phone plan."

And now the sulky lip went out. "Am I going to get anything that's on my Christmas list?"

"There are already some presents under the tree."

"None of them are big enough to be a dog. And none of them are small enough to be a phone. They're probably socks and underwear."

"I'm sure you'd be really good with a pet, sweetie, but you know we can't have a dog in our apartment." She pulled the car up next to the sidewalk at the corner of the theater building. "Hold on a second. I propped the door open in case I couldn't find you out here. I need to go close it so we don't get in trouble with the college. Sit tight. Lock yourself in until I get back."

After pulling her lime-green mittens back on and tying her scarf more tightly around her neck, Katie climbed out, waited for Tyler to relock the doors and hurried back to the exit. She glanced through the woods and walkway for the stray dog or a more menacing figure, but saw no sign of movement among the trees and shadows. But she slowed her steps once she shifted her full attention to the door. It was already closed, sealed tight. Had she not wedged the broom in securely enough?

Pulling her phone from her pocket again, Katie checked the time before turning on the camera. She'd only been gone a few minutes, hardly enough time for the security guard to make his rounds. And if he'd been close by already, why wouldn't he have answered her shouts of distress or turned on a light for her to see?

Who had closed this door? The same unseen person

who'd flipped on the running lights and hidden in the dark theater?

The man who'd run off into the woods after knocking her off her feet?

No matter what the answers to any of those questions might be, Katie worked around enough cops to know that details mattered. So she moved past the door and angled her phone camera down to take a picture of the disturbing message.

Her breath rushed out in a warm white cloud in the air, and she couldn't seem to breathe in again.

The message was gone.

The marks of her heeled boots were clear in the new layer of snow. But the rest of the footprints—boy-size tennis shoes, paw prints, the long, wide imprints of a stranger running away from the theater—*Stop before someone gets hurt*—had all been swept away.

A chill skittered down the back of her neck. She was bundled up tight enough to know it wasn't the snow getting to her skin. This was wrong. This was intentional. This was personal.

Katie backed away from the door. The man inside the theater had come back. He could still be here—hiding in the trees, lurking on the other side of that door, watching her right now. Waiting for her.

She glanced back and forth, trying to see into the night beyond the lamplights and the snow. Nothing. No one. She hadn't seen the man who grabbed her the night she'd been kidnapped, either.

She was shaking now. Katie didn't feel safe.

Her son wasn't safe.

"Tyler." She whispered his name like a storm cloud in the air as she turned and raced back to the car, banging on the window until Tyler unlocked the door and she could slip inside. She relocked the doors and peeled off her mittens before reaching across the seat and cupping his cheek in her palm again. "I love you, sweetie."

His skin was toasty warm from the heater, but she was shivering inside her coat as she shifted into gear and sped across the parking lot to the nearest exit.

"Mom? What's wrong?"

Tyler's voice was frightened, unsure. She was supposed to be his rock. She was a horrible mother for worrying him with her paranoid imagination. She was putting him in danger by not thinking straight.

"I'm sorry, sweetie. I'm okay. We're both okay." She shook the snowflakes from her dark hair, smiled for him, then pulled out onto the street at a much safer speed. "Why don't you tell me more about Padre."

"CONFOUNDED WOMAN." Trent slowed his pickup to a crawl once he saw that the parking lot outside the Williams College auditorium had nothing but asphalt and snow to greet him after his zip across Kansas City to get to Katie and Tyler.

As he circled the perimeter of the empty lot, just to make sure he hadn't misunderstood the location of the distress call, and the tiny Rinaldi family truly wasn't stranded someplace out in the bitter cold, Trent admitted that Katie Lee Rinaldi knew how to push his buttons—even though she never did it intentionally. It was his own damn fault. If he hadn't felt especially protective of Katie ever since she'd decided back in high school he was the one friend she could rely on without question, and if all the hours he'd spent with Tyler didn't make him think he wanted to be a father more than just about anything—

more than making sergeant, more than playing for the Chiefs, more than wishing he didn't have the time bomb of one concussion too many ticking in his head—then he wouldn't charge off on these fool's errands to protect a family that wasn't his.

He pulled up at the sidewalk near the auditorium's back entrance and shifted the truck into Park. He'd left before finishing a perfectly good workout to find out what Katie's phone call had been about when he'd barely been able to work up a polite interest in lingering on Erin Ballard's doorstep and trading a good-night kiss. Erin was an attractive blonde who could carry on an intelligent conversation, and who'd made it perfectly clear that she'd like Trent to come in out of the cold for some hot coffee and anything else he might want. Erin wasn't impulsive. Her wardrobe consisted of beiges and browns, and nothing she'd said or done had surprised him. Not once. Cryptic phone calls, leading with her heart and putting loyalty before common sense were probably foreign concepts. If it wasn't on Erin's planner in her phone, it probably wouldn't happen. Erin wasn't interesting to Trent.

She wasn't Katie.

No woman was.

The proof was in the follow-up buzz in his pocket. Trent checked his phone again, admitting he was less frustrated to read the Are you mad at me? text from Erin than he was to see that he hadn't heard boo from Katie since she'd called about witnessing something *weird* and had sounded so afraid.

No. Busy. With work, he added before sending the text to Erin. Maybe the woman would get a clue and stop pestering him. He'd already turned down her efforts to take a couple of dates to the next level as gently as he could, and he was done dealing with her tonight.

But he wasn't done with Katie.

After pulling his black knit watch cap down over his ears and putting his glove back on, Trent killed the engine and climbed out for a closer look. Because he was a cop and panicked phone calls about something *weird* happening at the theater tended to raise his suspicions, and because it was Katie, who was not only a friend since high school but also a coworker on the cold case squad, Trent wasn't about to ignore the call and drive home without at least verifying that whatever problem had prompted her call was no longer anything to worry about.

Not that he really knew what the problem was. Trent pulled a flashlight from the pocket of his coat and shined the light out into the foggy woods at the edge of the lot before clearing his head with a deep breath of the bracing air. The snow drifted against the brick wall of the building and crunched beneath his boots as he set out to walk the perimeter and do a little investigating before he followed up with Katie to find out what the hell she'd been babbling about.

Katie had been frightened—that much he could hear in her voice. But she'd never really answered any of his questions. He didn't know if she was having trouble with her car again, if something had happened to Tyler, if she was in some kind of danger or if she'd gone off to help a friend who needed something. With his interrogation skills, he could get straight answers from frightened witnesses with nervous gaps in their memories and lying lowlifes who typically avoided the truth as a means of survival.

But could he get a straight answer from Katie Rinaldi?

He checked the main entrance first but found all the

front doors locked. He identified himself with his badge and briefly chatted with the security guard, who reported that the campus had been quiet that evening, that the on-campus and commuter students alike had pretty much stayed either in the buildings or made a quick exit in their cars as soon as evening classes had ended. Nobody was hanging out any longer than necessary to tempt the weather or waste time in these last days before finals week and Christmas break. After thanking the older man and assuring him he was here on unofficial police business and that there was no need to call for backup or stop making his rounds, Trent followed the lit pathway around the rest of the building. Other than the campus officer's car, the staff lot to the south was empty, too.

Unwilling to write the call for help off just yet, Trent circled to the back of the auditorium. But when the chomp of snow beneath his steps fell silent, Trent looked down. "Interesting."

What kind of maintenance crew would take the time to clear a sidewalk at this time of night when the snow wasn't scheduled to stop falling for another couple hours? Trent knelt and plucked a bristle broken off a corn broom from the dusting of snow accumulating again beneath his feet. And what kind of professionals with an entire campus to clear would bother with a broom when they had snowblowers and even larger machinery at their disposal?

Had there been a prowler near the building who'd swept away any evidence of lurking on campus? Was that what Katie had called him about? Had she seen someone trying to break in? Had the perp seen her? With his hackles rising beneath the collar of his coat, Trent pushed to his feet, noting where the new snow had been swept away— around the locked back door and down the sidewalk into the trees. He'd qualify that as *weird*. The scenario fit some kind of cover-up.

"Katie?" There'd better not be an answer. He raised his voice, praying the woods were quiet because the Rinaldis were safely home, asleep in their beds. "Tyler?"

His nape itched with the sensation of being watched, and Trent casually turned his light down along the path between the trees. Was that a rustle of movement in the low brush? Or merely the wind stirring the branches of a pine tree? The lamps along the sidewalk created circles of light that made it impossible to see far into the woods. With his ears attuned to any unusual sound in the cold night air, he moved along the cleared walk down toward the frozen creek at the bottom of the hill. "KCPD! You in the trees, show yourself."

His deep voice filled the air without an answer.

"Katie?" His gloved fingers brushed against the phone in his pocket. Maybe he should just call her. But the hour was late and Tyler would be in bed and a phone ringing at this hour would probably cause more alarm than reassurance. Besides, if she wouldn't give him any kind of explanation when she called him, he doubted she'd be any more forthcoming when he called her. He'd give this search a few more minutes until he could say good-night to the suspicions that put him on guard and go home to get some decent shut-eye himself.

When he reached the little arched bridge that crossed the creek, *weird* took a disquieting turn into *what the hell?* Trent stopped in the middle of the bridge, looking down at both sides—the one that had been deliberately cleared from the back door of the theater down to this point, and the two inches of snow on the sidewalk beyond the creek marked by a clear set of tracks. There were two skid marks through the snow, as if someone had slipped on the bridge and fallen, then a trail of footsteps leading up the hill on the opposite side. One set of tracks. Man-size. More than that, the distance between the steps lengthened, as though whoever had left the trail had decided he needed to run. A man in a hurry—running from something or to some-thing or because of something. A student in a hurry to get to his dorm or car? Or a man running away from campus security and a cop who might be curious about why he'd want to erase his trail?

Where had this guy gone, anyway? The snow was com-ing down heavily enough that those tracks should be noth-ing but a bunch of divots in the icy surface if they'd been there when classes had been dismissed or Tyler's rehearsal had ended. These were deep. These were recent. These were—

Trent spun when he heard the noise crashing through the drifts and underbrush toward him. He'd pulled up his coat and had his hand on the butt of his gun when a blur of tan and white shot out between the trees and darted around his legs. "What the...?"

Four legs. Black nose. Long tail.

After one more scan to make sure the dog was the only thing coming at him, Trent laughed and eased the insu-lated nylon back over his holster. "Hey, pup. See anybody but me out here tonight?"

The dog danced around him, whining with a mixture of caution and excitement. Apparently, Spot here was the only set of eyes that had been watching him through the trees. The poor thing wore no collar and needed a good brushing to clean the twigs and cockleburs from his dark gold fur. Feeling a tug of remembrance for the dogs his family had always had growing up, Trent held out his hand in a fist, encouraging the dog to get familiar with his scent. "You've been out here awhile, haven't you, little guy?"

Of course, standing six foot five made most critters like this seem little, and once the dog stopped his manic movements and focused on the scent of his gloved hand, Trent knelt to erase some of the towering distance between them and make himself look a little less intimidating. When he opened his hand, the dog inspected the palm side, too, no doubt looking for food, judging by the bumpy lines of his rib cage visible on either side of his skinny flanks. The stray wanted to be friendly, but when Trent reached out to pet him, the dog jumped away, diving through a snowdrift. But as if deciding the big, scary man who had no food on him was more inviting than the chest-deep cold and wet, he came charging back to the sidewalk, shaking the snow off his skinny frame before sitting down and staring up at Trent.

"What are you saying to me?" Trent laughed again when the dog tilted his head to one side, as though making an effort to understand him. "I'm Trent Dixon, KCPD. I'd like to ask you a few questions." The more he talked, the more the dog seemed to quiet. He thumbed over his shoulder toward the auditorium. "You know what happened here? Have you seen a curvy brunette and a little boy about yea high?" When he raised his hand to gesture to Tyler's height, the dog's dark brown eyes followed the movement. Interesting. Maybe he'd had a little training before running away or getting tossed out onto the street. Or maybe the dog was just smart enough to know where a friendly snack usually came from. "Your feet aren't big enough to make those tracks on the other side of the bridge. And I'm guessing you spend a lot of time around here. What do you know that I don't?"

The dog scooted forward a couple inches and butted his nose against Trent's knee. When he got up close like that, Trent could see that the dog was shivering. With his stomach doing a compassionate flip-flop, he decided there was only one thing he could do. Katie Rinaldi might not need rescuing tonight, but this knee-high bag of bones did.

"Easy, boy. That's it. I'm your big buddy now." Extending one hand for the dog to sniff, Trent petted him around the jowls and ears with the other. When the dog started licking his glove, desperate for something to eat, he grabbed him by the scruff of the neck. Other than jumping to his feet, the dog showed no signs of fear or aggression. Maybe the mutt had made friends with enough college students that he didn't view people as a threat.

"I'm afraid I'm going to have to take you in," Trent teased, standing and lifting the dog into his arms. Craving either warmth or companionship, the dog snuggled in, resting his head over Trent's arm and letting himself be carried up the hill to Trent's truck. "I'll get you warmed up and get some food in you. Maybe you'll be willing to tell me what you saw or heard then."

The dog was perfectly cooperative as Trent loaded him into the cab of his truck and pulled an old blanket and an energy bar from his emergency kit behind the seat. "It's mostly granola and peanut butter but…okay."

Taking the bar as soon as it was offered, the dog made quick work of the protein snack. "Tomorrow I'll get you to the vet for a checkup and have her scan to see if there's an ID chip in you." He got a whiff of the dog's wet, matted fur when he leaned over to wrap the blanket around him. "Maybe they can give you a bath, too."

Trent shook his head as the dog settled into the passenger seat, making himself at home. "This is temporary, you know," Trent reminded him, starting the engine and cranking up the heat. "I'm a cop, remember? I'll have to report you."

Stinky McPooch raised his head and looked at Trent, as though translating the conversation into dogspeak. His pink tongue darted out to lick his nose and muzzle and he whined a response that sounded a little like a protest.

"Don't try to sweet-talk your way out of this. You owe me some answers. So what's your story? No warm place for the night? Anybody looking for you?" The dog tilted his head and an ear flopped over, giving his face a sad expression. Trent turned on the wipers and shifted the truck into gear before driving toward the street. "Sorry to hear that. I'm a bachelor on my own, too. You can call me Trent or Detective. What should I call you?" When he stopped at the exit to the parking lot, Trent reached over the console to pet him. Pushing his head into the caress of Trent's hand, the dog whimpered in a doggy version of a purr. "All right, then, Mr. Pup." He pulled onto the street. There wasn't much traffic this time of night, so it was safe enough to take his eyes off the road to glance at his furry prisoner. "Did you see anything suspicious at the theater tonight?"

The dog barked, right on cue.

When Trent moved both hands to the steering wheel, the mutt put a paw on his arm, whimpering again. Trent grinned and scratched behind the mutt's ears, loving how the dog was engaging in the conversation with him. "Tell me more. I like a witness who talks to me. I think you and I are going to get along."

His interrogation skills were intact.

Now if he could just get a certain brunette to tell him what the hell had panicked her tonight.

Chapter Three

Trent was a man on a mission when he stepped into his boss's office at the Fourth Precinct building. Lieutenant Ginny Rafferty-Taylor was out somewhere, but he'd spotted Katie going in earlier and wanted a few minutes of face-to-face time with her before the morning staff meeting started.

Instead of asking a pointed question about last night's phone call, however, he paused, unobserved, in the doorway as she dropped to the floor.

"Where did I put that stupid pencil?"

He did a poor job of keeping his eyes off the bobbing heart-shaped curves of Katie Rinaldi's backside as she crawled beneath the conference table in search of the accursed writing instrument. Thank goodness Lieutenant Rafferty-Taylor was nowhere to be seen, because he was failing miserably at professional detachment. He stood there like a man, not a cop, admiring the view, savoring the stronger beat of his pulse until Katie's navy blue slacks and the mismatched socks on her feet disappeared between two chairs.

With temptation out of sight, Trent's brain reengaged and he swallowed a drink of his coffee. The hot liquid burned a little more common sense down his throat, reminding him that he was at work, the fellow members of KCPD's cold case squad were gathering in the main room outside with their morning coffee and case files, and Katie had made it clear that—no matter how she twisted up his insides with this gut kick of desire—she only wanted to be friends.

I love you, Trent. I always will. But I'm not in love with you.

Man, had that been a painful distinction to make.

He'd felt an undeniable pull to this woman since he was fifteen years old and she'd moved in with her aunt across the street from the home where he'd grown up. Although he'd been a jock and she'd been into the arts, proximity and a whole yin and yang thing of opposites attracting had played hell with his teenage libido. When she'd gotten pregnant their senior year, his idealistic notions about the dark-haired beauty had dimmed. But when she disappeared, and he'd played a small role in helping her get safely home, an indelible bond had been forged between them, deeper than anything raging teenage hormones could account for.

After her return, she'd talked him into singing in a musical play with her and he'd discovered he liked driving her back and forth to rehearsals and hanging out with her. They'd dated a few times their senior year of high school. Well, he'd been dating, hoping for something more, but Katie had always pulled back just when things were getting interesting.

She didn't mean to be a tease, and had always been straight with him about her feelings and concerns. It just wasn't easy for her to trust. He understood that now better than he had ten years ago. She'd grown up with an abusive father, witnessed her mother's own murder at his hand.

She'd survived a kidnapping, but lost the good friend she'd been trying to help when she'd gotten involved with the kidnappers in the first place. She'd had an infant son before graduation and had to learn about being a mother.

Katie had every right to be cautious, every right to insist on standing on her own two feet, every right to protect herself and her son from getting attached to someone who'd thought he was going to make a career for himself in another city. She wouldn't risk the stability she provided for Tyler. She wouldn't risk either her or her son possibly getting hurt. He'd admired her for her stubborn strength back then. Still did. Understanding why she wouldn't give them a chance, Trent had accepted the dutiful role of friend and gone off to play football in college and take his life and dreams in a different direction. Some dreams died or morphed into other goals. He'd come back to Kansas City, come home to be a cop.

He might be a different man than the teen he'd once been. But the rules with Katie hadn't changed. One wiggle of that perfectly shaped posterior, one flare of concern that all was not right in her world, shouldn't make him forget that.

Besides, a man had his pride. Yeah, being built to play the defensive line made him a little scary sometimes. But he wasn't completely unfortunate in the looks department. He had a college degree and a respectable job, and his parents had taught him how to treat a lady right. He didn't have to pine away for any woman. He dated. Okay, so a lot of those dates—like Erin Ballard last night—had been set up by Katie herself, but he could get his own woman when he had to. He'd even been in a couple of long-term relationships. It wasn't as if he was a saint—he enjoyed a woman's company.

Trent drank another, more leisurely sip of coffee, cooling his jets while he remembered his purpose here. He anchored his feet to the carpet, bracing himself. From the grumbling sounds beneath the table, Katie was on a tear about something this morning. A civilized conversation might not be possible. But he'd gotten information from less cooperative witnesses in an interrogation room. He just had to stay calm and make it happen.

A chair rolled across the utility carpet as she popped out on the other side of the table. "You and I need to talk," Trent stated simply.

Her head swiveled around and her blue eyes widened with a startled look, then quickly shuttered. She knew he was talking about last night. But she blithely ignored the issue between them. "I have to find that pencil first." It was hard to feel much resentment when her bangs flew out in a dozen adorable directions after she raked her fingers through the dark brown waves and stood. "It's the second one I've lost today. I don't have time for this. I'm making my presentation to you guys this morning and—"

Trent tapped the back of his neck, indicating the bouncy ponytail where an orange mechanical pencil had been speared through her hair.

She buzzed her lips in a frustrated sigh and pulled the pencil from her hair. "Thanks."

He stepped into the room to keep their conversation private from their friends gathering outside the office. "You called me—"

"Trent, please." Katie gestured to their team leader's empty desk. "I have to get everything ready for the meeting before the lieutenant gets back."

Fine. He'd ease into the questions he had for her. As long as he could get her talking to him. Trent glanced over at the empty desk where the cold case squad's team leader usually sat. "Where is she?"

"The lieutenant got called into Chief Taylor's office for an emergency meeting. She said she'd be back in time for the team briefing."

"Emergency?" That word and news of an impromptu meeting with the lieutenant's cousin-in-law, aka the department's top brass, wasn't something a cop wanted to hear at the beginning of his shift. He eyed the other members of the team through the glass window separating Lieutenant Rafferty-Taylor's office from the maze of detectives' desks on the building's third floor. Max Krolikowski, his partner, along with Jim Parker and Olivia Watson, stood together chatting, apparently as unaware as he as to what the emergency summons might be. Katie's frenetic movements weren't exactly reassuring. "Any idea what's up?"

"Not a clue." She unplugged a cord, inserted a zip drive and pulled up a file on her laptop. When she looked up at the dark television screen at the opposite end of the conference table, she groaned and circled around the table to fiddle with the TV. "It's not my job to keep track of every bit of gossip that comes through the KCPD grapevine. The lieutenant was heading out when I came in. She told me to go ahead and set up for the staff meeting. So, of course, the wireless connection is on the fritz, and I had to track down extra cords. Then I realized I left one of the files in my bag and hadn't uploaded the pictures yet, so I had to go back for that. And now the stupid TV—"

"Take a breath, Katie."

"*You* take a breath," she snapped, spinning to face him.

"Really? That's your witty repartee?"

"I mean…" Her eyes widened like cornflowers blooming when her gaze locked on to his.

Accepting the remorse twisting her pretty mouth as an apology, Trent crossed the room to inspect the closed-circuit television. He tightened a connector on the side of the TV and turned the screen on for her. "There. Easy fix."

"Thanks." She bent over her laptop, resuming her work at a more normal pace. "I'm sorry. That was a dumb thing to say. I was going on like a chatterbox, wasn't I?"

"There's something buggin' you, I can tell. But it's just me, so don't sweat it."

"I'm not going to take advantage of your cool, calm collectedness. You didn't come to work so you could listen to me vent."

"But I do want to hear about last night."

She arched a sable-colored brow in irritation. Okay. Too soon to press the subject. Just keep her talking and eventually he'd get the answers he needed.

Trent reached around her to set his coffee and notebook in front of the chair kitty-corner from hers. Although Katie was of an average height and curvy build, she'd always seemed petite and fragile. It didn't help that she'd kicked off her shoes beneath the table, while he'd tied on a pair of thick-soled work boots this morning to shovel his sidewalks, blow the snow off his driveway and walk the dog he'd taken in around the block. Despite her uncharacteristic flashes of frustration and temper, and the static electricity that made the strands of her ponytail cling to the black flannel of his shirt, she seemed pretty and dainty and far too female for the cells in his body not to leap to attention whenever he got this close to her.

"You seem a little off your game this morning." He spoke over the top of her head, backing away from the enticement of making contact with more than a few wayward strands of hair. "You know something about the lieutenant's emergency meeting that you're not telling me?"

"Nope. She was business as usual."

"Is Tyler okay?"

"He's fine. I swear." Katie tilted her gaze up to meet his, confirming with a quick smile that that much, at least, was true. Then she went back to work on her laptop. She swiped her finger across a graphic on her screen and loaded the image of several mug shots up onto the larger screen. "I guess he's a little ticked at me. There's this stray dog that he's gotten attached to running around the theater this past week. He wants a dog so badly, it's at the top of his Christmas list. But our landlord won't allow pets. I mean, the dog is friendly enough, but he's skin and bones. I feel so bad for him, especially in this weather. Apparently, Tyler's been feeding him."

"A tan dog with a white stripe around his neck?"

"Yes. How did you…?" Her cheeks heated with color as she tilted her face up to his. "You went to the theater last night. I told you everything was fine."

Trent propped his hands at his waist, dipping his head toward hers. He matched her indignant tone. "No, you told me you'd *handle* whatever it was. If everything is fine, you wouldn't need to handle anything."

"Well, I don't need you to rescue me every time something scares me."

"What scared you?"

She paused for a moment before waving off his concern and turned back to her computer. "That's not what I meant."

"Then give me some straight answers. Something hinky was going on outside that theater. Either you saw something, or you at least suspected it." He wrapped his fingers around the pink wool sleeve of her sweater and softened his tone. "Something that *scared* you, and that's why you called me."

She hesitated for a moment before shrugging off his touch. "You were on a date."

"The date was over."

"Because of me?" She turned in the tight space between the table and chair, her forehead scrunched up with remorse.

He tapped the furrow between her brows and urged her to relax. "Because I wanted it to be."

She batted his hand away, dismissing his concern. "Trent, I don't have the right to call you whenever I need something. I'm not going to wimp out on being a strong woman and I don't want to take advantage of our friendship. We shouldn't have that you're-the-guy-I-always-call-on kind of relationship, anyway. You need to…find someone and move on with your life."

"I'll make my own decisions, thank you. I call you when I need something, don't I?"

"Sewing a button on your dress uniform is hardly the same thing."

"Look, you and I know more about each other than just about anybody else. We've shared secrets and heartaches and stupid stuff, too. That's what people who care about each other do. Now—as a friend who doesn't appreciate phone calls that make him think something bad has happened and he needs to drop everything without even taking a shower and speed across town in a snowstorm—"

"You didn't—"

"—I need you to tell me exactly why you called last night. And don't tell me you were frightened of that sweet little dog, who, incidentally, is spending the day at the vet's office while the Humane Society is checking to see if he's been reported missing."

Her eyes widened again. "You rescued the dog?"

"You wouldn't let me rescue you. Now answer the question. What scared you last night?"

"Nothing but my imagination. I'm sorry I worried you. The dog's okay?"

She changed topics like a hard right turn in a high-speed chase.

Trent shrugged. This woman always kept him on his toes. "I fed him some scrambled eggs and gave him water. He spent the night whimpering on a blanket in my mud-room, but he didn't have any accidents. Don't know if he's housebroken or just too scared he'll get into trouble and get dumped out someplace again. I took him to the vet's this morning for a thorough checkup and a much-needed grooming. My truck still smells like wet, stinky dog."

"Thank you." Her lips softened into a beautiful smile. When she reached out to squeeze his hand, he squeezed right back. "Thank you for saving him. I wanted to, but I'm not sure Tyler would understand having to take him to a shelter instead of taking him home."

"It looks like I'll be fostering Mr. Pup for a while. Until the Humane Society can find out if there's an owner or put him up for adoption. Maybe Tyler can come visit him."

Katie shook her head, whipping the ponytail back and forth. "Don't tell him that. He'd be at your house every day after school."

"You know I don't mind having Tyler around."

"I know. But… Mr. Pup? Tyler calls him Padre."

Trent nodded. The name fit. "Like a priest's collar. That's what I'll call him, then. Now, about last night…" He could do the sharp right turns, too. But her frustrated huff warned him he'd have to coax the answers out of her, just like he'd coaxed Padre into trusting him. "You have to give me something, Katie. You know I won't quit."

"I know." Her blue eyes tilted up to meet his briefly. Her gaze quickly dropped to the middle button of his shirt, where she plucked away what was most likely a couple of dog hairs. The nerves beneath his skin jumped as her fingers danced against his chest. But he couldn't allow himself to respond to the unintended caress. This was distraction. Nervous energy. Something on her mind that kept her from focusing. There was definitely something bothering Team Rinaldi this morning. "I have to get ready for the meeting."

"Every morning, you've been bragging about Tyler and the play you guys are doing. This morning, all you're doing is apologizing and fussing around like it's your first day on the job." Outweighing her by a good hundred pounds wasn't the only reason he wasn't budging. He covered her hand with his, stilling her fidgeting fingers. "Talk to me. Use words that make sense."

"Calling you was an impulse," she conceded. "Once I got my act together, I realized I shouldn't have bothered you."

Nope. He still wasn't budging.

Trent felt the whisper of her surrendering sigh against his hand. "They didn't need me backstage last night, so I was doing some work on my laptop out in the theater auditorium. I found a connection between an old double missing-person case and some new stuff we're working on. I got caught up following the trail through the reports and I lost track of the time."

This was remorse talking, maybe even a little fear, he thought, as she slowly tilted her gaze to his again. "I couldn't find Tyler when I was done. I mean, eventually I did. He was by himself in the parking lot, waiting for me. Everyone else had left and he was locked out of the building. And then I thought I heard… I swear someone was…"

"Someone was what?" He gently combed his fingers through her scattered bangs, smoothing them back into place.

"I thought someone was watching me. The lights went out, so it was pretty dark, and while I was looking for Tyler in the dressing rooms, some guy pushed me down and ran outside."

Trent's fingers stilled. His grip on her hand against his chest tightened. "A man attacked you? Are you hurt?"

She brought her other hand up to pat his, urging him to calm the blood boiling in his veins. "This is why I don't tell you things. It wasn't an attack. The dark always freaks me out a little bit, and my imagination made things seem worse than they were. Once I found Tyler with Padre, everything was fine."

"You don't know what that guy was after."

"He wasn't after me. Maybe I interrupted a break-in. Or some homeless guy snuck in to get out of the cold and he got scared by the blackout, too. He just wanted me out of his way so he could escape. Doug Price is going to give me grief tonight for not picking up the mess I left in the dressing room, but I wasn't hurt. I was more worried about Tyler."

He didn't care about whoever Doug Price was, but if he gave Katie grief about anything, he'd flatten him. "Did you report it?" She hadn't. "Katie—" His frustration ebbed on a single breath as understanding dawned. "You called *me*." Hell. He should have investigated inside the building instead of letting the dog distract him from his purpose. He should have gone straight to Katie's apartment when he didn't find her and Tyler at the theater, even if it was the middle of the night and he woke them out of a sound sleep. "I'm sorry. If I'd known what kind of danger you were in—"

"It wouldn't have done any good. By the time I found Tyler and went back to take a couple of pictures, anything suspicious I'd seen was gone." Katie quickly extricated her hands from his and nudged him out of her way. "I wasn't in any real danger. I was being a lousy mom last night. Guilt and reading that file about the missing teen and her baby made me imagine it was something more." She picked up a stack of briefing folders and distributed them in front of each chair around the table. "Except for that message."

Oh, he had a bad feeling about this. "What message?"

She tried to shrug off whatever had drained the color from her face. "Some prankster wrote something creepy in the snow behind the theater."

"And then he swept it away."

Katie spun to face him. "Yes. But how did you…? Right. You were there. And you don't quit."

He propped his hands at his waist. "What did the message say? Something about breaking in to the theater?"

She hugged the last folder to her chest. "I don't know if it was even intended for me."

"What did it say?" he repeated, as patiently as he'd talked to Padre.

"'Stop or someone will get hurt.'"

He dug his fingers into the pockets of his jeans, the only outward sign of the protective anger surging through him. "Stop what? Who'll get hurt?"

Her shoulders lifted with silent confusion. She didn't

have those answers. "Maybe he thought I was chasing him. I wasn't. The darkness freaked me out and kept me from thinking straight, and all I wanted to do was find Tyler to make sure he was safe. If I hadn't panicked, I'd have handled things better, and I wouldn't have ruined your evening."

Trent plucked the folder from her grasp and set it on the table. "You lost track of your son. That's supposed to frighten a parent. Don't beat yourself up about it. You said he's okay, right?"

She nodded. "We're both fine. Thanks for worrying."

"Thank you for sharing. Now maybe I won't worry so much."

She moved back to her computer and manipulated the pictures again. "I'll believe that when I see it."

They *did* know each other well. "Honey, you know I'm always going to worry—"

"You shouldn't call me *honey*." Katie glanced toward the window to the main room. "The rest of the team is here. I need to finish setting up."

Chapter Four

If that woman worked any harder at pushing him away, she might as well slam Trent up against the wall. "At least promise me you'll keep a closer eye on the people around you. If somebody was lying in wait for you—"

"I promise. Okay? Just let it go." Katie stepped around him as Max, Olivia and Jim came in, their animated conversation masking the awkward silence in the room.

"You're killing me here, Liv," Trent's partner, Max, groused. "A Valentine's Day wedding? You're already making me shave and rent a tux."

Olivia breezed past the burly blond detective, the oldest member of their team, taking her seat at the table. "Just because you and Rosie eloped to Vegas doesn't mean the rest of us don't want to share that special day with friends and family."

Max jabbed his finger on the tabletop, defending his choice in wedding arrangements. "Hey. I wanted to make an honest woman out of Rosie. And you know how her last engagement turned out. She wasn't interested in dragging out the process any more than I was."

Max's new wife had barely survived the nightmare of her first engagement to an abusive boyfriend and had become a recluse as a result. Meanwhile, Max had been fighting his own demons when the two had first met and clashed during the investigation into her ex-fiancé's unsolved murder. Mixing like oil and water, it was a wonder the prim and proper spinster and the rugged former soldier had ever gotten together at all. But Trent had never met two misfits who were a better match for each other. Max brought Rosie out of her shell, and she'd uncovered a few civilized human qualities that Trent's rough-around-the-edges partner had lost in the years he'd been dealing with post-traumatic stress. Max had been shot twice and Rosie nearly drowned solving that case. But the close calls had made them willing to risk everything and seize the love they'd found.

Trent might be a little envious of his older friend settling into the sort of relationship he'd once wanted with Katie Rinaldi, but he was happy for his partner. And he had been honored to fly out to Las Vegas to stand up for the couple.

"As soon as the doctor cleared me to travel, I made the reservations. There wasn't time to send out invitations." Max reached over to thump Trent's shoulder as he pulled out a chair to sit beside him. "At least I took the big guy with us."

Trent grinned, thinking he'd better join the teasing banter before anyone questioned the tension between him and Katie. "And then you put me on a plane back to KC twenty minutes after the ceremony so you two could get started on the honeymoon."

Max grinned. "Hey, I'm ugly. Not stupid."

Olivia was smiling suspiciously, working her cool logic on Max. "Maybe, since you cheated Rosie out of the whole white-wedding thing, she'd like to put on a fancy gown and see you all dressed up for once in your life. I've yet to see a man that a tuxedo couldn't make look good."

"I'd love to see her in a beautiful dress like that." Was the old man on the team blushing? Who'd have thought? Still, Max grumbled, "You're determined to make me miserable, aren't you?"

Jim Parker grinned and pulled out the chair beside his partner. "Maybe he's worried you're going to make him dance with you at the reception, Liv—after Gabe, your dad and your brothers, of course."

"And Grandpa Seamus," Olivia added. She pointed to Max. "But you are definitely on my dance card after that." She wiggled her finger toward Trent. "You, too, big guy. You all agreed to be our ushers, so it's tuxes and boutonnieres for everyone."

Max put up his hands in surrender. "There's only so much froufrou a man can take, Liv."

Jim propped his elbow on the arm of his chair, leaning over to back up Olivia. "I don't know, Max. There are few things I like better than slow dancing with my wife. Natalie's pregnant enough now that when we're close, I can feel the baby kicking between us."

Max scrubbed his palm over the top of his military-short hair and muttered a teasing curse. "Okay, Parker. Now you've gone too far, buying into all of Liv's romantic mush." Knowing full well he was going to eventually buy into it, too, Max turned back to the lady detective. "I thought you were a tomboy."

Olivia smiled wistfully. "My wedding day will be the exception. I'm the only female in my family. You don't think those boys all want to throw a big party for me? Dad insists on me wearing the veil of Irish lace that Mom wore at their wedding, and I want to. It's a way of honoring her memory and making me feel like she's there with us." The mood around the entire table quieted out of respect for Olivia's mother, who had died when she was just a child. But the detective with the short dark hair didn't let the room get gloomy. "Besides, Gabe looks gorgeous in a tux, and I refuse to have him looking prettier than me."

"Impossible," Max teased. "But if you're going all formal, then I guess I can put on a tie."

"Thank you for your sacrifice." Olivia smiled before turning her attention to Trent. "What about you? Will we see you dancing the night away at the reception?" She snapped her fingers as an idea struck. "You should bring Katie."

The brown ponytail bobbed as Katie's head popped up from her laptop screen. "Me? Like a date?"

Trent groaned inwardly at the pale cast to her cheeks. Did she have to look as if the possibility of attending a friend's wedding together was such an out-of-left-field idea?

"If you want." Olivia chided the low-pitched whistle and sotto voce teasing from Jim and Max before smiling at Katie. "Stop it, children. Believe me, I understand better than most about the department's no-fraternization policy. But even though we're part of the same team, technically, you work in two different branches—information technology and law enforcement. Besides, I was thinking practicality. Trent's an usher and you're still going to be one of my bridesmaids, right?"

"Of course. I was honored you asked me to be a part of the ceremony, but…" Katie's apologetic gaze bounced off Trent and back to the bride-to-be. "I was going to bring Tyler as my date."

Olivia seemed pleased by that answer. "Even better. I'd

love to see the little man again. All three of you should come together."

Even though they hadn't gone out on a date together in nine years, it seemed as though everyone thought of Trent and Katie as a couple. Maybe the others even took it for granted that they were destined to be a family unit one day. The only people who knew it was never going to happen were Trent and Katie themselves.

Sinking into his chair, Trent took another long swallow of his coffee. He watched the strained expression on Katie's face relax as the two women talked about Tyler. Her round face and blue eyes animated with excitement as they wagered whether her nine-year-old son would make as much of a fuss about dressing up for the special occasion as Max had. Katie was a different woman when she talked about her son. Her eyes sparkled and the tension around her mouth eased into a genuine smile.

No wonder she'd been so upset about losing track of Tyler last night. Tyler was her joy, her reason for being— her number-one excuse for shunning Trent and any other relationship that threatened to get in the way of taking care of her son. It wasn't that she didn't care about Trent as a friend, but she'd given her heart to another male nine years ago.

Max's fist knocked on Trent's chair below the edge of the table. Trent took another drink before meeting his partner's questioning look. "You okay, junior? You're pretty quiet this morning."

"You're loud enough for the both of us."

Max grinned at the joke as he was meant to, but his astute blue eyes indicated he wasn't buying the smiles and smart remarks. "There's that whole tall, dark and silent thing you do, and then there's stewing over in the corner.

You two were duking it out in here before we came in, weren't you?" His gaze darted over to Katie and back to him. "Seriously, what's the problem? Is it you? Katie? Is the kid okay?"

Trent swore under his breath. There was no subtlety to Max Krolikowski, no filter on his mouth. When he saw a problem, he fixed it. When he cared about something or someone, he went all in. Hell of a guy to have backing him up in a fight, but best friend or not, Trent wasn't sure the man he'd been partnered with on the cold case squad was the guy he wanted to confide his frustration and concerns about Katie to. "She basically told me to mind my own business."

Max dropped his voice to a low-pitched grumble. "You think something's up?"

Even if Trent wanted to share his suspicions about blackouts and prowlers and threats in the snow, he wouldn't get the chance to. All conversations around the table stopped as Lieutenant Ginny Rafferty-Taylor rushed into her office. "Are we all here?" The petite blonde officer set her laptop and a stack of papers at the head of the table before going back to shut the door. "Sorry I'm late."

Trent set down his coffee and turned everyone's focus to the police work at hand. "Ma'am. Katie said you had an emergency meeting with Chief Taylor?"

The older woman nodded. "Seth Cartwright from Vice and A.J. Rodriguez from the drug unit were there, too. I'll get right to it since it affects investigations in each of our divisions."

"What affects us?" Jim asked.

"Leland Asher."

Trent's mouth took on a bitter tang at the mention of

the alleged mob boss whose name kept popping up in several of their unsolved investigations.

Olivia leaned forward at the familiar name. "What about him? Gabe's first fiancée was writing a newspaper exposé about Asher when she was killed." Olivia and Gabe had solved that murder, but they hadn't been able to prove Asher had hired the man who'd shot the reporter.

Even Katie, who had never dealt with Asher directly, knew who he was. "His name shows up as a person of interest in several investigations in the KCPD database. Has he been arrested for one of those cases?"

"Not likely," Max said. "He has a great alibi for any recent crimes. He's currently serving a whopping two years for collusion and illegally influencing Adrian McCoy's Senate campaign."

"Not even that, I'm afraid." Lieutenant Rafferty-Taylor shrugged out of her navy blue jacket, hanging it over the back of her chair before sitting. Her back remained ramrod straight. "Asher's case went to appellate court on a hardship appeal. The chief just got word that Asher is being released from prison early, on parole. That's what good behavior and a pricey lawyer will do for you."

A collective groan and a few choice curses filled the room.

"Any chance the judge made a mistake?" Trent asked.

Their team leader shook her head. "It's the holidays, Trent. I think Judge Livingston was feeling generous. Chief Taylor wanted to alert us that Mr. Asher will be back on the streets, albeit wearing an ankle bracelet and submitting to regular check-ins with his parole officer, sometime tomorrow or Thursday."

"Well, merry Christmas to us," Max groused, folding his arms across his chest. "Just what we need, a mob boss heading home to KC for the holidays. I bet the crime rate doubles by New Year's."

For a moment, the petite blonde lieutenant sympathized with her senior detective, but then she opened her laptop, signaling she was ready to begin their morning meeting. "I know we believe Leland Asher is the common link to several of the department's unsolved or ongoing cases. The chief wanted us to be fully informed so we can keep an eye on him. Without our efforts turning into harassment, of course," the lieutenant cautioned.

"I'm willing to harass him," Olivia volunteered with a sarcastic tone. Max pointed across the table and nodded, agreeing with the frustration-fueled plan. "What's the point of solving these old cases if a judge is going to let the perpetrators go with little more than a slap on the wrist?"

Trent could feel the tension in the room getting thicker. Cold case work wasn't an easy assignment. Sometimes evidence degraded or got lost. Witnesses passed away. Suspects did, too. Memories grew foggy with age. And perps who'd gotten away with murder or other crimes that hadn't yet reached their statute of limitations grew confident or complacent enough over the years that they weren't likely to confess. So when the team built a solid enough case to convict someone, it sure would be nice if they'd stay behind bars for a while.

"Are we moving any cases we think Asher might be a part of to our active files?" Trent asked.

The lieutenant nodded. "We should at least give them a cursory glance to see which ones to follow up on. I believe we can use this to our advantage. Katie, will you flag those files and send each of us copies for review?"

"Yes, ma'am." Katie's head was down and she was already typing. By the time she looked up to see Trent grinning at her geeky efficiency, she was hitting the send button. She smiled back before turning to the lieutenant. "I just ran a search for Mr. Asher's name, and all those files should show up on your computers by the time you get back to your desks."

Trent gave her a thumbs-up before turning back to the others. "It'd be a hell of a lot easier to prove Asher's connections to those crimes by seeing who he interacts with on the outside."

Lieutenant Rafferty-Taylor nodded to him, probably appreciating how his suggestion cooled the jets of the others in the room, especially his perennial Scrooge of a partner, Max. Then she gestured to Katie at the opposite end of the table. "Speaking of connections, Katie, you said you've come up with something we need to look at in your research? Shall we get to work?"

"Yes, ma'am." Katie shoved her bangs off her forehead and glanced around the table as everyone waited expectantly. Trent winked some encouragement when their gazes met. She smiled her thanks for his support before looking down at her laptop. She highlighted the first picture on the television screen and turned to point to the gathering of mug shots she'd posted there. "Detailed information is in the folder in front of you, but you can follow the gist of what I think might be a significant discovery up on the screen." As Trent settled in to listen to the presentation, the rest of them did, too.

"As you all know, Lieutenant Rafferty-Taylor has had me copying and downloading all of our old print files of unsolved cases into a database and cross-referencing them. There are still more boxes in the archives, but those are cases that are thirty years or older. I'm focusing on more recent crimes where the perpetrator and potential witnesses are likely to still be alive."

Max whistled. "You've already been through thirty years of open and unsolved cases? Hell, you're making the rest of us look like a bunch of goldbricks."

"Not a chance, Max." She laughed at the gruff man's teasing compliment. "I've been doing this pretty steadily since spring. And I didn't get shot up and have to go on sick leave, either."

Trent nudged his partner. "Or run off to Vegas to get married before reporting back for active duty." Katie's dedication explained a lot of her late nights and the pale shadows under her blue eyes. But was all this unpaid overtime she'd put in the reason she had no time for a relationship? Or was it the thing she chose to do to fill up the empty hours in her life so she wouldn't miss those relationships? "What did you find out?"

Katie curled a leg beneath her to sit up higher in her chair. "When Olivia was investigating Danielle Reese's murder last spring, she came up with her *Strangers on a Train* theory, and it got me to thinking."

Olivia nodded. "*Strangers on a Train*, as in the Alfred Hitchcock movie where two people meet and agree to commit murder for the other person."

Her partner, Jim, continued, "But since they've never met before and don't run in the same social circles, the one with the motive can arrange for an alibi, while the one who actually commits the crime won't pop as a suspect on the police's radar because he or she has no motive to kill the victim."

"That's why we arrested Stephen March for Dani Reese's murder." Olivia braced her elbows on the table and leaned forward. "The evidence says he's good for it.

But he had no motive. I still believe he was blackmailed into doing it, or—"

"He murdered her in exchange for somebody else killing Richard Bratcher," Max finished. Trent reached over and rested a hand on his partner's shoulder. March and Bratcher were sensitive subjects for the stocky detective because Stephen March was his wife's younger brother, and Bratcher had been the bullying fiancé who'd abused Rosie Krolikowski. Max nodded his appreciation at the show of support. "We got Hillary Wells for Bratcher's murder, even though she barely knew the guy." He turned his attention back to Katie. "Are you saying that you did your brainy thing and finally found where March and Dr. Wells could have met and set up their murder bargain?"

"Not exactly."

"What exactly are we talking about, then?" he asked.

"I designed a program to search for commonalities between cases by looking for key words or names or places. What I discovered is a pattern between several crimes that occurred over the last ten years."

"A pattern?" the lieutenant asked.

Katie nodded. "I haven't been able to prove that they're all linked to one particular case, or even to just one person, but I've made some interesting connections between these six suspects and—" she swiped her finger across her laptop, changing the images "—these six victims."

Trent recognized the pictures of both Dani Reese and Richard Bratcher, the victims Stephen March and Hillary Wells had killed. He also recognized the stout cheeks and receding hairline of Leland Asher. "It's not an exact swap where Suspect A kills Victim B while Suspect B kills Victim A. It's more as though they're links in a chain."

The lieutenant urged her to continue. "Do you have specific examples of those links?"

"Yes, ma'am." Katie adjusted the display to bring the twelve images up side by side before she twirled her chair to the side and got up to touch the television screen. Her ease in front of an audience reinforced Trent's suspicion that whatever had had her so flustered earlier had to do with the details about last night, maybe something that she still hadn't shared with him—not a presentation to her boss and coworkers involving multiple murders. "It's a painstaking process, but as I put in more information from the reports, I've come up with links from unsolved cases to people or events from murders you all have closed earlier this year. Some of these seem pretty random, but in a place the size of Kansas City, the fact that these people may have come into contact with each other at all seems compelling to me."

Olivia tried to follow Katie's line of reasoning. "Some of the connections are obvious. Stephen March killed Danielle Reese. Dani was investigating Leland Asher. Hillary Wells murdered Richard Bratcher, and he was the man who was abusing Stephen's sister, Rosie March."

Max swore under his breath. "Don't remind me."

She pointed to the photo of a distinguished white-haired gentleman. "This is Dr. Lloyd Endicott, Hillary Wells's former boss and mentor. He died in a suspicious car crash that has yet to be solved. We suspect he's the man Dr. Wells wanted to have killed, since she took over his company and the millions of dollars that went with it."

Although Trent sometimes worried that Katie's knowledge of all these dusty old cases bordered on the obsessive, he couldn't deny how useful it was to have a walking, talking encyclopedia working on their team. He pointed to the image of a professional woman with short dark hair. "Does Hillary Wells or any of those other suspects or victims connect to Leland Asher?"

Katie nodded. "You might be surprised to know that before she died, she worked out at the same gym Matt Asher does."

"Leland's nephew?" Trent shifted his gaze to the image of a young man in a suit and tie who wore glasses and bore a striking resemblance to Leland Asher. "You think the two of them knew each other?"

She shrugged. "I can't say for certain unless I dig into the gym's schedule, class and personal trainer files, but the opportunity to meet was certainly there."

"It would be easy enough to go to the gym and ask some general questions to see if anyone ever saw the two of them together," Trent offered.

The lieutenant nodded. "Make a note to do that."

"Yes, ma'am."

"I don't have any evidence that Hillary Wells and Leland Asher ever met." Katie pointed to the nephew and then to Leland Asher. "But Max discovered that Matt regularly visits his uncle in prison."

Olivia nodded. "I'm guessing he's in the family business, although we haven't been able to prove that he's guilty of anything illegal. But he's down in Jefferson City nearly every week, so you know he must be passing messages to and from his uncle. Leland could have ordered Hillary to kill Richard Bratcher."

Jim Parker agreed. "It'd make sense for Matt Asher to keep the family business running while Uncle Leland is incarcerated. Where are his parents? Is his father involved in any of Leland's criminal activities?"

"There's no father in the picture. I did a little research

through Social Services and found what I could on his mother. She's Leland's sister—never married. It's in your folders. Isabel Asher overdosed when Matt was eleven—ten years ago." Katie pointed to the image of a blonde woman who had probably once been a knockout before the blank, sunken eyes and sallow skin in the photograph marred her beauty. "That's why she was in the system—she was fighting an ongoing addiction to crack cocaine, was in and out of rehab. There were several calls from teachers about neglect. After Isabel's death, Matt Asher went to live with his uncle."

Max tipped his chair back and said what they all suspected. "The dope was probably supplied by her brother's import business. If not, he'd certainly have the money to buy her whatever she wanted."

Jim concurred. "Access to her brother's wealth would make her a prime target. Let me guess, there's a boyfriend she used to shoot up with. Asher blamed him for his sister's death and that guy's in one of your dead files?"

"Well, Francisco Dona did have a couple of arrests in his packet, but he can't be involved in any of our more recent crimes." She highlighted the mug shot of a dark-haired lothario with long, stringy hair and a goatee. "He died in a motorcycle accident shortly after Isabel's death."

"Are we sure it was an accident?" Trent asked.

Katie drew a line from Francisco Dona to Lloyd Endicott. "Well, even though one rode a motorcycle and the other drove a luxury car, the sabotage to the engines was similar."

"As if both crimes had been committed by the same person?" Max sat up straight, his gruff voice incredulous. "Wow, kiddo. You're thorough."

"It's a thing I do. I like to poke around. Solve puzzles. It's just a matter of getting access to the right database."

Lieutenant Rafferty-Taylor threw a note of caution into the mix. "And having the legal clearance to access that database?"

"Yes, ma'am." Katie's lips softened with a sheepish smile. "Either I've got departmental clearance or it's public access. I haven't needed a warrant to put together any of this information, although there are places I could dig deeper if I did have one. I've sent out feelers to businesses, doctors, private citizens and so on to update our records. Some are eager to answer questions and help. Others don't even respond. Of course, I could find out more if…" She twiddled her fingers in the air, indicating her hacking skills. Trent had no doubt that Katie could access almost any information they needed—but the way she'd obtain it wouldn't stand up in court and no conviction would stick.

The lieutenant smiled. "We'll work within legal means for now. Continue with your report. This is already good stuff we can follow up on."

Trent read through the slim report on the dead socialite. "Says here the detectives assigned to the case suspected foul play in Isabel Asher's death. They thought it might be a hit by a rival organization to send a message to Asher. So you think Francisco Dona made a deal with someone to kill her?"

Katie nodded. "There was no conclusive evidence in her KCPD case file, although that's an angle the detectives in the organized crime division investigated before it was closed out as an accidental death."

Olivia thumbed through the information in her folder. "You *have* been busy. These deaths all happened within a general time frame, six to ten years ago. It makes our *Strangers on a Train* theory plausible."

Jim dropped his folder on the table, shaking his head. "But there are six murder victims here. And we've only solved two of them. And we haven't linked either of those conclusively to Leland Asher ordering those murders. You said this guy is getting out this week. If we can't pin something solid on him, we'll never get him back in prison." The blond detective looked from the lieutenant back to Katie. "Is there any place else where all of their killers could have met with Asher? Even randomly?"

"You mean like sitting together at a ball game? I haven't found anything like that yet, but…" Katie sat back in her chair and drew lines from one picture to another on her computer screen, giving them all a visual of her extensive research. "Leland Asher was diagnosed with lung cancer two months ago. The doctors suspect he's been suffering longer than that."

Their team leader nodded. "That probably helped prompt his early release as well—so the state doesn't have to pay for his medical treatments. What else?"

"Either Matt Asher or Leland's girlfriend, Dr. Beverly Eisenbach, have been to see him every week while he's getting radiation treatments and chemo shots." Katie drew another line. "Matt and Stephen March both saw Dr. Eisenbach as teens for counseling. Hillary Wells ran Endicott Global after Dr. Lloyd Endicott's death, and Dr. Endicott belonged to the same country club as Leland." The grumbles and astonished gasps around the table grew louder as the links of this twisted chain of murder fell into place. "Isabel Asher was Leland's sister and Matt's mother, of course. Roberta Hays was the DFS social worker assigned to Matt's case. And…"

Trent looked up from the notes in his folder when she hesitated. "What is it?"

She circled the image of a haggard-looking man with graying hair. "I found a connection to me in here."

"What is it, kiddo?" Max asked, voicing the others' surprise and concern.

"Roberta Hays's brother is Craig Fairfax."

Ah, hell. Trent recognized the name from Katie's past. *That* was what had truly scared her. He sat forward, extending his long arm to the end of the table. He reached for Katie, his fingertips brushing the edge of the laptop where her hands rested on the keyboard. But she curled her fingers into a fist, refusing his touch. That didn't stop him from asking the question, "You discovered Fairfax in your research last night?"

Her gaze landed on his, and she nodded before explaining the significance of that name to the others. "He's the man who kidnapped me when I was seventeen. He tried to take Tyler from me as part of an illegal adoption ring. He and his sister Roberta—who used her position with Family Services to scout out potential candidates like me—are both serving time now."

No wonder she'd gotten obsessed with her work and lost track of both Tyler and the late hour last night. Trent was already sending a text of his own, verifying that Craig Fairfax was still locked up in a cell in Jefferson City and not running loose on the Williams College campus.

"What's his connection to cold case?" the lieutenant asked, gently reminding Katie of the focus of the team's investigation. "Does he fit in with our *Strangers on a Train* theory? Can we tie him to Asher's criminal organization?"

Katie nodded. "Mr. Fairfax was diagnosed with prostate cancer earlier this year." She drew one last line on the computer screen from one sicko to another. "He's in the same prison infirmary with Leland Asher."

Chapter Five

"You need me there to back you up?" Max Krolikowski's voice was a deep growly pitch over the cell phone Trent slipped beneath the edge of his black knit watch cap as he climbed out of his truck at the Williams College auditorium.

"Nah, brother," Trent answered, flipping up the collar of his coat against the clear, cold night. He turned his back to the bitter wind blowing from the north and strode across the cleared pavement toward the massive brick building. "This is personal. We're off the clock."

"Doesn't mean I won't be there in a heartbeat. I owe you for helping me keep an eye on Rosie this summer." Max chuckled. "Besides, I decided I like ya. I'd hate to have to break in a whole new partner."

Trent laughed, too. "Nobody else would have you, you grumpy old man."

"Bite me, junior."

"Love you, too." Stretching out his long legs, Trent stepped over the snow piled between the sidewalk and curb. He noted that the parking lot was crowded with cars and the pavement and sidewalk had been cleared from one end to another by plows. There'd be no footprints to follow tonight unless the perp he believed had been spying on Katie was dumb enough to trek through the drifts. But if the guy who'd shoved her to the floor was that kind of dumb, Trent intended to be here to have a conversation about keeping his distance from the Rinaldi family. "Hey, did you ever hear back from the gym Matt Asher belongs to?"

"I thought we were off the clock."

"I'll stop thinking about these unsolved cases when you do."

Trent's booted feet quickly ate up several yards walking around to the front lobby doors of the building while Max grinched around in the background. When his partner came back to the phone, Trent knew he'd been checking the facts in his notebook. "Since the manager didn't seem to know much when we visited this morning, I stopped by on my way home and chatted up the afterwork crowd. Several people recognized Matt Asher and Hillary Wells, but couldn't remember if they'd ever seen them in a conversation with each other."

Trent figured with the discrepancy between their ages—Matt barely being twenty-two and the late Dr. Wells being a professional woman in her forties—that any conversation more intimate than a polite greeting between the two of them might stand out enough to make an impression on at least one of the other gym members. When he suggested the idea, Max concurred. "Asked and answered. No one I spoke to could recall either Matt Asher or Hillary Wells being in the same room together, much less sharing that they were looking for a way to have someone killed."

The sharp wind bit into Trent's cheek when he turned to the front doors. He hunched his shoulders to stay warm. "So that's not our connection between the two of them.

Still, eliminating the gym doesn't mean she didn't have some other connection to Leland Asher."

"So we keep digging."

Trent nodded. "I'll ask Katie if she's come up with any-place else that can tie the two of them together."

"Or tie Dr. Wells directly to Asher." Trent heard a soft voice in the background, then something that sounded suspiciously like lips smacking against each other. Max's gruff tone softened. "Rosie says to tell you hi—"

"Hey, Rosie."

"—and invite you over for dinner sometime before Christmas."

"I accept. Will you be there, too?"

"Wiseass." Trent grinned at the reprimand he heard in the background. "Um, the missus says I need to mind my manners. Maybe Friday before we all go see the little man in his play?"

"Sounds like a plan."

"Give me a call sometime to let me know if anybody else tries to bother Katie. She's part of the team, too. I don't like the idea of anybody messin' with one of us."

"That's why I'm here. If nothing else, I'm going to make sure she and Tyler aren't the last ones here and walk-ing by themselves to their car again." Trent held open one of the glass front doors for a pair of chattering, bundled-up coeds who must have been leaving an evening meeting or practice in one of the fine arts classrooms. He barely saw their bold smiles and flirty eye contact. He silently be-moaned the idea that their interest in him sparked amuse-ment rather than any fraction of the pull that a few ponytail hairs clinging to his shirt had that morning. "Ladies," he acknowledged to some silly giggles before they hurried past him and he signed off on his call to Max. "I'll keep you posted."

As soon as he stepped into the lobby out of the wind, Trent pulled off his cap and stuffed it into a coat pocket along with his phone. He removed his gloves and unzipped his coat before heading across the worn marble floor to the auditorium's dark red doors.

He stooped a little to peer through the cloudy glass window near the top of the door and saw a hazy tableau of the Cratchit family lifting their pewter mugs in a toast. He smiled when he spotted the little boy with the old-fashioned crutch tucked beneath his arm. Tyler's smudged face was easily the most animated of all the children onstage as he said his lines. There was a lot to admire about Katie's son. Trent didn't remember having that much confidence at that age, except maybe playing sports—but certainly not speaking in front of an audience. "Way to go, Tyler."

Trent shifted his gaze to the sloping rows of seats in the shadows between the lobby and the brightly lit stage. There wasn't much of an audience to be nervous about tonight. There was a skinny, graying man in a turtleneck pacing back and forth between the curved rows of seats. There were some obvious family of the cast scattered around, one running a handheld video camera, another snapping pictures with her phone. And there sat Katie beside a pile of coats in a chair in the middle of it all. Her downturned head made him think she was working on something in her lap instead of watching the rehearsal. Her laptop? Didn't that woman ever take a break from work? Was there something obsessive about learning the truth about that long-missing girl? Or was Katie reading more about Craig Fairfax, the man who'd tried to steal an infant Tyler from her and murdered her high-school pal Whitney Chiles?

"Come on, Katie Lee." His low-pitched whisper reverberated against the glass. She carried the weight of too much life experience on those slim shoulders. She didn't need to take on any more trouble. "Just enjoy the show."

If Katie was going to put in overtime making sense of the cases the team was working on, then he should do the same. Remembering his main reason for driving out here tonight, Trent detoured up the stairs to the tech booth in the balcony. He pulled out his badge before knocking on the door. The two men inside running lights and sound seemed willing enough to chat.

"Detective Trent Dixon," he identified himself, learning the men's names were Chip and Ron. "You guys know anything about a power outage here in the auditorium last night?"

"Yeah, I heard about the blackout," Chip, a balding man in metal-framed glasses, answered. "And how Katie foiled a break-in. But that's not on me. I locked up the booth when I left. And the work lights in the auditorium and backstage were still on. I walked out with Doug Price, the director. He turns everything off when he leaves— after the cast and crew are gone."

Only an innocent woman had been left behind in the dark. "Is there a way to turn off the work lights but turn on the rope lights to see backstage?"

Chip pulled down the lights at the end of the scene, then raised them slightly for the stage crew to come on and change the set for the next scene. Then he nodded. "The rope lights just plug in. Unless there was a power outage and everything in the building was dead, it'd be easy enough to throw a few switches backstage yet leave those on."

So the details Katie had shared about last night meant the blackout was deliberate. But whether the intent had been to trap her inside the theater or to cover up an intruder's escape, it was impossible to tell. "Did you see any signs of someone tampering with your light board?"

"It was just like I left it."

Ron, the sound guy with his cap sitting backward on his head, agreed. "The booth was locked up tight when I came in at six to set the microphones for rehearsal tonight. If anybody was in here, he had to have a key."

"And the director is the only person in the play with a key?" Trent would make a point of introducing himself to Doug Price.

Ron shrugged. "Except for campus security. Or maybe someone in the theater department. But all their productions are done for the semester. That's why we can be in here now."

The crew left the stage and both Chip and Ron went back to work. "Lights up."

Trent thanked them for their cooperation and went back down to the auditorium, sneaking in the back while Ebenezer Scrooge and the ghostly Spirit of Christmas Future walked onstage. After his eyes adjusted to the semidarkness, he spotted Katie's hot-pink sweater and headed down the aisle toward her. When he got closer, he could see that she was looking at a crumpled piece of paper instead of the flat screen of her laptop.

So she wasn't working. But her head was down and she was rubbing her fingers back and forth against her neck beneath the base of her ponytail, as if a knot of tension had formed there. She was so intent on whatever she was reading that she jumped when he slipped into the seat beside her.

"Sorry." He nudged his shoulder against hers to apologize for startling her, then nodded toward the paper she was quickly folding up. "What's that?"

"What are you doing here?" She dropped her voice to a whisper to match his before turning to the coats beside her. "Oh, shoot. I left my bag backstage." Without missing a beat, she stuffed the paper inside the pocket of her coat.

Okay. So that wasn't suspicious. He eyed the navy wool coat where the letter had disappeared. If that was some kind of threat… "Everything okay?"

"What? Oh." She pulled her lime-green scarf from the pile and folded it neatly on top of the coat, burying the missive beneath another layer. Right. So they were back to her keeping secrets and suffering on her own when he knew damn well he could help. "It's Tyler's letter to Santa. He said he doesn't believe in Santa Claus anymore but that he wrote the letter for my sake. I've always sent one out for him…mostly so I can read it and see what's tops on his wish list."

It was a plausible explanation for the frown between her brows. "That's a hard transition to go through the year they stop believing in the magic and hope of Christmas."

The frown eased a tad and she leaned toward him so they could talk without their voices carrying up to the stage. "He's still got plenty of hope, judging by the extent of that wish list. But other than some bad grammar, he sounds…" She sank back against the chair on a whispery sigh. "In a lot of ways he's still my little boy. But in some ways he's growing up way too fast."

Trent stretched out and slipped a friendly arm across

the back of her seat. "That growing-up stuff is inevitable. You do know that, right, Mom?"

She gave his ribs a teasing tap with her fist. "I know. And it certainly beats the alternative." That brief glimpse of a smile quickly faded. "When I think of some of those cases I've read through this year, like that missing teenage girl and baby—like my friend Whitney back in high school—I know we're lucky to be here. But I can't help thinking I've cheated him somehow, that I haven't given him everything he needs, that he feels he has to be all grown-up to take care of me. He doesn't, of course. But maybe he doesn't believe that I can take care of him."

"You're a terrific mom, and he knows that. All little boys want to try on being a man for a while, especially when they know they've got someone there to back them up in case the experiment isn't as exciting or safe as they thought it would be." Trent dropped his arm around her shoulders and pulled her to his side in a friendly hug. "Tomorrow, he'll be a kid again. I promise." When she leaned against him, her fresh-as-a-daisy scent drew his lips to her hair and he pressed a kiss to her temple.

"Don't do that." Her hand at his chest pushed him away and she sat forward in her seat, moving away from the touch of his arm, as well. "If Tyler sees, I don't want him to get the wrong idea about us."

"The wrong idea?" Well, hell. "That peck was just a show of support between friends. A woman is damn well gonna know when I intend my kiss to mean something more."

She turned with a surprised gasp. "Trent, I didn't mean to insult—"

He put up his hand to silence her apology. Yet when his gaze fell on the naturally rosy tint of her lips and lingered, the spike of resentment firing through his blood blended with a yearning he hadn't acknowledged in years. She shouldn't draw that pretty mouth into such a tightly controlled line, and he shouldn't have this urge to ease it back into a smile beneath his own lips. Maybe he had crossed a line without realizing it. Because, right now, every male cell in his body was wishing for a little privacy so he could kiss her just once the way he'd always longed to. But he hadn't had the skills as a teenager, and as an adult he didn't have the permission to even try.

For a long time now, he'd imagined if they could share one real, passionate kiss, he'd find out that this desire simmering in his blood was just the remnants of a teenage fantasy. He'd discover the spark wasn't really there. He and Katie would share a laugh over the awkward encounter, and he'd finally be able to get this useless attraction out of his system. Inhaling a cautionary breath, Trent pulled his hand back to rest on the arm of the seat, letting his shoulder form the barricade she wanted between them.

"It won't happen again." At least, he hoped he could keep that promise. "I'd never do anything to jeopardize my friendship with you or Tyler."

But as Trent faced the stage again, adjusting his long legs in the narrow space between the rows of seats, his eyes were drawn to the show's director, Doug Price. The pacing had stopped and the older man's dark eyes were trained on the seats where he and Katie sat. Tyler wasn't the only one she needed to worry about seeing and misinterpreting a quick kiss.

So, did the temperamental artiste simply dislike the hushed tones of a whispered argument near the back of the theater interfering with him watching his play? Or was there something more personal in the territorial sneer he aimed at Trent and Katie? Did this guy have a thing for Katie?

The flare of jealousy was fleeting, there to acknowledge but quickly dismiss. If there was one thing Trent understood about Katie Lee Rinaldi, it was that it wasn't *him* she was loath to have a relationship with. She didn't want a relationship with any man.

There was no competition here. Trent acknowledged the man's displeasure with a nod and scrunched down in his seat in an unspoken assurance that he wouldn't disrupt the rehearsal again.

But there were even curiouser things afoot when he noticed the Grim Reaper wannabe onstage repeatedly tugging on his mask, using the adjustment of his costume to peer out at the director. And, though it was impossible to track the exact direction of the actor's glare beneath the black hood and mask, Trent would bet money that the guy was taking note of Doug Price's interest in Katie, too.

Trent leaned his head toward Katie and whispered, "Who's the guy onstage?"

She guessed he wasn't talking about Mr. Scrooge. "Christmas Future is Francis Sergel. I made his costume. He's probably getting ready to complain about something that itches or doesn't fit him." She finally relaxed and settled back into the seat beside him. "He's good at that."

"Complaining?"

"Oh, yes." He grinned at the subtle sarcasm that bled into her tone. Although it still rankled that she would have such a strong reaction to that innocent kiss, Trent appreciated her attempt to return them to their normal footing with each other. He wasn't about to completely drop his guard and relax, though, not with the director and twitchy man onstage each sliding them curious looks. "So what's on Tyler's list? You know I like to get the little guy a present every year."

He felt the momentary stiffening in her shoulder where it brushed against his, but she didn't try any awkward evasion of the question this time. "A bunch of video and computer games. I'll give you a list. And a dog. If I'm not careful, he's going to run away from home and move in with you now that you're fostering Padre. That's *his* dog. In his nine-year-old brain, anyway. He barely talks about anything else."

"You know I've got two extra bedrooms at my house. And a fenced-in yard. Tyler is welcome to come over to visit anytime. They can play outside. That dog loves jumping and snuffling around in the snow. I think the cold in his nose makes him a little hyper. He needs somebody Tyler's age who can keep up with him. Heck, maybe I'll even put Ty to work picking up Padre's messes in the backyard."

Katie laughed out loud, then quickly slapped a hand over her mouth when Doug Price swung around to glare at her again. She quickly dropped her voice back to a whisper. "Do it. That'd be the reality check Ty needs to understand that owning a pet is a lot of work and responsibility. It's not just the landlord's rules or me being mean."

"I'll make the offer."

"Douglas!" Trent sat up straight when Francis Sergel jerked the black hood off the back of his head and stepped out of character and walked to the edge of the stage. "I can't work like this."

For a split second, Trent instinctively went on the defensive, worrying that his accusatory whine was targeted at Katie. It wasn't until he felt her hands through the thick sleeve of his coat that he realized he'd thrown his arm out in front of her.

Now, *that* was a look that warned him he'd overstepped the boundaries between them again.

Francis pulled the mask off his face and shook it at the director. "This needs another elastic strap sewn in. It keeps shifting on my face and I can't see."

Doug Price turned his face toward the catwalk near the ceiling and griped, "Spare me from working with these dime-store divas," while the actor playing Ebenezer muttered something similar. Then the director swung around and snapped his fingers. "Katie. Grab your sewing kit and take care of that."

The squeeze of her hands around his forearm kept Trent from answering back about talking to her in that dictatorial tone. Apparently, Katie hadn't been singled out, because the director used the same tone with the actor onstage. "Give your mask to one of the crew, Francis, and finish the scene."

"I need the mask to get into my character." The bearded man with black circles drawn around his eyes needed more than that Grim Reaper robe and makeup to get his creepy on?

"All you have to do is hit your blocking marks and point. Rise to the challenge." Doug gestured to the temperamental actor, then turned again. "Katie? Sooner rather than later, if you would. I'm trying to get an accurate running time on the show tonight."

"My sewing kit is in my bag in the greenroom."

"Then get it." His gaze slid past her to Trent. "And this is a closed rehearsal. Tell your boyfriend to buy a ticket if he wants to watch."

That's it. The need to stand up to that idiot jolted

through Trent's legs. But Katie's hand on his shoulder and a warning look kept him in his seat. She stood and beamed a smile at the director. "He already has."

Trent could have choked on the honey dripping from her voice, but the sweetly veiled retort seemed to appease Mr. Price. With a nod to Katie, the director turned back to the actors onstage. "All right. Let's take it back from your entrance, Francis."

He hissed a whisper behind her back as she moved in front of him toward the aisle. "So kissing you on the head is off-limits, but letting your director think I'm your boyfriend is okay?"

"That's Doug's interpretation, not mine. He saw your picture with Tyler on my computer and..." She looked down at him, her mouth twisted with another apology. "I didn't correct his mistake. Misleading Tyler is one thing. But sometimes, Doug is a little friendlier than I—"

"How friendly? Someday you're going to have to explain the rules—"

"Mom?"

Trent heard the loud whisper from the corner of the stage and peeked around Katie to see Tyler's smudged face peering from the edge of the heavy velvet curtain. The tiny dimple of a frown appeared between his feathery eyebrows, reminding him of Katie when she was stewing over a problem. Had he heard Price yelling at her? Had he seen the two of them arguing? Did he think he needed to protect his mama?

"Douglas? Now I have to deal with this?" When Mr. Death up there pointed to the little boy showing his face onstage, Trent shot to his feet, grabbing Katie on either side of her waist and moving her to his side. If he turned that snooty temper on Tyler...

But Katie Lee Rinaldi had already made it clear she could protect her son her own self, thank you, very much. "It's okay," she said in full voice. She stayed Trent's charge to her defense with a hand at the middle of his chest. She nodded to the actors and stopped the director before he could open his mouth. Then she curled her thumb and finger into an okay sign and winked to her son. "I'll be right there."

When she tapped either corner of her mouth and modeled a smile for him, Tyler's moment of concern disappeared and he smiled back at her. The boy smiled at Trent and thrust his hand out at waist level, sneaking a not-so-subtle wave to him. Trent put his fingers to his forehead and returned a salute, offering his own reassurance that the child didn't need to worry about his mom or anyone else while he was here.

As quickly as he'd popped out, Tyler disappeared behind the curtain.

"And this hobby is fun for you?" Trent dipped his chin to meet Katie's whispered thanks.

"The creative part of it is. But on this production, some of the people…" Katie's gaze shifted back and forth between Price and Sergel. "Not so much. But don't go all alpha on me. I can handle Doug and Francis. I already know how to deal with children."

His throat vibrated with a chuckle at her sarcasm. "Yeah, but yours behaves better."

Her fingers tangled together with his in a quick squeeze. "Duty calls. Thanks for stopping by. I know Tyler is happy to have you here to watch him. Although I think you make him a little nervous."

Trent tightened his grip to stop her as she scooted past him, surprised at the admission. "I do? I don't mean to.

The whole team is coming to opening night. Will he be okay with that?"

She smiled away his concern. "Relax. Having a few nerves onstage is a good thing. Seeing you will keep him on his toes. He wants to do a good job for you."

Katie made it impossible not to smile back. "Tyler's always first-string in my book."

"He knows that."

"Katie!" Doug yelled. "I need this fixed before the next scene." Trent released Katie's hand and straightened to all six feet five inches of irritated man before shrugging out of his coat and hanging it on the back of his seat, making it clear without saying a word that he was staying and that the lashing out at her needed to stop. The director seemed to rethink whom he could push around by adding a succinctly articulate, "If you please."

"Trent..." She knew what he was doing.

"Go on. I'm doing this very beta style, I promise. I'm just going to sit here until the show's done so I can give Tyler my critical opinion."

"And make sure these guys mind their manners?"

"It's what a boyfriend would do, isn't it?" Trent doffed her a salute, too. He also intended to be here to walk her to her car after rehearsal was done and to make sure nothing *weird* happened tonight. He folded his big body into the seat as if it was the most comfortable chair in the world. "I know Tyler will be my favorite thing about the play."

"Thank you." She turned into the aisle and hurried down to the stage.

Frankly, he wouldn't put up with the bossy overlord and the whiny string bean onstage. But he was here to support Katie and Tyler, not to audition or volunteer backstage for anything himself. All the more reason to find out who had trapped her in the theater and separated her from her son last night. If it was just one of these bozos trying to intimidate her, his presence could put a stop to that. And if it was something more sinister, then the scene of the crime was the best place to look for the answers Katie wouldn't give him.

Like what was in a letter to Santa that could upset her like that?

Once Katie took the mask from the stagehand and disappeared behind the curtain, Trent reached across the empty seat into her coat and pulled out the letter that had dented a worried frown on her smooth forehead. If that story had all been a lie and it was some kind of threat related to last night, and she didn't think she needed to tell him, then… He read the addressee on the envelope out loud. She hadn't lied. "Santa Claus?"

He pulled out the crumpled letter and smoothed it against the thigh of his jeans before reading.

Dear Santa,
I think you might not be real. My friend Wyatt says that his mom is Santa Claus but I know you are not a girl. I'm writing this letter just in case because Jack says your real, and because Mom asked me to write you a letter and it makes her happy when I do what she says. If you do come by on Christmas Eve, I want a dog, a cell phone, the action figures from the movie I saw this summer, gamer cards and a dad. Uncle Dwight is fun to do stuff with, but he is cousin Jack's dad. Jack is in second grade at my school and is fun to play with. Jack's not really my cousin, but it's weird to have an uncle younger than me and Dwight's more like a grandpa. Mom says

our family dynamite is complicated. I want a dad
who can play baseball and computer games, but I
don't want him to be so good that he beats me all the
time. Mom won't let me play any battle games, but I
like the racing games and the ones where you have
to collect stuff and get speshul powers. I found a
dog named Padre at rehersal. He can be mine if you
want. If you can catch him. He likes peanut-butter
sandwiches. A dad with a dog would be the best.
Your friend,
Tyler Rinaldi
PS: I live in an apartment, so you will have to come
in the front door because we don't have a chimney.
I can leave it unlocked.
PSS: Jack wants a racing car set and boxing mitts.
PSSS: I don't want one of those little girlie dogs
with a bow in her hair.

A dad? Tyler had asked Santa for a dad? No wonder
Katie had fretted over the letter. There were at least two
things on this list she couldn't give her son, and that had
to be difficult for a single mom who wanted to give the
world to her child. And yeah, Tyler did sound a little like
a cynical grown-up in a couple places. But this was still
the voice of a little boy speaking from his heart.

Trent felt a few sentimental pangs pulling on his heart,
too. He'd known Tyler since the boy was an infant and
his neighbor Maddie McCallister—now married to DA
Dwight Powers—had taken the rescued baby in to care for
him until she and Dwight had tracked down the missing
Katie and broken up that illegal adoption ring.

The illegal adoption ring headed by Craig Fairfax.

Craig Fairfax, the man who'd ordered the murder of

their high school classmate Whitney Chiles. The man who'd tried to kill Katie, and Maddie and Dwight, too.

Craig Fairfax, the man who shared a prison infirmary with reputed mob boss Leland Asher, the prime suspect in several of the unsolved cases their team was investigating.

If Katie's thoughts had taken the same dark trail, then she was probably more worried, unsure and afraid than she was letting on.

Trent's nostrils flared with a deep, quiet breath as the cop in him took over once more. He was here to keep Katie and Tyler as safe as they'd let him and to put a name to any threat that might mean them harm. Whether that threat was a frightened intruder; a cast or crewmate with some kind of bitter feelings or obsession toward Katie or Tyler; a convicted killer who might be using a mob boss and his connections to take revenge on the family who'd put him away for life; or even the mob boss himself, who was taking advantage of the inside knowledge he could gain on Katie in some bizarre plan to thwart the cold case squad's investigation into him and his activities—he couldn't leave the family alone and unguarded. No matter how awkward things got between him and Katie, no matter how angry she got at his interference—no matter how painful it was for him to be close and not have what he'd once wanted—he wasn't going anywhere.

The Rinaldis and finding answers to this complicated mix of unsolved cases were his number-one assignment now.

Trent carefully returned the letter to the pocket of Katie's coat and smoothed everything back into place. Then, while the Spirit of Christmas Future and Ebenezer Scrooge resumed their journey through the bleak future that awaited a man who refused to change his miserly ways, Trent pulled out his phone and sent a couple of queries to the KCPD database, checking to see whether Doug Price or Francis Sergel had any kind of criminal record or had been listed as a person of interest in any ongoing cases.

Interesting. Francis Sergel's name didn't show up anywhere until about ten years ago on a DMV app, and the guy had to be in his late forties or fifties. That most likely meant a legal name change for any number of reasons, from annoying enough people in his previous life and needing a fresh start to entering witness protection or something more nefarious. A man with only a recent past also meant a search through databases that Katie would have to access for him. But who would change his name to Francis? Or Sergel? Unless there was some kind of personal significance to the name. That was something else Katie could find quick answers to if he put her on the hunt.

And then there was Douglas Price. His fingerprints were in the system because he used to be a public school teacher. But there was nothing more than a few speeding tickets in his history.

Scrooge was dancing a jig with his nephew's wife and celebrating Christmas when a shadow fell over Trent.

"Don't get on my case about working when I'm off the clock if you're going to do it, too." Katie plopped down in the seat beside him, hugging her bulky canvas carryall bag in her arms. "Did something come up?"

Trent brushed his finger over his phone to darken the screen. "I was doing a little background check on a couple of your friends here." The dent between her delicate eyebrows instantly appeared. But he wasn't going to lie to her about his concerns. "Did you know Francis doesn't show up in the system until around ten years ago?" He nodded toward her bright green-and-blue bag. "You got something in that magic computer of yours that can tell me why he changed his name and who he used to be? Or at least give me an idea why he'd pick that name?"

"Francis?" She opened the flap of her bag and pulled out her laptop. "You think he's suspicious?"

"I'm a cop, Katie. I'm suspicious of everyone until I have an explanation that makes sense." He clipped his phone back onto his belt and rested his forearm on the chair between them. "I just want to make sure we've got nothing to worry about from any of the people around you."

"I told you last night I probably got in the way of an intruder."

"Then why mess with the lights? Why go to the extra effort to threaten you?"

"You think someone here… That Francis would…?" She pulled out a smaller remote gadget, turned it on and set it on the chair beside her. Then she dropped her bag to the floor and set her laptop on her knees. "Okay. What do you want me to look up? Legal cases? Witness relocation? Criminal profiling reports?" She reached over and tapped the back of his hand as she turned her open laptop toward him, urging him to look at the display screen. "Trent?"

"Son of a bitch." Trent felt his temperature go up, even as her fingers chilled against his skin.

There was a message scrawled in lipstick across the screen.

Stop what you're doing.

"That message last night *was* meant for me."

Chapter Six

Max Krolikowski strode onstage to join Katie, Tyler and the other members of the production company Trent had gathered to ask a few questions. Max dangled a plastic bag with a tube of lipstick inside. "I found this in the makeup supplies in the dressing rooms. The tip's worn flat and it looks like a match to the color on Katie's laptop. The case has been polished up, though." He glanced down at Katie, sitting in one of the dining table chairs on the set. "Either you guys are fanatics about cleaning up, or somebody's wiped it for prints."

She appreciated Trent's partner answering the call as soon as Trent had phoned and requested backup— "Somebody got to Katie again."

But right now she was wishing Max wasn't such a good cop and that the evidence relating to that disturbing message hadn't been so easy to find. Katie shook her head, not liking the implication. "We're not fanatics."

There was no longer a plausible option to dismiss the weird things that had happened to her at the theater. Someone was watching her. Someone was taking advantage of the opportunity to frighten her. And he was succeeding. She'd made a life for herself behind the scenes now—at work, at the theater—putting her son first. Being thrust into the spotlight by an anonymous stalker didn't feel so good.

Trent thanked the mother who'd been taking pictures with her phone and dismissed her and her daughter. "Let's take the tube, anyway. Maybe the lab can get a latent or DNA off it or the laptop." His big shoulders lifted with a shrug that Katie didn't find very reassuring. "So far, everybody's been cooperative, but no one saw anyone or anything that seemed out of place backstage. That makes me suspect someone here, whose presence wouldn't be questioned. Someone who's better at lying than I am at detecting it. I'm not sure where to take this next."

"You'll figure it out, junior. We just keep asking questions," Max advised, dropping the lipstick into the paper sack where her computer had already been tagged and bagged as evidence. He rolled up the top of the sack, then paused when he saw Katie watching him. "You're okay if I do this, kiddo? Will you need this for work tomorrow? I know you and your computer are attached at the hip."

Attached at the hip, hmm? Apparently, not closely enough.

"It's okay, Max," she assured him. "I ran a quick diagnostic myself. It doesn't look as though anyone messed with any of the files or programs, and I have everything backed up on a portable hard drive. Plus, I have a desk computer at home and at work."

Katie rubbed her hands up and down her arms, trying to erase the chill beneath her cardigan and blouse. She couldn't help but let her gaze scan the faces of the remaining cast and crew sitting onstage or in the audience seats. Had the makeup kit from the dressing rooms merely been an item of opportunity for an outsider? Or was someone involved with the play a better actor than anyone suspected? And what did any of this have to do with her?

Trent's cool gray eyes passed over her, winking a silent version of *hang in there* before he turned to Doug Price and repeated the question he'd already asked. "Did you see anything that looked out of place earlier this evening? Anyone you didn't recognize?"

Doug's grayish-blond eyebrow arched up with disdain. "Besides you?"

Max folded his arms over his sturdy chest. "Answer the question."

Perhaps thinking better of crossing the detectives who'd taken over his rehearsal, Doug eased his taut features into an imitation of a smile. "Look, I'm as concerned about Katie's safety—about the safety of everyone here— as you are, Detective. The entire cast and crew were here tonight. In fact, I think it's the first time since we started rehearsing that no one's been absent because of illness or a conflict. The kids all have a parent or guardian who comes to rehearsals with them, too. I won't allow any of the little minions to be unsupervised."

"So you're saying there were more people than usual here tonight," Trent clarified. "And you knew all of them?"

Doug considered his answer for a moment before crossing to the edge of the stage and pointing to the back corner of the auditorium. "There was a man here filming the scenes with the children. I'd never seen him before. I assumed he was a father who'd come instead of the moms who are usually here."

"Oh, my God." Katie's stomach twisted into a knot. There'd been a strange man filming Tyler and the other children? She instantly sought out her son, playing a card game with Wyatt on the stairs leading down to the seats.

He must have felt her concern because he looked up at her and frowned. Damn it. She was worrying him again. Better than most, she knew what it was like to be afraid for a mother's safety. She shouldn't be scaring him.

A large hand closed over her shoulder. She glanced up at the sudden infusion of warmth and support. But Trent was asking her for information as much as calming her fears. "Did you recognize this man?"

Her gaze drifted out of focus, trying to visualize the man she'd only glanced at in passing. "I didn't know him. But I assumed the same thing—that he was someone's dad."

"Can you describe him?"

"The camera was in front of his face when I saw him. Brown hair. Brown wool coat. Um, dress shoes instead of snow boots." She blinked her eyes back into focus. "His camera was a digital Canon with a mini zoom lens. Black woven strap around his neck. Sorry, that still doesn't give you a name or face."

Trent grinned. "Leave it to you to notice the tech. And don't apologize. This is a lot more than I knew a second ago." Even as he jotted down the limited description, she saw him checking the people remaining in the theater. Katie didn't see anyone who matched her vague description, either.

"Trent?"

A tug on Trent's sleeve turned him away from her. Katie watched her son's eyes tip up to the man who towered above him.

"What is it, buddy?" Trent dropped to one knee, putting himself closer to eye level with Tyler. "Do you know the man I'm asking about?"

Tyler shook his head. "There wasn't any dad here

except for Kayla's. She gets to stay with him this month, and it was his turn to watch us backstage. He doesn't have much hair at all."

Trent nodded at the matter-of-fact explanation. "What's Kayla's dad's name?"

"Mr. Hudnall."

When Trent glanced back at Katie, she filled in the blank for him. "Willie Hudnall. We all signed up to take different nights to supervise the children backstage. He was in the greenroom with the kids when I went back to fix Francis's mask."

"So he was there when your laptop was unprotected. He could have written that message there."

She hated to think the man she'd been grateful to for checking on Tyler twenty-four hours ago might now be a suspect. "My point is, I would have recognized him if he'd been the man in the audience. We all would have. Plus, Mr. Hudnall was wearing hiking boots, not dress shoes."

Max nodded to Trent and pulled out his phone. "I'll give the description we have to campus security. Find out if they've seen anyone like that."

While Max took a few steps away and made the call, Katie gestured to the others remaining for this official Q and A. "There are more than two dozen people backstage at any given time. More if you count the crew. Any one of them could have..." She pulled Tyler onto her lap and hugged her arms around him. She looked again. Looked closer. Maybe the enemy was right here. A friend in disguise. One of the people she trusted—one of the people she trusted with her son.

Trent rose in front of her, reading her distress. "Any one of them could have left you that message."

"But why? What am I doing that's such a threat to

anyone? I'd rather think it was that stranger. I know these people. I've been hanging out with them almost every evening for weeks now. Some of them have become friends." She shoved her fingers through her bangs, willing some sort of clarity to reveal the truth. "What does it mean? What am I doing that I have to stop?"

A noisy harrumph from the front row drew Trent's attention. "You got something to say, Mr. Sergel?"

Francis might have cleaned off his makeup, but wearing street clothes as black as the costume he wore in the play, and taking the stairs two at a time on his long, spidery legs, he still bore an ominous look that would keep Katie from ever trusting the man. "Just that Ms. Rinaldi keeps flirting with our director."

"Excuse me?" What was wrong with this guy to give him such a petulant mean streak? "I don't flirt with anybody."

Although he spoke to Trent, his beady, dark eyes were focused squarely on Katie. "Maybe someone resents that she's drawing attention to herself and trying to make her or Tyler Doug's favorite."

Katie shot to her feet, holding on to Tyler's shoulders to keep him from tumbling to the floor. "Are you kidding me? I haven't done anything to make Doug think—"

"Doug's the one who keeps hitting on Mom," Tyler piped up.

The director's head swung around, as if he'd dozed off during the part of the conversation that didn't concern him. "I beg your pardon?" He took a step closer. "I was simply being friendly. You keep to yourself so much, I wanted you to feel included."

"My mom doesn't even like you, and you're too old to be a dad," Tyler argued. "You should leave her alone."

"Tyler!" More shocked by her son's choice of defense than by Doug lying about his interest in her, Katie turned him to face her. "What do you know about men hitting on women?"

"Mo-om." Tyler rolled his eyes. "I watch TV. I know stuff. And I watch you, too. Doug's always asking you to go somewhere after rehearsal."

"And I always say no."

Trent stopped the mother-son conversation with a hand on her arm and turned their attention back to Francis. "Are you jealous, Sergel?"

"I only have the best interests of this production in mind."

"If the boss is paying more attention to the pretty lady than to the show onstage, that bothers you?"

"Well, of course it does. I think it bothers all of us."

"So you have a problem with Katie and Mr. Price being friends," Trent reasoned. "Would you like her to stop doing that?"

Francis lifted his pointy chin. "I am not answering any more questions without my attorney present."

"Have you done something to make you think you need an attorney?" Francis was tall. But Trent was taller. And bigger. He forced Francis to take a step back just by leaning toward him. "Did you deface Katie's computer? Maybe wanted to teach her a lesson? Remind her of her place? You were backstage for most of the play."

"Stop twisting my words around."

But Trent Dixon didn't back down. "I saw you snap at more than one person tonight, including Tyler and Katie. Maybe you're the one who wants to be the director's favorite."

"I refuse to answer any of your accusations. I only want the best show possible, and these two amateurs—"

"We're all amateurs, Francis." Doug Price pulled Francis back beside him. "Stop talking before you say something you'll regret." He turned to the others watching from the audience. "Everyone, please. Detective Dixon, there are children here and it's late. May I send them home? This is all very upsetting and counterproductive to putting on a successful play, and opening night is Friday. I don't think you'll find out anything more tonight. You can get everyone's contact information from Katie's cast-and-crew list if you have more questions. No one knows who this man with the camera was, but I promise you, if he shows his face again, I'll demand he identify himself."

"I want to know what he took pictures of, too."

"Of course." Doug clapped his hands, ensuring that everyone was following his directions and moving toward the backstage exit. "Shall we? I'm sure campus security is waiting to lock up after us."

Trent nodded. "Tell them to go ahead. We'll be right out. Thank you to everyone for your cooperation." Although his smile included the cast, crew and parents filing past them, he had nothing but *I'm watching you* in his eyes for Francis, who didn't move until Doug gave him a nudge and a warning glare.

Doug himself was the last one of the interview group to leave the stage, but he paused and brushed his fingers against Katie's elbow. When she flinched, his grip tightened in a paternal squeeze, and she looked up into light brown eyes that seemed genuinely concerned. "I'm sorry this is happening to you, dear. I hope you'll do whatever is necessary to stay safe."

"Thank you, Doug."

He released her to give Tyler's chin a playful pinch. "Be sure to keep our Tiny Tim safe, too."

"I will."

Trent urged the director to follow the rest of the cast and crew. "Good night, Mr. Price."

Doug's cajoling smile disappeared. "Good night, Detective."

As soon as Doug had disappeared offstage with the others, Tyler rubbed his knuckles back and forth across his chin. "I hate when he does that. He treats me like I'm a little kid."

Salty tears stung Katie's eyes as her *little kid* showed yet another sign of growing up too fast. Despite his token grumble, she pressed a kiss to the crown of his hair and ruffled the dark curls before nudging him to the stairs. "Get your coat on and gather your things. Don't forget your library book for school."

She felt Trent's compassionate gaze on her but couldn't look up to meet it. Not without the tears spilling over. Refusing to turn into an emotional basket case of fear, fatigue and regret, Katie picked up her own coat off the back of the chair and slipped into it.

She was pulling her knit cap on when Max ended his call and rejoined them. "Campus security hasn't seen anybody matching Katie's description of the unknown man tonight, but they'll keep an eye open for anyone matching his general description. I took the liberty of encouraging them to track Sergel and Price's whereabouts when they're on campus, as well. I gave them the plates, make and model of their cars and texted the same to you, in case either one shows up someplace they shouldn't."

Trent was bundling up to face the wintry night, too. "You read my mind, brother. I'll follow up with Katie's list to see if anybody else jumps out as having some kind of motive." He thrust out his hand. "Thanks."

"I'm keepin' tabs on what you owe me, junior. Don't worry." Max laughed as he shook Trent's hand. "I'll make sure everybody else has left before I head to the lab." His goodbye included Katie. "See you two in the morning."

"Good night, Max. Thanks."

The burly detective dropped a kiss on her cheek. "Take care, kiddo." He exchanged a couple of fake boxing moves with Tyler. "You be careful, little man."

"I will. Bye, Max."

By the time the work lights were out and they said good-night to the security guard, Katie's car and Trent's pickup truck were the last two vehicles in the parking lot. Trent set Tyler's book bag in the backseat and knelt down in the open doorway to buckle him in and steal a quick hug while Katie stowed her own bag and started the engine. "You did a good job tonight, Tyler. For a while there, I forgot it was you onstage and thought you were Tim Cratchit. I can hardly wait to watch the whole show on Friday. I'll be sure to tell Padre what a good job you did, too."

"Padre?"

Trent grinned. "Yeah. Your mom told me that was the name you gave him. I picked him up last night. He's going to be staying with me for a little while, until he gets some meat on his bones."

Tyler made no effort to hide his gap-toothed smile—or stifle the yawn that followed. "Tell Padre I said hi. And that I want to come see him Saturday. And don't give him away to anybody until I get there, okay?"

"I won't. I'll tell him you're coming."

Katie looked across her son to the big man kneeling

there and mouthed, *Thank you*. Even though his eyes had drifted shut, her son was still smiling. She buckled herself in. "Good night, Trent."

But when Trent started to leave, Tyler's eyes popped open. "Mom? Do you think anything scary will be written on your computer at home?"

He must have been more aware of tonight's events—and more frightened by them—than she'd realized. She reached across the console to cup his cheek, hating that a nine-year-old should have a worry mark on his forehead. "No, sweetie. I don't see how anyone could get into our apartment. We'll be fine."

He roused himself from his sleepy state and sat up straight. "What if that man who took pictures of us is there? Can we call Trent if we see him?"

Katie was at a loss. How could she make Tyler's fears go away when she wasn't sure what was happening around her and whom she needed to be afraid of? "Sweetie, if you see that man...or anyone who... Of course, we'll call the police. I don't want you to be afraid. I—"

"And you'll stop doing whatever is making him so mad?"

She looked past those wide blue eyes into Trent's, wishing she knew how to answer Tyler's question. Trent's eyes had darkened like steel at the worried timbre in Tyler's voice. He reached into the car and palmed the top of Tyler's head. "Tell you what. I'll follow you and your mom home. Give the place a good once-over before you lock up. I'll make sure nobody's there who shouldn't be." He pulled his gloved hand into a fist and held it out to Tyler. "Sound like a plan, buddy?"

With a nod, Tyler bumped his small fist against Trent's and settled back into his seat.

Trent's gaze sought hers this time. "Are you okay with that?"

Okay with Trent reassuring her son and making sure they were both safe?

Katie nodded. "I'll see you at home."

Chapter Seven

Tyler's head had lolled over onto his shoulder and he was snoring softly in a deep sleep when Katie pulled into her parking space at the apartment complex where the two of them lived near the Kauffman and Arrowhead stadium complex. Trent had pulled into a visitor's space and joined them by the time she had her and Tyler's bags looped over her shoulder, and she was leaning into the car to unbuckle her son.

"Wait." A gloved hand closed around her arm and pulled her aside. "Let me." Trent took her place at the open door and reached in to lift her sleeping child into his arms. "Lock up and lead the way."

With a nod of thanks, she closed the door and locked the car. Then she reached up to tug Tyler's scarf and collar around his face to protect him from the cold night air. Katie was just as aware of Trent's bulky frame blocking the wind as he followed behind her as she was his constant scanning back and forth to ensure that no one seemed unusually interested in the trio coming home late at night. Trent's intimidating stature and the gentle surety with which he carried Tyler against his chest made her feel at once protected and a little nervous. She'd known the teasing Trent, the caring Trent, the solid-as-the-earth

Trent most of her life, and there was a deep comfort in that familiarity. But there was a harder edge to the cop who didn't back off from asking tough questions, his quick ease at taking charge and asserting an authority that allowed no argument, a staunchness under fire that was both exciting and a little unsettling.

Still waters run deep.

The observation lodged in her head and refused to recede as she tapped her key fob against the lobby's automatic door lock, and again to get inside to the bank of elevators that would take them to the second floor. The elevator doors closed and her nose filled with the crisp scents of snow and cold on their clothes, the sweeter scent of a little boy who'd eaten red licorice backstage in the greenroom, and a muskier scent that was male and sexy and not any kind of *boy* next door or old-friend-like in the least.

What was wrong with her tonight? Had those threats stripped away a layer of composure she needed to keep her world in order? Why couldn't she stop analyzing the subtle changes she'd noticed in Trent tonight? He'd matured into a powerful Mack truck of a man who bore little resemblance to the lanky teen she'd once hung out with. The shadow of his late-night beard emphasized the angles and hollows along his cheeks and jaw. He moved with the easy yet purposeful stride of a predator guarding his territory. She'd gotten a glimpse of his temper tonight and been reminded that he was more complex than the nice guy who could make her laugh or make her feel safe. Had she just not allowed herself to analyze his size and scent and changeable demeanor before? Why had she overreacted to a simple kiss to her hair earlier? Why should her curious mind be so fixated on the man riding silently in the elevator beside her?

Even seeing Trent step out of the elevator first to look up and down the hallway to make sure it was clear felt different than all the times she'd had him over for a home-cooked meal or a bit of mending in exchange for putting together a bike for Tyler's birthday or teaching him how to hit a pitched ball or helping her replace a headlight on her car. And when had his jeans started hugging those muscular thighs with every long, sexy stride? *Stop looking!*

Feeling something very close to lusty attraction, and uncertain she wanted to feel anything like that for any man, Katie darted around Trent with her key to get the door open. Her soft gasp of breath at the rustle of her wool sleeve brushing against his nylon coat was like a mental alarm clock, waking her from this ill-timed fascination with the man.

"Make sure it's locked before you insert the key," Trent whispered. "Any sign of a break-in and we're turning around."

Feeling less sure of her relationship with this version of Trent Dixon, Katie obeyed his direction. She twisted the knob and felt the solid connection there. "It hasn't been tampered with."

After unlocking the door and pushing it open, she waited for a few seconds after he carried Tyler past her and inhaled a deep, senses-clearing breath before bolting the door behind her. She bought herself another second to shake off this discomfiting awareness that fogged her brain by taking off her gloves and cap and tossing them on the kitchen table with their bags before following Trent down the hallway to the two bedrooms there.

Trent had Tyler's gloves and hat off and had her son

half sitting on the edge of the bed, half leaning against him. Smiling at the sweet picture of man and boy, and refusing to acknowledge the pang of feminine awareness that instantly warmed her body, Katie knelt beside them. With Tyler's head resting on Trent's ample shoulder, Katie peeled off his jacket and clothes and changed him into the superhero long johns he wore for pajamas.

Katie tucked Tyler under the matching bedspread and sheets and bent over to kiss his soft, cool cheek. "Good night, sweetie. Pleasant dreams."

"G'night, Mom," the sleepy boy muttered. "'Night, Trent."

"Good night, buddy."

Katie turned on his night-light before joining Trent at the open doorway. They watched Tyler for a minute or so until he sighed and rolled over, fast asleep, secure in his own bed. Exhaling her own sigh of relief, Katie backed out of the room and pulled the door to behind them. "Thank you for helping with him," she whispered.

"Never a problem." Trent stuffed his cap and gloves into the pockets of his coat as he followed her to the kitchen. She pulled out a stool at the counter and invited him to sit while she hung her coat, along with Tyler's, over the back of a chair. Then she opened the top of Tyler's book bag and pulled out his homework folder and the remnants of his lunch. Trent unzipped his coat and settled onto the stool while she checked to make sure Tyler had completed his schoolwork at rehearsal.

"Is it too late to offer you a cup of coffee?" she asked, making the effort to sound as normal as she would on any other night Trent visited, despite battling the disquieting urge to shoo him on out of the apartment so she could sort through all these feelings buzzing to the surface tonight and get herself back in order again. "A couple of cookies, maybe? We baked Christmas cookies with Aunt Maddie this past weekend."

"I'm not hungry." He took out his notepad and pen. "I thought of this on the drive over. Before I leave, I want you to check your bag again. Tyler's, too. I want to make sure I've got all the details before I write up my report."

Katie squeezed the brown lunch sack in her fingers and turned to him. "You don't think this is about me? You think he got into Tyler's stuff, too?"

Trent's eyes had cooled from that intense storm cloud from earlier in the evening to an ordinary, calming gray. "I've got no evidence to think that, but I know the best way to get to you is to do something to that little boy. So humor me, okay? I want to make sure I cover all my bases."

Any last chance at reclaiming normalcy vanished at the idea of Tyler receiving one of those disturbing threats. She immediately dumped the squished sack and sorted through a sandwich bag with bread crusts and pretzel bits and an empty applesauce container. She thumbed through the folder of papers, scanning each page to make sure there were no extra messages or bright red lipstick scribbled on one. Checking each pocket of the bag, she found the deck of gaming cards he had been playing with earlier at rehearsal. All the children took books and games to keep them occupied when they were backstage waiting to go on. "This looks like the normal mess I unpack every evening."

"Now yours. Is there anything missing? Anything that's been tampered with besides your laptop? Anything been added that wasn't there before?"

"Some loose things spilled to the bottom of the bag when he pulled the computer out. But it's all my junk."

Katie opened the matching navy, white and lime-green billfold and fingered through some ones and a twenty, along with the receipts she'd tucked in with them. She checked her debit and credit cards, pulling the cards halfway out of their pockets and pushing them back in. "I don't think whoever it was stole any…"

Katie's mind sorted through several snapshots of memories that hadn't meant anything at the time. She touched the clear plastic window where she kept her driver's license and a couple of punch cards for a local coffee shop and pretzel cart. Her shoulders tensed. Oh, no. No, no.

"What is it?" The wood stool creaked as Trent rose to stand beside her. "Katie?"

"These two punch cards are switched around, and the corner of this one is bent. I'm sure it wasn't before. And my license isn't centered like it was before. I think he pulled them out and stuffed them back in. He searched through my things."

"He pulled out your driver's license?" He reached around her to lift the billfold from her grasp and inspect the cards.

"Maybe." She looked up at him over her shoulder. "Do you think he was looking for my home address? If it was someone from the play, our numbers and addresses are already on the cast-and-crew list. Why would he need to check my license?"

"To throw us off the scent? Because he was gone the day Price handed out the contact list? Because he isn't a part of your show?" Trent muttered something under his breath. "Maybe because this twisted perp has some kind of obsession with you?"

Like the bitter wind blowing outside her windows, a chill swept through Katie, freezing her right down to the bone. "Obsession?" Hugging her arms across her waist, Katie shivered. "My father was obsessed with my mom. He didn't like her to be with anybody when he wasn't around. He barely tolerated her being with me. And when she tried to get away from him, to help me get away…" Joe Rinaldi had killed her mother. Katie's vision blurred with tears. "What if this guy shows up here or does something to Tyler?"

Katie was rattled. She was exhausted. And she was afraid. When Trent put an arm around her shoulders, she turned in to his hug. Pressing her cheek against the soft nap of his flannel shirt and the harder strength underneath, she slid her arms around his waist beneath his jacket and let the heat of his body seep into hers.

The other arm came around her at the first sniffle. "I won't let him hurt you, sunshine. I won't let him hurt Tyler, either."

She nodded at the promise murmured against the crown of her hair. But the tears spilling over couldn't quite believe they were truly safe, and Katie snuggled closer. Trent slipped his fingers beneath her ponytail and loosened it to massage her nape. "What happened to that spunky fighter who got her baby away from Craig Fairfax and helped bring down an illegal adoption ring?"

Her laugh was more of a hiccup of tears. "That girl was a naive fool who put a lot of lives in danger. I nearly got Aunt Maddie killed."

"Hey." Trent's big hands gently cupped her head and turned her face up to his. His eyes had darkened again. "That girl is all grown-up now. Okay? She's even smarter and is still scrappy enough to handle anything."

Oh, how she wanted to believe the faith he had in her. But she'd lost too much already. She'd seen too much.

She curled her fingers into the front of his shirt, then smoothed away the wrinkles she'd put there. "I'm old enough to know that I'm supposed to be afraid, that I can't just blindly tilt at windmills and try to make everything right for everyone I care about. Not with Tyler's life in my hands. I can't let him suffer any kind of retribution for something I've done."

"He won't."

Her fingers curled into soft cotton again. "I don't think I have that same kind of fight in me anymore."

"But you don't have to fight alone."

"Fight who? I don't know who's behind those threats. I don't even know what ticked him off. It's just like my dad all over again."

"Stop arguing with me and let me help."

"Trent—"

His fingers tightened against her scalp, pulling her onto her toes as he dipped his head and silenced her protest with a kiss. For a moment, there was only shock at the sensation of warm, firm lips closing over hers. When Trent's mouth apologized for the effective end to her moment of panic, she pressed her lips softly to his, appreciating his tender response to her fears. When his tongue rasped along the seam of her lips, a different sort of need tempted her to answer his request. When she parted her lips and welcomed the sweep of his tongue inside to stroke the softer skin there, something inside her awoke.

Katie's fingertips clutched at the front of Trent's shirt, clinging to the warm skin and muscle beneath. She tried to keep things simple, to indulge herself in a little comfort without forgetting the rules that kept her world in order. But with fatigue, charged emotions and the history between them to combat, the rules suddenly didn't make much sense, and the friendly embrace gave way to a real, passionate kiss.

Sliding her hands up, she smiled at the ticklish arousal of her palms skimming over the scruff of his beard. Trent tasted the width of that smile with his tongue before touching his padded thumb to the corner of her mouth and demanding she open fully for him. With a breath-less moan in her throat, she obeyed. As he plunged his tongue inside to claim her, she was quickly consumed by the searing heat of his kiss.

Trent unhooked the band of her ponytail and sifted the falling waves through his fingers. For a moment, Katie thought they were falling. But she quickly found the an-chor of Trent's shoulders as he sank back onto the stool at the counter and pulled her between his legs. Drawn to the heat that instantly flared between them, she pushed the cool nylon of his coat down his arms and moved in closer. He released her only long enough to shrug the coat off and let it fall to the floor before he gathered her close again. Katie wound her arms around his neck, and his hands slipped down to palm her butt, lifting her squarely into his desire, letting her body fall against his.

Katie melted into his strength. Tears were forgotten as she surrendered to the shelter of his arms and the forth-right desire in his kiss. Each tentative foray between them was welcomed, rewarded. Surrounded by Trent's arms and body, cogent thought turning to goo by a sudden crav-ing for his lips on hers, Katie felt her fears and a lifetime of worry and regret slipping away until there was only a man and a woman, and Trent's heat chasing away the chill of the long night. Such strength. Such gentleness. Such patient seduction. The mother in her went away. The weariness diminished. The loneliness disappeared.

Katie had been kissed before. She'd been kissed by Trent. But he'd been a teenage boy then. She'd been little more than a girl herself. This Trent was all grown man, with hard angles and knowledgeable hands. Her breasts grew heavy and pebbled at the tips, rubbing in frustrated need against the layers of clothing between them. His fingers tugged at the hem of her sweater and blouse, then slipped beneath to sear her skin. He palmed the small of her back, dipped his fingertips beneath the waistband of her jeans and panties to brand the curve of her hip. Denim rasped against denim as he adjusted her between his strong thighs and bulging zipper, stirring an answering need deep within her. This was a different kiss. A deeper kiss. It was a kiss that sneaked around her defenses and made her forget that she was anything other than a woman who hadn't been kissed or held for a very long time.

She reveled in his strength. The passion arcing between them jump-started her pulse and refueled her energy. His raw desire renewed her own confidence and strength. She needed this. She needed Trent.

"Katie," he gasped against her mouth. Her lips chased his to reclaim the connection. This wasn't the time for talking. She heard the deep-pitched chuckle in his throat even as he nipped at the swell of her bottom lip. "Sunshine. The counter's digging into my back. Can't we find someplace a little more comfortable?"

A woman is damn well gonna know when I intend my kiss to mean something more.

Her fingers stilled in the tangle of his hair. This wasn't right. Trent Dixon wasn't supposed to be so all-fired manly and irresistible. She wasn't supposed to want him like this. Katie turned her mouth from the sting of his lips and a kiss brushed across her cheek instead. She brought her hands down to brace them against his shoulders and put a little space between them. Her nerve endings seemed to be short-circuiting. She slid down his body until her toes touched the floor, but she wasn't sure her legs would hold her upright. There were reasons a kiss like this had never happened between them before. She'd forgotten what was important. She'd forgotten Tyler.

She'd forgotten the threats.

Katie needed the cop. She needed the friend. She couldn't afford to lose either one from her life right now.

Finally coming to her senses, Katie blinked his grinning mouth into focus and shoved at Trent's chest. "What was that?"

She would have staggered away if his hands hadn't settled at either side of her waist to steady her. "Maybe it's the way things should be between us."

"No." Her hands dropped to the bulk of his biceps and pushed again. "I'm not going to make any more mistakes."

Trent's grip on her tightened, as if sensing her instinct to bolt. "Where's the mistake, Katie? I know you have feelings for me. And I've never made any secret—"

"I care about you, Trent. But I'm not—"

"In love with me." What was left of his smile disappeared. He set her away from him and reached down to snatch his coat off the floor. He towered over her when he stood. The drowsy timbre of his voice hardened like his posture. "Trust me, I know the difference." She hugged her arms around her waist and stepped out of the way as he shot his arms into the sleeves and shrugged the coat over his shoulders. "That wasn't the kiss of a woman who only cares about a friend. Deny it all you want, but there's something between us."

"Don't do this, Trent. Please. Not now. I don't want to fight."

"This is an adult discussion, not a fight. Maybe I've been reading you wrong all these years, thinking you were just too scared, too wounded to trust anyone completely—that you just needed time to heal. Maybe patience doesn't pay off." He stalked across the kitchen and foyer to the front door.

Katie followed, hating that he saw her like that, like some kind of small, wounded bird. "I don't need you reading me at all. I just need you to leave before I say something I'll regret."

He halted with his hand on the knob and spun around, startling her back a step. "What would you regret, sunshine? You regret having my help tonight?"

"No."

He leaned in closer. "You regret kissing me?"

"Like that, I do. Yes." Katie put up a hand to ward off his advance and planted her feet. "I regret being impulsive."

Trent walked right into the palm of her hand, forcing a connection between them. When she would have pulled away, he caught her hand against his chest. He reached out to brush her hair off her face, his callused fingertips stroking her skin as he smoothed the wayward waves behind her ear. "That's one of the things I've always liked about you. You may be a brainy chick, but you always follow your heart." He laughed, but there was no humor there. "Except with me."

Katie tugged her hand free and backed away from the taunt she felt in his touch. "I can't afford the luxury of being impetuous anymore. I'm not the same person I was when I was seventeen and I thought I could save the world.

I can't afford to be. Not with Tyler in the picture." She crossed to the table and picked up the remains of Tyler's lunch and carried it around the island to stuff it into the trash. "You know how many mistakes that's gotten me into in the past. It's what got me kidnapped by Roberta Hays and Craig Fairfax. It's what got Whitney killed."

"Caring about people isn't why you and Whitney—"

"If someone is targeting me for a reason we haven't figured out yet, then it's all the more important that I keep my head about me and not lose my focus and put Tyler at any kind of risk."

"I would never hurt Tyler. I love him—you know that."

"Yes, and he loves you, too." Funny, the big brute didn't look one bit smaller or any less irritated with her with the quartz counter and width of the kitchen between them. She gripped her own edge of the counter and willed him to understand why she couldn't handle another kiss like that. "What if you and I try to be a couple and it doesn't work out? Other than Uncle Dwight, who's like a grandfather to him, you're the closest thing Tyler has to a dad."

"A dad?"

"You know you're a natural at it. You're that perfect mix of buddy-buddy and making sure the rules get followed. You make him feel safe. And I know what it's like to be a child who doesn't feel safe. I won't put him through that." She blanked her mind to the memories of her father's violent rages against her mother before the remembered fear and helplessness could latch on and draw her back to the past. "If you and I take a stab at a serious relationship and it doesn't work out, then it's going to ruin our friendship and you won't be part of our lives anymore. If that happened, Tyler would be crushed. So would I."

"Why are you so sure we wouldn't work?" Trent crossed to his side of the island. "How do you know?"

"Because I screw things up, Trent." There. He knew that about her, but he'd forced her to say it, anyway. He straightened at the bald statement, his quiet rigidity sucking the charged energy from the room. It was a clever trick she'd seen him use in an interview room, creating an uncomfortable silence that a person felt compelled to fill with an explanation. "It's my fault Mom died. And because I failed her, I thought I could redeem myself by saving Whitney. I jeopardized the life of my own unborn child to help a friend, and she ended up dead, anyway. I nearly did, too." Katie raised her hands in a supplicating gesture. "I can live with my guilt and grief. I might even be able to handle a broken heart if I had to. But that's me. I would never ask Tyler to pay for my mistakes."

His eyes darkened like the shadows of the dimly lit room. "And you think you and me would be a mistake?"

"I can't afford to find out." Her arms flew out as the depth of her concerns pushed aside reason. "Get mad. Storm out of here. I'm sorry I can't be what you want me to be, but please… Think about where I'm coming from and try to understand. I need you to be my friend, Trent. I need you to be the rock in my life you always have been. Tyler needs that, too."

He nodded, as if finally seeing her point. But the man wasn't an interrogator for nothing. He set down his gloves and stepped back from the counter to zip his coat. "What if it *did* work out between us? What if you're robbing us of the chance to be happy—to be a family? I could be a real father to Tyler. And you know I'd be a damn sight better husband to you than your father was to your mom."

Katie carefully considered her answer. She had no

doubt that Trent would make a wonderful parent to her son or any other child. And that kiss? She circled the counter and crossed to the door to throw open the dead bolt and usher him out before those lingering frissons of desire could catch hold again. Common sense had to prevail. She had to make the right choices this time.

"One thing about us, Trent, is that we've always been honest with each other. Screwing up relationships is all I've ever done. And I don't want to fail at us. It would hurt too much. I forgot myself tonight. I was afraid and you were there for me. But I have to think about the future. I'd never want to mislead you, and I would never forgive myself if Tyler got hurt."

"You're asking a hell of a lot from me."

"I know. And it isn't fair. But maybe if we never give in, if we never start…"

She splayed her fingers on the closed door in front of her, feeling as though she'd been caught in a trap of her own making. They already had given in. The mistake had already been made with that little make-out session. Maybe the hurt was inevitable.

"You aren't a screwup, Katie Lee Rinaldi." She felt the heat of Trent's body behind her. "I'm not storming out of here in a temper, I'm not going to abandon you and Tyler when you need me, and I'm sure as hell not going to hit you."

"I know you would never—"

"For what it's worth, your mother's murder wasn't your fault."

"But it was." She spun around, seeing nothing but a wall of dark gray coat. The grit of unshed tears rubbed at her eyes. She hadn't blanked the memories, after all. It had been cold that night, too. There'd been so much yelling, so much pain. So much blood. "If I hadn't skipped my curfew that night, Mom wouldn't have been out looking for me. I was the reason Joe got so mad, the reason he blamed her. And when he slapped me and she said that she'd had enough and we were going to leave him—"

A large hand palmed the nape of her neck, lifting her onto her toes. Then Trent's mouth was on hers again. This kiss was hard and quick, a forceful stamp that drove away the nightmare. His face hovered near hers when he pulled away, and Katie couldn't look away from those dark gray eyes. "Your father was a bully and a bastard, and I'm only sorry that there was no one to stop him from hurting you and your mother back then. But it was *not* your fault."

"Trent—"

He pressed a thumb to her lips to silence any further discussion. "*Not* a screwup," he repeated before nudging her to one side and pulling open the door. Maybe as stunned by his unflinching support as she was by the power of that kiss, Katie hugged her arms around herself, trying to hold on to the warmth he'd instilled in her while he tugged on his cap and gloves. "I have to go home and let the dog out. Lock up behind me. Try to get some sleep. I'm going to put you to work on some research in the morning. In the meantime, I'll make sure someone's watching the building through the night."

"Have I scared you off with my neurotic fruitcake-iness?"

"You won't get rid of me that easily, sunshine." He stepped out into the hallway. There was a trace of the familiar grin she'd grown up with when he glanced back over his shoulder. "Who'd have thought you'd be the one to come up with so many rules? But I'll follow them. For now. You and Tyler will be safe."

The door closed behind him and she threw the dead bolt. But she sagged against the painted white steel when the full promise of Trent's words registered.

For now.

What happened when her by-the-book cop stopped following the rules she'd set down for their relationship? If Trent's patience ran out and he finally started pursuing her in earnest, how would she be able to resist the security and comfort he offered? Where would she get the strength to turn away from that simmering attraction that had bubbled to the surface tonight?

Katie pushed away to turn off the light and head back to her bedroom. She desperately needed some rest so she could be 100 percent in the morning when she saw Trent again—so she could keep their relationship at the normal she needed. If those anonymous threats didn't break her resolve to remain alone and avoid the temporary security of a relationship that was doomed to fail, Trent Dixon's seductive, unflinching determination would.

Chapter Eight

"Come on, Padre." Trent downed the last of the tepid coffee and set the thermal mug in the console between him and the dog curled up in the passenger seat of his pickup. "Are your muscles getting as stiff as mine?"

Well, *curled up* was a relative term. The moment Trent pulled his attention from the sun rising dimly on the horizon behind Katie's apartment building and spoke to the dog, the former Stinky McPooch leaped to his feet and straddled the center console to rest his neatly trimmed front paws on Trent's thigh. The dog's excited posture and wagging tail diffused the weariness permeating every bone in Trent's body. "You're hungry for some action, aren't you, pal?"

An eager slurp across the scruff of Trent's jaw indicated an affirmative answer. With a laugh, he reached over to attach the new leash to Padre's harness, which peeked through the bright red Kansas City Chiefs sweater he'd gotten to keep the dog warm and to make him an easy target to spot when the mutt dug into the snow he seemed to love so much. "All right, all right, I'm moving."

Padre was in his lap, ready to leap outside into the street, before Trent could turn off the engine he'd been running for the heater and pocket the keys. A slap of cold air and a brisk walk would do him some good, too, after sitting outside Katie's building for most of the night. Olivia Watson and her fiancé, Gabe Knight, had voluntarily ended their date early the evening before to stand watch while Trent went home to shower and try to get some shuteye. But he'd only lasted a couple hours before coming back to send Liv and Gabe on their way and watch over the Rinaldis himself. There was already more distance than he wanted between him and Katie, and though she was leery of taking any emotional risks and doubtful of her ability to make a relationship work, he had no doubt about what was in his heart. He wasn't going to let any harm come to the woman and child he loved. They were his to protect, even if they never got the chance to become the family he wanted them to be.

"All right, boy." He scratched Padre around the ears and looked into the dog's dark brown eyes, imagining he could talk more sense into him than he'd been able to with Katie last night. "Now mind your manners on the leash. Let's go."

Leading the dog to the sidewalk while he locked up the truck, Trent scanned up and down the block. Although it had been a relatively quiet night, there was plenty of activity this morning, with folks in the neighborhood out shoveling snow or sweeping the blowing flakes off their vehicles and warming up cars as they got ready to head to work or school. He wasn't the only brave soul out walking a pet, either, and there was even one diehard out for a morning jog who'd already worked up enough exertion to mask his face with a cloud of warm breath.

Trent negotiated a silent compromise with Padre by agreeing to walk faster if the dog stopped tugging on the leash. Besides working the kinks from his muscles after sitting in the truck for so long, Trent figured he could kill two birds with one stone, letting the dog manage his business while he scouted the perimeter of Katie's three-story building along with other buildings and patrons of the neighborhood.

While Padre snuffled through the snowdrifts, Trent took note of faces and locations and whether or not anyone was more interested than they should be in anybody else. On the way back, he located the windows to Katie and Tyler's apartment. Behind the curtains and blinds, the lights were on in the rooms he knew to be her bedroom and the kitchen. He slowed his pace when he saw the shadow moving at the kitchen sink and imagined what she might be doing in there. He wondered if she'd gotten any more sleep than he had.

When they'd kissed last night, Katie had given him a little taste of heaven. She'd forgotten the rules, lowered her defenses and clung to him with an abandon that was even hotter and more reality shifting than he'd imagined it would be between them. But then that brain of hers had to kick in. She'd gotten spooked by the possibility of their relationship deepening into something more, and she'd backed off all the way into her violent and unpredictable past. After all this time, Katie still didn't believe in him enough to trust that he'd be there to catch her when she stumbled. He believed in the two of them together enough for the both of them. But she wouldn't let it happen. She blamed herself for screwing up before there was anything between them to destroy.

Okay, so there were a few things about the woman that made him a little crazy—like holding back details after starting a conversation and refusing to explain herself. Like those damn rules, which he supposed were some kind of survival code in her mind. Still, those were just quirks he had to work around; they were challenges he was willing to meet. Trent tried to think of one thing she could do to make him not want her in his life and came up empty. But until she came around to the idea of a relationship, until these threats against her could be stopped, he'd better concentrate on the job at hand. And maybe get back inside the warmth of his truck. "Come on, Padre."

The tan-and-white collie mix trotted along beside him while Trent noted an older woman coming out of Katie's building, trading a friendly nod and a smile with the man who held the door open for her before hurrying in out of the cold. A businessman was backing out of his parking space in the lot while a family was bundling everyone into a minivan. One of the children said something to the mom and she grumbled, fishing her keys out of her pocket and sending him back inside the building to retrieve whatever he'd forgotten. The maintenance super tossed the last of his rock salt on the front steps and pulled the key fob from his retractable key ring to open the door and go in.

Trent glanced up at the kitchen window again. Katie's shadow had moved on to another part of the apartment, leaving him blind to her exact location. Losing track of her for a few seconds shouldn't make him antsy like this. His tired brain needed to tune in to what was off here.

His gaze shot to the front door again. The skin at his nape burned with suspicion. "Ah, hell."

The man who'd held the door for the older woman hadn't used a key fob to enter the building like everyone else. He hadn't needed to.

Trent's breathing deepened, quickened as he glanced around. Everybody else except for the jogger was dressed for the snow-shrouded December morning. But that man…

Brown hair. Long wool coat. *Dress shoes.*

The alarm going off in his head must have traveled down the leash. Padre danced around his legs and woofed.

"Padre, heel." Teaching the dog a new command, he gave a sharp tug on the leash. Padre broke into a run beside him as they made a beeline for the front door. Trent knocked on the window and peered through the glass to see if anyone was inside the lobby. Where had the man gone? "Katie?"

Then he turned to the bank of mailboxes and buzzed her apartment. "Katie? Tyler, you in there?"

When there was no immediate response, he shook the front door handle. He wondered if he could break the lock with a ram of his shoulder, or if he needed to fire a round into it.

"May I help you?" By now he'd gotten someone's attention. The super in the tan coveralls strolled across the lobby, pointing to the no-pets sign on the glass. "I'm sorry, sir. But that dog—"

"KCPD." Trent slapped his badge against the glass and made the startled man read *that* sign. "Open it now. You've got an intruder in there."

"An intruder? But this is a secure—"

"Now!"

"Yes, sir." Jumping at Trent's harsh command, the older man pulled the fob from his belt and swept it over the lock. "Are we in any danger?" he asked, pulling open the door.

"Katie!" Rushing past the super, Trent sprinted up the stairs to the second floor. Padre kept pace, whining with nerves or excitement when Trent skidded to a stop in front of the elevator. Just as he'd feared, the perp had gotten off on the second floor. Katie's floor. A door opened close by and Trent flashed his badge to shoo the curious tenant back into her apartment. "Police, ma'am. Get back inside."

With a quick scan up and down the hallway, Trent saw the rest of the doors were closed or were clicking shut as other curious tenants retreated at the sight of the hulking detective and vocal dog charging down to Katie's door.

"Katie!" His gaze dropped to the nickel-finished doorknob and easily turned it. Ah, hell. He traced his gloved finger over the telltale scratch marks there and on the dead bolt lock higher up, sure signs that both had been tampered with. He glanced up and down that hallway again. One of those closing doors might be hiding a stalker. One instinct said to pursue his suspicion, but another, stronger urge made him flatten his palm and pound on the door. "Katie Lee! Answer me."

"For Pete's sake, Trent, you'll wake the neighbors." The dead bolt turned and she opened the door. Pulling the dog along with him, he pushed her inside and quickly shut the door behind him and locked the dead bolt. "Come in," she muttered sarcastically. "Bring the beast, too. What's a little fine from the tenants' association? Were you the one buzzing to come up?"

"No one came in? No one's here but the two of you? Why didn't you answer?"

"Slow down, Detective."

Her irritation gave way to confusion as he handed the dog's leash off to her and pushed by to make sure everything was as it should be. A blue-eyed woman with damp, freshly shampooed tendrils bouncing against her neck was running around in gray slacks and a flannel pajama top, carrying a blouse she was probably getting ready to change into for work. Breakfast on the table. Lunch being packed. "Where's Tyler?"

"In the tub. Why is the dog here? What is going on?"

He went straight to the bathroom door, pulled off his watch cap and leaned his ear against the wood, relieved to hear the sounds of a little boy playing with ships in the water on the other side. He checked both bedrooms and the hall closet before rejoining Katie in the main room. "Someone tried to break in."

"Inside the building?"

"At your front door. I must have scared him off." Her knuckles turned white around the dog's leash. He should be outside, checking for signs of the intruder's escape route, making sure he wasn't still lurking in the building. But he couldn't leave Katie unprotected, not until he understood what the hell was going on and had a plan to deal with it. "He'd gotten your knob unlocked. Fortunately, you had the dead bolt in place. You didn't hear anything?"

"No. I was running a bath for Tyler."

Speaking of, a barefoot boy in superhero underpants ran out of the bathroom. "Padre!"

"Tyler," Katie cautioned, "where are your clothes?"

"Mom, Padre came to see me." Dropping to his knees, he hugged his arms around the dog's neck. There was licking and giggling and tail wagging and petting before Tyler jumped to his feet and the dog bounded after him. "Come on, boy. Let's eat."

Tyler paused to give Trent a quick hug around his hips, then ran back to follow the dog as Padre sniffed his way around the apartment. The little boy stopped at the table to scoop up a forkful of scrambled eggs and stuff it into his mouth. Then he stabbed another bite and dropped it to the floor, where the skinny dog gobbled it up.

"Tyler," Katie chided. "Not at the table." She hurried to the kitchen window, where Trent was pulling open the blinds to check outside. Where had that guy disappeared to? If he was still inside, Trent would have to do a room-to-room search, and with eighteen apartments in this building, the guy could stay one step ahead of him, sneaking out while he cleared each space. If he'd already made his escape… "Padre can't be in here. Tyler, you need to finish dressing before you catch a cold." She latched on to Trent's sleeve when he brushed past her to get another view from her bedroom window. "This isn't a friendly visit for Tyler's sake, is it? What's going on?" When she peeked out the window behind him, her tone changed from suspiciously annoyed to simply suspicious. "Who are you looking for?"

Trent looked over the top of her head to see a blur of movement. Son of a… The alarm in his blood reengaged. He caught Katie by the shoulders and turned her attention to the man in a long coat stumbling through the snow. "Him, Katie. Do you recognize him?"

Trent was already backing toward the door as she shook her head and faced him. "Who's that? Why is he running?"

"I intend to find out." Trent pulled open the apartment door. "Lock up behind me. No one comes in except me."

"Trent—"

"Lock it, Katie!"

He had to get to that pervert before he reached whatever vehicle he was headed for. Once he heard the secure click of the dead bolt sliding into place, Trent booked it into overtime, running down the stairs, skipping a few with each stride. He shoved open the outside door and rushed straight across the snowy ground. "Police! Stop!"

The man with the dress shoes might have cold feet, but he was fast. He dashed across the street and climbed into a black sports car. He had the engine revving before Trent reached the pavement. What the hell? Who was this guy? What did he want with Katie?

Trent held up his badge and pulled his gun. "Police! Get out of the car!"

But the perp showed no signs of cooperating. He jerked his wheels to the left and floored it.

Trent planted his feet and took aim as the driver swerved out of his parking stall. "Stop! Or I'll shoot!"

He squinted and turned his face from the pelting of slush and ice crystals. The car roared down the street, and by the time Trent could look back and get a bead on the fishtailing back tires, he realized he didn't have a clear shot. There were too many people around, frozen in their morning routines, some ducking behind their vehicles, others standing in open ground, staring at him—including the curvy brunette with her face pressed to the second-story window.

"Son of a…" His breath whooshed out on a frustrated curse as the car veered around the corner and sped away. There wasn't even time to get to his truck and get turned around to pursue the suspect.

But he wasn't about to give up on finding the answers he needed and putting a stop to the danger escalating around Katie and Tyler. With a wave of reassurance to the people around him, Trent holstered his weapon and pulled out his phone.

Max's gruff voice answered. "It's early, junior, and I'm in bed with my wife. This better be good."

"Apologies to Rosie. I need you to run a plate for me."

The tenor of Max's tone changed instantly and Trent imagined his partner rolling out of bed with an urgency belying his burly stature. "You need backup? Everything okay?"

"No. But I'm not sure what I'm dealing with yet." He strode back up the sidewalk "A guy just tried to pick the lock on Katie's apartment. He drove off after I chased him from the building."

"Hell, I'd run, too, if I had a defensive tackle chasing me down," Max teased, writing down the number Trent gave him.

His partner didn't even question that he was at Katie's this early in the morning. "The perp matched the general description of the guy taking pictures at the theater last night. I want to know why he was here."

"I'm on it. You stay with her. I'll call as soon as I know anything." He heard Max exchanging a kiss and muttering some kind of explanation to his wife. "Anything else?"

"Just get me the info, Max."

"Will do."

"Thanks, brother."

Katie was waiting for him when he knocked on her door. Trent pushed inside and locked it behind him. Baggy plaid flannel draping over those generous breasts shouldn't trigger this instant desire in him, but he'd had a lot of practice ignoring those traitorous impulses around Katie. It was harder, though, to ignore the concern in those wide blue eyes, or to turn away from the wary frown that dimpled her forehead. Trent pulled off his glove and brushed her hair away from her worried expression. He'd barely felt a sample of her warm, velvety skin before she pulled away from his touch.

"Did you catch him?" she whispered, darting her eyes toward Tyler and Padre playing on the floor beside the Christmas tree.

Right. The rules. Although Trent wanted nothing more than to take her in his arms and feel with his own two hands that she was safe, she was in touch-me-not mode this morning. He shook his head and unzipped his coat before crossing to check the lock on the kitchen window. "I got the plate number on his car, so hopefully it'll be enough to ID this guy."

He peered outside to see the sun glinting off the snow and the world turning back to normal before heading through the apartment to ensure that all the access points were secure. A parade of mom, dog and boy followed him through the apartment.

"How did he get in?" Katie asked.

"It's not that hard if you bide your time and have a charming smile."

"He conned his way in here?" She snapped her fingers and shooed Tyler and Padre across the hall when they reached her bedroom. "Clothes. Now, young man." Departing on a three-toned sigh, Tyler grabbed Padre's collar and went into his room. Once she was certain her son was changing for school, Katie tugged on the sleeve of Trent's coat and pulled him into her bedroom. "You're going to scare Tyler if you keep this up."

The fresh, flowery scent that was all Katie was stronger in here. But he conquered the urge to draw in a deep, savoring breath and crossed to the curtains to secure the window and fire escape outside. "The dog will distract him."

"Not entirely. He's a sensitive kid." He shivered at the touch of her fingers at the nape of his neck. But what he'd mistaken for a caress was pure practicality. She held up a palmful of road slush that was melting on his collar, then carried it over to the damp towel tossed across the bed from her morning shower to wipe her hand. "My God, you're a cold mess. You were out there all night, weren't you?"

"Most of it."

"I thought I saw your truck. I couldn't sleep, either, after our...discussion." She reached up and used the towel to dab at the moisture still beading on his neck and jaw. Ah, hell. Now, *that* was a caress. Goose bumps prickled across his skin in the wake of her touch, and her soft sigh teased something deeper inside. But she must have realized she'd crossed the very boundary she'd asked him to respect and quickly pulled away to stuff the towel into the hamper in her closet. Her shoulders came back with a forced resolve and she crossed to the desk she used as a home office. She picked up a stack of papers from the printer there.

"So I did some work, too. I compiled a list of Leland Asher's known associates and ran them through my database to see if there were any hits that matched up. I've been doing it backward—lining up the cases and then looking for connections between them to pop. This time I plugged in a bunch of suspect names we've been tossing around and ran them through the cold case data."

Fine. They were safe for now. He couldn't do a damn thing until he heard back from Max. So he let her turn the conversation to work. "Did you find anything?"

Katie nodded and handed him the papers. "Isabel Asher—Leland's sister—was a sorority sister of Beverly Eisenbach's at, get this, Williams College."

He thumbed through the stack. "The place where you and Tyler are doing the play?"

She pointed to the grainy printout from a twenty-five-year-old college annual. "The blonde in the front row is Isabel. Dr. Eisenbach is on the far left."

"Eisenbach's the shrink who counseled Matt Asher and Stephen March as teens?" He recognized the younger images of the two women who'd each held a spot on the person of interest board at the squad's team meeting earlier in the week. "You think that's how Dr. Eisenbach and Leland met? Through Isabel?"

"You'd have to ask Bev Eisenbach to find that out." She pointed to the date at the bottom of the photo. "But there's a reasonable chance that she knew the Asher family years before she counseled Leland's nephew. This is dated before he was even born. Maybe she's more than Leland's latest girlfriend. Having the previous acquaintance could be the reason he selected her to counsel his nephew, Matt. But if they've known each other since they were in their twenties, isn't it possible that their relationship has gone on for a lot longer than we realized? Maybe she counseled Leland for some reason—grief, stress, dealing with his sister's addiction? She might have confidential information on him that we could use in our investigation. Maybe he even confessed to some of his crimes, or the hits we suspect he paid for. Dr. Eisenbach's practice is one of the offices I've sent requests to for information. They confirmed that Matt Asher and Stephen March were former patients, but any requests for a complete patient list have been ignored."

"This is good stuff, sunshine. Maybe even enough to ask the lieutenant for a warrant to get a look at Eisenbach's records." Trent looked at another picture, this time of a young man with long blond hair or a blond wig, dressed in a Shakespearean costume. "What's this?" The actor's dark, beady eyes looked familiar. "Is this the Grim Reaper?"

Katie hugged her arms in front of her, clearly feeling a little less comfortable with this piece of information. "Francis Sergel about twenty-five years ago. I found him through my facial recognition software."

Trent squinted the name beneath the theater program picture into focus. "Frank Reinhardt?"

"Sergel must be a stage name he adopted. Looks like he's playing Hamlet."

Trent couldn't imagine that walking, talking skeleton of a man playing anything heroic. "He has ties to Asher?"

"Lieutenant Rafferty-Taylor didn't ask me to pursue him as a suspect, so I didn't exactly have permission to dig through criminal records. But after the last few nights at the theater, I wanted to know if I should be worried about him."

Was that what had her squirming inside her own skin— that she'd broken a procedure rule? "I'll request it."

She offered up a wan smile. "Thanks."

"Not a problem. I didn't like Sergel or that Doug Price, either. I want to make sure they check out." He flipped to the next page and skimmed the information. "So Sergel, er, Reinhardt, has a record?"

"Minor stuff. Nothing violent. Possession of narcotics. A DUI. He never went to prison. It was all time served and community service. And court-ordered NA meetings."

"Like Stephen March." And Isabel Asher. And any of a number of pushers and addicts who'd worked for and bought from and crossed paths with Asher's criminal empire.

"A decade earlier, but yes." She sank onto the edge of her bed as if her legs had grown too weak to hold her. She'd made the same realization he had. The team's idea of a *Strangers on a Train* setup behind several of their unsolved crimes could no longer be discounted as a mere theory. "It's a small world, isn't it?"

Trent knelt on the carpet in front of her, relieved to see that she didn't swat away a comforting touch when he rested his hand on her knee. "Cold cases are built on circumstantial evidence more than anything else. There are an awful lot of circumstances that your research has linked together. Now we just have to prove that Leland Asher is behind it all."

Her gaze met his and she tried to smile. "Good luck with that."

"Look, I'm going to take this information and run with it. I'll get Sergel and Price and Dr. Eisenbach and maybe even Leland himself all in for interviews. We'll get the doctor's patient list and see if she counseled Leland. We'll make a case against Asher and put him back in prison where he belongs." He stroked his fingers over the gray wool of her slacks. "But my immediate concern is those threats you've been getting. I've got a call in to Max to see if he can run down the name of that guy who got away. You didn't recognize him, did you?"

"From the back? Running away?"

"He was wearing dress shoes instead of snow boots. Like the photographer you saw at the theater."

The telephone on her bedside table rang and she jumped. Trent squeezed her knee before standing up and giving her the space to move around the bed and answer it. "So that's why he looked at my driver's license."

"If it's the same guy who defaced your laptop, yeah. It'd be easy to find you." Trent caught her by the hand before she left him entirely. "I don't suppose I could talk you into packing a bag for you and Tyler and moving in with me until this all blows over? It's hell sleeping in my truck, and your couch isn't big enough."

He needed her to read between the lines of his teasing tone and understand he was drop-dead serious. *I'm not going anywhere and I'm not leaving you alone.*

Her fingers trembled for a moment inside his grasp before she pulled away and picked up the cordless receiver from its cradle. "Hello? Yes?" Trent watched the color drain from her face. "Who is this? Why are you doing this to me?"

"Katie?"

She punched the button to put the call on speakerphone and held the receiver between them as an electronically altered voice filled the room. "—want to hurt you, Katie Lee. But you've left me no choice. I know what scares you. The dark. A syringe. Your murdering father. Losing your child."

Trent dropped the photos Katie had printed out and grabbed the phone from her hand. "This is the police. Who is this?"

He gritted his teeth at the answering laugh. "You were warned. Even your boyfriend's not going to be able to save you now."

The click of the disconnecting call echoed across the room. Trent hung up her phone and pulled his from his coat. He'd call Max again to find out who'd just dialed her number. Although he'd bet good money this wraith stalking Katie had used an untraceable cell.

Katie sank to her knees, crawling across the carpet to pick up the photos. "He's not going to hurt you, sunshine. I won't let him." His partner picked up. "Max?"

But Katie was more focused on some distant point

inside her head than in any kind of shock. She sat back on her heels and crumpled the papers in her fist. "It's these."

"Pictures? Printouts? The mess I made?" After relaying the message to Max, Trent picked up the rest of the papers and tried to understand the wheels turning in her head. "You're not talking to me, woman. What do you mean?"

She blinked and brought those cornflower-blue eyes into focus on him. "It's the research I'm doing on these cold case files." She braced her hand on his shoulder to stand and hurried to her computer. Trent followed, anxious to catch up on her train of thought. "I've opened up the wrong can of worms somewhere—I've breached some piece of information I shouldn't have. That's what he wants me to stop."

Trent looked over her shoulder as she booted up her computer, plugged in her portable hard drive and turned on the hot-spot security device. "The brass isn't about to stop a criminal investigation. Even if the lieutenant takes you off the case and reassigns you, we'll still be going after Asher. Are you sure?"

"Every time I ping another database, every time I send an email request—that's when he contacts me." With the equipment in place, she tucked her hair behind her ears and went to work. "I need to run a full system diagnostic. It may be on my computer at work, too. He's mirroring me."

"What does that mean?"

"Somebody's tapped into my computer. Or maybe the portable hard drive. Even if he's not copying my data, he can see what sites I go to. He's been tracking every movement I make online."

"How can you tell?"

She'd gotten into the belly of the programming now

and was scrolling through code. "Every time I get a little more information about Leland Asher, every time I discover another piece of the puzzle that can build our case against him, something happens. That man at the theater. Vandalizing my laptop. He's tracking me somehow. Either visually or online."

Stop what you're doing, the message had said. "They want you to stop investigating Leland Asher?"

She pointed to the gibberish on the screen. "It's all right here. But I've been too distracted to see it. It's a virus, a replicating virus that copies everything I do to another computer. Someone got close enough to my laptop or portable hard drive to plant it."

"At the theater? There's too much security at HQ."

"I don't know. I may be able to track down the source." Her fingers were flying over the keyboard, clicking on icons and typing in commands he didn't understand. "I need to notify tech support at work to sweep the systems, just in case they've found a back door into the KCPD network. But there are enough safeguards that that might be difficult, even for an experienced hacker. More likely, it's my personal account that's been…"

She picked up the hot-spot device and turned it over. "Do you have your pocketknife?"

Trent reached into the pocket of his jeans to retrieve the knife. He marveled at the woman's intelligence as she pried open the device. "Katie?"

She dropped the pieces onto the desk and sank back in her chair. Trent didn't have to be a genius like her to see that the innards weren't connected, so it hadn't blocked any intrusive signals. She could have been hacked almost anywhere if that wasn't working—at the coffee shop, at the theater, at home.

He pried the open knife from her grip. "Where did you buy that thing? Who would have access to disable it besides you?"

"Anybody. I bought it months ago. I keep it in my bag. If they could get to my laptop, they could get to the hot-spot device. Then I'd be as vulnerable as if I had no security on my computer components at all. I am so going to lose my job over this, aren't I?" She closed her hands into fists. "Such a screwup."

"You're not," he insisted. He dropped down on one knee beside her and captured her jaw between his thumb and fingers to turn her gaze toward his. "This just means there's somebody who thinks he's as smart as you out there. He's a lot more calculating and doesn't give a damn about who he hurts." He tightened his grasp and pulled her forward to meet his kiss. Katie's lips were full and sweet and shyly responsive in a way that shattered the caution around his heart and kindled a fire in his blood. "I believe in you, sunshine. Maybe this is a break in the investigation, an opportunity to trace it back to some hacker with ties to Asher. Now take a deep breath and figure this out."

Her hands came up to cup his face and she smiled. "I don't know why you're so good to me."

"That's easy." He leaned in to kiss that worry dimple on her forehead. "Because I lo—"

"Wait a minute." Trent reeled in the ill-timed confession as a new idea reenergized her. He folded the knife blade and returned it to the safety of his jeans pocket while Katie went back to her keyboard. "I should be able to track back to the date the device was disabled. The time should help us zero in on a location and who could have—"

She drew back with a gasp, her hands raised as row after row of words scrolled across her computer. After the first line, they were the same words, repeating over and over and over until they filled the screen.

Stop, Katie.
Die, Katie.
Die, Katie.
Die, Katie.
Die, Katie.
Die, Katie.

"Trent?"

"Son of a bitch." Trent pulled her to her feet. He wanted to smash the monitor to erase the threats she'd somehow triggered. He would have ripped the whole thing out of the wall and tossed it across the room if some little sane part of his brain hadn't remembered he was a cop, looking at a desk full of key evidence. "Log out of there. Do something. Fast."

Katie quickly shut down her Wi-Fi connection and pulled the cable connecting her router to the internet. He turned off the screen himself before she backed into him. His arms instantly went around her. "Easy, sunshine. You're okay."

She shook her head, the nylon of his coat rustling against her hair. "Why is this happening to me? I'm just one little cog on the team. I'm background. I'm nobody. We're all trying to solve cold cases and connect them to Leland Asher. All I do is the research. Why was that man here? Why is he trying to scare me?"

Probably because they were getting closer to the truth, closer to making a major case against Asher stick. And someone in Asher's camp was targeting Katie because she was the weakest link on the team—she hadn't had police training and she didn't carry a gun, but she was vital to proving that there was nothing alleged about the mob boss and his illegal activities. "Their time to shut us down is running out. Asher gets released from prison today."

She shook within his grasp. He knew the moment she decided she needed him more than she needed the distance between them. Turning in his arms, Katie shoved open the front of his coat and burrowed against his chest. Her fingers clenched in the layers of his shirts and the skin and muscle underneath. Trent threaded his fingers through her damp waves and cradled the back of her head, dropping his lips to the fragrant sunshine of her hair, holding her tightly against his strength.

"Mom? Are you okay?" a soft voice whispered from the open doorway. Despite the grip he had on Padre's collar, Tyler's eyes were wide with concern. Smart kid. He could see his mother was scared.

He just prayed the boy couldn't see that Trent was more than a little frightened for Katie, too.

"I'm okay, sweetie," Katie answered, her voice strong to reassure her son. "I just got some bad news." She tried to push away, but Trent wasn't budging.

Instead, he held his hand out to the little boy. "You're going to come stay at my house for a couple days, buddy. Okay?"

With a nod that didn't quite erase his frown, Tyler left the dog and ran across the room to hug Katie. She lifted her son into her arms and Trent wrapped them both in his shielding embrace.

Chapter Nine

Trent sat at his desk, staring at the twelve pictures on his computer. Six victims, six suspects. Plenty of circumstantial evidence to link one to another, but no real proof as to who was ultimately behind either the unsolved murders or the threats against Katie. But the key to solving the crimes attributed to Leland Asher and his criminal network had to be staring him in the face. If only he could get those pictures to talk.

That one of the police department's information technologists was being stalked and receiving threats promising to kill her or harm her son if she didn't stop poking around with her research meant the team had gotten too close to uncovering some long-buried truths. Their cold case investigation was heating up.

Maybe more than Trent wanted.

Not for the first time that day, his gaze wandered across the maze of detectives' desks to the cubicle where Katie sat, surrounded by a desktop computer, a stack of print files and a tall cup of some mocha-latte thing. She wore a pencil in her hair and a hands-free headset to talk on the phone with other tech gurus assigned to the department. The threats that had frightened her at home only seemed to motivate her now. Maybe diving into work was a way to distract herself from the fears for her and Tyler's safety. Or possibly, skipping lunch and never leaving her computer was some kind of atonement for allowing an outsider to breach her computers and gain inside information on the cold case squad's progress on different investigations. Or maybe there was still a little bit of that teenage girl who charged into battle left inside her, and instead of cowing her into submission, the danger that had come to her very doorstep had inspired her to take action—to save the investigation, to find justice for those victims whose murders had yet to be solved, to save her son.

Although Trent didn't understand all the jargon, Katie and the tech team at the lab had scoured all her computers, and, as she suspected, the mirroring had been done through the hot-spot device on her laptop and portable hard drive. The KCPD network was secure and only the public-record files she'd been using in her database had been accessed. Her laptop was back from the lab—unfortunately, with no usable prints but her own and his. And, with a legal warrant and approval from Ginny Rafferty-Taylor, Katie was back at work again, doing a little hacking herself to find out when the virus had been planted so she could determine her location at that time and identify anyone who might have had access to plant the bug in her system.

A paper wad smacked Trent in the forehead, drawing his attention back to the desk across from his. "Really?"

"Hey, I didn't want to be the only one working." Max Krolikowski had plenty of ammunition on his messy desk, but he pointed to the stray missile that had landed on the tidy expanse of Trent's blotter before hanging up his phone. "That's the number that called Katie this morning." Trent unfolded the note and smoothed it open to read the information Max had jotted there. "Just like you suspected. Disposable cell. It's been turned off so there's no way to trace it."

Trent slipped the paper into a folder and glanced down at the license plate number and name of the rental company that had leased the black sports car to a John Smith, aka Mr. Fancy Dress Shoes, aka he still didn't have any freaking ID on the guy who'd gotten far too close to Katie and Tyler that morning. Just a bunch more puzzle pieces and no big picture yet.

"However, it does belong to a type of phone sold exclusively at your favorite big-box discount department store over the past year."

Trent sat back in his chair. Like the anonymous John Smith with the fake license and credit card, that was almost worse than no help. "There are a dozen of those stores in the city. Assuming the perp bought it in KC."

"Yeah, but they all have surveillance cameras in their electronics departments."

"Are you willing to sit through twelve months of surveillance footage from all those stores to see who bought a phone and then try to identify John Smith or anybody else who's come up in one of our cases?"

"It's a long shot."

"It's worse than a long shot."

"But I'd do it for Katie."

Trent agreed. "So would I."

With an answering nod, Max picked up his phone again. "I'll start calling, see if the stores even keep security footage from that far back."

"I'll find out if this guy used his John Smith ID to buy the phone or anything else."

Trent closed out the pictures on his computer screen

but paused before picking up his own phone to help Max with one of the tedious, but necessary, demands of police work. "What's the point of threatening Katie? She's not going to be arresting anybody. This bastard should be coming after me or you or Liv and Jim, or anybody else on the team, if he wanted to misdirect us or slow down our investigation."

His partner hung up the phone without dialing. "You think this Smith dude tried to break in to her apartment to harm her? Not just to steal her computer or something like that?"

"I didn't give him a chance to finish the job. And he wasn't inclined to stop for a chat."

Max scrubbed his fingers over his jaw in a thoughtful sigh. "Are the threats affecting her work?"

Trent glanced over to see Katie riffling through the files on her desk before tapping her headset and answering whatever the party on the other end of the call had asked. "She seems as scatterbrained and brilliant as ever."

"Interesting." If Max meant something by that cryptic response, he didn't elaborate. "But the scaring part's working?"

Trent could still feel the marks on his skin where she'd finally turned to him for solace and held on to him until her trembling had stopped. And he'd never forget the worry stamped on Tyler's sweet, innocent face. "It's even getting to her son. I mean, Jim's at the school shadowing Tyler during the day, so we know he's safe for now. But how do I reassure a nine-year-old that everything's going to be okay if I don't even know what I'm up against?"

"I don't have kids— Hell, that's a scary thought, ain't it—me and kids?" Max propped his elbows on his desk and steepled his fingers together. "But I think you just need to be there for them."

"That's what Katie needs, too." Trent summoned half a grin, appreciating Max's attempt at deep philosophical advice. "But I won't lie. It's hard to be spending that much time with her, given our history."

"It's hard because you're a good guy. You think things through. You wait for an invitation. You don't just haul off and kiss a woman like I did Rosie when we first met and I was toasted out of my…" Max slapped his palm on top of his desk. "Well, hell's bells, junior, you *did* kiss her. And not one of those Dudley Do-Right pecks on the cheek, either, I'll bet."

Groaning, Trent tried to temper Max's stunned excitement. "They were a mistake."

"They? More than once?" Max swore under his breath. "You've been holding out on me. About time it happened between you two."

Trent glared at his partner. "Nothing happened."

"No fireworks?" Max looked disappointed. Oh, yeah, there'd been plenty of spontaneous combustion between them on that kitchen stool. But the *Die, Katie* bombardment on her computer screen had reminded Trent that Katie needed his protection, not his love. Max leaned forward and whispered, "Wrong kind of fireworks?"

Give his love life a rest, already. "It's Christmas, not Independence Day."

"Huh?"

"Wrong time for fireworks. I was taking advantage of a vulnerable moment." Of several vulnerable moments, it would seem.

Max grumbled a curse and sorted through the scattered papers on his desk. "Junior, you don't know how to take advantage. If Katie wasn't willing, you wouldn't—"

"Tyler's safety is her priority." Trent pulled a phone book from a desk drawer and started looking up numbers, as relieved to be ending the conversation and getting back to work as he'd been to air some of his concerns with his most trusted friend in the first place. "And it should be. It's my priority, too. I want to find out who this jackass is and put him in my interrogation room. I want to get him out of their lives so Tyler can just be a kid again and Katie can…"

What? Go back to being his buddy when he wanted to be her bedmate? Her soul mate? Her everything? Now that she and Tyler were staying with him, his worries about their safety had eased a fraction, but remembering not to push for everything he wanted from her grew harder with every passing minute.

"Earth to big guy." Olivia knocked on the corner of Trent's desk, pulling him from his thoughts. "The lieutenant wants us in her office. The press is covering Leland Asher's release."

Setting aside his troubling thoughts, Trent pushed to his feet, taking a moment to tuck in his corduroy shirt and the thermal Henley he wore underneath before following Liv and Max across the room. Katie ended her call and scooped up her laptop, darting into the office on a waft of flowery scent that reminded Trent of freshly shampooed hair and warm curves pressed against his body. Wisely avoiding broadcasting that woman's physical effect on him, he took a position standing at the back of the room while Katie set up her laptop and sat at the front of the group. When his gaze locked on to a sly glimpse of cornflower blue directed back at him, Trent wondered if Katie was making a point of keeping her distance, too.

"Let's see what our friend has to say." Lieutenant Rafferty-Taylor turned up the sound on the television screen as a twinkling of camera flashes captured the image of Leland Asher walking through the prison exit into the bright, cold sunshine of the wintry afternoon.

Looking like a politician on a campaign stump, Asher waved to the crowd of eager reporters, curiosity seekers and armed guards who were there to make sure nothing got out of hand before the alleged mobster left the premises. Although the once stocky man had lost a lot of weight, probably due to the cancer, there was a sense of entitlement to his carriage. Plus, he wore the impeccably tailored suit and dress coat of a man who still had access to plenty of money. The man with a briefcase beside him led the way to a small podium, where he identified himself as Asher's attorney and made a statement regarding his client's release.

But the words coming from the television were just white noise as Katie began to fidget in her chair. She drummed her fingers over her keyboard without typing anything and kept drawing her hair between her fists in a ponytail before letting it fall back to her shoulders when she realized she had no clip to secure it. What was buzzing through that brain of hers now?

An elbow butted up against his, diverting Trent's attention to his far too observant partner. "You up for this, junior? You want me to take over shadowing Katie?"

"No." He wasn't about to leave Tyler and Katie's security up to anyone else. "I want you to be there to take up the slack in case I can't get the job done."

"You not get a job done? Trust me, junior. That'll never happen."

Olivia sat on the corner of the table. She nodded to the TV. "He's on. Turn it up."

A dark-haired woman wearing a fur coat ran up to the podium to kiss Leland's cheek. The woman had a striking strand of white framing her face when she turned to the camera. And while she looked adoringly up at the gaunt, graying man, he wound his arm around her waist and held her to his side.

Katie pointed to the screen. "That's Beverly Eisenbach, Mr. Asher's significant other. She's the psychologist who counseled Matt Asher and Stephen March as teenagers."

"Any response to your query about whether or not Leland was ever a patient of hers?" the lieutenant asked.

Katie shrugged. "Talk to her attorney and get a warrant?"

Trent tuned out Asher's pontification about learning from his mistakes and how his incarceration hadn't affected his business investments one iota, as well as the updates on his health. Taking Lieutenant Rafferty-Taylor's lead, he turned the gathering into an impromptu staff meeting. "I tracked down the house mother from the sorority Bev Eisenbach and Isabel Asher belonged to. She's retired now, but she remembers the two of them taking classes and hanging out together before Isabel left school. Night and day, she called them. It wasn't just a blonde-brunette thing, either. The house mother said she never understood how two young women with such different personalities got along so well. Dr. Eisenbach was neat, organized, intent on keeping her scholarships and earning her degree, while Isabel was more of a free spirit who was there for the social opportunities."

The petite blonde who led the cold case group folded her arms in front of her and nodded, urging Trent to continue. "Does the house mother remember meeting Leland? Can we prove that Leland and Dr. Eisenbach knew each other twenty-five years ago? And does that information do anything to help our case?"

"The house mother remembers Leland coming on campus to attend events with Isabel. They had no parents, so he was more than a big brother to her."

Olivia chimed in. "We can trace suspected criminal activity to Leland all the way back to that time. He was already starting to amass his fortune, so I'm sure Bev would have been interested in meeting Isabel's big brother."

"Maybe that's what she liked about Isabel," Max interjected. "She could hook her up to a man who was destined to make a lot of money. Clearly, it paid off for her."

Trent thrust his fingers into the back pockets of his jeans. "The house mother remembers the guy Isabel Asher was dating, too. 'A prissy Italian guy' is how she described him."

"Francisco Dona." Katie supplied the name as she typed on her laptop and read the info off the screen. "He was a small-time dealer and user. Looks like they dated each other, or at least used together, on and off for several years until she died. He was questioned as a suspect in Isabel's death, but no charges were ever filed."

Trent picked up on a small detail. "You said *was*. He died in a motorcycle accident. Did anyone ever investigate his death as a possible homicide?"

Katie shook her head. "ME's report said he died of head trauma. He suspected Dona was under the influence. He found a trace amount of drugs in his system."

"But Mr. Dona passed about a month after Isabel's overdose," the lieutenant confirmed.

"There's nothing suspicious about the timing of that," Max groused with sarcasm. "Can anyone say retaliation?"

Trent agreed. "If Leland and Isabel were as close as the house mother claims, then it makes sense that he'd order a hit on Dona. It wouldn't be the first time an accident was staged to cover up a murder."

Katie continued to read the information on her computer. "Even if Francisco Dona didn't provide Isabel with the drugs that killed her, Asher could have still blamed him. According to this, there were no signs of anyone trying to revive Isabel after she collapsed. There wasn't even a 9-1-1 call until her son, Matt, discovered the body."

Even though they were talking about alleged criminals, Katie's voice trailed away in sympathy. She knew firsthand what it was like to deal with the death of a parent, and might even be remembering her own mother's murder. Trent pushed away from the wall where he was leaning, wanting to go to her. But the sharp blue gaze darting his way was a warning to keep his distance. Either she was telling him she could handle this or she was asking him to keep the complications of the relationship growing between them private.

"Great." Liv's sarcasm matched Max's. "Another murder we'd like to attribute to Asher that we can't prove. How does this guy keep getting away with it?" She turned to Katie. "Can we at least talk with the ME who wrote the report?"

"That would be Dr. Carson." Katie turned her focus back to her computer and pulled up the name on the report before shaking her head. "He retired with early-onset Alzheimer's a couple of years ago. Your brother Niall replaced him."

Liv groaned at the latest twist. "Does anybody else think that if we could just shuffle all these players in the right order that we'd solve a half dozen murders and put Asher away for good?"

Trent and Max and Katie all raised their hands and Olivia laughed before Lieutenant Rafferty-Taylor directed their attention back to the television. "He's leaving."

Hand in hand, Leland Asher and Bev Eisenbach walked to a waiting limousine, where another group was waiting for him. Trent recognized Asher's longtime chauffeur and bodyguard and spotted a couple more thugs watching the audience like Secret Service men. A young man with glasses—Leland's nephew, Matt—climbed out of the long black car and extended his arm. The two generations shook hands before Leland pulled his nephew in for a showy hug and whispered something in his ear.

Trent couldn't be certain, but had Matt Asher arched his brows over the rim of his glasses and made eye contact with Bev Eisenbach before the hug ended? Or was he alerting the group to the fans with more questions and accusations surging their way?

Either way, Leland remained coolly unperturbed by the rush of attention and turned at the people calling his name.

"One last question, Mr. Asher." A television reporter with long, dark hair thrust her microphone in his face. "How do you feel?"

"Like a free man." Leland laughed and pulled up his pant leg to show off the parole bracelet on his ankle. "Except for the new jewelry the state has so graciously given me."

He waved aside the follow-up questions and ushered

Bev into the limo before he and Matt and the bodyguard climbed in behind her. The network camera panned the crowd, getting shots of protesters and supporters alike, people who thought, like the cold case squad, that Asher had gotten away with murder, and others—friendly plants, perhaps—who waved signs and shouted about "freeing the innocent."

When the camera scanned back to the limousine driving away, a far too familiar image near the back of the crowd shot adrenaline into Trent's bloodstream. In three strides, he was across the office, tapping at the screen. "Are we recording this? Can we get a recording?"

Katie turned her laptop around and typed. "I can get a feed off the station's website. Wait…"

"What is it, junior?" Max asked.

She pulled up the website as they gathered around her. "I've got it. They're replaying the interview."

"Freeze it. There." Trent rested a hand on her shoulder and pointed to the man in the crowd who'd just snapped a photograph of the group at the limousine. Brown hair, long wool coat. Although he couldn't see the telltale shoes, he recognized the nondescript features and receding hairline. "That's John Smith. That's the guy who tried to break in to Katie's apartment."

"Is he part of Asher's entourage?" the lieutenant asked.

"Is he a reporter?" was Liv's guess.

"Hold on." Katie went for a more definitive answer. Using her mouse, she framed the suspect in the picture and clicked a screen shot of his image. "Now that we've got a face, I can blow it up and run him through recognition protocols. If he's in the system, I can track him down."

She pulled back when a private investigator's license

showed up on the screen, along with three different driver's licenses and a state ID card. John Smith apparently had several aliases he used, and not a one of them looked legit lined up like that. But there was at least one thing in common on two of the cards—an address.

Trent pulled his notepad and jotted it down. "That's downtown. Probably an office building."

Katie looked up at Trent. "Go get him."

Chapter Ten

Katie glanced over for the umpteenth time at her flow-ered bag sitting in the corner of the greenroom backstage, making sure no one had opened it to mess with the con-tents inside. Good. Still latched. Still safe.

Her research had indicated that her device had been hacked almost two weeks earlier. That day she'd taken Tyler to school, stopped by the coffee shop, gone to work, and hadn't left until it was time to pick up Tyler at his after-school club and go straight to rehearsal. And since she wouldn't count her son as a suspect, and no one at work had any reason to track her research since they could access the same info themselves, that left someone at the coffee shop or here at the show to have tampered with her hot-spot device.

Her money was on someone involved with the play—or who could hide out at the theater undetected. So her suspicions of everyone here were riding high. But since she was alone for the moment while Doug and the cast were onstage going over last-minute notes before tomor-row's final dress rehearsal, she figured it was safe to let the messenger bag out of her sight for the few seconds it would take her to hang up the costumes she was ironing in the women's dressing room.

She set the iron on its end and gathered up the long dresses she'd prepped for the last run-through before opening night and carried them into the women's dressing room. She could hear Doug Price's voice booming through the auditorium and was glad that Trent was in there with Tyler, maybe trading a wink or a thumbs-up to let her son know that Doug's dramatic speech about "moments" and bringing the audience to tears meant the temperamental director was pleased with the way the show had come together. She was doubly glad that Trent was there to keep an eye on Tyler, to make sure her son had nothing to worry about except remembering his lines and making his entrances.

Because they weren't safe. Not yet. The threat was still out there.

When Trent and Max had gone to John Smith's downtown address that afternoon, they'd found a ransacked office, a few drops of blood that indicated there'd been an altercation of some kind and no sign of Smith. A BOLO on the rental car hadn't turned it up yet, either. That meant Smith, whoever he really was, was still out there, still watching, still looking for a way to get to her. Whether he was a spy for Leland Asher or someone with a more personal interest in her, she felt less and less that keeping Trent at arm's length was a good idea. The only time she'd felt safe since finding that message scribbled in the snow, the only time that Tyler acted like a normal kid, was when Detective Dixon was around.

Katie caught a glimpse of her pale features in the bright lights of the dressing room mirrors and cringed. No wonder Tyler was scared for her. Sleep had been a rare commodity the past few days. She touched the shadows beneath her eyes and wished she had Trent's arms around her right now, so she could soak up the comfort of his warmth, be reenergized by the thrill of his possessive kiss and feel secure enough to drop her guard for a few moments and simply take a normal breath without looking over her shoulder or second-guessing every move she made and worrying about Tyler.

With the gun and badge on his belt, and the sheer size of those shoulders and chest, Trent didn't exactly fit the role of backstage parent. But he'd made it clear that until he could arrest John Smith and prove that the part-time private investigator/full-time con man was the person who'd threatened her, Trent was going to be spending a whole lot of time with her. His days, at work and here at the theater—and nights, too, sleeping just a few feet away from the guest rooms in his comfortable ranch-style house where he'd put her and Tyler.

Dear, sweet, solid...sexy, distracting, aggravating Trent. He made her feel all prickly inside when he caught her in the crosshairs of those steely gray eyes. And he hadn't been kidding when he'd told her a few nights earlier that a woman would know when she'd been kissed by him. After all these years—seeing him date other women, interacting with him herself—how had she missed discovering the difference between friendship and passion, between a chaste brush of his lips at her temple and that powerful stamp of perfection claiming her mouth?

And how was she was going to fit these deepening feelings for the man, this need for his strength and protection, this desire to hold and be held, back into the rules for emotional survival that had kept her safe and sane since her wild, violent and unpredictable youth? It was impossible to think of Trent as a friend while imagining what it would be like to give in to the temptation of his hard body and potent kisses again. Yet it was equally impossible to imagine how she could have gotten through this week in one piece without the friend she trusted implicitly at her side.

When she focused in on her reflection again, she realized she was stroking her own lips—missing, wishing, hungry for Trent's mouth on hers.

Good grief. Katie's cheeks flushed with emotion and she drew her fingers away from her sensitized lips. She was doing exactly what she'd told herself over and over that she shouldn't. She wasn't just attracted to Trent. She wasn't just turning to him as her cop friend to protect her from a dangerous situation. This wasn't just gratitude for helping her and Tyler time and again. She was falling for Trent Dixon. Falling for the vital, mature man her boy next door had become.

Laughter and the voices of numerous conversations and complaints woke Katie from her bothersome thoughts. Doug must have dismissed the cast and crew for the night, and they were making a mass exodus out the back workroom to the parking lot. Sliding her fingers through her loose hair, she pulled the waves off her face and groaned at the static electricity in the air that left her looking as if she'd just crawled out of bed instead of neatly downplaying the amorous turn of her thoughts. No amount of smoothing could give her a business-as-usual appearance, so she simply turned away from the mirror and hurried into the men's dressing room to pull the costumes that still needed ironing before anyone came in and questioned the embarrassed heat in her cheeks.

She exchanged smiles and a quick good-night with a few of the actors who'd left their coats or purses in the dressing rooms as she carried an armload of shirts and two of the specialty costumes out into the greenroom. She draped the shirts over the back of a chair and shook out the long black robe that belonged to the Spirit of Christmas Future.

A shadow fell over her as she spread the drapey material over the ironing board. Katie gasped, startled by the man in black standing between her and the exit door. She put her hand over her racing heart and dredged up a polite smile. "Hey, Francis."

His beady dark eyes didn't smile back. "I don't want any wrinkles in that, understand? I want it to flow as I move, so it looks as though I'm floating across the stage."

She watched the expressive gesture of his hand that demonstrated the undulating movement. "I do my best to make you all look good."

"And I appreciate that. I know I come across as a bit of a demanding actor, but my drive stems from wanting to put on the best production possible." His Adam's apple bobbed up and down as if the next few words were difficult to get out. "Your costumes have helped us achieve that."

Really? A compliment from Francis? "Thank you." He probably expected her to say something nice in return. "And, I must say, you're a very convincing Christmas spirit."

He clasped his hands behind his back, but left little more than the width of the ironing board between them. She didn't know if he was watching to make sure she pressed his costume to his specifications or if he was so socially inept that he was unaware of how his proximity and the musky smell of a long night under stage lights filling the air between them could make her feel so uncomfortable. "It was nice to have you backstage tonight, Katie. Not out in the audience where you distract Douglas."

So much for trying to get along with the man. Her hand fisted around the handle of the iron. "This again? Francis, what did I ever do to you? I'm a volunteer. I love doing theater. My son has made new friends and he's enjoying himself. I'm not looking for a relationship with any man here, and I'm certainly not interested in Doug."

"Protest all you want," he articulated in a disbelieving whine. "I see right through your little helpless-female-with-the-big-blue-eyes-and-perky-boobs act. Douglas doesn't want you for anything other than the thrill of the chase. And maybe to get lucky. If you're looking for a husband, I promise, he'll run as far from you as he can get."

"That's insulting. I am a self-sufficient woman. I have a career. I'm raising my son."

"That's probably why he cast him. Douglas took one look at you in auditions and—"

Katie shoved the iron at him, coming close enough to move him out of her space. "Shut up, Francis, or I will brand you."

"How quaint. Resorting to violence in a meager effort to defend yourself. I was only trying to give you a friendly warning."

"There's nothing friendly about these conversations. You want something from me. You're jealous or insecure or—"

"Heed my words." He leaned toward the ironing board again, perhaps sensing she wouldn't really make contact. "You're not the first pretty woman he's hit on, and you won't be the last. If you're thinking you'll be cast in a show, or your son will get a better part the next time

Douglas directs, you're mistaken. I know how power attracts women, and he's using his to entice you."

"He's not a CEO, he's directing a play." Katie plunked the iron down on the collar of his robe, ready to char an ugly hole straight through the heavy cotton if he said one more derogatory thing. She knew all about bullies like Francis. She'd grown up with one. "You need to heed *my* words. I am not the least bit tempted to sleep with Doug or whatever distasteful thing you're insinuating. If he turns you on so much, you can have him. With my blessing."

"You crazy…" Francis grabbed her wrist and the iron, snatching them away from the smell of singed material. "Stop what you're doing!"

"What?" Anger morphed into fear in a single breath. His particular choice of words surprised her far more than the pinch of his fingers on her skin. Katie tugged at his grip. "What did you say?"

"I said to stop what you're—"

"Mom!" Tyler ran across the greenroom, dropping his book bag at the argument he'd walked in on and dashing around the end of the ironing board to stand beside her and pull on her arm. Oh, Lord. Her little man thought Francis was hurting her. "Are you ready to leave? I am."

"Tyler—"

Francis set the iron down but left his fingers clamped over Katie's wrist. "Back off, Tiny Tim. I'm having a conversation with your mother."

"Not anymore you're not." A deeper voice entered the argument and ended it. Francis's eyes had barely widened with alarm before Trent was prying his grip off Katie's wrist.

Then he went up on his toes as Trent pinned Francis's

arm behind his back. "How dare you?" he sputtered through his bushy black beard.

"Don't make me take you in for assault and harassment, Sergel." Trent carried the vile man several steps away before positioning himself between her and Francis. The width and height of his shoulders and back completely blocked Francis from her line of sight. If the no-nonsense authority in his tone wasn't enough, Katie could well imagine the *just try something* challenge in Trent's expression that would keep any smart man at bay. "Whatever your beef with Katie might be, it ends now."

"I'll thank you kindly to keep your hands off me, Detective."

"I will if you keep your distance from Miss Rinaldi."

"Very well." Francis was rubbing his shoulder when he crossed the room to pick up his coat. "But don't say I didn't warn you, Katie." Francis pulled on his long black coat. "Don't trust Douglas. There's been something wrong with this entire production. Strange things happening. People who don't belong hanging around. He hasn't been himself. You and your son are the only thing different about this show and any other play I've done with him."

"Shut up, Sergel. Or Reinhardt or whatever your name is." Trent took a step toward him, and Francis hurriedly grabbed his hat and scarf. "Not one more harsh word to this boy, either. Understand?"

With a dramatic harrumph and flourish of his long dark coat, Francis swept out of the room.

Trent turned. His gaze went straight to the wrist Katie was mindlessly massaging. "Everyone okay in here?"

Katie nodded. Physically, she was fine. But her brain kept flashing with images of messages scratched in the snow or smeared in lipstick. "Francis told me to stop what I'm doing."

"What do you mean?" He reached over the ironing board and scrubbed his palm along the top of Tyler's head, reminding her son that the tension in the room had been neutralized and he could drop his guard and be a kid again.

Katie dropped her arm around Tyler's shoulders and hugged him against her hip, reassuring him with the same message, even though her mind was still racing with suspicion. "He used the exact same words—*Stop what you're doing.* That's just a coincidence, right? Do you think he could really hate or resent me so much that he would want to scare me by hiring that private detective or sending those threats?"

He nodded, giving her misgivings careful consideration. "I don't know. The threats could be some kind of weird jealousy thing—there's certainly something about that prima donna that's not right. But my money's still on Asher and your research." He crossed to the sofa to pick up his coat and shrug into it. "I'll make sure Sergel leaves. You get all your gear packed so we can get out of this place ASAP." After adjusting the hem of his short coat over his holster and badge, he plucked Francis's black robe off the ironing board and tossed it into the men's dressing room. "And forget about ironing that jackass's costume."

Tyler squinched up his face in curious frown. "Mom, what's a jackass?"

Katie squeezed her lips together to stifle her laugh at the innocent question. But a smile erupted anyway, and she walked Tyler around the ironing board to Trent. "You can explain that one, Detective."

"Sorry."

The stricken look on his rugged face stretched her smile farther. Feeling strengthened by his presence and taking pity on his uncharacteristic distress, Katie braced a hand on Trent's shoulder and stretched up on tiptoe. She didn't second-guess the impulse—she simply did what felt like the right thing to do. She slipped her fingers beneath his collar and slanted his head down to seal her lips over his. She might have started the kiss, but his warm, firm lips quickly moved over hers, completing it. The kiss was brief, and the link between the two of them warmed Katie all the way down to her toes. Trent's eyes were smiling above hers when he lifted his head. "So that's what I have to do to get your attention? Get in trouble?"

"You've always had my attention, Trent. I guess it's just taken me a long time to work up the courage to do something about it."

He combed his fingers through her hair and tucked it behind her ear. "I'm willing to take it slow, as long as I know you're on the path with me."

When he leaned in to kiss her again, they both suddenly became aware of the nine-year-old tilting his gaze from one to the other, silently observing the teasing, intimate exchange.

Trent cleared his throat and pulled away, probably worried that he was going to have to explain what was happening between his mother and best friend, too. "Mom, did you mail my letter to Santa?" Tyler asked.

Katie offered a nervous chuckle in lieu of an answer. What was going through that wise little man's mind now? "It's getting late."

Trent nodded. With a hand on her son's shoulder, he scooped up Tyler's book bag and coat and marched him toward the door. "I'll keep Tyler busy so you can finish up faster."

"Sounds like a plan."

He nodded and helped Tyler into his blue coat. "Come on, buddy. Let's bundle up."

"Is *jackass* a naughty word?" Tyler asked, following his big buddy into the backstage area without question.

"Let's talk."

Several minutes later, Katie had unplugged the iron and hung up the shirts, and even Francis's wrinkled costume, when her phone vibrated in the pocket of her jeans. She pulled it out to read a text from Trent.

We're outside. Distracting Ty with snowball fight. Hurry. I'm losing.

Grinning, Katie pulled on her stocking cap and coat and looped her flowered bag over her shoulder before texting a response.

Thanks. On my way. Duck. ;)

She knew a split second of panic when she turned off the light in the greenroom and stepped into the darkness backstage. The work lights were off on the stage and the running lights had been disconnected. She was in utter darkness. Her audible gasp echoed through the storage and work space.

"Is someone there?" a voice asked. Doug Price. As much as she hated to cast him as any kind of rescuer, she couldn't stand to be trapped in the dark again.

"Hello?" she called out. "Please tell me you're near a light switch."

She heard a shuffle of movement, and then a light came on by the exit door. Doug had set his briefcase on a chair and opened it to stuff his director's notebook inside and pull out his cap and gloves. "Over here, Katie. I'm sorry. I thought I was the last one here. I was just locking up."

What had he been doing that he hadn't seen the ambient light from the greenroom on the opposite side of the stage when she'd opened the door? And how had he made his way through the darkness back here? Ultimately, it didn't matter. She just wanted out of this place. "I'm sure I'm the last one now. Thanks for waiting."

Katie wove her way through the prop tables and set pieces that had been such obstacles in the darkness. Not that she completely trusted Doug after the things Francis had said, but she was anxious to get out into the open, eager to get to Trent and her son. But as Doug pulled his keys from the briefcase, they caught on some papers inside, and a thick manila envelope folded in half dropped out. Katie bent down to pick it up. It was heavy, as though there was a stack of large photographs or a couple of magazines inside. "Here. You dropped—"

"I'll take that." Doug snatched it from her hand. He quickly stuffed it into his briefcase and closed it. He took a deep breath, calming the brief outburst. "I'm sorry. Thank you."

Perhaps she was broadcasting her discomfort at being alone with the man, because Doug offered her a courteous nod and pushed open the steel door to a blast of swirling flakes and cold air. "Is it snowing again?" she asked.

"I think it helps set the mood for the play, don't you agree?" Hearing the squeals of a laughing child carried on the wind, Katie quickly slipped out past Doug. She spotted Trent and Tyler down by the footbridge, pelting each other with snowballs. She smiled and headed toward them, considering joining the fun, when Doug turned the key in the lock. "Hold up, dear. I'll walk you to your car."

Trent saw her and waved just before a dollop of snow hit the middle of his chest. He scooped Tyler up off his feet and jogged up the hill as Katie made her excuses. "That's very gallant of you, Doug. But my friend Trent is still here."

"Yes, of course." He switched his briefcase to the opposite hand, away from Trent's approach.

Maybe there was nothing suspicious about his behavior at all, and she was the one being paranoid. "Well, thanks. Only one rehearsal left."

Doug nodded. "We have a great show. Remember the cast party this weekend. I'd love to see you there." Trent arrived and set Tyler on his feet. The two were a pair of snow-dusted clothes and ruddy cheeks, demanding she smile at their boyish behavior. Doug seemed less amused. "You're welcome to come along, too, Detective. If you like that sort of thing."

Trent clapped his gloved hands together, throwing out a cloud of snow. "Oh, I love a good party."

"Yes, well, good night." Doug brushed away the few snowflakes that had fallen onto his shoulders and walked around the corner of the building to his car. She heard his engine start before she would have expected and the cold motor shifting into gear before driving away in a rush.

"It's a good thing he's a director," Trent deadpanned, "because he's not a very good actor. I don't believe he really wants me to come to your cast party."

"I guess he's in a hurry to find another date, then." Katie laughed out loud, feeling the stress of the day and those disturbing encounters with Francis Sergel and Doug

Price dissipate. She dropped her arm around Tyler's shoulders, linked her elbow with Trent's and led the way to the parking lot. "Come on, you two. Let's get your truck warmed up before all that snow soaks through to your skin and freezes you."

But she slowed her steps when she saw the other two cars left in the lot. They weren't campus police vehicles, and everyone else from the play had left already. Hadn't they? She eyed the silver sedan with the tinted windows parked near the exit, and the small black car parked beneath the nearest street lamp. Its engine was running, as though someone had parked close to the theater and was waiting to pick up a passenger. Only there was no driver inside.

She didn't have to be a cop to know that something wasn't right. "Trent? Doug and I were the last ones out of the theater."

Trent's hand on her arm stopped her. He pulled out his keys and thrust them into her hand. "Get in my truck and lock yourself inside."

He lifted his coat and pulled out his gun, too. Katie automatically pulled Tyler away from the weapon. "Trent?"

"Black sports car." He braced his gun between his hands and pointed it toward the car with the running engine. "The license plate matches. Call Max and tell him I located John Smith's car."

The man who'd tried to break into her apartment. "That's him? Why is he—"

"Go." Trent waved her toward his pickup and circled around to approach the car from the rear.

Katie hugged Tyler to her side and backed away. But not before she saw the hand on the steering wheel.

A bloody hand.

"Trent?" She pushed Tyler behind her and inched forward with a ghoulish curiosity. The man was injured. He needed help. No, she just needed answers. She wanted to ask him why he'd been terrorizing her. "Oh, my God."

There'd be no answers tonight. She saw the body slumped over in the front seat. She saw all the blood on his clothes and the car's upholstery.

She clutched Tyler's face against her chest and spun him away from the gruesome sight as Trent opened the car door and checked for a pulse. "Is that John Smith? Is he…?"

Trent nodded and pulled up his coat to holster his weapon. He held up two fingers, indicating the man had been shot twice, and mouthed the word *dead*.

"What's going on?" Tyler's question came from the face muffled against her breast. "Is that guy sleeping?"

With a heart that was heavy with the knowledge that her son had been anywhere close to this kind of violence, Katie exchanged a silent message with Trent and pulled Tyler toward the heavy-duty pickup with her.

"Katie! Get down!"

Katie heard three little whiffs of sound before Trent came charging around the sports car. By the time she saw the tiny explosions of snow spitting up from the pavement and heard a car door slam, Trent's arms were around her and Tyler, pushing them into a run. "Go, go, go! Run, buddy!"

Someone by the silver car was shooting at them.

When the side mirror shattered, Katie screamed. Trent swept Tyler up into his arms and grabbed Katie's hand, jerking her into a detour from the path of the bullets. "Into the trees!"

Mimicking his crouched posture, Katie pumped her

legs as fast as they would go. They zigzagged over the open pavement, taking the shortest path to cover. Katie nearly toppled when they plunged into the snow beyond the curb. It suddenly felt as if she was running in water, pulling her boots out of the sucking, frozen drifts. A bare branch splintered beside them, shooting icy crystals and shards of wood into their faces. Trent muttered a curse and jerked them away from the pelting cascade. She felt the blow of something hard against her hip and stumbled, but Trent's strong arm held her upright and kept her moving. When they reached the fallen trunk of an old oak, he leaped over the mound of rough wood, dead branches and snow and pulled Katie over the trunk with them.

She landed on her bottom, sinking waist-deep into a drift of snow. Trent shoved Tyler into her arms as another thwap of a bullet hit the far side of the tree trunk. "Stay down! Keep him covered!" he ordered.

Katie was already pulling Tyler beneath her, rolling onto her stomach on top of him and digging down into her bag for her phone. Trent peeked over the top of the tree trunk, drawing two more shots that smacked into the old wood before he ducked back down and drew his gun. Katie punched in 9-1-1 as Trent rose up again and fired off several rounds.

"Mom?" Tyler held his hands over his ears. She felt him jerk against her with every shot Trent fired.

"Stay down, sweetie." Three more shots and the dispatcher picked up. "I'm at Williams College with Detective Trent Dixon. Behind the old auditorium. Someone in a silver car is shooting at us."

Another shot pinged off a metal light by the sidewalk, turning a silver wreath into ribbons floating to the ground. Katie stayed on the line when she heard car tires squealing for traction against the wet, freezing pavement. A car door slammed and Katie's heart squeezed in her chest when Trent pushed to his feet and climbed over the top of the tree trunk. "Stay put!"

"Trent!" Katie shouted her fear as the man who meant so much to her left the shelter of the tree and chased after the car peeling out of the parking lot. She heard pounding boot steps as the ground gave way to asphalt. There were two more shots and the screaming pitch of a car sliding around a sharp turn and speeding away into the night. Katie reported to the 9-1-1 dispatcher that she and her son were okay, but that she couldn't see if Trent or anyone else had been hurt. "There's a dead body here, too. A man who's been shot. Probably by whoever was in the silver car. Send an ambulance," she begged, feeling her extremities shiver with a mix of cold and fear. "Send everybody."

"Max!" She heard Trent's long strides approaching them again and knew he was on the phone to his partner, giving him a sitrep on the shooting.

Although the dispatcher asked Katie to stay on the line, she stuffed her phone into the pocket of her coat, keeping the connection open while she dealt with the more pressing needs of hugging her frightened son and making sure Trent hadn't been hurt. "It's okay, sweetie." She wiped the chapping tears from her baby's cheeks. "Trent?"

"Right here, sunshine." He dropped over the top of the tree trunk and squatted down beside them. He stuck his gun into the back of his jeans before pulling her and Tyler out of the snow and into his arms. "The shooting's stopped. They're gone. There were two men. I think we walked into the middle of a hit."

"What? I wonder if Doug saw it, too. Maybe that's why he drove away so fast."

"Well, he didn't stop to call the police if he did. But Max heard your call on the scanner. He's already on his way. He'll get Liv and Jim moving, too, and notify the lab about our extensive crime scene. Everybody in one piece?"

Katie waited for a nod from Tyler before answering, "Wet, cold and scared out of our minds. But we're fine."

They were all on their feet now, making their way to the sidewalk and up the easier path to the parking lot. Moving forward and scanning the area for any other unwanted surprises never stopped until they reached Trent's disabled truck. Besides the shattered mirror, he had two flat tires and a cracked window. He opened the passenger door on the side away from most of the damage and reached inside to check a hole in the dashboard. "Good. We'll be able to get ballistics and have some concrete evidence for a change. I got a partial plate on the car, too, but it was moving pretty fast." He turned to pick up Tyler and set him on the seat, facing out, away from the bullet hole. "At least we'll be out of the wind here. I'm guessing campus security will reach us first. Then we can get a door unlocked and go inside."

She could already hear the sirens in the distance. Others had probably reported the sounds of gunfire, too. A chill set in as the adrenaline started to wear off and Katie started to realize the full import of what had just happened. But as Trent straightened in the open triangle of the door and truck frame, she saw the deep rip in the sleeve of his coat and the blood soaking into the layers of insulation and cotton underneath. She grabbed him by the forearm and turned his shoulder toward the street lamp above them, on alert once more. "Trent."

He pulled at the damp material to get a better look. "Oh, man, this was my favorite coat."

Katie smacked the uninjured side of his chest. "Trent Dixon, you've been shot and you're griping about your coat?"

His leather glove was cold against her cheek. But there was nothing but heat in the quick kiss he gave her before whispering, "I'm okay. We'll fix it at home."

She held on, looking up at him, and whispered back, "You're sure?"

"The shot grazed me when we were running." He winced beneath the white clouds of his breath and glanced down at Tyler. "There's a first-aid kit in the glove compartment. Let's not worry you know who."

"Then it *is* bad." Katie instantly released him and dived inside the truck to retrieve the medical supplies.

"Barely a scratch, I promise."

But she'd raised a smart kid who knew they were talking about him. Tyler swiped at the tears that were still falling, bravely taking control of his fear and confusion. "I can go to the hospital if we have to. I'll watch Mom." He sniffed and rubbed at the red tip of his nose. Katie kissed his cheek and handed him a tissue before tearing open a box of gauze pads. "I'm not scared. But real guns are loud."

Trent squeezed Tyler's knee. "They are, buddy, aren't they? Dangerous, too."

Tyler touched the cuff of Trent's bloody sleeve. "Does it hurt?"

"It stings. It's raw skin and it burns. But like I told your mama, this isn't bad. It could have been a lot worse."

"Like that man in the car?"

Katie's breath locked up in her chest and tears burned her eyes. No sense hiding the truth from him now. She hadn't been able to protect him from violence any more than her mother had been able to protect her. Trent glanced at Katie, then hunched down in front of Tyler for a man-to-man talk.

"Guns can do terrible things, Ty." Trent held out his heavy black Glock where the boy could see it without touching it before sliding it safely back into his holster. "The safety's on now, so it can't hurt you. But when it's not…"

Tyler listened in rapt attention to every word while Katie went to work, cutting away the shreds of Trent's coat sleeve, along with the flannel and thermal cotton underneath. "But guns can save lives, too. Someday I'll teach you how to shoot one safely. Until then, you don't mess with any of them, okay?"

Tyler nodded his understanding.

"But don't worry, buddy. Tonight, they aren't going to hurt you or your mom. I'm glad you're here to back me up. You can help me keep an eye out for that silver car that drove away, in case it comes back, okay? At least until Uncle Max gets here to pick us up."

"Okay."

Before Trent could straighten, Tyler threw his arms around the big man's neck and held on as he stood. Trent wound his good arm around her son and pulled him onto his lap as he perched on the edge of the seat.

Katie let him cradle her son and reassure him that the nightmare had ended, at least for tonight. Seeing her friend being so tender and protective with Tyler allowed her to breathe a little easier, too. Trent was right—the bullet had only grazed him and hadn't ripped through muscle or bone. But it wasn't an injury that was going to stop bleeding on its own anytime soon, so she pulled out a wad of gauze and applied pressure to the wound, willing it to stop, willing this good, wonderful man who clearly meant the world to her son—and to her, she was discovering—to be safe.

By the time she'd tied a longer piece of gauze around his biceps to keep the pressure bandage in place, a campus police car was pulling up. She could see lights flashing off the buildings and trees as KCPD cars and, hopefully, an ambulance arrived on campus.

"You don't think the shooters are coming back, do you?" she asked. "Are we witnesses now?"

"They won't be back tonight," Trent stated in a hushed, sure tone that inspired confidence. "My guess is that they wanted us disabled so they could make a getaway without me following them."

But she saw that he kept his hand on the butt of his weapon, just in case.

Chapter Eleven

Katie was clean and warm after her hot shower. But even in her flannel pajamas and robe and with a pair of socks she'd borrowed from Trent on her feet, she couldn't shake the chill that permeated her from the inside out.

"They doing okay?" Trent's voice was a deep-pitched whisper in the shadows of the hallway as he stepped out of the master suite and came up behind her to peek into the guest room where Tyler slept with Padre on the long twin bed.

Trent had towel dried his short hair without putting a comb through it and had the damp terry cloth hanging around his bare neck and shoulders above the fresh jeans he'd slipped on. She could feel the heat of his shower radiating off his skin, and breathed in the enticing smells of soap and man. But still, she hugged her arms around her waist and shivered. "They shot at my son."

Trent laid his hand over her shoulder. "The EMT said he was just fine—nothing a good night's sleep and a sense of security can't fix."

She turned her cheek in to the warmth and caring he offered. "You give him that."

"I think that sense of security comes from a mom who's always been there for him."

Katie grunted a small laugh of disagreement, and the tan-and-white collie mix lifted his head at the sound. She was the reason John Smith had become a part of their lives in the first place, although KCPD still wasn't certain who had hired him or why he'd been following Katie. For all she knew, Smith had been executed because he'd failed to break into her apartment and murder her, or retrieve whatever information she'd found that Leland Asher didn't want her to. Some security. More like the magnet for trouble she'd always been.

"Katie?" Perhaps sensing the guilty direction her thoughts had taken, Trent tightened his grip on her shoulder.

But she shushed him and walked into the room to pet the skinny dog that had been a blessing for Tyler to come home to. The two had eaten a snack together and played, and had separated only long enough for Tyler to take a bath and brush his teeth. She scratched the dog around his ears, then pressed a kiss to the soft fur on top of his head. "I'm counting on you to keep an eye on our boy, okay, Padre?" Then she lifted the covers and tucked Tyler's leg beneath the quilt and pulled it up to his chin. She brushed his dark hair off his forehead and kissed his sweet, velvety skin. It was a relief to see the tears had washed away and the frown mark had relaxed with sleep. "I love you, sweetie," she whispered, then winked at the alert dog. "Good boy."

As soon as Katie backed away from the bed, Padre laid his head down over Tyler's legs and she knew her son would be watched over through the night. If only she could let go of the uncertainty of these past few days and sleep so easily.

She looked up to see the big, half-dressed man filling the doorway. The gauze and tape on Trent's shoulder stood out like a beacon in the shadows cast by the lone night-light in Tyler's room, mocking his claim that she didn't screw up relationships, that the people around her didn't get hurt.

But it was too late and she was too raw to have that discussion again. So she grasped at the friendly banter and mutual support system that had always been there between them. "Okay, mister. You're next." She nudged him out into the hallway and pulled the door partly shut behind her. "The doctor said I should replace your bandage after your shower."

She stopped in her bedroom to retrieve her bag, where she'd stowed the extra supplies the doctor in the ER had given them, then followed him through the quiet house into the en suite off the master bedroom. While Trent hung up his towel, she filled a glass with water. "Antibiotics first."

"Yes, ma'am." With a weary grin on his unshaven face, he dutifully took the pill she handed him and swallowed it.

She got the distinct feeling he was humoring her when she closed the toilet lid and had him sit so she could peel the tape off the tanned skin of his upper arm and toss it and the soiled gauze beneath it into the trash. He only winced once and never complained about the pain he must be in as she made quick work of cleansing the open wound and applying a new layer of ointment before covering the injury with a clean gauze pad. But the tape twisted and fought her as she pulled it off the roll and tried to tear the pieces she needed.

"Where are those scissors?" After securing the gauze with one mangled piece of tape, Katie squatted down to open the bag and pull out the contents inside to retrieve the smaller items that had fallen to the bottom. "Just give me a sec." Wallet. Sunglasses. Squashed breakfast bar. Laptop. Mini toy truck. "There they are…"

Katie gasped. She'd been so intent on fixing up Trent and getting back to her own bed, where she prayed a dreamless sleep would claim her, that the damage done to the cover of her laptop almost didn't register. But then she trailed her finger over the small, perfectly round dent in the metal cover. A frightening realization swept through her with such force that it made her light-headed. She wobbled and sank onto her knees. She set the laptop on the tile floor and dug into her purse again. Not for scissors this time. It was… *Oh, my God.* There. Perfectly round and just big enough to slip her finger through. A bullet hole.

"Is something broken?"

Turning, she held up her bag with her finger still sticking through the hole. "I could have been killed. Tyler could have been killed. You could have…" Her voice faded with every sentence until there was barely a breath of sound. "I don't understand why this is happening.'

"Ah, Katie." Trent tossed the bag aside and pulled her onto his lap. "Sunshine, come here."

Dressing the wound was forgotten as she curled up on top of his thighs and leaned into him. His arms came around her and wrapped her up with the heat of his body.

With her ear pressed to the strong beat of his heart, Katie shivered. "I'm so cold."

His big hands moved up and down her back and arms, creating static friction as he rubbed flannel against flannel. But even that electricity couldn't seem to pierce the shroud of despair closing in around her. "You're going into a little bit of shock. Let's get you warmed up."

When he lifted her into the air, she remembered herself. "Your arm. What if it starts bleeding again?"

"Screw that."

"I need to finish dressing it."

He carried her out of the bathroom to the king-size bed where he slept. "Right now, you just need to let me take care of you." Her toes touched the floor only long enough for Trent to pull back the covers. Then he swung her up into his arms again and set her near the middle of the bed. Before she could think to protest, he'd stretched out beside her and pulled the sheet and thick comforter up over them both. He gathered her into his arms and threw one leg over both of hers, aligning them chest to hip, with her head tucked beneath his chin and their legs tangled together. "Think of it as doing me a favor." With her arms caught between them, he pulled her impossibly closer, wrapping her up in the furnace of his body. "I need a break, sunshine. This whole investigation is wearing me out. It'd be nice to not have to worry about you getting into trouble for a little while."

She almost giggled at the teasing remark, but she was too caught up in the drugging effect of his body heat seeping into hers. The tightness in her chest eased, and the shivering abated. The longer Trent held her, the longer he whispered those deeply pitched assurances in her ear, the stronger she felt. The panic lessened. Her jumbled thoughts cleared.

He stroked his fingers through her hair, pressed a kiss to the crown. "You're safe. You're fine. Tyler's fine. And I'm too big to bring down with a piddly-ass shot like this wound."

His wound. It needed to be properly tended. Katie stiffened her arms and pushed against his chest. "Trent—"

"I'm fine, too. You stay right here. This is what *I* need, remember?"

Katie wasn't sure if she'd dozed for a little while or if lying with Trent, bundled beneath the covers to chase away the wintry chill that had derailed her for a few moments, was all the healing she needed to feel more like her normal self again. To believe again that she and her son were safe. To feel as though the mistakes of her past couldn't touch her tonight. Not in Trent's bed. Not in his arms.

It was sometime later, when the wind of a winter storm outside rattled the windowpanes and startled her awake, that Katie realized she'd never returned to her own bed. And now that she was feeling rested and warm—and she couldn't hear any sounds of a boy or dog stirring—she admitted that she didn't want to leave.

"Better?" The drowsy male voice greeted her from the pillow beside her.

Katie smiled. "Much."

"This is nice, Katie Lee Rinaldi." Trent's fingers were stroking lazy circles along her back and hip, and Katie discovered her fingers taking similar liberties across the warm skin and ticklish curls of his chest. "But you know what else I need?"

Her hand stilled and she pushed herself up onto her elbow. Did he want her to finish taping his bandage? Did he need one of the painkillers the doctor had prescribed? "What is it? Anything I can do—"

"I need you to trust me."

"I do." She leaned over him, trying to assess the message in those gunmetal eyes.

"I need you to trust us—even if it's just for tonight."

Oh. Her body tingled in anticipation. "Trent, are you asking me to—"

He silenced her question with a sweetly lingering kiss. His patience with her was as maddening as it was exquisite. His lips ignited a slow burn that seemed to travel from her mouth to every point of her body where his hips and thigh and roaming hand touched her, creating a network of pathways that crisscrossed inside her, filling her with heat and an edgy sort of desire that demanded more than easygoing kisses and tender caresses.

"I know you need me to take things slow." He combed his fingers into the dark waves of her hair that brushed against his chest and tucked them behind her ear, cupping the side of her neck. "I need your brain to help me put Leland Asher away for good, but I need something else from you, too. I need to touch you to believe I didn't almost lose you tonight. I need to feel your confidence and caring to keep me strong. I need to feel your strength, holding me, accepting everything I want to give you and be for you. I'm not just asking for sex, sunshine. I need that closeness we've always shared. I—"

She shushed him with a finger over his mouth. "I think I need that, too. I want all the things I think you can give me. For tonight."

"It'll change everything between us."

Sliding her arms around his neck, Katie fell back onto the pillow, pulling him to her. "I think it already has changed."

And then there was no more conversation. There were only hungry lips and greedy hands and Trent's muscular body moving over hers.

He unwrapped her like a gift, untying her robe, unbuttoning her pajama top. He slipped his hands inside, searing her skin with every sweeping touch, every squeeze of a breast. With his thumb, he teased the sensitive tips to tiny pebbles, generating little frissons of electricity beneath every touch, feeding the current of heat and pressure stirring deep in her womb.

Carefully avoiding his injury, Katie swept her hands over the smooth skin of his back, felt the muscles of his chest quiver and jump beneath her exploring fingers. She sampled the sandpapery line of his chin and jaw, and smiled at the responsive cord of muscle at the side of his neck that made him groan deep in his throat each time she took a nip.

True to his word, he seemed to touch every inch of her body while his wicked mouth worked its magic on hers. He tugged her pajama pants down to claim her hip with the palm of his hand and pull the most feverish part of her body into the bulge thrusting behind his zipper. When he kissed his way down her neck, Katie thrust her fingers into the damp muss of his hair, releasing a spicy scent that filled her nose. She guided his mouth to the straining peak of her breast and whimpered at the bolt of heat that arced through her.

Every kiss was a temptation. Every touch a torment. "Trent," she gasped. "Now. Please."

He threw back the covers to shuck off his jeans and shorts and sheathe himself. The chill of the night had barely cooled her skin before Trent was back, tossing aside the flannel pants she'd kicked off and settling between her legs. "There's no turning back from this," he reminded her, stealing another kiss from her swollen lips.

Katie nodded and pulled at his hips, demanding he complete what he'd started. "I've made some bad choices in my life, Trent. This isn't one of them."

She lifted her knees and he slipped inside, slowly filling her with his length. His dark gray eyes locked on to hers as he began to move. She tried to hold his loving gaze, tried to memorize every second of this stolen time together, but soon the sensation was too much. She could only feel. He slipped his hand beneath her bottom and lifted her into his final thrust. Katie closed her eyes and surrendered to the heat bursting inside her. Seconds later, Trent gasped her name against her hair and followed her over the edge into the fiery inferno.

TRENT AWOKE TO the sound of a phone ringing and an empty bed.

He swung his feet to the floor, trying to orient himself to the long night and the early hour. He scratched his fingers through his hair, instantly remembering how Katie had played with it—and how her fingers had tightened against his scalp, holding his mouth to a sweet, round breast as she gasped for breath and squirmed with delight beneath him. Hell. Even remembering how she'd put her hands all over him with such hungry abandon was enough to make things stir down south this morning.

With a groan of resignation, he scooped up his shorts and jeans, fishing his ringing cell out of the back pocket and checking the number. Olivia Watson. She'd hold for a couple more rings, giving him time to go into the john to splash some cold water on his face and try to get his head on straight before taking a work call.

He'd known Katie had a rockin' body. What fool male wouldn't want to put his hands all over those decadent curves? But he hadn't expected how responsive she'd be to every needy touch. How eager she'd be to explore him, as well. That was the free spirit he'd imagined her to be in his youth. That was the Katie who'd first captured his young heart.

And he sure as hell hadn't expected this gut kick of pain when he realized their time together—a crazy mix of comfort, caring and passion—didn't mean as much to her as it did to him. Hell. She must have left before dawn. The painkiller in his system had knocked him out eventually, and he'd slept longer than usual, oblivious to her efforts to escape and erase any evidence of their time spent together.

The phone was still ringing in his hand when he strolled back into the bedroom and sat on the black-and-gold comforter that had been draped neatly back on the bed—after he distinctly remembered it sliding off onto the floor last night. Katie hadn't left so much as a dent in the pillow beside him this morning. She'd taken every stitch of clothing, even her damaged bag and the contents that had been scattered across his bathroom floor, leaving no trace of *them* behind.

Well, he'd gotten exactly what he'd asked for, hadn't he? One night with Katie Lee in his bed. If only the two of them had been lousy together. If only the hushed conversation and cuddling in between hadn't made him think that it had meant something life changing to her, too. Trent hadn't felt that right inside his own skin for ten years. But expecting Katie to suddenly love him the way he loved her…?

The bedroom door burst open and a nine-year-old and the excited dog chasing him jumped onto the bed. "Aren't you going to answer your phone?" Tyler asked, bouncing up and down on his knees. "It's been ringing forever."

"Tyler." Katie followed a few steps after, hanging back

in the doorway. She'd already dressed in a pair of jeans and a sweatshirt and had pulled the sexy waves of her hair back into a tomboyish ponytail. "I told you not to wake Trent."

"But, Mom, he was already awake." Tyler threw himself on the bed, which bounced like a trampoline with his light weight. "Padre and I peeked."

Katie shook her head at the bouncy boy and whining dog and frowned an apology at Trent. "I didn't know if I needed to answer the phone for you."

Was this entourage the reason she'd left him this morning? Letting Tyler see the two of them share a kiss was one thing, but explaining what it meant when Mommy and Trent slept in bed together was something else. Or was that just the excuse she was using for pretending as though last night had never happened?

"Nope. I got it." He punched the button on the phone and put it to his ear. "Olivia. What's up?"

"Sorry to wake you, Sleeping Beauty, but I'm at the ME's office at the crime lab. My brother Niall just completed the autopsy on your private detective. We got an ID on John Smith."

"Hold on a sec, Liv. Katie's here with me. I'm going to put you on speakerphone." Katie hustled Tyler out of the room with orders to finish his bowl of cereal and get dressed for school. Then she nodded and came back to stand beside Trent and listen in on the call. "Tell us about John Smith. Which one of those aliases was real?"

"None of them. None of those identities existed until about ten years ago. John Smith is the most recent incarnation. The man had a knack for reinventing himself."

Normally, all the details were important. But he was

only in the mood for straight answers this morning. "You said you had a match."

"We do. His fingerprints are in the system."

Katie pulled the phone down to her level and asked, "Then why didn't this guy's real identity pop when I ran the search on him?"

"Because Niall found the prints in the archives." Katie tilted her confused frown up to meet his. The KCPD archives were the files where cases that had been solved were stored. Or where crimes that had passed their statute of limitations—meaning the police could no longer pursue them—had been filed away. "Does the name Francisco Dona ring a bell?"

Katie's encyclopedic memory came up with the connection first. "Isabel Asher's boyfriend? The guy Leland blamed for her death?" She shook her head. "There was a motorcycle accident. Francisco Dona is dead."

"He is now." Olivia's sarcasm wasn't entirely for humor's sake. "The fingerprints don't lie. This guy has been able to fly under the radar for ten years. Somehow, he got his prints in a DB file and a John Doe was cremated in his place. He was reborn as a new man several times over, most recently as John Smith, private eye."

Trent tried to have some respect for a man who could change his identity as readily and completely as the WIT-SEC division of the US Marshals' office could. But all he could see was a criminal who'd gotten far too close to Katie and Tyler. "So if he knew we were tracking Leland Asher and putting together a case against him, Francisco Dona—Mr. Smith—would have a personal stake in finding out what we know."

Olivia agreed. "If Asher found out the man he blamed for his sister's death was still alive, he'd make fixing that mistake his number-one priority once he got out of prison. He'd certainly want to make sure the man paid before the cancer got him."

That dimpled frown had reappeared between Katie's eyebrows. "I get why Francisco Dona would come after me. I'm the information guru—I'd be his best source for finding out where we are in the Asher investigation and what the team's chances are of putting him back in prison for life."

"But?" Trent prompted, wondering what wheels were turning in that clever mind of hers.

"But if he had access to my laptop, which he did when he or someone else planted the mirroring program, then why threaten me? Why warn me to stop? He should want every piece of information he could steal from me."

"Are we dealing with two different cases here?" Trent suggested. "Smith might have been after Katie, but somebody else was after Smith."

Olivia had her own idea. "Or maybe trailing Katie was Smith's effort to try to escape from Asher's retribution one more time, but he failed. Still, how did Smith get access to Katie's computer in the first place?"

Katie spoke up this time. "I have a theory on that." She glanced up at Trent, perhaps offering an explanation for her hasty retreat this morning. "A couple of weird things happened at the theater last night."

"Besides finding a dead body and getting shot at?" What else had he missed besides Francis Sergel putting his hands on Katie?

"I did some research this morning. The bullet just dented my laptop—it still works." When she gestured for him to follow, Trent went into the spare bedroom with her. He tried to ignore that all her things had been moved in here and focus on the restraining-order record she pulled up on the screen. "There have been sexual harassment complaints filed against Doug Price. I found a record of a college student who went to a judge after she discovered Doug hiding a camera in a women's dressing room and taking pictures without her consent."

Trent borrowed one of Max's choice curses. "How does this guy get to work in community theater?"

"Because it's a volunteer position with a volunteer board, and sometimes it's hard to find people with the skills to organize and run a show who are willing to give up that much of their time." Katie shrugged. "And probably because people don't talk about it enough. I've found three different theater companies where Doug has volunteered in Missouri and Kansas."

"And you think he planted the device to sabotage your computer?" Olivia asked.

"He could have been blackmailed into doing it. It fits our *Strangers on a Train* theory about someone manipulating others to commit crimes for them." Trent was less than thrilled to hear about Katie's encounter with Doug Price last night. "He was eager that I not touch or see whatever was in that envelope. I wonder if they were photographs, or copies of them. And the price to keep them from going to the police or going public was tampering with my computer."

Olivia seemed to agree it was a strong possibility. "Do you think he killed John Smith? Or Francisco? Or whatever we're calling him now?"

"I don't think he'd have the guts to pull a trigger. But maybe he saw something and that's why he was in such a hurry to leave—especially if Smith was his blackmailer."

"You want me to bring Doug Price in for questioning?" Olivia offered.

"Yeah. Put Max to work, too." Trent had a feeling that after months of hard work and dangerous setbacks, a lot of cold cases were about to break wide open. "I want to know if John Smith was tracking Katie for his own survival or if someone else hired him. If so, who? And why?"

Katie nodded. "And if last night was a hit ordered by Asher, how did he find out John Smith's real identity?"

Trent headed back to his own room. "I want Leland Asher in my interrogation room. Today."

"I'll clear it with the lieutenant and have Max pick him up."

"Katie and I will stop by Smith's office to see what we can find there before coming in."

Trent hung up and went to work, unlocking his gun from the strongbox in his closet and sliding the weapon onto his belt. He started to pull on a thermal undershirt but realized the dressing on his wound needed changing. Unfortunately, it was a two-handed project. He pulled off the twisted tape and soiled gauze and dangled it at Katie's door. "A little help?"

"Come on in." She set down the blouse and sweater she'd been getting ready to change into and picked up her bag with the first-aid supplies. He sat on the edge of the double-size bed while she doctored him. "Jim's coming by to take Tyler to school again and watch him until we pick him up. And then I'll start pulling everything KCPD has on Francisco Dona and John Smith. I'll get a brief together on Asher and his minions before you run your interviews this afternoon, so you know who all the players are."

After the first piece of tape was secured on his shoulder, Trent caught Katie by the wrist. Even if she was going to pretend it hadn't happened, he needed to say something about last night. "Damn, you smell good in the morning." He watched the blush of heat creep into her cheeks as he lightly massaged the warm beat of her pulse. "You were amazing last night. But I missed you when I woke up. I gather you don't want Tyler to know what happened."

Katie twisted her wrist from his touch and cut another length of tape. "If he doesn't know how close we got, maybe he won't get his hopes up and think—"

"That you and I could be a real couple."

She positioned the tape over the gauze and gently smoothed it into place. "Trent. Last night was like a fairy tale. Tyler had a dad and a dog, and you were completely wonderful to me."

"But?" He was wary of where this explanation was going.

"Obviously, this isn't over yet. Between a mob boss and a dead private detective, there are still so many things that could go wrong. You've already been hurt. Tyler was frightened out of his mind. And, let's face it, I wigged out on you." She picked up his thermal shirt and helped him slide his arm into the sleeve without disturbing the bandage. "I've never been part of the story where they all live happily ever after. I'm afraid a few moments like last night, that idyllic perfection, aren't real."

He pulled his shirt on over his head and slipped the rest of it into place before standing beside her. He dropped his head to whisper against her ear, "It is for me, sunshine. As far as I'm concerned, the fairy tale is real." He inched in a little farther and pressed a kiss to her hair. "I just need you to decide when or if you're going to accept that I'm in love with you and that you're in love with me. I want to be a father to your son and a husband to you. And you know damn well that I'd be good at both."

He couldn't lay it on the line any plainer than that. With his heart and future in her hands now, Trent left her standing there in pale silence and returned to his own room to put on his badge and go to work.

Chapter Twelve

What John Smith's office lacked in decor, it more than made up for in messiness.

Katie helped Trent sort through the rows of file cabinets, looking for anything useful. Folders had been stuffed into drawers without regard to labels or alphabetizing. Whoever had gone through the office before them hadn't been there to rob Smith because they'd left behind a bottle of scotch and bag of marijuana that had been stashed in the back of one drawer.

She'd at least been able to make more sense out of his desktop computer. It appeared he'd used it mainly for word processing and internet research, so she'd easily tracked several of the searches he'd recently made—including a floor plan for the units in her apartment complex, news updates on Leland Asher's release from prison and several searches of medical sites to find the prognosis and life expectancy for a sixty-year-old man diagnosed with lung cancer.

"Looks like he's been tracking Asher for years," Katie reported.

Trent nodded, looking over her shoulder to read the monitor. "That clued him in on when he needed to change his identity again. If Asher got too close to finding out he was still alive, Francisco would go underground for a few months and reinvent himself as someone else."

"The medical searches probably meant he was hoping Leland would die soon. Maybe that was why he was at the press conference, to see with his own eyes whether the man who wanted him dead had long to live."

Trent went back to the file cabinets to continue his search. "Unfortunately for him, he miscalculated. Leland's men got to him first."

Katie rolled the chair away from the desk to help Trent dig through the remaining mess for other useful clues. There was one more piece of information she could get off Smith's computer—who had hired him to spy on her— but they needed a different warrant to breach the confidential agreement between investigator and client. While Lieutenant Rafferty-Taylor pleaded their case to a warrant judge, she and Trent were spending their morning in dusty cabinets, sharing terse, business-only conversation.

"Katie." His sharp voice pulled her from her thoughts. He set a bent folder on top of the cabinet and opened it. "Is this who I think it is?"

Katie joined him, reading the name scrawled across the top of the first page. "Stephen March." She flipped through the pages to see copies of March's time spent in drug courts and rehab, along with a criminal complaint Stephen March had filed against his sister's fiancé, Richard Bratcher, which had been thrown out of court. "This shows March's motive for wanting Bratcher dead, as well as blackmailable offenses that could be used to get him to kill Dani Reese." She dug farther into the drawer in front of her. "These are all people Smith investigated?"

"Looks like it." He peeled a tiny slip of masking tape off the inside of the drawer. "I wonder."

"What is it?"

He showed her the hyphenated list of numbers before crossing over to the safe behind Smith's desk. He knelt down and twisted the numbers on the dial. "This guy was resourceful, but I don't know that he knew much about security precautions." Trent opened the door and pulled out three thick manila envelopes and stacked them on top of the safe. He pulled a fourth one out and dumped the contents out beside the stack. Out tumbled bundles of money. Twenties, fifties, hundreds. "I'm guessing this was a cash business. Probably a smart idea for a man who had to change identities and bank accounts every couple of years."

"Trent." She pulled another folder from the file drawers. "This says Hillary Wells." There were other files in this cabinet that matched names in her own research. "That creep piggybacked off all my work. In some of these, he's gone to websites I checked and printed off the exact same information." She didn't know whether to feel angry that he'd stolen her months of dedicated research to use for some nefarious purpose or violated to think John Smith, aka Francisco Dona, had followed every thought, every move, she'd made on her computer—and she hadn't even known he'd been lurking, watching.

"I think we're onto something here, sunshine."

Katie snapped out of the emotional debate. Trent hadn't used her nickname since that conversation about fairy tales earlier that morning. In fact, he'd barely looked at her. And he certainly hadn't kissed her or held her or touched her in any way since dropping that bomb of an admission this morning.

I just need you to decide when or if you're going to ac-

cept that I'm in love with you and that you're in love with me. I want to be a father to your son and a husband to you.

That promise was everything she'd wanted growing up. But a life's worth of mistakes and tragedies made it difficult to believe in that promise. How was she supposed to do the right thing when she wasn't sure what that was anymore? How could Trent love her enough to risk a relationship with a woman with all her phobias and eccentricities and emotional baggage that came with the package? And was it worth the risk of her and Tyler losing him from their lives if the relationship didn't work? Then again, maybe she'd lost him already by not giving him the answer he'd wanted this morning.

And the idea of not having Trent's strong arms and stalwart presence and beautiful soul in her life anymore already felt like a very big mistake.

But Trent was talking work now, not their personal lives, where she got him shot and broke his heart. She circled around the desk to join him. "What did you find?"

He pulled another manila envelope from the safe and handed it to her. "Check inside. I'm guessing that envelope you saw with Doug Price held something similar."

Katie pulled out a stack of photographs. "Oh, my." These were images of scantily clad women, obviously taken by a hidden camera. She even recognized an image of the college student who'd sued Doug for harassment. "Oh. My."

"You blackmail a man into doing a job for you, then you keep an extra copy of the evidence for insurance purposes."

Katie stuffed the pictures back inside the envelope. "This man was horrible."

"Which one?" The phone in Trent's pocket rang before

she could answer. Katie waited in anticipation until he nodded. "Yes, ma'am." She sat at the desk again and booted up the private detective's computer, waiting for the order. "We've got the warrant. Do it."

One keystroke and she'd know who'd hired Smith to spy on her. She leaned back in the chair, surprised by the answer on the screen. "There's only one name here. One person who hired Smith to watch over all these people."

"Please tell me it's Leland Asher."

"No. Dr. Beverly Eisenbach."

TRENT GLANCED AROUND Ginny Rafferty-Taylor's office, as anxious to get this show underway as the drumming of Katie's fingers or Max's pacing would indicate.

Four suspects. Four different strategies. Four different plans of attack.

And if the team was as good as the lieutenant seemed to think, then Leland Asher would be on his way back to prison by the end of the night.

The petite lieutenant picked up the stack of folders Katie had prepared and handed them to Trent. "Are you ready to do this?"

"Yes, ma'am."

"How do you want to handle it?"

Trent glanced over to Katie's big blue eyes staring up at him. He couldn't, wouldn't put his heart out there again for her to torment until she decided whether she was going to live her life taking risks or holed up in the security of lonely nobility. But whether he got his fairy-tale ending or not, he'd be damned if anyone was going to hurt her or Tyler again.

He nodded to her, making that silent vow, and headed

out to Interview Room 1. "I'm going to pick off the little fish first."

In the grand scheme of things, Doug Price was an easy interrogation. Trent was twice the older man's size, and all he had to do was stand and dominate the room to get the play director to talk.

He tossed the stack of lewd photos he'd gotten from John Smith's safe and fanned them across the table in front of Doug and his attorney. "Anything look familiar to you, Mr. Price?"

His lawyer tried to keep Doug from saying anything, but the man already had some of that oversprayed hair falling out of place. He sat forward in his chair. "Where did you get these?"

Trent tossed a crime-scene photo of John Smith's bloody face on top of the other pictures. "From this guy."

Doug cringed and pushed the photos away. But he cracked like an egg. "John Smith. He's a private investigator. He told me he'd given me the last copies of those pictures when I saw him last night. I had no reason to kill him. I was doing him a favor." A favor in the sense that Smith hadn't given Doug any choice. "Smith said if I kept an eye on Katie and helped him get access to your team's investigations that he wouldn't turn any of those photos over to the police."

"So you sabotaged Katie's laptop and left those threats for her? You assaulted her in the women's dressing room?"

"It wasn't assault. I was removing a camera. I wasn't expecting her to be there. I just wanted to get away."

"I think we can safely say that your career in community theater is over." Trent pulled out a chair on the opposite side of the gray metal table. Doug started to relax, but Trent decided to stay on his feet and catch him off guard. He pulled three more photographs from the file Katie had prepared. Three more links in the chain of related crimes she'd dug up in her extensive research. He set the pictures down in front of Doug, one by one. "Do you know any of these people?"

"No. No." He pointed to the last one. "Her. I don't understand what she has to do with any of this."

Interesting. "Who is she to you, Doug?"

"My therapist. I saw Dr. Eisenbach for a few months years back. Court-ordered sessions. The judge said I had an addiction to pornography."

BEV EISENBACH AND Matt Asher clammed up behind their attorneys when they were separated into two interview rooms. But as Olivia slyly observed when she and Max *accidentally* allowed the two suspects' paths to cross in the hallway across from the restrooms, the twenty-two-year-old and the woman old enough to be his mother clearly knew each other. They'd called each other by their first names in a quick, hushed conversation, and their fingers had met in a quick squeeze.

Now, there was an odd couple.

They each truthfully claimed to have shared nothing with Trent, then whispered something about promising to remain silent.

So the two had a plan that they'd clearly been working on together for some time...while their uncle/boyfriend had been locked away in prison. Instead of kowtowing to the boss, they'd been plotting behind his back. Setting Leland up for murder? Or taking over the criminal empire from a dying man?

The information Olivia had fed Trent between interviews made him grin. Bev and Matt's conversation had given Trent some key intel to use as he moved on to his final interview with Leland. He grinned because while they acted as though Leland was on his way out of the business, and they were setting themselves up to take his place, someone had forgotten to tell Leland.

Trent's approach to a man of Leland Asher's self-appointed stature was different than the intimidation he'd used with Doug Price or the friendly charm he'd turned on his nephew and Bev Eisenbach. "How long do you have to live, Mr. Asher? Years? Months? Weeks?"

Leland smiled. "I like a man who's direct, Detective. I can talk to a man like that."

Trent leaned forward in his chair, matching Leland's confident posture. "Did you have any dealings with Craig Fairfax at the penitentiary infirmary?"

"Fairfax?" Leland scratched at his gaunt cheeks. "Poor bloke. Terrible cough. I always thought he was going to hack up a lung. Very difficult to have a conversation with him."

"So you did interact with him. Did you ever talk about Katie Lee Rinaldi?"

"Who?"

Trent steeled his gazed on Asher, knowing Katie was watching in Lieutenant Rafferty-Taylor's office through the closed-circuit camera overhead. This would be a tough line of questioning for her to hear, but since she was part of the team, she'd insisted on listening in. "A girl Fairfax kidnapped ten years ago."

"Oh, that Katie. Tragic upbringing from what I hear. Yes, I believe she's the district attorney's daughter now." Close enough. Apparently, Fairfax had been filling Asher in on Katie's family history. "Goodness knows, Mr. Fair-fax has a vendetta against that man. If he could get out of prison, I'm sure his first stop would be the DA's house, or perhaps his wife's school—or at the home of this Katie you mentioned. Yes, I remember he definitely has a score he wants to settle...*if* he were ever to be released from prison."

Trent's hand fisted beneath the table at the indirect but abhorrent threats, although he betrayed nothing to Asher. "Do you have a score to settle, Mr. Asher? With Francisco Dona, perhaps?"

"I have no comment."

"What about John Smith? Do you know anyone by that name?"

"Not very original, is it?" Trent waited until Leland answered the question. "No, I don't believe I do."

"But you know Dona."

"Knew, Detective. Past tense. Dona died in a motor-cycle accident several years ago."

"Did he?" Trent wasn't intimidated by the man's con-descending tone. "If you discovered Mr. Dona was alive after all these years, you'd want to do something about it, wouldn't you?"

Leland checked his brittle nails before leaning forward and resting the elbows of his tailored suit on the table. "I liked you better when you were straightforward, Detec-tive. You know as well as I do that Francisco is a sensi-tive subject for me. He turned my sister on to drugs and then killed her with them. At the very least, he was a cow-ard and let her die without raising a finger to help. Isabel was the light of my life. Francisco snuffed that light out."

He wanted straightforward? "Did you murder Fran-cisco Dona last night in retaliation for your sister's death? Or hire someone to murder him?"

"So he is dead." Asher leaned back in his chair and

smiled. "I'm a dying man. Whether it was ten years ago or yesterday, knowing he died before me makes me very happy."

Leland checked his watch and glanced at his attorney. "Will there be anything else, Detective Dixon? I have a dinner engagement I don't want to miss."

"Just one last question and then I can let you go."

"What's that?"

"Did you know that your girlfriend, Beverly Eisenbach, and your nephew, Matt, have been having an affair while you've been incarcerated in Jefferson City?"

Leland leaned over to whisper something with his attorney before answering.

"Yes."

KATIE KNEW SOMETHING was terribly wrong when the cast came out for curtain call at the final dress rehearsal. There were only five Cratchit children crossing to center stage. Where was Tiny Tim? "Where's Tyler?"

She ran down to the stage and straight up the stairs, pushing aside actors while the music was playing and they were still taking their bows. She wasn't going to lose him again.

"Wyatt? Kayla? Have you seen Tyler?"

The other children seemed startled to realize one of them was missing.

"No, ma'am."

"We were playing cards backstage at intermission. He said his last line, didn't he?"

Yes, her son had the last line of the entire show. Then the actors had all exited backstage to line up for bows, and now... "Francis." She caught the tall actor by the sleeve of his robe before he went back onstage. "Have you seen my son?"

She heard him snorting beneath his mask. "No director. Missing actors. Crazy costume ladies dashing across the stage. You know what they say—a bad dress rehearsal means we'll have a stellar opening night."

"Stuff it, Francis. Have you seen Tyler?" He tugged his robe from her grasp and ignored her question. "Then is Trent here yet?"

Francis snickered from behind his mask. "It's not my job to keep track of your child or that bruiser boyfriend of yours."

"Francis, please."

"That's my cue."

Trent had promised to be here by the end of the rehearsal. Maybe Trent had arrived early and he and Tyler had gotten to talking backstage and her son had simply missed his cue. Katie hurried back to the greenroom.

He'd had to stay late at the precinct office, walking Doug Price through booking, writing up reports on his interviews with Leland and Matt Asher and Beverly Eisenbach, and sitting down with the rest of the team to determine whether they had enough circumstantial evidence for arrest warrants yet. Normally, Katie would have been part of such a meeting, but Lieutenant Rafferty-Taylor had excused her for Tyler's benefit. With the threat of John Smith no longer in the picture, Katie had figured she could go to the final dress rehearsal without the benefit of a 24/7 bodyguard. Even so, Trent had insisted a uniformed officer accompany them, and he'd promised to join them at the theater as soon as he could get away from work. After all, Tyler still wanted him to be a part of his life, even if Katie needed time to decide how to respond to Trent's ultimatum.

But maybe that need for an evening of independence to figure out her future had been a mistake.

She hurried past Ebenezer Scrooge himself, knowing there would be no other actors behind him. The crew members thought Tyler was onstage or had made an emergency run to the bathroom and forgotten he had to go back out.

She found Tyler's street clothes still on the hanger in the men's dressing room, although his coat was gone.

Katie quickly slipped into her own coat and pulled out her phone. He wouldn't have been so foolish as to go out and play in the snow, would he? Just in case, she hurried across the backstage area and stepped outside. "Tyler?"

Not trusting her son's safety to anyone else, Katie punched in Trent's number and lifted the phone to her ear. It rang once before she saw the silver car, just like the night before, waiting in the crowded parking lot. She saw Leland Asher nod to her before climbing into the backseat. "Oh, no. Tyler!"

She started to run. But strong arms locked around her from behind, knocking her phone into the snow and lifting her off the ground. A rough hand and a pungent cloth muffled her scream, and within seconds, her knees grew weak and the world faded into black.

THE NIGHTMARE DIDN'T go away when Katie awoke.

It had just taken on warmer temps and a posher backdrop.

She was still a prisoner, like she'd been at seventeen. And her beloved little boy was once again in harm's way.

Instead of being handcuffed to a bed in a makeshift

hospital ward, waiting to deliver a baby, she was seated at Leland Asher's ornate walnut desk in the study of his mansion, hacking into a computer system for him. She didn't need to be drugged or kept in chains in order to cooperate. The two thugs who'd kidnapped her and Tyler had already shown her Matt Asher's dead body and promised to do the same to her nine-year-old son if she didn't do their boss's bidding.

There was something seriously twisted inside Leland Asher's head to make him order his bodyguards to lure Tyler outside the theater with a story about her getting hurt in the parking lot. Now he had them tie Beverly Eisenbach to a brocaded Queen Anne chair before thanking them for their years of service and dismissing them, promising each a healthy bonus in their bank accounts. Then he'd kissed his longtime girlfriend and stuffed his wadded-up handkerchief into her mouth to muffle her protests and pleas for mercy. With Matt Asher dead, Leland weakened by his illness and the hired help dismissed for the night, Katie even briefly considered standing up to Leland herself, maybe shoving the desk chair at him and making a run for it with Tyler, or whacking him over the head with this computer.

But as if sensing her tendency to tempt fate, he used the one thing she cared about most to force her to unlock code and break through firewalls and search through servers to access the information he wanted—he stood in the center of the room framed by windows and floor-to-ceiling curtains and simply rested one hand over the shoulder of her son and held a gun in the other.

Her sinuses reeled with a headache from the knockout chemical they'd used on her, but her synapses were firing on all cylinders. She'd been at the computer for about an hour since getting her instructions, but in reality, she'd gained access to Beverly's medical files within the first fifteen minutes. She'd spent the rest of the time fighting for survival in the best way she knew how. She prayed her desperate plan had worked and that it had worked quickly enough for her and Tyler to have a chance to escape.

She rested her fingers for a moment before looking up at the gray-haired man. "I'm in."

"I want you to access her private files."

Beverly screamed through her gag, rocking back and forth in her chair, pulling at the ropes that bound her.

"I need a warrant to do that," Katie explained.

Leland put the gun to Tyler's head and Katie bit her lip to stop from crying out. "Here's your warrant. Now do it."

Katie's fingers sailed over the keyboard again. "You keep looking at me, Tyler. Think about Padre. He's going to need you to give him some extra exercise tonight because we'll be getting home so late." She locked her gaze on to Tyler's red-rimmed eyes and smiled. "You focus right here, sweetie. I love you. Don't ever forget that, not for one second." He wiped his nose on the sleeve of his costume and nodded, trying so hard to be brave and remain calm for her.

She glanced down at her work, wanting to do everything she could to maintain Tyler's focus on her and keep him from witnessing a gruesome crime or becoming a victim himself.

Don't make a mistake. Don't make a mistake.

Since Leland hadn't questioned anything she'd done so far, Katie pretended the extra commands she typed in were necessary to retrieve the sensitive information that the law and a stubborn girlfriend wouldn't give him. The counseling office's patient list was already on her screen. But with her fingers flying over the keyboard, she embedded a message and sent it to Trent's phone. The message was sent and gone by the time she'd reached Bev Eisenbach's confidential files.

"Have you finished yet?" Leland was growing impatient.

She couldn't push her luck too much further. "Just about."

Leland kept his grip on Tyler but switched the gun back to Beverly as tears smeared her mascara and she whimpered for forgiveness. "Miss Rinaldi, I remind you that I'm a dying man."

"I'm in the system." *Find us, Trent. Find us.* "I'm pulling up the patient files now. What do you want me to look for?"

Leland smiled, pleased with her success. Keeping a grip on Tyler's arm, he walked over to Beverly and pulled the gag from her mouth. "It was quite a clever plan all those years ago that you came up with, darling. Care to explain yourself?"

Bev coughed for a few seconds before she could speak. "Leland, dearest, you know I've always had your best interests at heart. Look at all I've done for you. I convinced that tweaking drug addict to kill that reporter who was going to expose your connections to the senator. I did the world a service by having your men kill Lloyd Endicott so that Dr. Wells would murder that horrible Richard Bratcher. I found out Francisco Dona was still alive. I found out he was working as a private detective."

"No. No, dear. You kept that from me." He drew the gun across Beverly's forehead, and Katie nearly screamed at the horrible images he was exposing her son to. "All these years I thought I'd avenged Isabel's death, only to find out that my nephew—her own son—knew he still breathed air, and you two hadn't done a damn thing about it. I had to have my men take care of it."

Katie was a bit of a brilliant geek herself. She'd already tapped into her KCPD account and was mirroring everything that she was doing here on the department server. She'd pinged Trent's phone—Max's, Olivia's and Jim's, as well. Lieutenant Rafferty-Taylor received a notification of the new files uploading. Katie had even copied a notice to her surrogate father, the DA.

Look at Miss Katie Lee Rinaldi—taking a huge risk, bending the rules, doing whatever was necessary to protect the people she loved. She was charging into battle, taking on a known criminal to save her son and her own life one more time.

Read between the lines, Trent. Find us.

She'd always been able to get herself into trouble, but Trent would always be there to help her get out of it—to catch her when she fell, when she was frightened, when she was terrified her next mistake might cost her everything she held dear.

Be patient with me a little longer, babe. I love you. I need you. I'm in love with you.

A loud crash at the front door shook through the house. "KCPD! We're coming in!"

Tyler cried out with a startled yelp.

"It's okay, Ty," she reassured him. "They're using a battering ram to break down the door."

"At last." Leland smiled from ear to ear. "I wondered how long it would take the police to find you."

"Asher!" A deep, familiar voice echoed through the house.

"Mom!" Tyler recognized Trent's voice, too. She saw him pull from Leland Asher's grasp.

She put up her hand, cautioning him to obey. "Shh, sweetie. Remember you're playing a part. You're the good little boy who does whatever Mr. Asher says, right?"

Tyler's frightened eyes locked on to hers again and he nodded.

The next voice Katie heard was Ginny Rafferty-Taylor's. "Leland Asher. Your house is surrounded. Your chauffeur and bodyguards have been neutralized. It's just you and me and a lot of very angry cops."

"I'd be happy to talk with you, Lieutenant."

The team must be working its way through the mansion while the lieutenant stalled Asher. "I need to talk to the hostages first. I need to know they're okay."

"Are you?" Leland tightened his grip on Tyler's collar and Katie nodded. "Answer her."

"It's Katie, Lieutenant. Tyler and I are both fine. But Mr. Asher has a gun."

Leland laughed. "Of course I have a gun. All your police friends have guns—it's only fair. Please. Welcome to my home, Lieutenant."

Oh, God. Now his bizarre actions made sense. "He wants you to come in. He wants… Oh, God, please don't hurt my son."

"Did you find the evidence I requested, Miss Rinaldi?" Tears stung her eyes and she reached out for Tyler. "Miss Rinaldi."

She forced her attention back to the computer. "Yes. Dr. Eisenbach has notations in her patient files. Those with secrets she can use to blackmail them, those who need a favor and will do something in exchange for that favor." What more did the man want from her? "Could I please have my son?"

The lieutenant's voice sounded closer when she spoke

again. "Are you sure everyone is okay? Your nephew is here. He's been shot, Mr. Asher. He's dead."

"Yes, I did that."

He was confessing to murder with dozens of cops swarming the estate? With three witnesses who could testify against him right here?

Katie was more certain than ever that this monster intended to commit suicide by cop. He was a dying man, determined to set his affairs in order—to eliminate those who'd betrayed him and then die instantly himself, avoiding a lingering death.

But with her innocent boy smack-dab in the middle of all those guns? She couldn't let that happen.

"Don't shoot! Please don't shoot! There's an innocent child here." Katie reached out again. "Please, Mr. Asher. May I have my son?"

"Soon, Miss Rinaldi." He turned his attention to Tyler. "Would you like to go over and sit with your mother?"

"Yes, please."

"When she's done working. She's proven more loyal to her loved ones than my family has been to me." Leland looked around the room, perhaps seeing the movement of SWAT cops taking position outside the windows. "Did you find the information I was looking for, Miss Rinaldi? Has my beloved Beverly betrayed me?"

Katie looked at the incriminating evidence she'd pulled off Dr. Eisenbach's computer records. The notations Leland Asher had asked her to find were right there.

Francisco Dona, aka John Smith, is alive. Can use him to eliminate threats and provide surveillance to ensure jobs are completed as ordered in exchange for keeping his identity from Leland.

Matt Asher's hatred for his uncle can be used to my advantage. String him along with promise of helping him take over the business. He can do the dirty work and I can reap the profit. (I've earned it.)

Stephen March, Hillary Wells, Doug Price and many more—their names were all there. The psychologist had counseled all of them, forced them to do her bidding, first to please Leland—to become an indispensable ally with hopes of eventually becoming his wife or business partner—and later to eliminate Leland himself when his promises of power and position turned out to be lies.

But once Katie gave Leland the information he wanted, the bullets would start to fly. And Tyler—her son, her angel—would be caught in the crossfire.

"Miss Rinaldi. My time is running short. I'm sure your compatriots are closing in on my position and lining up kill shots even as we speak. Is the information there? Did my love betray me?"

Beverly wept in her bonds, begging to make amends. "Leland, please."

"Miss Rinaldi?"

Katie pointed to her face, silently telling Tyler not to look anywhere else, to hold fast to the love in his mother's eyes.

"Miss Rinaldi?"

"Yes. It's all here. Beverly and Matt have betrayed you."

"Thank you."

Without missing a beat, Leland shoved Tyler toward Katie. Beverly screamed as he turned and fired a bullet right into the middle of her forehead.

Katie lunged for her son and wrapped him in her arms,

dragging him beneath the sturdy walnut desk as a pair of smoke grenades crashed through the side windows, filling the room with a stinging gas.

"Close your eyes, Tyler. Hold tight to me." Oh, thank God, thank God. But Leland still had a gun. A lot of people still had guns.

"No!" Leland shouted in a rage. "Shoot me! Shoot me!"

"Drop your weapon, Asher!" That was Trent. His voice was muffled by the mask he wore, but there was no mistaking the deadly authority in his tone.

"Drop it!" Max was in the room, too.

"This one's dead," Olivia announced, moving away from Dr. Eisenbach's slumped body.

Jim Parker was there. Even Lieutenant Rafferty-Taylor had a bead on the man her team had finally brought down. "Drop it, Mr. Asher. You're surrounded. We have oxygen masks. You do not."

"No! You have to shoot me!"

Katie hugged her body around Tyler's as tightly as she could when she felt the barrel of Asher's recently fired gun singe the nape of her neck. "Don't hurt my son!"

Leland yanked on the collar of her blouse to pull her from beneath the desk. But six feet five inches of defensive tackle slammed into the older man and flattened him on the floor.

"It's over, Asher. You're done." She could hear him kicking Leland's gun away and pulling the handcuffs from his belt. "Sunshine, you all right?"

"Yes." The lieutenant helped her crawl out from under the desk and stand.

"Tyler?"

"I'm okay." Katie hugged her son tightly to her chest, assuring her boss with a nod as Max, Olivia and Jim circled around the imported rug where Trent was handcuffing a winded Leland Asher. "Mom, my eyes hurt."

"Keep them closed, sweetie. It's the cloud in the air. It's making Mr. Asher cry, too."

Lieutenant Rafferty-Taylor radioed backup that it was clear to enter and that they'd need two extra oxygen masks.

"Is Trent okay, too?" Tyler asked, hugging his arms tightly around her waist.

Trent Dixon, Katie Rinaldi's best friend, the man she loved—the man who didn't yet know how much she loved him—hauled Leland Asher to his feet and handed him off to Max and Jim. He peeled off his gas mask as the smoke in the air began to dissipate. "Read him his rights and arrest him for everything in the book."

Leland sneered at the much bigger man. "You're wasting your time, Detective. I told you I was dying. I was simply setting my affairs in order."

Trent leaned in. "You don't get to take the easy way out, Asher. You just confessed to two murders, and I bet we can close out a dozen more because of the evidence Katie sent us. More important, you threatened the lives of the two most important people in the world to me. Now, whether you have a year or a month or they find a cure for cancer and you live to a ripe old age, you are spending the rest of your days in prison."

Chapter Thirteen

The cold case squad and their loved ones filled up an entire row of the theater. Ginny Rafferty-Taylor and her husband, Brett, flanked the son and daughter who sat between them. Katie suspected they had a young starlet in the making with their daughter sitting on the edge of her seat for the entire show.

Uncle Dwight slipped his handkerchief behind Tyler's cousin Jack and poked Aunt Maddie, who wept silent tears at every poignant moment of the show.

Jim Parker and his very pregnant wife, Natalie, sat on the aisle so she could sneak out to use the restroom at several private intermissions. He wore a red tie and she had on a green maternity dress, adding a festive color to the group who'd all come to see Tyler in his debut role onstage.

Reporter Gabe Knight nodded sagely at several of the show's classic scenes, all the while holding hands with his fiancée. Olivia Watson might be a tough chick on the outside, but she was all smiles and thumbs-up to Katie as Tyler uttered the last line of the play.

Even Max Krolikowski, as gruff and Scrooge-ish as they came, draped his arm around the shoulders of his wife, Rosie. He nodded at something she whispered in his ear and pressed a kiss to her curly red hair.

They'd all been focused so long on closing KCPD's unsolvable crimes that it seemed odd to see this group of friends coming together to celebrate the holiday and show their support for a brave little boy who'd nailed every line and entrance, and whose very life was the best present a mother could ever have. Katie was grateful for her family and friends. They'd had each other's backs and saved each other's lives.

And when Tyler came out with the other children to take his bow, they all rose as one and joined the applause with the rest of the audience.

But it was in the quiet moments backstage, after the others had gone home and Katie was stuck in the greenroom ironing costumes and ignoring Francis's blow-by-blow critique of their opening night performance, that she got the best present of all.

"Low clearance, buddy."

Trent ducked through the greenroom door, carrying Tyler on his broad shoulders with the same joy and love that Ebenezer Scrooge had carried Tiny Tim through the streets of London on Christmas Day. Trent even shook Francis's hand and congratulated him on his performance, rendering the temperamental actor speechless for a few moments before he beat a hasty escape.

"You ready to go, sunshine?" Trent set Tyler on his feet and hurried him into the dressing room to retrieve his coat. "I promised this hot young actor that I'd take him out for ice cream if he stayed in character for the whole show."

"And I did, Mom," Tyler bragged, galloping back out to join them. "I'm getting a root-beer float."

"Sounds a little chilly for a December night. Do you mind if I tag along with you for some hot chocolate?"

Trent leaned over the ironing board to steal a kiss. "Maybe it's me who should be asking if I can tag along and be part of the family celebration."

Katie cupped the side of his jaw in her hand when he would have pulled away. She lost her heart in the depths of those dark gray eyes. "You will always be a part of this family, Trent. You saved our lives. You made my son feel safe and you helped me learn to not just trust, but to embrace what I feel."

"And what do you feel, Katie Lee Rinaldi?"

"That I love you. That I've always loved you. I'm just sorry it took me so long to realize I'm *in* love with you, too."

Trent took her hand and led her around the ironing board to pull her into his arms and claim her mouth with a kiss. "I'm in love with you, too, sunshine."

Several seconds passed before Katie remembered they had an audience and pulled away—but only to welcome Tyler into the circle of this loving man's arms.

"Mom, you don't have to mail my letter to Santa. I already got what I wanted for Christmas."

Trent agreed. "I think we all did."

"I haven't said yes to your proposal yet." She felt glaring eyes from above and below and laughed. "Yes. Of course, the answer is yes."

* * * * *

MILLS & BOON®

**If you enjoyed this story,
you'll love the the full *Revenge Collection*!**

**Enjoy the misdemeanours and the sinful world
of revenge with this six-book collection.
Indulge in these riveting 3-in-1 romances
from top Modern Romance authors.**

Order your complete collection today at
www.millsandboon.co.uk/revengecollection

'The perfect Christmas read!' - Julia Williams

Jewellery designer Skylar loves living London, but when a surprise proposal goes wrong, she finds herself fleeing home to remote Puffin Island.

Burned by a terrible divorce, TV historian Alec is dazzled by Sky's beauty and so cynical that he assumes that's a bad thing! Luckily she's on the verge of getting engaged to someone else, so she won't be a constant source of temptation... but this Christmas, can Alec and Sky realise that they are what each other was looking for all along?

Order yours today at
www.millsandboon.co.uk

MILLS & BOON®
The Billionaires Collection!

This fabulous 6 book collection features stories from some of our talented writers. Feel the temperature rise with our ultra-sexy and powerful billionaires. Don't miss this great offer – buy the collection today to get two books free!

Order yours at
**www.millsandboon.co.uk
/billionaires**

'High drama and lots of laughs'
—*Fabulous* magazine

Fed up with disastrous internet dates and conflicting advice from her friends, Ellie Rigby decides to take matters into her own hands. Instead of looking for a man for herself, she's going to start a dating agency where she can use her extensive experience in finding Mr Wrong to help others find their Mr Right.

Well, that is until a match with one of her clients, charming, infuriating Nick, has her questioning everything she's ever thought about love…

MILLS & BOON

MILLS & BOON®

Why shop at millsandboon.co.uk?

Each year, thousands of romance readers find their perfect read at millsandboon.co.uk. That's because we're passionate about bringing you the very best romantic fiction. Here are some of the advantages of shopping at www.millsandboon.co.uk:

* **Get new books first**—you'll be able to buy your favourite books one month before they hit the shops

* **Get exclusive discounts**—you'll also be able to buy our specially created monthly collections, with up to 50% off the RRP

* **Find your favourite authors**—latest news, interviews and new releases for all your favourite authors and series on our website, plus ideas for what to try next

* **Join in**—once you've bought your favourite books, don't forget to register with us to rate, review and join in the discussions

Visit **www.millsandboon.co.uk**
for all this and more today!

MILLS_WEB

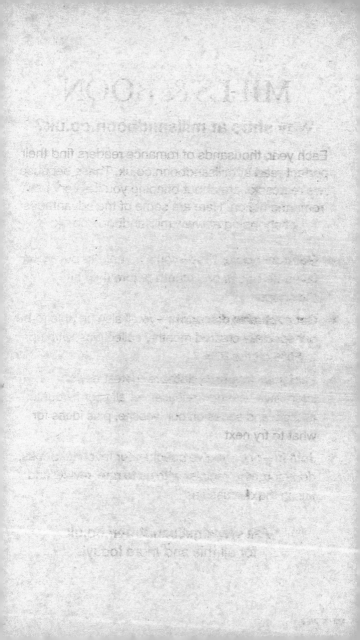